FRINGE
BENEFITS

FRINGE BENEFITS

*STRANGER MAGICS,
BOOK FIVE*

ASH FITZSIMMONS

Print Edition ISBN: 978-1-949861-09-9

Cover design by BespokeBookCovers.com

www.ashfitzsimmons.com

CHAPTER 1

Nine p.m. in Edinburgh, per the bedside clock, and the sun still hadn't had the decency to set. My body hurt with the fierce hunger that starts as a belly cramp and finishes with a raging headache, but I couldn't risk leaving my room until full dark. Even on the outskirts of the Old Town, I couldn't be certain that one of the Arcanum's assassins wasn't watching for me from a parked car or a shadowy alley, scanning the passing pedestrians for my wanted face.

Me, a detective inspector, *wanted*.

The brass back at the Durham Constabulary wouldn't have believed it, particularly if I'd told them who was hunting me, but then I'd always tried to keep the mundane and magical sides of my life separate. True, I'd wound up in Faerie once on a murder investigation, but that wasn't a matter I disclosed in my official reports. One does not go around the Constabulary declaring oneself a witch, after all.

Pity, that. As the Arcanum, the governing body of my magical betters, had put a target on my back, I wouldn't have minded having a colleague or two at my side over my months on the run.

Had I been a remotely competent wizard, I could have dulled the hunger, at the very least. A top-notch wizard could have produced a meal from thin air. But I was a mere witch, and the little talent I had was being employed to hold together the flimsy warning wards across my thin door and dingy window.

The hotel in which I'd landed was, by charitable estimation, dodgy as hell, but it was cheap, and the old Pakistani proprietor accepted cash and asked no questions. True, I was an oddity among his guests, a forty-seven-year-old woman in a hoodie and jeans, rubbing shoulders with barely legal prostitutes and backpackers desperate to stay anywhere but another hostel, but Mr. Patel was apathetic to us all unless the police stopped in. I'd given him no cause for concern, however, and no reason to enquire about my employer. Something told me he wouldn't be pleased to have a detective in the building, even one outside her jurisdiction.

The bedside clock showed only one minute had passed when I glanced up again, and I continued to work on my broken wand to distract myself for another hour. The sun set late that close to midsummer, which might have been a perk had I not been living on a vampiric schedule. With the short night, I'd hardly have six hours to eat, find provisions for the next day, and take care of business at the twenty-four-hour launderette I'd scouted out—also dodgy, but I'd reached my limit of rinsing my pants in the bathroom sink. The Internet cafés were closed by then, but the dodgy hostel down the road—there was a definite theme to the neighborhood—was willing to sell time at the public computers to non-guests. Not knowing if the Arcanum had somehow put a trace on my mobile or my laptop, I availed myself of the sticky hostel computers to check my mail every few days. There'd been nothing in weeks—well, nothing but messages from my super, who wanted to know how much longer my bereavement leave was going to last. By then, I suspected I was on permanent holiday, but I wasn't about to tell *him* that.

The downside of staying off my own equipment was that I had no secure way to access the Fringe network. I couldn't very well log in from the hostel lobby, and if my mobile was being traced, I couldn't risk alerting the Arcanum to my presence. Then again, it had been two and half months since the Fringe unraveled, and I doubted that anyone was lurking on the network besides whatever watchers the Arcanum had assigned to lie in wait. Sure, I itched to make certain, but that was out of the cards. I hadn't even attempted to ring another Fringer since I went on the run, though I'd staked out a few of the pubs across Edinburgh where we used to congregate. Nothing, of course. The Fringers of the city were dead, captured, or in the wind, and no one was lingering around the old hangouts, waiting to have a pint with a friendly face.

Still, I'd held on to the irrational hope that I'd stumble across a crafter in my nocturnal wanderings. I'd fallen down a flight of stairs and broken my wand while outrunning a pair of Arcanum assassins in York, and the electrical tape I'd used to put it back together was barely doing the trick. The gaffer tape I'd first tried had been a disaster, and I'd spent the better part of an afternoon picking precious motes of dragonscale off the tape when I removed it to try another fix. Though electrical tape conducted magic, it did so poorly, which made my wand nearly useless to me. Plus, the tape had a nasty habit of melting and dripping off after only a short use, meaning I had to scrape my fractured wand clean and repair it anew every few days. Complicating that was the frustration of my degrading wards. I simply didn't have the power to build them properly, and the ones I'd erected on the fly had all the structural integrity of a paper airplane in a hurricane. But they were my best hope of an early warning, and as I couldn't rebuild them without a functional wand, I made my repairs and tried to ignore my growling stomach.

By half-nine, I'd finished wrapping the rowan in black tape, and I gave the wand a test flick before tackling the ward situation. The stick thrummed in my hand more faintly than usual, but at least it was working. Willing the sun to hurry up and sink before I starved, I rose from my bed-*cum*-workbench and inspected the spell I'd worked around the door two days before. It wasn't a complete loss, not yet, but I could pick out weak spots in the construction, holes in the fence that could admit an assassin while I tried to sleep.

As I considered ways to shore up the failing spell, my mobile rang.

My hand clenched instinctively on the wand, and I whipped around as if expecting to find a wizard standing by the wardrobe. But the room was empty and still, the only sounds the chirping ringtone and the blood pounding in my ears.

No one had tried my personal mobile in weeks. Not the Constabulary, not my few non-Fringe associates—so who the devil was ringing at half-nine?

Shaking my hand to loosen its death grip, I fished the phone from my pack and checked the screen. On reading the caller ID, I let out the breath I hadn't realized I'd been holding, dropped the wand onto the stained duvet, and tapped the button. "Seamus," I said, trying not to sound like a scared teenager in a haunted house. "Hello, love. How's life?"

"Badger?"

His voice seemed strained, higher than I recalled, and I frowned as I sank onto the rumpled bed. "Yes, it's me. Are you all right?"

"It's happened again. Badge, it's happened *again*."

My empty stomach knotted at the fear in his tone. "Are you all right?" I repeated.

"I don't know, I...I think I may have killed him."

"Where are you, Seamie?"

"On my way home. Please, I don't know what to do, I don't...you've got to help me, I don't know—"

"I'm in Edinburgh," I said quietly, praying that my paranoia was unwarranted. "I'll text you the address. Are you driving yet?"

"Hired a car. I flew into Teesside."

"Okay. It's going to be fine," I said, as much for him as for myself. "I'll expect you about midnight." I paused, listening to his uneven breathing. "Love you, Seamie. Be safe."

I hung up before he could decide whether to echo the sentiment, then shot him my address and reassessed the night's plans. My backpack was ready, my hunting knife was strapped in place under my trousers, and the Taser I wasn't supposed to have was securely in my jacket pocket. The pants situation could be addressed later. I needed food, and I needed to fix the wards before Seamus crashed back into my life.

And I had less than three hours to figure out the best way to tell my panicked ex-partner that he wasn't strictly human.

"Sorry, Dad," I muttered to the silence, then stood to face the door wards, pushed up my sleeves, and raised my battered wand.

Of the two of us, I'd always been the one with the lead foot, so I was surprised to get a text from Seamus not two hours later, telling me he was parking down the street. He'd *flown* up the A1, I realized, doing the quick approximation, and tossed the rest of my soggy chips in the bin in a fit of last-minute tidying. *You're being ridiculous*, I berated myself even as I straightened the duvet. Seamus was coming to me with blood on his hands, not to reminisce about old times. He wasn't going to give a damn about the condition of my room…or, I thought, pausing in front of the cracked mirror, my face. If he was scared enough to hop a plane home for the first time in twenty-two years, he wasn't going to critique my graying roots or the dark circles beneath my eyes, the ones that not even concealer seemed to faze those days.

I forced myself away from the mirror and made certain that my weapons were stowed out of sight. Why should I care what Seamus thought, anyway? He was the one who'd run off to Belfast on two weeks' notice, not me. He couldn't be bothered to spend a single holiday with his parents, no matter how many times they asked him to come home. Hell, he hadn't even offered to make the trip when the Arcanum murdered my parents—he'd sent a sympathy text, nothing more. If he wanted to see me again, he had no room for criticism of what he found.

So what if the motel room was dusty and smelled of cheap vinegar? The last time I'd checked, *he* wasn't the one on the run from murderous wizards.

But just the same, I couldn't keep myself from tugging a brush through my bob and checking my teeth for stuck crumbs. As I did, my eye caught the tiny bulge from the gold necklace under my shirt, and I threw on a hoodie to hide it. There was no reason for him to know about *that*.

I stilled at the sound of squeaking floorboards in the hallway—a song I'd come to know, but played up-tempo that night—and braced myself at the rapid, heavy rapping on my door. "Coming," I said, struggling against my racing heart, and threw back the bolt.

And there he was. Seamus—*my* Seamus—in a gray anorak and brown trousers, looking as if he'd stepped straight from my memory. He slouched slightly, hunching his shoulders at my neighbors' raucous laughter, and his dark blue eyes searched my face, betraying his nerves with their twitching. I knew that look—I'd seen it hundreds of times, replayed over and over whenever my thoughts turned to him.

I'm sorry, Badger. Please don't follow me.

My throat clenched. He hadn't changed. In twenty-two long years, Seamus hadn't changed...

But no—there, in his black hair, the telltale silver threads at the temples. Perhaps he was just baby-faced after all, blessed with good skin and favorable genes. If he was graying, then Dad was wrong about him, and maybe...

"Hello, Badger," he said, shoving his hands in his pockets—quickly, but not quickly enough for me to miss the leather gloves he was wearing. "It's, ehm...it's good to see you."

I'd imagined that moment for years—sometimes giving him a curt speech and a slap in the face, sometimes letting him lift me off my feet and twirl me in the rain like a silly girl in a sappy movie—but when he was finally standing before me, scared and tired and haunted, I threw my arms around him and pulled him close, as if I could hold him against vanishing again. I shut my eyes and felt his arms encircle my back. As we stood in the doorway in our silent embrace, my righteous anger ebbed, and I buried my face in his crinkling jacket.

"Welcome home," I murmured, forgetting for a moment that I was living in a veritable whorehouse, on the run from the most powerful magical organization in the world. Seamus was home, my friend, my partner, my lover, and everything would be good again if I held on tightly enough.

But the moment couldn't last, and I released him as his arms dropped. "Come in," I said, beckoning him out of the hall, and latched the door behind him. Making a mental note to flip on the repaired door wards, which I'd disabled in anticipation of his arrival, I turned to watch him take stock of my quarters and considered the reassuring gray. Seamus was aging after all, Dad had been mistaken, and whatever was plaguing him could be fixed. I smiled and hugged him again, then reached up and ran my fingers through his neat hair while he held me, just as if the intervening years had been a moment's fancy. Whatever had happened in Belfast, we would get through it together...

The light from the bath made his gray strands shine—gray strands that abruptly darkened at the roots, a cruel inversion of the situation on my own scalp. I stiffened, and Seamus, noticing the change, stepped back as I retracted my searching fingers.

"You dyed your hair," I said, feeling as if I'd been sucker-punched.

His darting eyes told me he was trying to think of a good answer. "Not well enough, eh?" he replied with a weak laugh. "Suppose I missed a few—"

"You dyed it *gray*." I stopped him with a shake of my head before he could further the lie. "I know roots, Seamie. You can't just color the bits on top and hope no one takes a closer look."

He deflated under the scrutiny. "Is it that obvious? I tried to be subtle—the guys were teasing me about looking like I'm twelve, so I fixed it. You know how hard it is to get respect when everyone thinks you're still a PC?"

In that moment, as the bath light hummed behind me, I shoved my hopes aside and truly saw Seamus. The face of a man twenty years too young, unblemished and without a trace of the five o'clock shadow any other dark-haired man would have borne. The gloves he'd worn since our school days, protection against his bizarre metal allergy, unwarranted on that warmish June night. Only his eyes, now slightly sunken and glazed with weariness, showed me that the apparition slinking toward the wardrobe wasn't the product of my tired, overworked mind. I'd never seen him look so hopeless, so...*lost*.

"Forget it," I said, closing the door to the bath. "It's not important. Tell me what happened."

I sat on the edge of the bed, and he leaned against the wardrobe with his arms folded, staring at everything but me. "I was interviewing a suspect two days ago. Rape. Bad business, the girl was ten."

"Jesus."

He nodded. "Youth football league. We're still waiting on the lab work, but she said the assistant coach did it." He snarled as if he'd tasted something bitter. "So we brought the bastard in, and I took his statement. Well, I *tried* to. He was mouthy—said this was absurd, we had nothing, you can't believe a little girl, you know the rest. And then..."

"Yes?" I prompted after his silence continued to

stretch.

Seamus swallowed hard. "I opened the folder. Showed him her picture. The bruises around her throat. Her mam had taken her to hospital, and the girl was so scared when we showed up to talk to her. Didn't want to get in trouble." He paused again, then finally met my eyes. "She has your hair, Badge. Same lock, same place."

Automatically, my hand rose to tuck the white streak behind my ear. I felt for the girl—while it hadn't been a social stigma for a while, my prematurely white forelock had opened me up to a variety of taunts as a child, when any deviation is cause for teasing. *You're not ugly*, Seamus had assured me then. *You're like a badger. It's neat.*

His fingers dug into his upper arms as he recalled the interview. "Did he crack?" I replied.

"Yeah. He said she'd been asking for it." Seamus squeezed his eyes shut. "And the next thing I knew, he was on fire."

"Oh, *Seamie*," I whispered.

He wouldn't look at me. "I froze. He was screaming, and I...I backed up to the wall, and the smoke detector went off, and then the sprinkler. And he kept burning. One of the sergeants hit him with a fire extinguisher, and that did the trick, but..."

"How badly was he hurt?" I asked when Seamus's voice faded.

"Word is he's not going to live. I had to get out of town." When he opened his eyes again, I saw the plea in them. "They're not blaming me, *no one* ever blames me, but I saw the video, and...and spontaneous combustion doesn't happen like that." He took a deep breath and slowly released it. "I'm on leave. They're worried about trauma, you know. Seeing a man burst into flames not two meters away..." He slid onto the bed beside me and clutched my arms. "Help me, Badger. *Help me*. I thought it was over, but if it's coming back...if I set him on fire..."

I gripped his shoulders and met his frantic stare. "If I

could help you, I would. You've got to believe me. But I don't know—"

"You're the witch! Can't you—"

I shook my head to silence him, then cocked my thumb toward the paper-thin walls. "Exactly. I'm a witch," I muttered. "Which means I'm useless in this situation."

Seamus huffed in agitation as he released me, then rubbed his temples and stared at the stained carpet. "Can you at least tell me why I'm cursed? What did I do? How do I stop this from happening again?"

The neighbors started blasting pop in the next room, and I knew the smell of marijuana wasn't far behind. "You're not cursed," I explained as the wall sconces rattled with the thumping bass. "You're not ensorcelled, as far as I can tell. I mean, there's a possibility of some really top-end magic at work on you that I just can't see, but—"

"I'd have seen it by now," he interrupted, holding up his arms and letting them flop into his lap. "I've looked." He turned to me again and searched my carefully composed face. "Why can I see it? See *that*?" he added, pointing to the warded door. "Your dad never gave me a straight answer. Just…"

Frustrated and afraid, Seamus reached toward me, and I took his hand as always.

"I need the truth," he said, giving my hand a squeeze. "Whatever it is, however bad it is, I need the truth. Be my friend and tell me what I need to know."

My eyes began to prick, and I blinked the evidence away. "You won't believe me."

At that, Seamus laughed incredulously. "I believe that you're a *witch*, Badge. You showed me real magic. What could be harder to believe than that?"

He was waiting, and I felt the familiar pressure of his strong, bony fingers entwined with mine. No matter how little I liked it, I couldn't lie to him, not when the truth was becoming more obvious with every passing year. "Okay," I sighed, holding his gaze. "I think there's about a ninety-nine percent chance you're fae."

"Huh?"

"Fae. A faerie. All the signs are there, and Dad—"

The shrill wailing of my window wards cut short my explanation, and I yelped and pulled Seamus to the floor as the glass exploded inward. Scrambling, I grabbed my wand and stood, only to find a man perched on the sill, a young redhead sporting the black uniform of the Arcanum's assassin corps. His wand—which, unlike mine, bore no reinforcing tape—swiveled to my chest and held its position as he leapt to the floor. "Hannah Parsons," he said, brushing a shard of glass off his outstretched arm, "I've been authorized to take you to Montana for your own protection. Drop your wand and come peacefully, or—"

"Or *what*?" said Seamus, rising from a crouch with a pistol in his hands.

The wizard paused, momentarily flummoxed, and stared at the muzzle pointed in his direction. "Who the hell—"

"Seamus Malone, PSNI, and yes, that's a loaded Glock. Put down your weapon, get on the ground, and keep your hands where I can see them." When the wizard hesitated, he added, "I survived the Troubles, boyo. You won't be the first idiot I've shot. Now *get down*."

By then, the startled wizard had recovered enough presence of mind to smirk at Seamus. "Police, are we? I hate to tell you, mate, but you're outclassed. Drop the gun and stand down, and I'll let you walk away from this."

"Do as he says, Seamie. Stay calm. Listen to him," I said, putting my wand on the bed, and slowly squatted with my hands raised. "That's a trained wizard. He can run circles around me."

"But does that make him bulletproof?" Seamus replied, holding the gun in place. "Shall we find out?"

My knees hit the floor beside my loaded backpack. "This is no time to be clever. Those wands are deadly."

"Funny, so's the Glock. You know, I believe we have ourselves a proper Mexican standoff."

The wizard swiveled his wand to face Seamus. "Not for long, we don't. Last chance—"

That was all I needed. With his attention distracted, I ripped open the pack's outer pocket, pulled free my Taser, and fired over the bed. The wizard jerked with the electric shock, then collapsed and began to spasm. "Let's go," I said, dropping the weapon, and grabbed my backpack. "While he's down. Move!"

Seamus stared at the writhing wizard, then at me. "Bloody hell, woman, where did you get that?"

"Friend of a friend, and that's all you need know. Come on. Where did you leave the car?"

"Out front. One moment." He glared down at the wizard, then stomped on the man's wrists until I heard the crunch of bone. "Not going to be shooting anything if you can't hold your hand steady," he told the would-be assassin. "Bit of police brutality for you. Sorry, *mate*." With that, he followed me into the hall, not bothering to holster his weapon.

I threw my room key on the front desk as I ran outside, hoping the maimed wizard would be gone by the time Mr. Patel got around to investigating. Two of the usual drunks were loitering by the door, passing a bottle in a paper sack, but neither seemed particularly concerned to see me in a hurry or Seamus leading with a gun. Then again, the local policy was best summed up as "see nothing, say less," so no one protested as we made our way into the night.

"There," said Seamus, catching my elbow, and pointed me toward a black Skoda parked on the next block.

As he fished the fob from his pocket, I yanked it from him and hurried toward the driver's side. "Get in, I'll get us out of here."

"It's in my name—"

"And you've not driven around here in *how* many years?"

He slid into the passenger's seat without further complaint as I tossed my bag into the back, but I noticed that he kept the gun at the ready as I peeled out into the night.

Twenty minutes later, the city was behind us, and I sped west along the quiet roads. "Just curious," Seamus ventured as he finally tucked the gun back into the holster under his jacket, "but would you like to tell me what the hell is going on?"

I gritted my teeth and focused on the strobing lane divider to calm my thudding heart. "Did Dad ever mention the Fringe?"

"What, the festival?"

"No. It's an organization for those of us with subpar magical ability. Support, assistance, information, et cetera. Dad was a regional coordinator, and I took his slot when he retired."

He nodded beside me. "All right…"

"No, it's not all right. It went to hell at Easter. There was a rogue faerie with an army, and then turmoil in the Arcanum—that's the worldwide governing body for the real wizards, the Arcanum. They chose a new grand magus—lovely girl, probably too young—and in short order, one of the top magi staged a coup. Decided that witches are more trouble than we're worth. That man who broke into my room is an assassin. They've been hunting me since March."

"Christ," he muttered. "Your parents—"

"Early casualties. It was never like Dad to go without a fuss." I paused to fight down the lump in my throat. "I missed the first raid—training down south, it was an all-day narcotics seminar on the bank holiday, you know, and I…sorry. Sorry, that's—"

"Take your time, Badger."

I gripped the wheel to steady myself. "So I went to the training, and I turned both of my mobiles off that day. Bad reception in the building, and we were doing hands-on work. Anyway, the seminar was about to end, and someone pulled me to the phone. Commissioner broke the news about my parents—your dad found them. They were supposed to go for dinner together that night."

"He told me." Seamus cleared his throat, then said, "I'm sorry I didn't come sooner. If you'd told me you were on the run—"

"This isn't your mess."

I tried to focus on the road to get the crime scene photo out of my head. Officially, I couldn't touch the case, but one of my colleagues had thought I'd want to see for myself, and I found the e-mail waiting when I turned my work mobile back on. Though someone had put sheets over the bodies by the time the photo was snapped, my mother's right hand was exposed, and the black-rimmed hole through her palm told me everything I needed to know. Nothing but a wand or a high-powered laser could make a burn wound like that.

She'd tried to defend herself. My poor, mundane mother had seen the wand and raised her hands, trying to shield herself from the fatal shot. The bastard who'd attacked them had killed a defenseless woman, and my dad, a witch with paltry wand skills, surely hadn't given him much trouble.

I'd skipped the planned group dinner and locked myself in my hotel room, frantically trying to find answers on the Fringe network. Surely, I reasoned, someone would know why a wizard had come after my parents—my dad had been retired for ten years, and they were no threat to the community. At the very least, I had a responsibility to pass on to my people the warning that an armed maniac was on the loose. But when I logged in, I saw the flashing red panic indicator around the edge of the screen, and I knew I'd stumbled online too late.

The Fringe had unraveled, and it was all over before I even knew it had begun. The video feeds had gone black, and the chats were abandoned. I pored over the flurry of messages posted that day to make sense of the situation. A coup in the Arcanum. The grand magus missing. Assassins striking simultaneously worldwide. Witches snatched, lesser bloods and coordinators murdered. Mass evacuations into Faerie. Survivors disappearing with cryptic signoffs or simply silence. I'd missed it all, weathering Armageddon in blissful ignorance while taking notes on synthetic opioids. And when it hit me that I was alive only because I'd been out of town, I crouched on the bathroom floor and trembled, then emptied my stomach and cried for the family I'd not been able to save.

Then I'd picked myself up, washed my face, and checked out early. I'd driven straight back to Durham, stayed in another hotel until morning, then closed my bank account and popped by the office just long enough to fill out the necessary leave paperwork. With that in order, I'd grabbed my spare chargers and my Taser, exchanged my overnight suitcase for a backpack at a camping store on the outskirts of the city, and headed south to York, intending to hide until I could formulate a plan that wouldn't end with me on the wrong end of a wand.

Two weeks later, an assassin found me, and I'd fled north again, minus my car—a shot intended for me had hit the petrol tank, and I'd escaped in the chaos of the resulting fire.

Seamus touched my shoulder, jerking me from my thoughts. "It's my mess now, too," he murmured. "What's the plan?"

I glanced at his gloved hand, then pulled the car onto the side of the road and cut the engine. "Go home," I said, tossing the keys into his lap. "Be safe. Try to stay calm."

He shook his head. "Badger, let me—"

"No. This is me protecting you," I shot back, feeling a flicker of satisfaction as he twitched. "Don't follow me,

Seamie. I'll ring you when I can."

As he sputtered protestations, I slid out of the car, grabbed my bag from the back, and started off along the road. I didn't know where I was going, but there were lights in the distance, and where there were people, there was bound to be a bus or train. With the initial adrenaline rush past, weariness was setting in, but I kept my eyes on the horizon. Half an hour to the nearest bright spot if I hurried, an hour if I took my time…

Footsteps thudded in the dirt behind me, and Seamus called, "Badger, wait!" I tried to shrug him off when he grabbed my arm, but his grip was a vise. "No," he said when I turned to glare at him. "*No.* That's not how this works."

"Oh, really?" I snapped. "I remember the script. Let me go."

"Not unless you get back in the car."

I twisted and stomped his foot, then pulled free while he was distracted, put a few steps between us, and raised my palms to hold him at bay. "I'm trying to keep you alive. Get out of here."

The light of a passing car revealed his pained expression. "You honestly expect me to leave you on your own, with a hitman on your trail, and fly back to Belfast like nothing's wrong? Are you mad?"

"Seamie—"

"Forget it. Wherever you're going, I'm coming with you."

"That's not your decision."

"Says who? Get in the car, Badge."

Exhaustion, frustration, the hour, and the emotional bomb of seeing my former fiancé conspired to start my tears anew. "No. That's not fair," I said, swiping at my eyes, "you don't make that call. I'm not getting you into this. Just go, get as far away from me as you can, and—"

He stepped closer and hugged me again, muffling my orders against his jacket. "I'm not going anywhere," he mumbled into my ear. "And I'm sorry I didn't come weeks ago. I'm so sorry, love." When I didn't pull away, he said, "You're about to collapse. At least let me drive you to somewhere with a bed, eh? Come on, we can fight about this in the morning."

My body decided before my mind had time to consider the ramifications, and I let Seamus lead me back to the car. "In with you," he said, opening the rear door, and I curled up in the too-short back seat as he slid my pack onto the floor. I closed my eyes and heard the doors close and open and close, then tucked myself against the cushion as the car rumbled back to life. "It'll be all right," said Seamus over his shoulder. "Sleep, now."

And a few minutes later, lulled by the rocking of the road, I did.

CHAPTER 2

The unmistakable bouquet of bacon and black tea coaxed me back to consciousness.

Once I was aware enough to recognize what I was smelling, I bolted upright and looked around, disoriented and surprised to find myself tucked under a fluffy white duvet in a sunlit bedroom. A hotel, I realized after a second's panic, but a far nicer one than my last place of residence, a room with decorative sheers and a flat-screen television and carpet that was still its original color. A little two-seat table was positioned beside the window, and atop the table were a pair of covered dishes and a ceramic teapot, the source of the heavenly odor.

As I tried to piece my situation together, the bathroom door opened, and Seamus stepped out, wiping his hands dry against his borrowed robe. "Thought that might do the trick," he said, grinning as I rubbed the crust from my eyes. "Hungry? Thirsty? Please don't tell me you've gone vegetarian in my absence."

"Where am I?" I croaked, looking in vain for a clue in the room's generic furnishings.

"Inverness. Wait there." He returned to the bathroom, then emerged with a glass of water and passed it to me. "You don't remember arriving?"

I thought back over the hole in my memory as I drank, but judging by the light, I'd lost at least a few hours. "No. *Inverness?*"

"Seemed as good a place as any, and I was getting tired of driving." He sank into one of the chairs and poured a cup of tea. "You were pretty groggy when we checked in. Barely had your shoes off before you were snoring again."

Glancing under the duvet, I saw with a burst of relief that my clothes were as I'd remembered, minus the dirty trainers on the carpet. "I don't snore."

"Oh, I'd say that some things never change. Are we feeling peckish yet, or should I eat your breakfast, too?"

I climbed out of bed and slid into place at the table, and he lifted the metal covers with the aid of a cloth napkin, revealing enough eggs and starches to satisfy a teenage boy. "There's a restaurant in the lobby," he explained as I tried to choose a starting point. "They'll do room service as long as you don't mind picking it up yourself. Suppose that defeats the purpose, but I didn't know if you'd be up to leaving bed before noon."

I grunted in the affirmative and tucked in.

Seamus chuckled, and I looked up as he plunked a hard plastic knife and fork on the table. "You're a regular vision this morning, Badger."

"Starving," I replied between bites.

"Mm." He began to work on his bacon. "Eat your tomato—when did you last have anything remotely vegetable?" he chided. "And lettuce doesn't count."

"Tomato's a fruit."

"It's close enough. I can't imagine you've been eating well of late," he said, popping a bite in his mouth. "Not if you've been playing hide and seek with the murder wizards." He chewed thoughtfully as I continued to make short work of my plate. "Feeling any better? You looked like shit last night."

Stung, I dropped my fork and glared at him across the table. "Like *shit*? Maybe you haven't noticed, but this is what forty-seven looks like, you—"

"Whoa, hold on," he interrupted, briskly shaking his head, "no, that's not what I meant. You're gorgeous. You just looked like you'd come off a week of double shifts, that's all I was saying. God, I…" He cut his eyes to the ceiling and grimaced. "I'm sorry. That came out all wrong, didn't it?"

"Yeah," I muttered, mollified enough to resume my meal. "And since when am I gorgeous, Seamie?"

"Since always."

"Ha."

"As far as I'm concerned," he protested.

"Get your eyes checked, love." I peered at him more closely over the teapot. "Not looking so good, yourself. Did you sleep?"

"Not yet. Someone needed to be up in case of murder wizards, right?" He downed his tea, squeezing his eyes shut at the shot of hot liquid, then automatically poured a refill. "Now, if you're able to think straight again, we need to talk. What's the plan?"

"The plan," I replied between bites of toast, "is for you to get your arse on the next plane off this island."

Seamus smirked back at me over his cup. "Try again."

"You're not getting involved with—"

"Whitt's Rule Number One. Remember?"

I frowned. "No hits to the bollocks unless you mean it?"

"Right, sorry. Rule Number Two, then. No lone rangers."

I thought of our old instructor, a little man with dandelion fluff hair and gapped front teeth, and smiled in spite of myself. "Whitt never squared off against the Arcanum."

"The rule still applies. You need a partner. Come on, then," he said as I began to protest, "when was the last time you had a solid night's sleep? April? March?"

Pushing my plate aside, I reached across the table and took his free hand. "I appreciate it, but no. You've got no idea what you're doing, and I can't protect you."

One eyebrow quirked. "You're telling me they're immune to lead?"

"How did you get a gun here, anyway?"

"Checked baggage, credentials, luck, and stop changing the subject," he replied, squeezing my hand. "Here's the long and short of it, Badge: you're stuck with me, at least until I'm sure there's not a bounty on your head. Now, what's the plan?"

"You know," I said, holding his steady stare, "as I recall, you ran off to protect me. I'm running off now to protect you. This is what we call reciprocity. Fair's fair."

He refused to blink first. "First, I didn't *run*. I removed myself from your general vicinity so as not to accidentally kill you."

"My general vicinity? You went to fucking *Belfast!* Twenty-two years, Seamus! I've been telling you to come home—"

"And I just crisped a man to death, didn't I?" He put his cup down and took my other hand. "What if that had been you?" he murmured, his bone-crunching grip belying his apparent calm. "I couldn't live with myself if I hurt you."

"You *did* hurt me."

"Not like I could have." Releasing me, he took up his fork and stabbed his cooling eggs. "I was the problem, so I left. This is different."

"Yes, now *I'm* the problem! I'm a walking target—"

"The maniacs with wands are the problem, not you. And I'll be damned if I stand by and do nothing." He glared out the window as he swallowed a bite. "If I go off again, maybe I can aim it at one of them. I mean…" He hesitated, suddenly unsure. "Look, if you don't want me around, I understand. I wouldn't want me around, either. But if you're willing to accept a risk of sudden inferno, I want to help you."

My chest clenched, and I stalled for time with tea. "I just want you to be safe, Seamie," I said when I trusted myself again.

"And you." He shrugged. "Here, listen, this is your show, yeah? I'm along to make sure you eat and sleep and watch your back." He cocked his teacup toward the city outside. "So, Inverness. What are our chances of being killed in our sleep if we stay here?"

"Worse with every passing day," I muttered, pushing my untouched sausage around the plate. "They'll track me here eventually. I'll slip up, or they'll get lucky. I mean, they're based in Glastonbury, so it may take them a while, but I know they're looking for me. Seems coordinators are high on the hit list."

"Glastonbury?" He snorted. "Figures. And *why* are they trying to exterminate witches?"

"Not just witches—all of us in the Fringe. And I wish I knew. We've never been a threat to the Arcanum. I mean, I certainly can't take a wizard in a fair fight."

"Taser worked nicely. So, how long can we stay here, then? Couple of days? Week?"

I massaged my temple with two fingers. "Don't know. I'm still trying to find a crafter, but no luck there."

"What sort of crafter?"

"Did you notice my wand last night?" I asked, pushing back from the table, then rose and retrieved it from my backpack. "The tape isn't an upgrade. It's getting weaker every time I patch it."

Seamus held out his hand, and I dropped the wrapped wand in his palm. "Huh. How do you fix it?"

"Don't know if it *can* be fixed, actually. I may need a new one," I explained, returning to my seat. "So I've got to find someone with a supply of rowan and dragonscale, and the know-how to—"

"Wait, *dragonscale*?"

"Excellent conductor, but expensive as hell. It's rare."

His brow furrowed as he considered that. "Like…"

"Dragons exist," I said, discerning the cause of his consternation. "Not here—outside this realm. That's why you don't see many wands like mine. A gift from my grandparents." I beckoned for the wand, and Seamus passed it back to me. "They didn't want anything to do with us, but at least they sprung for a wand for me. I'm too weak a witch to work with anything less than dragonscale."

Seamus frowned as I inspected the degrading tape on my wand. "When we were kids—"

"My power faded. Or maybe it didn't grow with me."

"Ah." He watched me tuck the wand back into its pocket, then sighed. "Badger?"

"Yeah?"

"Are you ever going to tell me what you were trying to tell me last night, or am I going to have to beg it out of you?"

I zipped the bag closed and straightened to find him watching me intently, expectantly—perhaps fearfully—with his hands wrapped around his half-empty teacup. "Yeah," I mumbled, sitting on the edge of the rumpled bed. "What I was trying to say is that Dad was convinced that you're fae. I think he's right."

"You've got to give me more than that."

"I know. Thinking about the best way to do this," I muttered, then steeled myself and met his worried eyes. "All right, you accept that witches exist, yeah? And wizards are like us witches, but more talented."

"Okay."

"Well, wizards and witches...we're human, but we've got the ability to work with magic, see," I explained. "Runs in families, like being short or redheaded or whatever." He nodded, and I pressed on. "But...you know what I was saying about dragons, how they're not in this realm? There are two other realms. One we call the Gray Lands, and it's best avoided unless you like monsters. The other is Faerie."

"As in..."

"Exactly what you think. There's a race native to that realm who look like us, but they're different. Incredible magical talent. Immortal. Forever young." I paused and tried to read his inscrutable expression. "See where I'm going with this?"

But Seamus shook his head. "You can't seriously think—"

"There are two easy litmus tests for figuring out if you've got a faerie on your hands," I said, cutting him off. "One, they can't touch iron or silver. I think you know better than I do what that result is."

With Seamus's gloves off, I'd seen the old scar on the back of his left hand, the result of a run-in with an exposed nail when we were six. It had faded, but the sunlight revealed the brand of scar tissue that lingered, and many more besides. Nor had it escaped my notice that he was still traveling with his own utensils.

"Two," I said, "animals can't stand them."

Seamus's cheeks began to color. "I'm not good with them, that's all—"

"Remember Sweetie? You weren't in the car with her more than twenty seconds before she tried to take a chunk out of your arm."

"She was *vicious*."

"She was a geriatric German Shepherd with two feet in the grave. Be honest with me, Seamie: have you ever successfully pet a dog? A cat? Anything?" His silence was answer enough, and I sighed. "I can't be absolutely positive, but all the signs point to fae. Dad thought you're probably half-blooded. The full-blooded ones are impossible to deal with. Psychopaths, really."

He said nothing for a long moment, then put his cup down and rested his head in his hands. "You think I'm not human," he mumbled.

"Probably half."

"That's not reassuring. And you...I mean, you knew about this? Brian told you?"

"Yeah," I admitted.

"When?"

"After Doug Stewart—"

His head jerked up again. "*Jesus*, Badger! Why the hell didn't you tell me?"

I tried to project calm as Seamus's red face worked. "Because Dad asked me not to. He said it was the best thing to do for you, and I trusted him. In retrospect, I think he was trying to make you someone else's problem, but I only wanted to help you, Seamie. You've got to believe that."

"Do Mam and Dad—"

"They're aware. They trusted Dad on this, too."

"But w*hy*?" he demanded. "Why did no one—"

"Because no one in the Fringe knew what to do with a half-fae child. We've plenty of lesser bloods—quarter-fae and below—but there was no one around who could have trained you. Not safely. And sometimes, if you don't expose a sensitive to magic, he won't realize his own ability. That's why I stopped showing you things after Doug," I explained, wincing at the hurt in his eyes. "Dad said that if you forgot about magic, you might not figure it out." Seamus continued to stare at me, and I spread my hands. "He thought it was best. *Everyone* in his circle thought it was the right thing to do. He wanted you to have a normal life for as long as you could."

He turned away, scarlet and trembling, and I held my breath while he collected himself. Finally, Seamus muttered, "You knew."

"I'm so sorry. I should have—"

"I'm some sort of goddamned monster," he yelled, "and you—"

"I was going to marry you, wasn't I?"

Thrown by the interjection, Seamus froze, and I pressed my luck. "Yeah, I knew," I said softly, "and I didn't care because I loved you. I don't think you're a monster, Seamie. And I was wrong not to say anything, but I wanted so badly to help you." Suddenly feeling vulnerable under his stare, I folded my arms and looked out the window. "Wish you'd come home sooner. We had a girl in the States of late—both parents half fae, and all her brothers. She would have known who could train you."

He grunted. "Arcanum killed her, I take it?"

"No. I think she made it into Faerie, but I can't give you more than that. I don't have her number. Don't even know if it's possible to make a call into that realm, to be honest. I kept the queen's number, but it's not as if I've tried."

"Queen?"

His shaking, at least, seemed to have abated when I looked back at him. "Court system. The queen heads one, the king the other. They're not a couple," I clarified. "He's surprisingly reasonable in person, and she was more than civil when we talked—I investigated her husband's murder, long story. I'm sure *they* would know what to do," I mumbled. "But I haven't heard of a faerie in this realm since the Arcanum went on the offensive."

"Why not call, then?" I frowned at the question, and Seamus rose to join me on the bed. "You said they let witches in over there, yeah? Try to ring up this queen of yours. Better hanging out in someone's spare room than hiding for your life over here."

I shook my head. "Doesn't work like that. First rule of dealing with faeries is that you never, *ever*, ask for a favor. I haven't got anything to bargain with, and even if I had, I'm significantly outclassed against them."

"You think it would be worse than murder wizards?" he retorted.

"There are stories. Safer to keep running."

We sat beside each other in silence, listening to the lift rumble and chime down the hall. After a few moments, I felt Seamus's fingers brush against mine and took his hand.

"Is that why you don't want me here?" he asked quietly. "You think I'm going to come back and bite you someday?"

"Of course not. I'm trying to save your life, you dolt. If the Arcanum finds out about you…"

I left that statement unfinished, but Seamus squeezed

my hand in understanding. "Whatever else I may be, I'm a good shot. And I'm going to keep you safe, Badger, if it's the last thing I do. Whatever it takes." I felt his eyes on me and turned to look at him. "I'm still your partner," he said with a half-smile. "So what do you say we think about a plan?"

My plan that morning consisted, first and foremost, of a hot shower. The flophouse where I'd been staying never provided anything better than tepid water, so within a couple of minutes, I'd steamed the white-tiled hotel bathroom into foggy oblivion. Standing under the pounding massage head, rubbing half a sample bottle of vaguely floral shampoo into my dirty hair, I closed my eyes and tried to choose a next step. After all, no matter how pleasant that moment was, I had to come out of the shower eventually.

Edinburgh wasn't safe, that much was clear. Perhaps in a month or two, but not for the immediate future. Glasgow was probably also a bad choice. Sure, I could blend into the crowd there, but any large urban area would be an obvious target. I couldn't very well stay in the Highlands, though—an Englishwoman with distinctive hair would be remembered, especially if she went about in the company of a man half her age. Someone's tongue would wag to the wrong ear eventually.

Suppose I pressed south, aiming for Leeds or Liverpool—hell, why not London, if I was going that route?

Or I could try to hide out in the backwoods of Wales, pick a town with an unpronounceable name and buy a wig. No, Wales was too close to Glastonbury for my taste— really, anything in the UK was too close for my comfort.

Ireland, then. Seamus knew the north, and perhaps we could get by in the south, maybe choose a hiding spot in the far west and wait out the storm by the Atlantic. But getting there would mean using my ID, and the last thing I wanted to do was ping on anyone's radar. As much as I doubted that the Arcanum had got its hooks into Visas and Immigration, I didn't want to risk it. Besides, if Seamus went back to Belfast, wouldn't he be caught up in the investigation about his unfortunate suspect? Even if he wasn't a suspect in the bizarre death, he'd have to return to work…and I could only imagine the questions his workmates would have if I was lurking about.

Leave, then. Take a chance and make the hop to France or Spain. I could hide among the tourists, or perhaps I could push west, look up my mother's distant cousins in Texas and Oklahoma and try to camp with them. But no, Mama's "people" were strangers, and I couldn't see the wisdom in venturing closer to Montana. Texas was big, but at least now I had an oceanic buffer between the silo and myself. Then again, a fat lot of good an ocean would do me if a sufficiently strong wizard opened a gate from afar to step out next to me.

Maybe, I decided, reluctantly shutting off the taps, this didn't have to be sorted that day. We could stay in this lovely room a bit longer, have a few good nights' sleep, and eat meals slightly more healthful than my recent diet, which had consisted mostly of chips and crisps. Seamus could get his head on straight, and I could…well, *breathe*.

My mind made up, I tucked a towel in place and stepped into the room in a cloud of steam, dripping but feeling a bit closer to human. "What do you say we—" I began, then spotted Seamus's head on the pillow I'd recently vacated.

As long as I could remember, he'd been a master of the art of the catnap, pulling all-nighters for three and four days in a row and sneaking off during lulls to crash at his desk or in a car. He'd done it again while I was bathing, and he was sound asleep in the mussed hollow I'd left in the middle of the bed, curled onto his left side with his right arm flung toward the edge of the mattress.

Like always.

For a fleeting instant, I pictured myself throwing off the towel and sliding into the space—*my* space—beside him, tucking myself against his body and under his arm, and drifting off with his warm breath in my hair. It hurt to force the notion aside, but I clutched my damp towel and turned away to clear my head. No. Whatever he looked like, however desperately I wanted someone to hold me and tell me everything was going to be just fine, the man in the bed wasn't the Seamus who had skipped out of my life two decades before.

I kept telling myself that as I stared out at the late-morning traffic of loch-bound tourists and apathetic locals, but my heart refused to be convinced.

The bedding rustled behind me, and I turned as Seamus stirred awake. "Feeling better?" he asked through a yawn.

"Cleaner, at least." I stepped away from the curtains before someone passing below could look up and get an eyeful. "Go back to sleep, I'm just going to get dressed."

"Mm." He hoisted himself onto his elbow and grinned. "Thoughts about the day's activities? Any other revelations you might need to share with me?"

"Not yet," I said, heading for the bathroom.

"In that case, and since I don't see any murder wizards lurking about, want to do something ridiculous?"

I closed the door and raised my voice. "Probably not."

"We could do Loch Ness," Seamus continued. "I don't know about you, but I've never been out there, and that seems a shame. Isn't there a tour boat?"

"Yeah, but forget it." Dropping my towel, I wiped a streak of mirror clean with my palm—just enough to show me my face without revealing the bits of myself I found even less appealing. "You won't catch me out there."

Seamus's voice grew louder, and I assumed he'd pressed himself against the door, just as he had in our old flat. "Not afraid of Nessie, are you?" he teased. "Come on, we'll play tourist and get your mind off of this mess."

"Actually, I've got a healthy respect for Nessie," I replied, running a brush through my wet hair. "All of them."

"Huh?"

"Nessie's real." I squinted at my crooked part, then brushed it straight. "We think there's a natural gate into the Gray Lands deep in Loch Ness. The Arcanum's done tests, and my understanding is that the dark magic readings are seriously elevated near the middle of the lake. Actually, we sent a group out not ten years ago, and they managed to take a few pictures. *Good* ones, mind. Whatever's lurking out there isn't a plesiosaur, and 'it' is definitely a 'they.'"

Seamus pounded on the door, and I put my modesty towel back in place before opening it a crack. "Yes?"

He gaped at me through the gap. "Slow down, back up. Nessie *exists*?"

"Uh-huh. And since those who avoid the Gray Lands tend to live longer, we're not going for a boat ride."

"But…but there's a sea mon—"

"*No*, Seamus. Go if you want, but you're going alone. Besides," I said, closing the door as he sputtered, "getting trapped on a boat is low on my list of good ideas. If it's all the same to you, I want to lie in bed and watch a television that gets more than three channels."

Before he could offer a counter-proposition, my mobile began to ring in the next room. "Bloody *hell*," I muttered, tightening the towel, and brushed past Seamus to pull the phone from my backpack. The ID knew the caller, and I hit the button with a sudden fluttering of hope. "Hello, Gerri?"

"Badger? Oh, my God, *Badger*! It's you! Where are you?"

I sat on the edge of the bed and pressed the phone to my ear, nearly bursting with the excitement of hearing another Fringer's voice for the first time in weeks. Gerri Tidwell had never been particularly active in the organization, but I'd been round to her house a few times when my travels took me near Berwick-upon-Tweed. When we first met, she was living in a renovated semi-detached house in Spittal with her son, but having bought the other half, she'd since put in a few doors and was running a modest B&B, a perfect place for the coordinator on the go to crash. "I'm still around," I told her. "More importantly, where are you? Are you safe? Hurt? Are you alone?"

Gerri's enthusiasm waned a degree as she spoke. "I'm all right, dear, but our Tommy's on the run. And I...I can't stay here long."

"What's happened?"

Her voice dropped to a whisper. "Wizards about. I've seen them in the shops. I've got to run soon, they're going to find me—"

"If they haven't yet—"

"And I need you to take the Endicott twins."

My guts twisted, knowing what was to come, as I asked, "Why do you have the twins?"

"Bastards killed Elaine and Marty," she replied, her voice hard as diamond. "And they burnt the house down to cover their tracks. Didn't know the girls were hiding in there."

Had I not been sitting, my knees would have buckled. "Jesus, Gerri. Are they—"

"They're healing, but I can't do this anymore. I can't run with the girls in tow," she said, almost begging. "Please, you've got to do something. Help me. I can't hide them much longer, not with wizards in town..."

I took a deep breath to steady myself, then loosened my painful grip on the phone and nodded. "I'll come to collect them tonight. Say midnight. Be safe, love, and don't do anything rash. Look for me."

"Bless you, Badger," she replied, and the phone went dead.

I only realized I'd been sitting in silence and staring at

the wall when Seamus squatted in front of me and waved his hand across my face. "Badge? All right, then? Who was that?"

I blinked, bringing the world back into focus, and met his worried eyes. "Another Fringer. I've got to take a couple of children out of harm's way before the Arcanum finds them."

His brows knit. "You think the murder wizards would—"

"I *know* they would kill the girls if they found them," I said, and pushed myself off the bed. "They're witch-bloods."

"Come again?" he replied, following me toward the bathroom.

"Witch-blooded fae. Mix a faerie with a wizard or witch, and presto. Marty Endicott was a witch, and Elaine Davies was quarter-fae. The Arcanum's preferred method of dealing with fae-blooded Fringers of late has been eradication, so the twins aren't going to stand a chance on their own. They're six, if I recall," I added, closing the door again to throw on my clothes. "Elaine was active on the network, and I know her mother is still around—well, she was a few months ago. If she's alive now, she's in Faerie."

"So can we contact Granny?"

"I don't know," I said, pulling on my T-shirt, then slipped my necklace back in place beneath it. "But for now, they're my responsibility."

"Why you?"

I sighed and buttoned my trousers. "Because I'm the regional coordinator. For all I know, I may be the only one left in the UK. The job means looking out for people. Helping them. When there's a crisis, they turn to you." I threw on my hoodie, assuming the extra fabric at the neck would soak up the worst of my hair drippings. "How quickly can we get to Berwick? Three hours? Four?"

"Probably," said Seamus, "but I think it all rather

depends on which of us is driving. Are you sure you're up to this? The road goes back through Edinburgh, you know."

"So it does. But don't you suppose there's somewhere along the way that we could exchange your car?"

I opened the door again to find him waiting just outside. "Aren't we clever?" he said, smirking.

"You may find this hard to believe, Seamie," I replied, pushing him out of the way, "but they don't call me 'Detective' for my good looks."

"Or charm."

"Cheeky," I muttered, and tossed my wet towel at him.

CHAPTER 3

With nearly twelve hours to kill, I suppose I could have spared the time to primp before hitting the road, but I've never been one to waste the energy with a job on the line. By one, Seamus had found a place to exchange his Skoda for a blue Focus—not an ideal getaway car, but relatively inconspicuous and large enough to hold the twins. We took our time at lunch, and as I drummed my fingers on the steering wheel, waiting for Seamus to adjust his seat, he glanced at me and shrugged. "What's your hurry? We've got hours."

"If Gerri's right and there are Arcanum agents around her, I want a chance to scout before going in tonight."

"Which they're probably anticipating if they've kept a tail on her. Why don't we hang back and save the final approach for full dark?"

I started the car and pulled away from the restaurant. "What makes you think they're anticipating me? Gerri's not a major Fringe player—she's probably panicking over nothing."

Seamus was quiet for a moment, then said, "It's all rather convenient, though, isn't it?"

"What are you talking about?"

"Well, they located you in Edinburgh last night, but they botched the pickup. And they know you're on the move again—only a fool would have stayed in the city—but they don't know where you've gone. Now, out of the blue, you get a call from one of your people and swoop in to her aid. Do you get these sorts of calls often?"

"Not since Easter," I admitted. "Gerri's the first to ring me. But we've all been hiding—maybe now, if a few more reach out, we can start to reconnect—"

"The first person to try your number does so *now*? She just so happens to decide that today's the day to get the band back together?"

I heard the incredulity in his voice and knew without looking that one of his eyebrows had migrated halfway to his hairline. "You don't get it. The Fringe is a *family*. I'd trust any one of them with my life, and they'd trust me. They *do* trust me," I added. "Gerri wouldn't contact me if she didn't think I'd keep her safe."

"Mm. So part of this family dynamic is foisting inconvenient kids onto your sisters and brothers, is it?"

"She's nearly sixty-five," I replied, trying not to sound defensive. "And she has a bum leg. Her son lived with her and helped out around the place, but he's on the run now. If she's been watching over those girls since March, then I think she's done her fair bit." When that garnered no response, I said, "We're all we've got, us Fringers. We've no one else to turn to. Faerie doesn't exactly want us, and the Arcanum's been apathetic until now. If we can't trust each other, who *can* we trust?"

"I hear you," said Seamus, "but I still think this smells rotten."

"Sure, the timing could be better, but Gerri's a nice lady. You'll like her, you'll see."

Seamus grunted, but he let the matter drop as we sped toward the Cairngorms. As we passed yet another flock of disinterested sheep, he cleared his throat and took a swig of his Coke. "So...while I've got you captive, I've been thinking of a few questions."

"Is this going to distract me from driving?"

"I've seen you multitask. Okay, first question."

"Shoot," I muttered.

"Flying brooms. Who the hell thought that would be a good idea?"

"Those have really gone by the wayside—"

"So they *do* exist?" he interrupted, pouncing on the opening.

I sighed. "Yeah. Definitely more of a wizard thing—if you catch a witch atop a levitating object, he probably didn't put himself there." I stole a glance at Seamus, who was opening a bag of peanuts as I spoke. "Going to share?"

"If you keep talking."

I held out my hand and felt a few nuts hit my palm. "Right," I said, popping the lot in my mouth at one go. "So, you know, it's bloody hard to cast a successful levitation spell on yourself. Inanimate objects are much simpler, and a good wizard can make other people levitate with sufficient work and planning, but if you need to rise quickly, just levitate the nearest object and sit on top of it. Brooms are fairly universal, yeah? They're a literal pain in the arse over long distances, or so I hear, but they work in a pinch. I heard—and this is all third-hand, mind—but I heard that a wizard once ensorcelled a proper saddle after a bad broom trip."

Seamus chuckled. "Like, flying around atop a saddle, feet in the stirrups, nothing underneath?"

"Exactly. Can you imagine the sight?"

"Unfortunately." He drank again and tipped another handful of peanuts my way. "Next question: what's the deal with black cats? Familiars and all that rubbish?"

"Nothing demonic." I cringed with the memories of Halloweens past. "Cats are useful creatures—mousers, yeah? And people are funny about black animals, so black cats were cheaper to come by, and there was less chance of having them stolen."

"So, pest control, then?" he replied, sounding disappointed.

"Not…exactly." I glanced at Seamus, wishing he'd chosen another topic. "Animals are a fantastic early warning system. A cat's useless for telling you when another witch or wizard is around, but get a faerie anywhere near one, and the cat will either hiss and claw or run for the rafters. Know what I mean?"

"Maybe," he mumbled into his Pepsi.

"They're also sensitive to anything out of the Gray Lands. Basically, if it's not from this realm, animals are going to be twitchy around it." I hesitated, then said, "This isn't about you, Seamie. This is about giving people who are barely competent with magic time to head for the hills—"

"When something wicked this way comes. I get it."

"Seamie…"

"It's all right, Badge."

We sat in uncomfortable silence for a few minutes, and then I shifted in my seat. "My turn."

"Not yet, this is my chance at Q&A—"

"Why haven't you visited?" I blurted over his protests. "Forget about me, why not your parents? They're not getting any younger, and it breaks their hearts every Christmas when you're not around."

"I did mention what I left back at work, didn't I?" he said stiffly. "You think I want to put my own family at risk of incineration?"

"One incident in twenty-two years—"

"That's all it would take!"

I cut my eyes to the passenger side and watched his chest heave as he struggled against his outburst. Seamus's face had crimsoned, and he glared out the windscreen as if he had a deep, personal hatred for the Scottish countryside.

"Once in all that time," I resumed when the echoes of his shout no longer rang in my ears. "The odds are decent. Just stop by before you go back to Belfast and surprise them. They'd be thrilled to see you again, you know they would."

He continued to stare straight ahead. "I'm not taking that chance."

"And yet, here you are, riding around with me. I'm not sure whether I should be pleased or insulted to have warranted a visit."

That, at least, made his head swivel in my direction. "Do you honestly think I'd have come home if I weren't desperate?"

"Well, given your track record thus far, I'd say no."

Seamus's hand tightened around his peanut bag, crinkling the wrapper into a dense ball. "Badger," he finally said with some difficulty, "the only reason I've put you in danger now is because you're the one person I know who might be able to stop me before I accidentally kill someone. Again," he muttered, then sighed and looked away. "I don't know, you've done well against the murder wizards. You'd probably be safer on your own. If you want me to—"

I whipped onto the side of the road and threw on the brakes. "No," I said, grabbing Seamus's arm as the seatbelt yanked him back from an impact with the dash. "You are *not* running out on me like that again, goddammit!"

"What are you—"

"I've waited all this time to see you, and you're not going to pull that 'I'm protecting you' nonsense," I snapped. "If you want to go, fine. You'd be safer if you weren't with me. But don't say it's for my own good. *You* don't get to make that decision, understand?" I said, tightening my grip until he winced. "No more shitty heroic sacrifices. If I don't feel safe around you, I'll damn well let you know, and *I'll* take the appropriate measures. I'm not some pathetic little girl you need to protect. So be on your way, if that's what you want. Go with my blessing—I want you to be safe. But don't you *dare* say it's for my own good."

Seamus blinked at me for a moment, digesting my speech, then murmured, "I've never thought of you as a pathetic little girl. Not ever. I just...Badge, I don't know what I'd do if I hurt you."

I released him and shifted back into gear. "It seems we both survived that scenario, so I wouldn't worry."

"You know what I mean," he replied, exasperated. I gave him a look, and he protested, "You're still alive! That was the goal!"

"Yes, fine, whatever. But don't sit there and think you didn't hurt me."

In the uncomfortable quiet that followed, Seamus seemed to lose his appetite for interrogation, and I tried to concentrate on the road instead of the scene replaying behind my eyes, the movie that always popped up at inopportune moments.

In my mind, old Sergeant Norrell was walking the new guy, the unfortunately-named Richard Smallwood, around the floor once more, making the introductions. I was sitting at my desk—a picture-less desk, a recently depersonalized desk—eating a quick ham sandwich, and Norrell caught me with my mouth full and cheeks puffed like a mumps patient. *And this is Hannah Parsons*, he'd told Dick, who'd watched with mild amusement as I'd tried to swallow half a sandwich in one dry gulp. *Better mind yourself around this one, lad. She scared her last partner so badly, the poor boy ran off to Belfast.* I'd laughed along with Norrell's guffaws because the alternative was sobbing, and one did not cry in front of one's superiors when one was female and working toward a promotion.

Every new male hire got a similar spiel when he met me. In some ways, I suppose it helped—better to be thought a nail-tough ball-buster than a pushover, especially when one was a head shorter than most of the men in the building—but I can't say my reputation did anything to improve my social life. As for the female hires, they found out eventually, and a few even had the sense and decency to ask me for the truth of the rumors. *Fiancé got cold feet*, I'd always tell them, and that was enough. They sympathized. Most said I was better off without the wanker or worse, and I would smile noncommittally.

"Hey, Badger," Seamus ventured, penetrating my unpleasant reverie, "look, I…I just want to say I'm—"

"Can we talk about something else, please?"

"Sure," he said too quickly. "So…how did you plan to kill time around Berwick?"

"No idea," I muttered as a herd of cattle flashed past in a blur of windblown brown hair. "Let's get there first, okay?"

"Okay."

I felt more than saw his hand as it moved toward mine, then paused and retreated.

Despite Seamus's misgivings, I was eager to scout around Spittal and hurried down the coast toward England. But realizing I could do what I needed in that town in far less than the seven hours we had to burn, I compromised and pulled into the car park at the Berwick Pier. Neither of us was yet hungry, nor particularly talkative, but the walk to the lighthouse was a diversion and a needed stretch of the legs.

The afternoon sun shone deceptively brightly as it popped in and out from behind the clouds rolling overhead. I was grateful for my hoodie, though the wind cut straight through the cotton and nudged my hands into my pockets for warmth. Seamus adopted a similar posture to mine—slightly hunched, hands tucked away, eyes set on the horizon—and together, we strolled out above the sea, letting the waves, the wind, and the squawking birds carry the conversation for us.

Part of me—the mature, sage coordinator who could arbitrate disputes with the best of them—chided me for my silence. This was *Seamus*, she insisted, my Seamus, and didn't I want to let bygones be bygones? He was scared and confused, he needed support right now—and that was my job, wasn't it? Be the leader. Be the rock others cling to in the storm. Put the past aside, put your stupid feelings aside, and do the job. Someday, perhaps, when you weren't being hunted like an escaped convict by magically gifted assassins and Seamus wasn't unintentionally crisping people, you could have a sit-down with him and talk about the many ways in which the end of your engagement could have been better handled, but now was not that time.

But another part of me countered that by showing the coordinator a select pair of fingers, and I had to admit that I liked her style.

The lighthouse wasn't far, and soon we found ourselves huddled at the edge of the pier, staring out at the blue-gray water. Somewhere out there, on the other side of the North Sea, was Denmark. I'd never been—Seamus and I had talked once of spending a short break in Copenhagen, back when we were young and the idea of staying in a hostel was still exciting, but on my own, I'd never given the place much thought. Not that I'd ever had time for travel between the Constabulary and the Fringe. When I wasn't in Durham, I was making the rounds through the north or tucked in with my computer at home, reading the latest from the network. I had contacts worldwide—the sun never set on the Fringe—but I'd spent precious little time out of the UK. A few holidays on the Med when I was at my bikini best, a long weekend in Paris and Vienna and Rome to put tick marks on my mental list, but that was the farthest I'd been from home.

Well, that and two brief ventures into Faerie—one to question the queen, the other to meet with the ill-fated young grand magus—but leaving the realm itself almost didn't count. Any voyage seemed less real without a passport and at least one irate baby on a plane.

Maybe now was the time to spread my wings and start my delayed globetrotting, I mused, as the wind blew cold salt against my cheeks. Take the girls and flee somehow, find sanctuary in some far-flung corner of Europe without a sizeable expat community and start afresh. I didn't know if Seamus was a part of that plan, but at that moment, his future was lower on my list of concerns than that of the orphaned Endicott twins. I owed them whatever help I could provide, but Seamus...

He ran, that other, angrier part of me said. *You owe him nothing.*

Before I could agree with her again, a third voice—a younger voice I vaguely recognized as having been my own, once upon a time—whispered, *This is Seamie you're talking about. Are you really never going to forgive him?*

Not yet, I told her, looking for Denmark in the distance. *Maybe not for a good, long time to come—*

"Badger?"

I jerked, startled from my thoughts, but maintained my composure. "Yeah?"

Seamus slid closer to me as the other walkers moved past us. "I thought you'd understand why I left," he murmured.

"I do."

"Then why are you so angry with me?"

He sounded genuinely perplexed, and I could feel my temper rise as I turned to look at him. "I said I understood why you left," I replied, keeping my voice low. "I never said it was the right decision."

"Badge—"

I held up my hand to cut him off. "Stop. I don't want any more explanations, and I don't want any excuses. We can talk about this later if you're still around. Right now, I've got far more important things to think about than reliving the past, so..."

He nodded and took a step to the side, giving me a measure of space. "All right," he said softly. "Okay. Work first, yeah?"

"Yeah."

We watched a bird swoop and dive, breaking the surface just long enough to snatch a wriggling silver fish from the shallows and carry it away.

"I don't know about you," said Seamus, "but I could

do with a cuppa."

"Yeah," I mumbled, and turned toward the shore. "Yeah, me, too."

Tea at a sea-view café turned into dinner when neither of us could think of a better option, and then we piled back into the car for a reconnaissance drive around Spittal.

"Can you at least tell me what you're looking for?" Seamus pleaded during my third pass through town. "Unless you'd like me to count postboxes, I'm useless."

"Anyone like that guy from last night," I replied, pausing to let a knot of pedestrians cross the road.

"So…all in black, waving a wand? Should be tough to spot."

I ignored the sarcasm. "Nothing that obvious. If they're here, walking around in daylight, they'll be going about in civilian garb."

"Then how am I supposed to—"

"They have a look about them, okay?" I said, gripping the wheel to keep myself from snapping at him. "Most British wizards do. Old-blooded ones, anyway."

"What sort of look?"

"Well, there's not much genetic diversity, if you catch my drift."

"Ah," he muttered. "Inbreeds."

"No, not exactly, but…you'll know what I mean once you've seen a few. There's a certain similarity among them, especially if they're old Arcanum. A lot of the magi and other strong ones are. It's like…you know, like breeding show dogs. A spaniel and a spaniel make other spaniels, right?"

Seamus snorted. "You know how inbred some of those show dogs are?"

"Bad example. It's…" I sighed, struggling to find an easy way to encapsulate Arcanum blood politics. "Okay, the first thing you have to understand is that wizards marry wizards. It's what's *done*. If you're particularly strong, you're pressured to marry someone at least close to comparable and have a large family. Combine the best genes and multiply, yes?"

"Fucked up, but yes."

"I never said this was *normal*. All right, ideal situation, strong wizard from a long line of wizards marries someone just like him and produces a litter. Now, to complicate this, you have new-blooded wizards in the mix—new mutants, if you like, or their descendants. Anyone who doesn't have wizards at least five generations deep is considered new-blooded. Follow me?" Seamus nodded, and I rounded a corner past a line of small inns. "Well, new-blooded or old, a strong wizard is a strong wizard, but there's more prestige in marrying someone from an established family."

"Like old money and new money," he offered.

"Precisely. So, further complicating this, sometimes you get two well-papered wizards together, and they make a witch. Dad, for instance—my grandparents had five children, four solid wizards in a row, and then there was little Brian. It happens from time to time," I explained, "but it's, ehm…it's not something families talk about. Especially not one like his."

Seamus frowned. "Yours, don't you mean?"

"*His.* They've never wanted anything to do with me. Well, one thing." I pulled up at an intersection and glanced at my confused passenger. "My wand, remember? A little gift from my doting grandparents to make me quietly go away. Hush money, if you like." His brow only furrowed more deeply, and I looked aside as the road cleared. "Half of the reason for the Fringe's existence is that witches are not too subtly encouraged to go off and build lives for themselves that don't include the Arcanum. There's no place for us in the organization. So you'll see witches marry other witches or mundanes…sometimes lesser bloods, but that's rare. The Endicotts were the poster children for making *that* work. Anyway, that's why most of your better wizards share a certain resemblance, at least around here."

As I headed out of town again, aiming for Tweedmouth, Seamus twisted in his seat to rummage through the bags behind us, then reappeared with my taped-up wand in hand. "Mind if I have another look?"

I rolled my eyes. "Asking a bit late, aren't we?"

"Not at all. You were less likely to say no this way." He held it lengthwise in front of him, two fingers of his left hand supporting the base and his right index finger supporting the tip, and peered at the spiraling black tape. "Is it just me, or is it supposed to feel weird when you touch it?"

"It's not just you. Tape aside, that's a *really* powerful wand. It's almost like holding a live wire...well, it was before I broke it."

"So if I were to start waving it around, would—"

"Probably not, but do us a favor and point it away from my face, hmm?"

He obliged with a mumbled apology. "And this crafter you need to find—any leads?"

"None," I sighed.

"What if we found a hardware store and bought some wood glue? Not tonight, I mean, everything's closing soon, but in the morning?"

There was no point in making another pass, I decided; I was killing time more than hunting wizards as the light shifted toward orange and pink. "It's not that simple. Just the fact that the grain's broken could make the wood irreparable, and it's been hemorrhaging core material for weeks. When you're working with magic-conducting materials, you've got to know what you're doing, or else the finished product won't work properly. And besides," I added, slowing at an intersection, "witches and wizards always muck it up when we try. All crafters are witch-bloods. Most of them can't use magic, but they can manipulate the tools we need."

Seamus considered that for a moment. "So what happens when the murder wizards kill all the witch-bloods, then? Who's going to make their wands for them?"

I could only shrug. "They may have kidnapped some of the crafters. Whether they can force them to make wands is another matter." Cutting my eyes to him, I allowed myself to smirk. "It would be too bad if the materials the Arcanum had on hand weren't up to snuff. Crafters are so *particular* about what they use."

"Now more than ever, I suppose." He shook the wand like a skinny maraca, and I grimaced at the sound of moving grit at its core. A proper wand core was nearly as dense as the wood around it. At the current rate, my wand was going to be less than useless in another month.

Seeing my unease, Seamus put the wand back in its pocket, made himself comfortable, and cracked his knuckles. "Were you planning on circling Spittal all night?"

Before I could answer, I spotted a shopping center and pulled into the mostly deserted car park in front of Argos. "Not all night," I replied, shutting off the car, and the engine ticked as it began to cool. "Thought I might take a nap, if you'll watch for me."

"Sure," he replied, and I climbed out and into the back seat, which, while not the best bed I'd ever appropriated, would do the trick. I made myself relatively comfortable and closed my eyes, and I'd almost drifted off when I heard Seamus's seat creak in front of me. "Hey, Badge?" he whispered.

"Mm?"

"What happens if you can't find someone to fix your wand?"

"Then I'm screwed," I mumbled into my crooked arm.

"Because I was thinking that if we came across another wizard, we could jump him and take his wand. Or is there a way to put a trigger lock on those things?"

"No, and no."

"Why not? Seems fair to me."

I cracked one eye open and found him watching me from the front seat. "Unless we robbed another witch, I wouldn't be able to use any wand we nabbed. I need another rowan-dragonscale—it would be like wearing glasses in the wrong prescription."

He frowned in thought. "And you're sure no wizard would be carrying one?"

"Positive." I twisted on the bench to tuck myself against the back of the seat. "The only other wand a witch can use, and I'm not even sure if I could, is oak and unicorn horn. Dad had one, but given how poorly I fare with mine, I doubt I could make his work."

"*Unicorn?*"

"They shed their horns like deer—we're not horrible. Well, I mean, there are a few merrow-skin wands in circulation, but those are all antiques."

The look of incomprehension on Seamus's face deepened. "What the hell is merrow?"

"Polite term for a mermaid," I replied, "and before the Arcanum recognized them as people, a few crafters specialized in working with merrow skin. It's a good conductor, but making new merrow wands is strictly forbidden. Like ivory, I suppose."

"That's…oh, God, that's—"

"Disgusting, yeah, I know, but it's one of the six proven wand combinations—the ones that always work," I explained. "Rowan and dragonscale, oak and unicorn horn, ash and phoenix blood—kind of rare, since it's tough to raise phoenixes—willow and merrow skin, maple and amber, and pine and quartz. Magi and assassins and anyone else with real talent go for the pine wands—they don't do much, magically speaking, but what you save in getting a cheap core you can use to trick out your wand. Carvings, a nice handle, maybe a decorative amethyst set in the tip if you're feeling fancy. You'll know a magus's wand when you see it," I said, closing my eyes again. "They favor flash. Wake me in an hour?"

"Got it."

I heard him sigh as he shifted down in his seat, and then I knew nothing until I woke to his hand on my shoulder in the darkness and a murmured, "It's time."

Gerri Tidwell's B&B was off a quiet side street, a narrow lane lined with stone houses and too-tall shrubbery that set my paranoia on edge. I pulled into her circular driveway and cut the lights, then sat still and watched the shadows for movement. But there was nothing to disturb the night, and with a nod to Seamus, I let myself out of the car.

We slipped past the front door and around into the little fenced garden, which offered a door into Gerri's back parlor. I stood close to the house, hiding myself from insomniac neighbors, and quietly rapped on the glass. A long moment later, I heard a latch turn, and the door opened to reveal Gerri's drawn face. "Oh, thank heavens," she whispered, "come in, come in."

"My friend," I explained, seeing her eyes flick to Seamus. "Are the girls awake?"

"I was just finishing the packing," she replied, locking the door behind us in a fluttering of housecoat. Her hand trembled, and as I reached out to turn the lock for her, she gave me a grateful smile. "I'm so sorry, I'm being a silly old woman, but I can't shake the feeling that they're close..."

"You're not silly at all," I said, and gave her a quick, tight hug. "It's good to see you again, Gerri."

"You too, Badger. You, too." She stepped back, brushed a stray gray lock from her eyes, then pointed to the ceiling. "Five minutes, and you can be on your way. The girls are in the kitchen."

As she hurried upstairs, I beckoned for Seamus to follow me, then flicked on the hall light to show the path. What little I could see of the house looked as it always had—furniture a few decades out of fashion, plastic floral arrangements, and questionable wallpaper—but the blinds were down, the curtains drawn, and the house silent but for our footsteps on the wooden floor and the high-pitched susurrus coming from the kitchen. "They're dear little things, but they may be shy. Let me make the introductions," I told Seamus, then opened the kitchen door and gasped in spite of myself.

One of the Endicott girls—it was impossible to say which was which—looked up from her place at the kitchen table, her dark eyes large in her gaunt face. Of the beautiful blonde curls she'd formerly sported, there was nothing but a few patches of short regrowth scattered across her scalp. I had no idea whether her sister's hair had suffered the same fate, as she wore an oversized hoodie that fell nearly to her eyebrows…or, rather, to the place her eyebrows should have been. One appeared to have vanished, while the other, and the eye below it, were covered by a beige patch.

I froze for an instant, then remembered I was supposed to be the comforting one and dropped to my knees. "Hester, Esther, sweethearts," I said, holding out my arms.

The burn-scarred twins hesitated only a moment before sliding out of their chairs and running toward me for a hug. "Badger!" the bare-headed one whispered, squeezing my neck.

Her one-eyed sister hugged my chest, though her little arms barely reached halfway round. "Gerri said you were coming," she mumbled into my sweatshirt. "We have to hide now."

The girls each grabbed one of my hands and tugged, and I awkwardly stood again. "No more hiding," I told them, trying to sound cheerful. "We're going to go on a little holiday while Gerri takes care of some things here…"

But the girls shook their heads, and the one-eyed twin turned her gaze on Seamus. "Where's Gerri?"

"Upstairs," he told her. "She's just gone to pack your things."

The twins looked at each other in a moment of silent communication, then at me. "*No*," the bare-headed one told me. "She's going to get the bad men."

"What bad men?" I asked. "Darling, there's no one here to hurt you. This is my friend Seamus—"

Her sister interrupted by tightening her grip on my hand. "The bad men who hurt Mummy and Daddy. She's going to get them."

As I looked at their maimed faces in the dark kitchen, I recognized the emotion written there as terror. "It's all right, you're in no danger," I soothed, "Gerri will be right back—"

"Shh," Seamus suddenly interjected, then held up his finger for quiet and cocked his head toward the ceiling.

The floor creaked once, twice, a squeaky spot in the middle of the upstairs corridor.

And then it creaked again—the same pattern, going the same direction.

My heart stopped as the realization hit, and then the little hands wrapped around mine snapped me back to that instant. I heard the unmistakable percussion of footsteps on the staircase, and I pulled the girls toward Seamus with a hissed, "Car. Get them in there, I'm right behind you. If I don't come out, drive for—"

"Fuck that," he muttered, and pushed me away from the kitchen door. Before I had time to quarrel with him, the door flew open, showing me a pair of black-clad wizards with sparking wands. They stood silhouetted against the hallway light for only an instant before a blast of gunfire erupted once, twice, again and again. The wizards staggered backward and collapsed, and behind them, a woman screamed.

In a few eternal seconds, it was over, and Seamus held his pistol at the ready as he approached the motionless men. "Stay here," I told the girls, sliding free of their grip, and followed him into the hallway.

Seamus gave one body, then the other, a few judicious

kicks, but neither showed any sign of life, and the blood pooling below them drove the point home. "Right, they're armed," he said, gesturing to the utilitarian wands with the barrel of his gun. "May as well take them."

"I told you, I can't use them."

"Then maybe we can trade them with someone who can. It can't hurt to have them, can it?"

As I pried the wands from the dead assassins' fingers, Seamus continued down the hall to a moaning lump I recognized as Gerri. He peered down at her for a moment, then nodded and stepped back. "That's not fatal if you hurry to hospital," he told her. "Give me a reason not to change the situation."

She looked up at him in horror, then at me. "Badger, please...let me go, I'm begging you—"

Gerri was pathetic, but I could summon no pity. "Why?" I mumbled, watching another flicker of pain cross her face. "Why would you do that?"

"They have our Tommy. Said they would give him back if I"—she paused to draw an anguished breath—"if I helped them. Find you. It's Tommy, I had to...had to help for Tommy..."

"They were going to kill us," I told her, too stunned to feel anything but numb. "The girls and me. You know that, don't you?"

"And what makes you think they would have kept their bargain?" Seamus asked. "You're making deals with the people who did *that*." His left hand jutted back toward the kitchen, where the silent Endicott twins waited past the pair of corpses. "Who set those little girls on fire. Do you honestly think your son is anything but dead?"

Seamus's arm tightened, but not before I saw its tremor. "Call an ambulance," I said to Gerri, drawing Seamus back in case his trigger finger was growing impatient. "Tell your handler we escaped."

Her eyes widened in fear. "They'll kill me if you—"

"You threw your lot in with them," I snapped. "Let's

see how your friends take this news."

I was picking my way past the bodies when Gerri spoke again: "They'll find you. They took blood samples from the twins. You can't hide them."

I looked back at her and shrugged. "All I have to do is outrun them. Good luck, Gerri. You may need it more than I do."

"Badger, wait. *Badger!*" she cried, but I scooped up one of the twins, stuffed the pilfered wands in the back of my jeans, and nodded toward the door. Seamus grabbed the other girl and led the way with his gun outstretched, and he slammed the back door on Gerri's cries.

CHAPTER 4

The car wasn't equipped with proper seats for six-year-olds, but I didn't care. While I sat behind the wheel and tried to come to terms with what had just transpired, Seamus buckled the girls in, murmured reassurances, then climbed into the front beside me. "Where now?" he asked, touching my shoulder to pull me from my trance. "We can't stay here, Badge. Where do we go now?"

I shrugged and shook my head. "Doesn't matter. Arcanum's got their blood."

"So?"

"Blood trace," I mumbled. "They'll set up a spell to find them. Gerri's right—we can't hide the girls. Arcanum can find them anywhere."

"Maybe she was lying…" He paused, then twisted to look into the back seat. "Did anyone take blood from you? Either of you?" he asked the twins.

They nodded in unison in my rearview mirror. "The bad men," said the one-eyed twin.

"And the nurses," added the other. "There were nurses. They stuck needles in our arms, and it *hurt*."

"Nurses?" Seamus echoed, adjusting his awkward pose to better see them. "Right, ehm…which of you is which? I'm Seamus, and you're…"

"Esther," said the bare-headed twin.

"Hester," the one-eyed one piped up.

"I'm older," Esther offered.

"Two minutes," Hester muttered.

"Esther, Hester. Great," said Seamus, who sounded

remarkably calm for having just shot three people. "So nice to meet you. Now, Badger's going to drive us out of town, and I need you two to answer a few questions for me. Do you think you can you do that?" They nodded again, and Seamus patted my arm. "Come on, love, it's time to go. Before the ambulance arrives."

"I don't know where—"

"North. Let's go back to Inverness and regroup."

"But once they have a blood trace—"

"It's harder to hit a moving target, yeah?" He studied my face, then leaned close and murmured, "You're not going to sit here and wait for them to come to you. Keep fighting, Badger."

Though still dazed, I managed to turn on the car and pull away from the crime scene we'd left behind. My internal compass, running on autopilot, navigated me toward Berwick and the A1, the fastest route out of England. The four-lane coast road was scenic by day, but just past midnight, it was dark and quiet, and I kept my foot close to the floor.

Seamus, who had been making small talk with the girls while I headed for the main road, finally got down to business. "What happened to your parents?" he asked. "Where are they now?"

Glancing in the mirror, I saw the twins look at each other, and then Hester spoke. "The bad men came."

"To your house?"

"Uh-huh. Mummy made Easter dinner, but it was going to be late, and we were taking a nap."

"Not really," said Esther. "We were *supposed* to take a nap, but we were playing Barbies. You have to tell the police the truth," she added, turning to her sister. "It's a rule."

"He's not police," Hester protested.

"He's got a gun," Esther countered.

"Police haven't *got* guns."

"Well, Badger's police, so you still can't lie."

"It's a special police gun," said Seamus, breaking up the argument, "and you're right, Esther, you must tell the truth. That's a *very* important rule. But don't worry, you're not in any trouble for skipping a nap," he added in a conspiratorial whisper. "Used to do it all the time, myself. Now, then, you were in your room, yes?" They nodded. "When did the bad men come?"

Hester continued in her role as designated spokes-twin. "Daddy ran upstairs while we were playing, and he looked scared. He said we had to go...and then someone rang the bell," she said, puzzling through her memory, "and he told us to hide. We knew all the good places, and we hid in Mummy's closet."

"Long dresses," Esther explained. "No one ever looked behind them."

"And it was hard to hear through the door," said Hester, "but the bell kept ringing. And then there was a big *boom*, and it sounded like someone broke a glass. And a man said something. I couldn't tell what, but it was a man talking. And then..."

She fell silent, and Seamus gently prodded, "What happened next, love? What did you hear?"

Hester sniffed, and her voice was choked when she managed to resume. "Daddy screamed. Like he was hurt. And Mummy screamed, and..."

"And we kept hiding," said Esther when Hester faltered again, "because Daddy told us to. It got quiet, and we thought the bad men were gone, but then the house caught fire, and it came up the stairs, and we couldn't get out."

"Then the firemen came," said Hester, "but we got burnt first."

"And we went to hospital. It hurt a lot," said Esther. "The nurses stuck us and put plasters on, and then a lady told us Mummy and Daddy had gone to Heaven."

"We told her about the bad men," Hester continued, "and she wrote it in a notebook, and she asked us about our family."

"What did you tell her?" asked Seamus.

"To call Gerri. Mummy said that if anything ever happened to them, Gerri was going to take care of us."

"But what about your grandparents?" he pressed. "Aunts and uncles?"

Again, the girls looked at each other, and I said, "It's all right, you can tell him."

"Daddy's family doesn't like us," Esther explained, "and we're not supposed to talk about Granny with strangers."

"But Gerri came to see us," said Hester, "and she made us leave. The doctors wanted to keep us, but she said we had to go, the bad men killed Mummy and Daddy with magic, and they were going to get us if we stayed."

Esther chimed in. "So we hid in her house, and we didn't go outside, and Gerri was really scared because the bad men took Tommy away—"

"And they came in one night," Hester interrupted. "Gerri woke us and said the nice doctors needed to do some tests on us, but they wore all black, and they *weren't* nice."

"One was American," said Esther. "They didn't look like doctors."

"And we saw their wands," Hester continued, "so we knew they were the bad men. They left, but they came back early today, and they told Gerri that they wanted to find Badger. They said they'd bring back Tommy if she helped them. And she said okay."

Feeling suddenly nauseated, I pulled the car onto the side of the road, mumbled an excuse, then hurried into the grass to be sick. A door opened behind me while I retched, and then Seamus was smoothing my hair back from my face as I knelt in the weeds with a burning throat. "It's all right," he murmured, "it's going to be all right, let it out..."

When my stomach was empty, I squeezed my eyes

tightly shut against the darkness to keep from crying, but a little sob escaped anyway, and with that, the leaking dam ruptured. Seamus pulled me to my feet and held me while I shook, rubbing my back in an ineffective attempt to calm me. After a moment, when the worst was past, he said, "It's over, Badge. It's over. I'm sure she called for help in time—"

"I'm not upset over that," I interrupted as I rubbed my eyes dry. "The Fringe is supposed to be a *family*, Seamie. We help each other, we work for the greater good. That's what we're about. Ever since Easter, I've been looking for survivors, *any* survivors, and…and then I find one, and it's Gerri, and…"

"Every family has its asshole cousins," he replied when I couldn't finish. "The rest of them are out there, love. We're going to find them. We'll take care of the twins, and we'll find the rest of your people, and everything will be all right. I promise."

But I shook my head, even as he tightened his hug. "You can't promise that. I don't even know where to begin…"

"Well, then, you have me. Best I can do for now, but I'm not leaving you, Badger."

"It's not safe—"

"I know that, but if you're in the middle of this, then so am I. Besides, I can't bloody well go back to Belfast— bullets fired from *my* gun just happen to be lodged inside a couple of corpses in Spittal. How would you like me to explain that one?"

"Dump the gun," I suggested. "Wipe the prints and throw it into the sea."

"Yeah, well, I'd still have a lot of paperwork waiting, at the very least. Come on, let's keep moving. No sense in making this any easier for the murder wizards, eh?"

I let him lead me back to the car and the worried twins, but I pulled my personal mobile from my bag before I merged onto the road and began to scroll through my saved contacts as I pushed the car well beyond the speed limit. "Erm…would you like me to do that for you?" Seamus offered.

"No, I've got it."

"Who are you possibly calling at this time of night?"

I found what I was looking for in the R section, but my finger hesitated above the screen. "Remember when I said I had the queen's number?"

"Yeah. You also said it might be a bad idea to ask her any favors."

"Unfortunately, I'm all out of good ideas," I replied, and hit the green button before I could lose my nerve. "Let's find out if Faerie has phone service."

I pressed the mobile to my ear and held my breath through one ring, then another. As I resigned myself to an empty line, I started to pull the phone away, and then I heard the click of an answered call, followed immediately by the anxious voice of a young woman: "Detective? Is that you?"

She sounded shocked, but in a good way, and I forced myself to launch into my hastily scripted speech. "Dr. Richar—erm, Lady Eleanor, this is Hannah Parsons from the Constabulary. I'm, ehm…I'm in a bit of a situation—"

"You're *alive*! Thank heavens, I'd hoped you were hiding somewhere. It's Detective Parsons from Durham," she said, I assumed to someone with her in the room.

"Put her on speaker," a faint, vaguely American-sounding baritone replied, and a few seconds later, I heard the handset land on a table. "Hannah?" he said more loudly. "It's Coileán. Where are you?"

"Heading north from Berwick. I've got the little Endicott twins with me—"

"Isabel Davies's granddaughters?" Eleanor interrupted. "You've *found* them?"

"Yes. They're injured, and—"

"What about their parents?" asked Coileán.

I gripped the steering wheel to calm myself. One excited faerie was bad enough, but I had two on the other end of the line, talking over each other and me. "Killed. The girls have been in hiding since Easter. But it's worse than that," I pressed on, raising my voice before they could interject again. "Long story short, the Arcanum has blood samples on the girls. I'm on the move, but we're fighting the clock before someone thinks to run a trace."

Coileán swore unintelligibly, and Eleanor, turning away from her phone, made a similarly indecipherable comment. "I've sent for Isabel," she explained a moment later. "She's been worried sick. Now, we must get you out of that realm before the blood trace works. How long do we have?"

A door slammed open in the distance, followed by the sound of running footsteps and a muffled female voice. Coileán answered her, and with a muttered, "*Goddammit*," the new voice crescendoed toward the phone. "Hey, Badger, it's Toula. What am I hearing about a trace?"

I wasn't surprised to learn that the Arcanum's problem witch-blood had landed in Faerie, but it was still reassuring to have confirmation that she'd made it out alive. "Arcanum has samples on my passengers, and since my friend just killed their retrieval party, I assume they'll be after us before long. How much time have we got?"

"Depends on who's running the trace and how badly they want you found. Also, your friend killed how many wizards, exactly *how*?"

"Two wizards, two rounds to the chest. He's another detective."

"Buddy system. I like it." She drummed her fingers on the table, then gave a frustrated huff. "Okay, here's the sitch—and you two jump in if I screw this up. The Arcanum has Carver and a bunch of Fringers stashed away somewhere as hostages for the courts' good behavior. The new grand magus is a real piece of work," she muttered. "Opening a gate to you might be a bad idea."

"In case anyone's monitoring the background," Coileán

explained. "If you're close to Scotland, you're far enough from Glastonbury that it might not be a problem—"

"Emphasis on *might*," Eleanor interrupted. "To summarize the current situation, if the Arcanum thinks we're making incursions into that realm, the hostages die. Or so they say."

"I don't know what specific tools Glastonbury is using," Toula added, "but it's totally possible that they could detect fluctuations in Scotland. We need to get you through a natural gate. Hang on, I'll call the guys."

Before she could go far, another woman's voice echoed across the room, and Eleanor responded in kind. "Hello?" the newcomer said in a soft Welsh accent as she neared the phone. "Hello, are you—"

"Isabel? It's Badger from the Fringe," I replied. "I've got—"

"The girls?" she said hopefully. "I was told you—"

"They're in the back seat." I cupped the handset against my shoulder and glanced in the rearview mirror. "Got your gran on the line. Say hi," I told the twins, and held the mobile up for them. The girls shouted a greeting, and I put it back to my ear. "They've been injured pretty badly," I told Isabel, "but I'm trying to bring them to you."

"Bless you," she murmured. "And…and my daughter? And Marty? Any word of them?"

I hesitated, then said, "I'm so sorry, and I hate to tell you like this, but—"

"No, no, don't be sorry. I'd expected it, but…" She paused to clear her throat. "Thank you. For the girls, I…the babies mean the world to me, and to have them safe…"

As her voice faded, I heard another door, more footsteps, and a couple of male voices in the distance. Toula spoke to them, and then she returned to the phone. "Badger? I've got Aid here. He has the file on natural gates."

No further introduction was necessary. I'd not had

direct dealings with Faerie's short-term teenage king, but the Fringe had tracked his doings during the year in which he'd searched for Oberon's heir, leaving a trail of Eleanor's rattled siblings in his wake. Aiden might have seemed intimidating were it not for the fact that he'd also been an integral part of our tech support of late, and it was fundamentally difficult to fear anyone in IT. "Hello, there," I said. "Sorry, I don't think we've actually met."

"Uh, hi," said a young man with a distinctly American accent. "Badger, yeah? You're the missing coordinator, right?"

"I…suppose…"

"Well, there's only one on Vivi's wall chart, so glad to hear from you. Where are you?"

"Just over the border into Scotland. We left Berwick half an hour ago."

"Burk?" he asked, sounding puzzled.

"Berwick-upon-Tweed," Coileán offered. "Here, open the map, I'll show you."

I heard the sound of flipping pages, then a muttered, "*Ah*. Okay," Aiden said more loudly, "that's…not ideal, actually. Um…well, there's the natural gate on the Glastonbury Tor—"

"Which is right out," Eleanor interrupted. "We're not making her drive into the lion's den. What else?"

"Unless you want to head to Edinburgh and catch a flight to the mainland," he continued, "your next best option is just off the coast of Skye."

"Skye," I sighed, propping my elbow on the door. "Nothing closer?"

"Nope. There used to be one near Aberdeen, if I'm reading these notes correctly, but it seems to have closed. But Skye doesn't look so far away…"

"Farther than you'd think. A lot of it is winding two-lane roads," Eleanor explained. "Detective, what's your time?"

"Quarter to one in the morning. Traffic isn't a serious

problem," I said with more levity than I felt.

No one laughed at my feeble attempt at a joke. "You're a few hours ahead of us, then," said Eleanor. "What's the driving time?"

"Hold on, I'll route it. And where, exactly, am I going?"

After a moment's pause, she said, "The closest named place is Duntulm. You're heading for the castle ruins— they're just off the road."

I motioned for Seamus's mobile, then dropped mine into my lap as I programmed the route into his. "About six and a half hours at the speed limit. We should be there by seven if the roads stay clear."

"Come, now," Coileán interjected, "I *know* you can do better than that."

"I've got improperly restrained children in back," I replied, "and I did mention that it's the bloody middle of the night, yes?"

"Be careful, but hurry," said Toula. "If you can push it…"

"Is that enough time to get a tracking spell going?" I asked her.

"If they start now. We'll meet you on the other side. If things get dicey, call back, and we'll…figure something out. Let me give you my number—"

"I can't take it, I'm already juggling two mobiles and a car. Ehm…one last thing." I paused and cut my eyes to Seamus. "My friend, the one who shot the wizards? He's with me now, and…" I hesitated, struck by the fleeting surety that saying the words would make them real, and I could continue to ignore the blatant truth if I just kept my mouth shut. But the moment passed, and I spoke before I could rethink my decision. "I strongly suspect that my friend is half fae. He needs to be trained."

"If he's at all fae," Eleanor replied, "he needs to get out of that realm. Bring him with you."

I let out the breath I'd been holding and squeezed the phone. "Thank you. I'll phone you when we reach Skye."

"Be safe," she said, and the line went dead.

I put my mobile away, fighting the tremor in my hand, then looked at Seamus, who was holding our map. "Skye," I explained. "There's a gate on the island. We're expected."

"Nothing closer?"

"No." The dashboard clock glowed the early hour, and I felt weariness begin to settle over me again. Shaking it off, I blinked and focused on the dark road ahead. "Look for a petrol station. We could do with another top-up. Also, I don't know about you, but I'm not going far without coffee."

"Can we have crisps?" one of the twins asked.

"Sure," I said, flipping on the radio. "Not as if you two were planning to sleep tonight, were you?"

Sunrise found us northeast of Fort William, me with one hand locked on the wheel and the other wrapped around an oversized bottle of room-temperature Coke, Seamus facing backwards and leading the girls in a spirited, if off-key, rendition of "Rio." The radio wasn't much help in the wee hours, but the twins were young enough to not completely turn their noses up at Duran Duran, and both found Seamus's affected squeaky falsetto to be riotously funny. Under ordinary circumstances, I preferred a quiet car, but Seamus and I had agreed with a shared look that keeping the little ones entertained through the long night was of paramount importance. They were getting tired— hell, we all were—but as they were strung out on Coke and snacks, they were far too hyper to sleep.

The song ended, and I cringed a little as "Take On Me" queued up, knowing full well what was ahead. The road had long ago narrowed to two lanes, and I stared ahead, watching the first light of morning glint off the green trees and fields. Soon we would bend to the north, leaving the Spean to follow Loch Lochy, then push west again, wending a path past lakes and through the verdant

Highland hills. Even with the overcast morning sky, I began to relax a degree as the world illuminated once more—in truth, I'd worried about driving the narrow roads in the dark, and the pale light was a welcome development. Less than two hours to Kyle of Lochalsh and the long, arching bridge to Skye, I estimated, and from there, all I would need do is follow the main road through Portree and up the peninsula to Duntulm.

My Fringe rounds seldom took me as far as the islands, and I racked my brain to recall anything of significance about Duntulm. Aiden had said the gate would be in the castle ruins. Vaguely, I recalled a pile of stones near the edge of a cliff, but little warranting interest. Dunvegan Castle was lovely, now—I'd done the tourist thing on occasion in my Fringe travels, when time permitted—but Duntulm seemed less than promising. Still, I reasoned, if someone knew of a natural gate into Faerie, it would be one of the fae.

As I rounded a bend in the road, I caught a brief flash of light in a meadow to my right as we sped past. I'd seen nothing but sheep over there as I approached, and I checked my mirror to see if I'd missed a metal sign that would gleam when the clouds broke overhead.

There was no sign. There *were*, however, a man and a woman in black jumpsuits, looking about them confusedly, and a lightning-rimmed hole in space behind them.

"Oh, *shit*," I whispered, and snapped off the radio. "Girls, unbuckle, get on the floor. Seamie, duck down. Has anyone got a hat?"

"Ski cap in my bag," Seamus replied, slumping low in his seat. "Esther, love, could you dig around in there and find it?"

He sounded relaxed, as if hiding from passing traffic were part and parcel of everyday life, but I met his eyes and saw the worry etched there. "I'm sorry, girls, but I need you to stay under the windows for now. We have to play a hiding game," I said, glancing in the mirror at the empty back seat. "Can you do that?"

"Do we have to be quiet?" Esther asked, passing me Seamus's green hat.

I slid it over my head, hiding my distinctive forelock. "No, just stay low," I told her. "And Seamie, what are you doing with a hat like this in *June?*"

"I keep that bag packed," he explained. "Suits you."

"Liar."

"Want to tell me why we're hiding?"

I considered the twins behind me, then realized there was nothing I could do to soften the truth. "Gate opened back there. I saw a couple of wizards on the side of the road."

"F—udge," he muttered, catching himself before he could expand the girls' vocabulary. "Can we get off this road?"

"There's no point. They're homing in on the twins— they'll follow us anywhere. This is the fastest route to Duntulm, yeah?"

He nodded. "So what do we do, then?"

My broken wand was in the bag behind me, as were the two I'd taken from the downed wizards. Weighing the likelihood of my success in a fair fight with two Arcanum assassins, I stomped the accelerator.

The roads of the Highlands are known for their scenic beauty, not their appropriateness as racing straightaways. The girls whimpered when I passed one hundred thirty kilometers per hour, and even Seamus gripped the door handle when I hit one hundred forty. At least our car had decent tires. The last thing I wanted to do was wind up in a scenic Highland ditch, but slowing was out of the question. The Arcanum gates were popping open with more regularity, at least once every ten minutes—and what was worse, they were anticipating our route. Then again, there isn't exactly an abundance of major thoroughfares in western Scotland, so their job wasn't particularly difficult.

I'd already decided that if a gate opened in front of us, I was mowing the stupid bastards down. Vehicular homicide wasn't on my bucket list, but I was driving for our lives, and as far as I was concerned, the assassins were fair game.

Through the mountains and down to the coast they dogged us, always close but never in a good position to disable our car. I swerved into oncoming traffic as the situation warranted, and twice I took us off-roading, but the few shots they were able to aim missed us. I took the Skye Bridge at one hundred twenty, praying no oblivious pedestrians wandered into my path, and looked to my left in time to see a gate open over the water...and a wizard run through and fall straight into the sea.

"Stay on the A87," Seamus told me from his position below the window. "Hugs the coast to Sligachan, then makes a beeline north to Portree. You're going to miss the town and head to the northwest."

"How far?"

"You'll pick up a secondary road just past Uig. If you hit the water, you've gone the wrong way."

"Time?"

"At sane speeds, an hour and a half." I caught him reaching into his jacket for his gun. "What can I do to help?"

"Stay down and pray the sheep don't get out," I replied, staring at the mountains rising ahead.

We blew past Broadford and Dunan, Luib and Sconser, all of them wide patches on a narrow road, then sped north toward the island's main settlement. I'd spent a pleasant afternoon in Portree one summer, sitting by the picturesque harbor and enjoying the cool air, but I pushed the memory aside and focused on the task at hand as another gate opened behind us. I left it in our dust, then skirted Portree and headed into the less inhabited parts of Skye. The twins made not a peep, and I risked a glance behind me to spot them kneeling in the floor, holding hands across the middle of the car.

If anyone had been timing me, I'd have had my license yanked, shredded, and cast into the sea. Just before seven, I swerved onto the little road to Duntulm, then followed the western coast of the peninsula toward its tip. Cursing at the gleam of another gate, I grabbed my mobile and rang Eleanor again. "Nearly there, and we have followers," I said as soon as she answered. "Where's the gate?"

"We're waiting for you," she replied, then paused. "Ehm…I'll let Aiden give you the directions."

Her phone changed hands, and Aiden's voice returned to the line. "Okay, here's the deal," he said as I dodged a sea bird out for a stroll. "The gate is just off the island, past Duntulm."

"*Off?*" I yelped. "I'm in a car, the road's going to run out, I haven't got a boat—"

"You don't need one. Uh…how do you feel about heights?"

"Heights?"

"Look," he said in a rush, "get to the castle, and head for the edge of the cliff it's on. Just over the edge, about twenty feet down, is a small gate. You can jump through it."

"*Jump?*"

"I know, I know, it's not ideal—"

"You expect me to hit a target like that? With the girls?"

"If you jump straight out and—"

The phone was pulled away from him, and another man with an American accent took over. "Coileán says we'll widen it. You'll have a ride waiting."

"What sort of ride?"

"Her name's Georgie, and she's not going to hurt you. Bye."

I hung up and tossed the mobile to Seamus. "This is a bloody disaster," I told him. "The gate's only accessible if you jump off a cliff, so they're sending someone to meet us."

Seamus frowned. "I thought they couldn't come through."

"They're *faeries*," I snapped. "Capriciousness comes with the territory." I paused, replayed what I had said, and met his eyes. "Sorry, nothing personal, I'm just—"

"Stressed. Drive. Don't kill us."

"Right. Sorry."

The engine finally began to overheat as I neared the tip of the peninsula, and then, with a wave of relief, I spotted the ruined castle in the nearing distance, set back a short walk from the road. "There," I told Seamus, pointing with my chin. "It's there, we're going to make—"

Something massive and black shot up from behind the castle, spreading leathery wings like a creature ripped from a nightmare, and I screamed and slammed on the brakes. The car fishtailed, then slid off the road, leaving deep gouges in the grass until it came to a stop.

"The *fuck…*" Seamus whispered, staring out the windscreen as the beast flapped its wings and settled to the ground.

A dragon, I dimly realized, as every impulse in the deep part of my brain bellowed at me to run. That thing—that was a *dragon*. A real dragon. An enormous, scaly dragon with a mouth full of fangs and curving claws as long as my hand, an overgrown, flying lizard the size of a jumbo jet. As I caught my breath and gawked at the creature, it cocked its horned head like a dog, and then, slicing through the tumult of my thoughts, I heard a voice that was not my own.

Hi! Are you ready?

Seamus jumped in his seat beside me. "Jesus, did you hear—"

"I think it's a telepath." With shaking hands, I unbuckled, pulled my broken wand out of my bag, and stepped out of the car. As the dragon stared me down, I tucked the wand into the back of my waistband and held up my empty palms to show I was no threat. "Ehm...hello," I said, edging away from the safety of the vehicle. "You, ehm...are you—"

I'm Georgie. The dragon's head bobbed, and it—*she*, I remembered—bent her long neck backwards to nose the brown saddle hooked around her. *Climb up, let's go.*

By then, Seamus had got out as well and was coaxing the twins from their hiding spot. "We're supposed to ride *that?*" he asked, wide-eyed and, if I wasn't mistaken, slightly paler than usual.

Georgie cocked her head again, then sank onto her belly and snorted a puff of gray smoke. *Do you not know how? It seems pretty easy—just hold on, and I'll do all the work.* Her red eyes swiveled toward the twins, who hugged Seamus's legs in terror. *It's okay*, she thought, *I'm not going to eat you. Promise. I had a late-night snack.* She awkwardly opened her mouth, revealing a serrated row of clenched teeth, and it suddenly occurred to me that the dragon was trying to smile.

"Up you go, now," I told the twins, taking a no-nonsense tone to hide my own fear. "Seamie, help them. I'll get the bags—"

Before I could finish my thought, I heard the unmistakable crack of an opening gate behind me, then wheeled about in time to see the flash as it ripped through the air. "Go. Go, *run!*" I shouted, motioning the girls on, then drew my wand with my left hand and jabbed my right toward Seamus. "Gun, now."

"On it," he said, taking aim at the gate as it materialized.

"No, give me the gun." He started to protest, but I shook my head and pointed at the waiting dragon. "Get the girls to safety. I'll cover you."

"Badger—"

"*Gun*, Seamie." When he hesitated, I grabbed his shoulder and glared at him. "Listen to the witch, okay?

Give me the gun. I'll be right behind you."

With reluctance, he passed me the weapon and stepped back. "Are you sure—"

"*Go.*"

Seamus spared me one last look, the sprinted for the dragon. I had time only to see him scoop the girls up and throw them toward the saddle before the gate solidified and two young, athletic-looking wizards stepped through.

The male of the pair raised an eyebrow in surprise as he looked over my shoulder toward the monster by the ruined castle, but the female disregarded the threat and trained her wand on my chest. "It's over, Parsons," she said, keeping her eyes locked on me. "You've got nowhere left to run."

"Ehm...Connie," her partner began as Georgie launched herself from the ground with an ear-splitting screech and dove off the cliff.

"Forget them. Hannah Parsons," she continued, "you have flouted the authority of the grand magus and the Council. Your death has been authorized. Lay down your weapons—you know this standoff is futile."

"Shield," I whispered, throwing my will into the thrumming wand. It sparked in warning, but a faint shield manifested in front of me, albeit one barely the size of a medieval buckler. With my shield raised, I steadied the unfamiliar gun as well as I could and tried to pretend I had the matter in hand. "Listen to me," I told the assassins. "Listen to yourselves. What have I done? What have *any* of the Fringe done to you? Certainly nothing deserving execution!" Slowly, holding them in my sights, I stepped backwards toward the ruins. "We've nothing to do with Arcanum politics. Why are you doing this?"

"Grand magus's orders," the male assassin replied, sounding as nonchalant as if he were discussing the weather. "Pruning the vines, as it were. You're more trouble than you're worth, you know—"

"Tim, enough." The tip of Connie's wand glowed, and

she gave me an almost pitying smile as I continued my slow retreat. "Let us make this easy on you," she told me. "We can make it painless. Look around you—there's no escape." She chuckled and began to close the gap I'd widened. "Your ride's left you, I see. There's nothing over the cliff but a short fall and a bunch of rocks. Now, put down your weapons."

I took another step back. "No."

Connie rolled her eyes. "Look, we both know you're not going to *shoot* us—"

That was as far as she made it before I pulled the trigger.

Shocked, Connie threw up a shield, and Tim followed a second later. Now suddenly on the defensive, the wizards watched me warily as I edged toward the castle. "You're a *police* officer!" Connie cried. "Murdering a civilian—"

I shot again, but the bullet ricocheted off her shield. "Self-defense, love. This is your chance to stand down and get out of here."

Her tone turned toward mockery. "Who would ever believe you? I mean, shooting a civilian armed only with what, a stick? How could you possibly be in danger from a stick?"

While my attention was on Connie, Tim seized the chance and fired a bolt directly at my little shield. My wand hand took the remnant of the blast as the shield cracked and failed, and I cried out, feeling like I'd punched a brick wall. Now unshielded, I slid the useless wand back into my waistband and forced both hands around the gun, willing my injured wrist to stop throbbing.

Connie's smile returned with predatory flair. "You've got fight in you, Parsons, but this is where it ends." In an instant, her shield had dropped, but only long enough for her to shoot a killing blast of magical energy my way.

I froze as I watched it near me, a red and orange wave against the background magic swirling about us, and my left hand shot forward as if I could block it. *This is how*

Mama died was my last thought before the impact.

I felt the blow, but I felt it a meter in front of me as the bolt struck something solid and splintered into useless fizzles. There was a shield, I realized, staring dumbly at the translucent air in front of my outstretched hand. A proper shield, a *big* shield, and my wand—my ruined, taped-up wand—was behind me.

Connie gaped at me, momentarily puzzled. "But...you're a *witch*—"

I decided to question the provenance of the miraculous shield later. While the wizards were distracted, I reached my gun hand around my shield and emptied Seamus's pistol in their direction, bellowing as if that would improve my aim. Most of the shots missed, but before I turned to run for the ruins, I heard the wizards grunt and cry out as a pair of bullets hit home. Tim fell to his knees, and I sprinted toward the castle, running for my life before they could give chase.

"You stupid *bitch*!" Connie cried, and I jerked as a bolt hit the ground beside me.

With my heart jackhammering, I vaulted the protective fence, flew past the warning sign, and wove my way through the stones and crumbling piles of masonry toward the cliff's edge. When I reached the lip of the land, I grabbed onto one of the remaining walls for support and looked down, scanning the area for a sign. A fall from that height would end messily on the rocks below—I didn't know if I could jump out far enough to reach the water— and I panicked, thinking that the gate had closed when the dragon passed through. But no, *there*—if I stood in just the right place and looked at the proper angle, there was a small patch of blackness, an oblong that didn't match the ground beneath it. It could have been a shadow had the sun been high enough and uncovered, but I knew I was seeing a gate, a hole through the realms into featureless blackness, an impossibility twice as wide as my shoulders, hanging a few meters below the cliff's edge.

I couldn't do it. I couldn't safely make that leap, and I had no idea what awaited me on the other side. My mobile was in my pocket—I could phone Eleanor again and ask for a pickup, but with the twins safely through, would she even answer my call?

"Parsons!" came Connie's nearing shout. "It's either my way or the long way down! Last chance!"

Even if she was injured, the wizard was coming for me with a wand at the ready. I had a broken wand and an empty gun to my name, and I had nowhere to left to go.

With a prayer to any kind deity that might have been listening, I took two running steps and leapt from the cliff.

CHAPTER 5

I was no diver, and my form largely consisted of pinwheeling my arms as if I might achieve flight with enough thrashing. But luck was on my side, and I slipped through the gate feet-first, accelerating as I plummeted into blackness.

Suddenly, my body was jerked as if I'd been caught by an invisible harness, and I hung in midair, blinking as my eyes adjusted to the night. There were lights below me—small, bright orbs that floated above the heads of a modest crowd. One shone down on the youthful-looking man standing under me, who watched through the splayed fingers of his upraised hand as I got my bearings. "Are you hurt?" he called, his voice clear but his accent unfamiliar.

I shook my head, then remembered the general lack of light. "Out of breath. They're following—"

He twitched a finger at the sky, and the gate above me sealed shut. "Not anymore," he said, and lowered me to the ground.

I landed gently on all fours and felt soft grass beneath my hands. Pushing myself to my feet, I winced as I put pressure on my sore wrist, then looked around for Seamus and the twins. A dragon couldn't be that difficult to hide, even in the dark...

The man who'd caught me moved to my side. "They are safe. Isabel is with the children." He pointed to a little clump in the near distance, which consisted of a kneeling blonde who appeared to be all of twenty-five and the twins, who alternately talked over each other and hugged the woman. "And your friend is…uh…" He gestured in the other direction, and I could just make out Georgie's bulk against the trees at the edge of the clearing in which I'd landed. Beside her, illuminated by one of the floating orbs, Seamus gesticulated wildly at the dragon, while a bearded young man and an older teenager—Aiden, I assumed—appeared to be making an effort to calm him.

"Good," I sighed, absently rubbing my wrist. "Thank you, ehm…"

"Val. Give me your hand." He beckoned with two fingers, and I hesitantly extended my hurt arm. Prodding it, he took note of when my face scrunched with the pain, then nodded and held my hand steady. I watched as a web of enchantment coalesced around my wrist, simultaneously numbing and bracing it. "Not broken, just bruised," he declared as the healing enchantment took its final form. "Give that a day to work before you remove it."

I turned my arm back and forth, examining the active magic around it. "I don't think I could remove it if I tried," I admitted. "Witch, you know."

"Then I will remove it when it's ready." He flashed a tight smile, then cut his eyes to Eleanor and Coileán, who stood by Toula, rubbing their temples. "They will be more sociable in a moment. The realm can be deafening when she's displeased."

"*She?*"

He nodded. "Sentient. She has, shall we say, firm opinions."

The knot in my stomach, which had just begun to loosen after the long night, cinched tight. "She doesn't like me?"

"You?" he replied, surprised. "No, she has no quarrel with you. She understands the refugee situation." He dipped his head slightly toward the group standing by the dragon. "Your friend is another matter."

I waited until Val's dark eyes met mine again, then murmured, "I *thought* Seamus was fae, but I could be mistaken—"

"Oh, no, he's fae. Emphatically fae." He folded his arms and frowned in thought. "Do you know something of the courts, uh…"

"Hannah. Badger. Detective Parsons. I answer to anything. And yeah, a bit," I said, shrugging. "What about them?"

"Once," he murmured, "and not very long ago, there were the Three. Coileán followed Titania, and Eleanor followed Oberon."

"We're caught up on those two," I replied, nodding along, then hinted, "The Fringe database does have a pretty fair hole concerning Mab…"

"Which is why you don't see the problem. She angered the realm and was driven out, and the remnant of her court scattered after she was killed," Val explained. "More importantly, the realm now refuses to recognize the existence of a third court, and she sounds the alarm every time one of Mab's crosses the border. Like so," he added, pointing to the queen and king. "She can be placated, but she doesn't *like* it."

"So…you're telling me Seamus is—"

"Affiliated with Mab's court, at least by blood. Do you know anything of his family?"

I shook my head. "He was abandoned as a newborn. No one's ever come forward to claim him—well, no one *I* know about. I mean, he's been in Belfast for twenty-odd years, but if his long-lost biological parents have come knocking, he hasn't told me about it."

Val sighed and rubbed his neck. "My sister can look at his aural signature, but finding a match is unlikely. Ah, well." He thumbed one hand at the others and said, "Perhaps we could move this meeting somewhere that isn't the middle of the woods."

"Hang on," I said as he started to walk off, "I thought aural comparison was high-level *spellcraft*, not enchantment. That's wizard territory."

"It is," he replied, then pointed to Toula. "My sister. One moment, let me speak with them," he added, and slipped away.

I stood alone in the dark, piecing together the fragmentary information I'd been handed. Seamus was definitely fae, and at least one of his parents had belonged to *Mab's* court. That alone was worrying, especially if the realm itself was rejecting him. Toula could find out for certain—and Toula, I knew, was Mab's actual blood. So if Val was her brother, and the construction mending my wrist was clearly enchantment, the fae form of magic...

He was also Mab's, I realized as the tumblers fell, and the enchantment he'd effortlessly made was far too tidy to be the work of a beginner. Toula was perhaps a decade my junior, so that meant Val was probably the elder of the two, and—

Yeah, he's Mab's heir. He doesn't like to think about it, came Georgie's mental voice. I jumped and wheeled around to pick her out of the darkness, and her teeth flashed in the orb light. *Sorry, I was bored. Seamus is having trouble coping with my existence, and Joey and Aiden are calming him. You looked perplexed.*

"Just...it's a lot," I muttered.

I have no idea what you said, but I think I picked up the thought behind it. Your friend is going to be fine. The realm is calming down, and I can't imagine Coileán and Eleanor throwing him out—not with that stunt you pulled. The Arcanum probably wouldn't be happy to see him, would they? But don't worry, I'm sure that someone here can help him. She wrapped her tail around her nose and watched me over the top. *You have many feelings.*

I nodded.

Is he your mate?

"He was."

I felt her rummage through my thoughts, and then she snorted. *I'll never understand you people and your mates. Come together, mate, separate. It's not difficult. There's no reason to keep the other one around once the mating's over.* As I fumbled for a rebuttal, I could sense the mirth in the alien voice. *I know, I know, it's different for you, but honestly, our way makes more sense.*

Before I could be drawn into a discussion of monogamy with a dragon after pulling an all-nighter, Toula left her huddle to fetch me. "Hey, Badger," she said, giving me a quick hug. "Glad you made it. Any interest in a bed?"

"Well, yeah, but Seamus—"

"*That* can wait for dawn. Come on." She wrapped one arm around my shoulders and led me toward a gate that had opened near the queen. "Eleanor said you two can camp with her for now until we get things sorted out with your buddy."

Too weary to protest, I let Toula escort me through the gate and into a long corridor with a thick red carpet, periodic crystal wall sconces, and tasteful marble nudes on little tables. She pushed open a door into a candlelit bedchamber, then flicked a finger. The heavy window drapes closed, blocking out the night, and the white duvet folded itself back in invitation. "Bathroom's that way," she said, indicating a paneled oaken door on the far right, "and Seamus will be one suite over. Get some sleep, eh?" she added, giving my face a quick study. "You look like you've been going for hours."

"I had a nap in the car—*the car*," I said, grabbing Toula's arm. "Seamus hired our car in Inverness. We left it in Duntulm—"

"Someone will find it eventually. *You're* not going back for it." She smiled and nudged me toward the bed. "You're safe now, Badger. Sleep well."

A million thoughts were running through my mind when I stripped and climbed beneath the covers, but the moment my head hit the pillow, I knew nothing but dreamless sleep until a rapping at my door woke me.

I bolted upright in bed, blinking in the faint light that had slipped past the curtains, then remembered where I was and that I was in my underthings, and hurried back into my clothes. "Come in!" I called as I tugged my T-shirt into place and smoothed my bed-mussed hair.

The door cracked open, and Eleanor peered through the gap. "Sorry, Detective, did I wake you?" she asked, glancing around the room. "Seamus is up and restless, and I didn't know if you needed more time…"

"I was up," I lied, then looked down at myself and realized my shirt was inside-out. "Ehm…just going to shower, if that's all right."

"Oh, certainly. Of course."

Looking at Eleanor in the relative gloom of my guest suite, I could imagine that she was just another young woman, a slight girl with a vibrant red French braid and understated diamond studs. She wore a thin purple shirt over dark leggings, topped by a long, cream-colored cardigan that she hugged around herself as she watched me. She was anxious, then—her body language betrayed her—but about what, I couldn't say.

The disjunction between what I was seeing and the truth of the queen's age took a moment to process. At a distance, in the shade, she could have been anyone wandering the high street on a Saturday afternoon with an armful of bags from H&M and Topshop. But I had seen Eleanor up close, unglamoured, and I'd seen the age in her eyes. Beautiful green eyes, but ancient. Mundanes might find her oddly striking—there was something not *right* about her—but any Fringer with sense knew she was seeing an older faerie. Granted, Eleanor wasn't ancient by fae metrics, but according to our database, she was at least seven hundred years old.

So what, I wondered, could someone like that possibly be worried about?

"Is everything all right, my lady?" I ventured.

"Fine," she said, smiling too quickly. "Freshen up, and I'll see you downstairs in the main dining room when you're ready." She turned to go, then paused with her hand on the door. "Did Coileán ever give you the lingua franca?"

"I don't recall…"

"You would if he had. Here." Before I could argue, Eleanor put her fingertips against my temples and closed her eyes. "This won't hurt, dear."

It didn't—it felt like a flash of lightning went off behind my eyelids—but the moment left me disoriented and clutching the dresser for support. "What…what did you—"

"Do you understand me?"

"Sure, I…" I paused, actually hearing the words, and realized what she had done. "You…put Fae in my head? You uploaded an entire language?"

"That's not a bad way of looking at it," she replied, and grinned. "Take a shower, Detective, you'll feel loads better. And the weirdness fades," she added in English as she headed for the door. "I doubt you'll notice by dinner."

Easy for her to say. My scrambled brain barely knew up from down, and throwing another language into the mix was the last thing it needed that morning. I'd shifted time zones—whether several back or quite a few forward, I couldn't guess—and the light diffusing through the frosted bathroom windows gave me no indication of what time it was supposed to be. Beyond the temporal issue, I'd been on the run for weeks, and my mind refused to accept that a stranger with a wand wasn't about to break down the latched door. Even as I showered, I fought the urge to keep looking over my shoulder, just in case someone had sneaked in behind my back.

I was hungry, but I couldn't say what meal I was craving. I'd thrown an extra pack of crisps in my bag during our pit stop the night before, but my luggage was long gone, left behind in the car on the cliff at Duntulm. Taking a quick mental inventory, I tallied my belongings and came away with the clothes on my back—well, on the brass towel rack and the door hook at that moment, being slightly steam cleaned—and my phone, plus Seamus's empty gun and my damaged wand, which, I feared, had helped me through its final spell. Connie's bolt had rendered it next to dead during our standoff, and unless someone in Faerie dabbled in wandcraft, my usefulness as a witch was virtually nil.

Closing my eyes to rinse the lather from my hair, I remembered the shield that had saved my hide at the last—the wandless construction strong enough to withstand an assassin's bolt. Where had that come from? Certainly not from me—my broken wand had been nowhere near my hand at that moment, and the notion that I could make something like that shield empty-handed was ludicrous. I was wielding dragonscale for a reason. But other than the Arcanum agents, I'd been alone on the cliff. So who, then, had shielded me? And why?

It was a relief to find that whoever had stocked the glass-walled shower had also thought to leave a toothbrush and comb for me, though a hairdryer was nowhere to be found in the otherwise opulent guest bath—which, incidentally, was the size of a studio flat. Then again, Eleanor had no reason not to be lavish with her accommodations, seeing as money was no object in Faerie, and the rules of physics were at the very least negotiable. Still, being accustomed to hotel rooms on the modest end of the spectrum, I found it disconcerting to wend my dripping way through the palatial suite, hoping to remember where I'd dropped all of my few belongings before the queen sent a runner to drag me to the table.

After locating both shoes, by some miracle, I hurried down a curving marble staircase, then followed the sound of voices through echoing hallways to a dining room vast enough to comfortably seat at least the House of Commons, and probably half the Lords besides. Row upon row of heavy mahogany tables and ornately decorated chairs marched up the length of the vaulted hall, bisected by a wide central aisle. The head table perched on a short dais, giving the favored diners a view of the assembled, or at least of those at the first dozen tables. As I stood on the threshold of the cavernous room, gawking at the soaring ceiling and the multi-story windows, I heard Eleanor call my name as clearly as if she'd been standing beside me. Jolted, I looked around until I spotted a tiny figure waving at the head table, then heard her speak again: "Down here. Sorry about the walk—you'll build an appetite, yes?"

"Sure," I said, though I didn't know if she could hear me in turn, and half-jogged the length of the room to join the two diners on the dais.

When I'd neared to proper hailing distance, Eleanor gestured to the empty chair beside Seamus, who was shoveling bacon down his throat like he'd only just discovered the joy of well-prepared pork products. "This wasn't my first choice," she explained, "but my staff were using the smaller rooms, and I didn't want to inconvenience anyone. Hungry?"

"Starved, actually," I replied as I ran up the staircase. "I'm sorry to keep you waiting, but I—"

She waved the apology aside. "Don't worry, dear—you had a long night. Sit down, help yourself. Catch your breath."

I plopped into my seat, and Seamus automatically slid me the teapot and a platter of fried potatoes. "It's all good," he mumbled through a mouthful of eggs. "Probably slimming, too."

Eleanor glanced our way and grinned. "I wouldn't go that far, but I wouldn't fret about it, were I you. You, ehm…you've lost weight since we last met."

"Maybe. I wouldn't know," I replied, reaching for a basket of toast. "I haven't been watching my figure of late."

"Well, seeing as you've been playing hide and seek with

the Arcanum, that's entirely understandable. You poor thing," she murmured, and refilled her teacup. "No offense intended, but I can't believe you lasted this long on the lam."

"Honestly, neither can I." The tea was perfectly steeped, the bread golden, the eggs fluffy, the bacon thick and just crispy enough to crunch on the edges, and my awakened stomach demanded tribute. "Thank you for letting us sleep over," I said between bites. "I don't know the plan at this point…"

"We thought you might want to join the rest of the Fringe once you've found your bearings," said Eleanor. "There's a…" She paused, and her mouth quirked like she'd tasted something bitter. "I hate calling it a refugee camp. There's a Fringe *settlement* near Coileán's place. We've made great progress in the last month. There's a proper neighborhood now, a community center, work space, a pool—a start, you know, but everyone's still adjusting. Vivi has a command post, too, and I'm sure she'll be thrilled to share it with an actual coordinator."

I lowered my laden fork and peered around Seamus at the queen. "There isn't another coordinator here?"

She shook her head brusquely. "The hitmen targeted most of you in the first assault. A few are still unaccounted for, and we think at least one may be in Arcanum custody—Slim?"

"He's *alive?*"

"They took him before Coileán could convince him to evacuate. I wouldn't bring the matter up around Coileán right now," she added in a low murmur. "He's rather fond of the fellow."

I nodded and returned to my brunch. "How many of us are still out there? Fringers, I mean, not just coordinators."

At that, Eleanor could only shrug. "Vivi keeps the records, you'll have to ask her. And there's been no communication since the evacuation, so anything she has is out of date. But that's not a matter you need to worry about at the moment—eat up, Detective, build your strength."

While Seamus and I continued our mostly uninterrupted attempt to clear the laden table's offerings, I sneaked glances at Eleanor, who drank her tea and picked at a piece of buttered toast. When my distended stomach began to warn me against taking another helping, I pushed my plate aside and watched her until she looked my way and frowned in query. "What aren't you telling me?" I asked. "I don't mean to be rude, my lady, but something's bothering you."

She sipped, biding her time as Seamus looked up from the scraps of his meal, then said, "I'd hoped to wait until the others arrived before we discussed…matters."

"Matters?" Seamus echoed. "That's nice and vague. Want to give us a hint, then?"

Eleanor smirked at him over her cup. "Now, which of you is meant to be the bad cop?"

"Ah, see, you're changing the subject," he countered. "Come on, what's the problem? We can take it."

But she shook her head. "The rest will join us shortly. Until then, child, do try to find a modicum of patience."

Seamus knew well enough when a subject wasn't about to crack, and he resumed his feast. Stuffed, I poured another cup of tea to aid my digestion, then stiffened when I heard Eleanor's voice in my head: *Keep drinking. Don't look at me, just listen.*

On instinct, my eyes darted her way, but Seamus was oblivious, and the queen was concentrating on her toast.

I understand that you and Valerius had a chat last night while Coileán and I were indisposed.

Unsure of how I was supposed to respond to that, I formed the words in my thoughts and waited: *A brief one. He stopped me from going splat.*

To my relief, Eleanor picked up on my end of the conversation, and I felt more than heard a flicker of amusement in her reply. *A fate best avoided, splatting. What did he tell you about Seamus?*

I thought about the chaotic night, piecing my memory back together as the caffeine did its work. *He said he's fae and one of Mab's, and the realm isn't happy. Is that why you're on edge?*

More or less. She's still peeved with us, as she continues to make perfectly clear. Eleanor grunted and reached for a pot of jam. *We've told Seamus nothing yet. I was hoping to avoid having this conversation by myself.*

I hesitated, trying to discern the subtext from that inaudible statement. *If you send him back, they'll kill him. They've got enough now to track him—the car, if nothing else. My wallet, at least, is still in there. If he surfaces, they won't hesitate.*

We're aware of that.

He can't defend himself, I thought with greater urgency. *Seamie's been lucky with me—they'll catch him without his gun, shoot him in the back, go after him at work—*

Yes.

He's not the enemy. Please, I only brought him here because I thought you could help him—

"Seamie"?

There were several enquiries behind that quick thought, most of them personal. *We go back,* I explained, trying to blank my mind of anything embarrassing. *Grew up as neighbors.*

Eleanor made no reply, and I sipped my cooling tea, hoping she'd drop the subject. But before I could relax, I heard her yet again: *You love him.*

It wasn't a question, but I tried to hedge. *I...have loved him.*

You love him, she repeated with a hint of surprise. *You knew, and you still pursued him?*

Even as I stared into the distant corner of the hall, I felt the pressure of her eyes on me and nodded. *I'm not the first, am I?*

There was no reason for me to think of her late

husband, a witch who'd answered to Charger in Fringe circles—Eleanor knew damn well whom I had in mind. Perhaps realizing she'd hit something raw, she retreated and left me to my tea until the distant door opened for a small crowd of figures that quickly grew and differentiated into faces I recognized. I picked Coileán out of the pack, then Val and Toula to his right, and Aiden and the bearded man just behind them, walking with Monkey—"Vivi" here, outside the Fringe channels in which I'd previously encountered her. Suddenly, the door opened again, and two small streaks thundered up the aisle past the others, squealing as they raced.

"*Girls!*" cried a mortified female voice from the back of the room, but it was too late for decorum. Laughing and heaving for breath after their sprint, the Endicott twins scrambled up the dais and ran around the table to hug Seamus and me.

"Hi, Badger!" one of them chirped as she jumped onto my lap. "Are you going to stay with Granny, too?"

"There's *loads* of room," said the other as Seamus hoisted her off the floor. "Granny said we could have our own bedrooms, but we want to stay together, so there's another bed for you and Seamus."

From the corner of my eye, I saw his cheeks redden at the offer, but my attention was otherwise focused on the girls—the beaming, cherubic, brown-eyed blondes with matching cascades of beribboned curls halfway down their backs. Gone were the disfiguring burn scars, the eyepatch, and the frizz of new hair, and I looked back and forth between them, marveling at the transformation.

As I gawped, their frazzled grandmother appeared at the foot of the dais, clutching her chest and glowing scarlet. "My lady," she panted, "I apologize, the children—"

"Are children," Eleanor interrupted, smiling indulgently at the twins. "Are you hungry, girls?"

The one in Seamus's lap—Hester, if I'd had to guess—

turned around and nodded. "We had breakfast, but my tummy's talking again."

Eleanor squinted in quick thought, and a child-sized table appeared beside Isabel, set with scaled-down china and crystal and laden with a tower of tiny pastries. "Be careful," she cautioned, pointing to the little teapot. "The chocolate may be a bit warm."

The adults forgotten, the Endicotts clambered down from the dais and set about inspecting their bounty, and Eleanor chuckled to herself as she stood.

"That's some incredible healing work," I said, watching Isabel coax the girls into the chairs while they grabbed at the choicest bites.

"Glamour," Eleanor murmured, coming up behind me, then pointed over my shoulder toward the bobbing heads. "Look closely and you'll see it. No healing enchantment is that effective. I've yet to encounter one that could replace a limb...or an eye, as the case may be."

I turned to look up at her. "You mean..."

"I saw the damage last night. With time, the scars should fade, but never entirely. Still, there's nothing to be gained by confronting them with their injuries every time they look in the mirror, is there? Nice of you to join us," she said, straightening as the others neared. "Busy morning?"

"You know, it might have been kind to let them sleep in," Toula retorted. "How's it going, Badger?"

I hoisted my teacup. "Better now."

"If you wanted to eat, you're out of luck," Seamus added, spreading his hands over the denuded platters. "Sorry."

The bearded man smirked as the plates refilled and Seamus's jaw dropped. "You must be new here," he said, then looked at me and sobered. "You're Badger, right? Joey Bolin. Have you heard anything about Helen?"

His name rang a bell—the new grand magus's fae-blooded husband, if the reports I'd seen were accurate.

"Nothing in weeks," I told him, shaking my head as he climbed to our table. "Not since the unravelling. I'm so sorry."

His face fell, and I gave it a quick study, trying to ascertain the truth of the rumors. He was too young to look anything but his age, and the neat beard he sported told me that whatever fae blood he had was diluted. But that was neither the time nor the place to question him about his background. "We're going to find her," I said. "Give me a few days to rest up, and I'll be back at it."

The others spoke at once, a cacophony of surprised voices, and Seamus grabbed my arm. "Are you *insane*?" he said, leaning close to be heard. "We only just got out of there! They'll kill you if they—"

I met his panic with forced calm. "I have a responsibility. As long as there are Fringers in hiding, someone has to find them. If I stay here, I'm no use to anyone."

"But…but you called—"

"I called for the twins and for you. My place is back there."

"Now, Detective," Eleanor began, "let's not be hasty. We're all concerned about the missing Fringers, but there's no reason for you to go back into that mess. Better to tick one name off the list. A bird in the hand and all of that, yes? You'll be comfortable here until the Arcanum comes to its senses."

"I appreciate that," I told her, "but you said yourself that I'm the last remaining coordinator. This is my duty."

"You have no duty to commit suicide," Coileán interrupted, "which is exactly what a return trip would be. Forget it."

I stiffened, then stood to look down at him from the dais. "Are you telling me I'm a prisoner here, my lord?"

"No, of course not—"

"Then I'm going back. I ask your leave for a few days here to lick my wounds, and then I'll be on my way."

He rubbed his face and sighed, a sound far too weary for his apparent youth. "I'm not going to chain you to the wall," he said slowly, "but I strongly advise you to give this some thought. Going back there alone—"

"Oh, she's not going *anywhere* alone," Seamus interjected. "I'm with Badge."

I couldn't miss the look Eleanor and Coileán exchanged at that. "No," I said, turning to Seamus, "you're staying here. Or did you want to explain the shootings in Berwick to your chief? The abandoned car?"

"Forget the sodding car. You need a partner."

"I can manage perfectly well without—"

"Hey, guys? *Hey*," said Toula, raising her voice as Seamus and I began to bicker. "Whoa, there. Nothing has to be decided today, all right? And before you two lunatics decide who wants to go out in a blaze of glory, how about letting us do what we came here to do?"

Seamus frowned down at her from his seat. "What's that, then?"

She folded her arms and met his stare. "So, it's pretty blatant that you're fae, bub. We just need to figure out how much of a pain in everyone's ass you're going to be." Val gave her a sharp look, and Toula shrugged. "What? You can pussyfoot around this all day, or we can rip the bandage off. Five-O can hack it, right?"

Taken aback, Seamus blinked in surprise, then prodded his chest. "You…are you talking to me?"

Joey rolled his eyes. "You'll get used to Toula-ese. Don't fight it, man—that only makes it worse."

Eleanor left Isabel and the twins to their meal and ushered the rest of us into a richly appointed sitting room, complete with silk carpet, oversized tapestries, and a black grand piano. The floor-to-ceiling windows overlooked a little lake, on which a pair of white swans were swimming in lazy circles. I'd have given the rolling landscape a longer study if not for the fact that Seamus was waiting for me on one of the leather couches, his face paper-white.

"So," said Toula, sounding too cheerful by half, "what do you know about your family?"

Seamus's fingers touched mine, and I squeezed his hand in reassurance.

"My parents live in Durham," he told her while the others watched from their ring of chairs and couches. "Dad's a doctor, Mam's a nurse. They don't work together," he added, beginning to babble. "Mam's in the infirmary at our old primary school, and Dad and his partner have a surgery in town. Ehm…Dad's family's all local. Mam came from Belfast for uni and stayed—"

"I think she means your birth parents, Seamie," I murmured.

"Oh." His face colored. "Nothing. I don't know anything about them."

"You were adopted?" Coileán asked.

Seamus's voice hardened a degree. "Abandoned. They left me outside Dad's front door."

Eleanor hesitated before following up. "This may be a sensitive subject, but have you never sought them out?"

"Why would I?" he muttered, his grip tightening on mine. "They obviously want nothing to do with me, so why should I bother with them?"

"Well, now, you don't *know* that for certain," she protested.

He tried to disguise his hurt with rough laughter. "Whoever my mother was, if she gave a damn about me, she'd have gone through a proper adoption. It was 1969," he said, growing more agitated as his old anger resurfaced. "*All* the unwed mothers did it. She could have gone to the nuns if she wanted to be sure I'd never find her. But she didn't care. She left me on the steps of the surgery like a milk crate. Dad thought I wasn't two days old."

The awkward silence that followed hung in the room for a moment as Seamus reburied his feelings with deep breaths and a steady glare at the wall beyond Toula's head. When she saw that no explosion was imminent, she pulled her chair toward our couch and waited until he met her eyes. "I am *so* sorry," she murmured. "If you want to talk about parental abandonment some time, I'll be happy to tell you about my mother. She left me with my father to raise, which might have worked had he not ended up in Arcanum custody early on."

"She had little use for any of her children," Val muttered.

Toula gave him a knowing nod, then turned her attention back to Seamus. "Yeah, not particularly maternal, that one. But look, we're not here to one-up you over sob stories. I was asking about your birth family because there's a decent chance that you've got at least cousins out there, if not siblings. *Finding* them may be a challenge, but I'll do what I can."

"And there's a possibility that bears noting," Eleanor said softly. "I was born of a rape. So was he," she added, pointing to Aiden. "Coileán, erm…"

"Gross misrepresentation," he offered.

"It's unfortunate," she told Seamus, "but many of us were forced upon one parent or the other. All I'm suggesting is that there may have been a reason for your abandonment. If I had to venture a guess, I'd say your mother was probably mortal. Perhaps she couldn't face reliving that attack. Or she could have had you in secret and dropped you off where someone was bound to find you. There are any number of possibilities."

"If your father was the mortal one, he may never have known about you," said Coileán. "But then again, the fact that you're alive at all suggests that your mother probably wasn't fae. If she'd been fae and she didn't want you, it would have been far simpler for her to either enchant her way to a miscarriage or just kill you at birth. Not that uncommon."

Seamus blanched again, and Toula stepped in before

Coileán could provide examples. "What I'm going to do is run an aural analysis spell. Quick and painless, color-coded for my convenience. It'll tell us *what* you are, but if we're lucky, it may also tell us where you come from. All right?"

He looked at me uncertainly, and I nodded. With a sigh, he turned back to Toula and muttered, "Don't suppose I have a real choice, do I?"

"If you don't want—"

"No, no, that's fine," he interrupted, and squeezed his eyes closed. "Sorry. Give me the worst."

While he tensed for the blow, Toula whispered and stretched out her hand. A misty ball began to coalesce over her palm, then solidified into a hollow sphere, a jumbled lattice of blue and red threads like colored string thrown haphazardly around a balloon. "Okay, hard part's over. You can open your eyes," she said, and Seamus slowly did as she bade.

He scowled at the glowing ball cupped in her hand. "What is—"

"That's you. Don't bother trying to make sense of the lines—what we look for in doing aural analysis are the components of a given lattice. An aural signature is made of the combined lattices of the parents." She tossed the sphere into the air and spread two fingers in a V, and the lattice split into single-color spheres. "What you've got here is a classic half-fae signature. The blue lattice belongs to your mundane parent, the red to your fae parent. *That*," she continued, pointing to the red sphere, "is why you'll never take up blacksmithing."

"There are workarounds," Aiden protested.

"Yes, gloves can do wonders for the masochistic faerie," she retorted, "but something tells me you don't play a lot of horseshoes, right, Seamus?"

He had eyes only for the orbs. "So...practically speaking, what does all of this mean going forward?"

"It means you need to be trained," Val interjected. "You are a danger to yourself and everyone around you until you can control your own abilities." He turned to Coileán. "With your permission, I'll see to his education."

From the corner of my eye, I caught Joey and Aiden's twin grimaces and suspected I could guess the cause.

"That would probably be for the best," Coileán replied, then turned his attention to Toula. "Any match?"

She tapped her quartz ring, which began to glow and rapidly flash a series of colorful lattices above her hand. "Searching my database," she explained to Seamus and me. "I've got so many stored in here that I need a separate spell just to run the cross-check, especially since we're hunting a needle in a haystack." She watched a stream of red lattices appear and fade, then exhaled slowly and studied Seamus while the spell did its work. "How much do you know about the courts?"

He shrugged. "Until yesterday, nothing."

"Okay. Officially, there are two." She cocked her head toward Coileán and Eleanor. "He heads one, she heads the other. Allegiance is generally something you inherit. Basically, those two keep the anarchy here to a minimum."

"With varying degrees of success," Eleanor mumbled.

"Anyway, there *was* a third court," Toula continued. "Which Mab ran—our oh-so-loving mother," she added, jutting her thumb at Val. "Long story short, she broke the peace, her followers recently tried to invade, and the realm gets twitchy whenever anyone affiliated with that court comes over, but that's mostly Gramps and Ellie's problem. Now, given how strongly the realm complained last night, we assume that your fae parent was one of Mab's. If that's the case, then you don't currently belong to a court, and more annoyingly, the odds that I've collected a signature related to yours are slim…"

Her voice faded as a red orb appeared and lingered, rotating slowly above the back of her hand. "Maybe I spoke too soon," she muttered, then pulled Seamus's red half over for comparison. With a wave of her finger, the two flattened. She stacked them, then frowned and separated them again. "Not the *parent*," she mumbled, and Seamus's orb split again into two red orbs, one of which was the twin of the orb from Toula's ring. She checked the identical lattices from all angles, then leaned back in her chair and sighed. "Well, shit."

"Now, *that's* reassuring," said Seamus. "What's wrong?"

"I got a match, that's what's wrong. I only have one signature from that court, and it's Mab's." She gestured toward the blue orb and two smaller red ones from Seamus's signature. "Whatever faerie produced you was a sibling of ours. I can't narrow it down more than that—"

"There were at least two hundred," Val interrupted. "All gone but for the two of us."

"So if you were hoping to meet that parent someday, I'm really sorry," Toula resumed. "But, uh…for what it's worth, we're your aunt and uncle. Um…so, uh…" She rubbed the back of her neck. "Hi?"

CHAPTER 6

"As far as I'm concerned, Faerie can get over herself," said Vivi. She leaned against the desk housing three monitors and folded her arms. "There are plenty of Fringers here with connections to Mab's court, and she hasn't raised a stink yet."

"Maybe because they're Fringe," I ventured, taking in the rest of the command suite. The room was cold—a precaution for the computers, Vivi had warned me on our walk over—and the walls that weren't lined with monitors or stacks of equipment were hung with white dry-erase boards covered with names and other data. I only needed to read a few before I had the color-coding system down. Purple denoted deceased, and one board was strikingly violet.

"Yeah, maybe. But if she's listening—*as I know she is*," she added, glaring at the ceiling, "she can cut Seamus some slack. Dude's a cop—I don't see him causing a real problem. Here, sit down," she offered, pulling a wooden chair on casters from its spot under one of the desks. "I'll show you what we've got."

I sank into the chair and pushed myself closer to Vivi's matching seat. "I just wanted to help him. Thought I was doing the right thing—"

"You did. He'll deal with it." She typed a rapid sequence of passwords into one of the computers, and I watched with a pang as the familiar Fringe interface appeared. "Look," said Vivi, giving me a tight smile, "Hal, my dear, sweet, entirely mundane husband got yanked out of Virginia ahead of a pack of monsters out of the Gray Lands, and then he got dumped on my parents' doorstep for Thanksgiving. With all *twelve* of my big brothers. I hadn't told him about the faerie thing until then, and you know what? He survived. Even married me. So yeah, I get it that Seamus is a little shell-shocked, but he'll adjust. And he's in good hands," she added as she slid to the next monitor over and pulled up a spreadsheet. "Val's old as dirt, and he knows his stuff. He'll get your friend squared away."

"He's got his work cut out for him." My thoughts flashed to the moment just before I'd parted from Seamus, as Toula dubbed his hair dye a "critical glamour failure" and cackled.

"Eh, he's a pro. Unlike yours truly." Vivi pushed back from the computer bench and pulled her glasses off to wipe them clean on her shirt. "Going to be honest with you, Badger, I feel kind of like a squire who's found a sword and is trying his best to pass as a knight. I'm in so far over my head, I can't even see the surface anymore."

"You've done a remarkable job," I replied, and pointed to the window, which overlooked a tree-lined street of small storefronts and a manicured park. "This place is a wonder."

"Thanks, but I don't take any credit for that. My brother Robbie's an architect. He's had his mitts in a dozen planned communities over the last thirty years," she explained. "Once we got a headcount, he started laying this place out. Built a bunch of it himself. Well, I mean, he drafted the boys in for some of the actual construction, but he's been overseeing the development. And I just sit up here and play switchboard," she sighed, resting her elbow on the desk. "Useless on the magic front, but for some reason, the Fringe is willing to listen to me. Boggles the mind."

"Please," I scoffed, "we all know what you did in Montana—"

"Nothing extraordinary. I'm not Rick," she mumbled as she turned back to her computers. "Somebody with experience should be doing this, not me. Someone like you."

"You know," I said as she typed, "the only way to get experience with a thing is to do it. None of us has had to face a situation like this before—you're more experienced already than anyone."

"Ha." She found what she wanted in her spreadsheet, then looked my way again. "Tell me you're not really going back. Chief's right, it's suicide."

"It's my job, Vivi."

"But we need you here. Look." She jabbed her finger at the screen, and I slid closer to examine the columns of names and numbers. "I'm the de facto mayor of a town of five hundred and thirty-nine," she said as I read. "It was only five hundred and thirty-seven when we started. Two of the evacuees were *very* pregnant. Anyway, I've got people out there of all ages, all nationalities, witches and lesser bloods and witch-bloods alike, thrown together into faux suburbia and trying to put their lives back together. No one knows when the Arcanum is going to come to its senses, no one knows when we can go home again, and no one leaves the settlement for fear that some asshole faerie will disregard the 'do not fuck with the Fringers' directive. Don't get me wrong," she continued, "everyone's been great thus far, and conflict's low, all things considered, but people are *scared*, okay? They need someone to steer them through this. You're a coordinator—they need you."

I scrolled through the spreadsheet, connecting faces to the few names I knew. "How are you even communicating? Finland, Pakistan, Chad…"

"Quick jolt of Fae to the skull works wonders. Better than memorizing conjugations, yeah?"

"True." I looked up from the screen and found her watching me, her face drawn. "But what about the ones left behind? And the ones the Arcanum's taken—what about them? Who's looking out for the others?"

Vivi could only shrug. "We can't do anything for the ones in Arcanum custody. As for the others…well, look at the board behind you."

I turned and read through the long list of blue names, all written in a tight, neat hand. The board was only half-covered, but there were at least a few hundred people listed.

"The missing," Vivi explained before I could ask. "Unaccounted for. Could have been taken, could be dead, could be in hiding. We just don't know. And until people start getting back on the network, we have no way of finding out."

"You think anyone's actually going to trust it again? The net's been compromised."

"Aiden and I are working on a new setup, but it's going to take time to get it off the ground and sufficiently secured. And even then, getting the word out to anyone left over there is going to be close to impossible. That's why I check the old network from time to time—just in case." She gave the monitor a pat and stood. "I've called a town meeting for tonight. Please tell me you'll speak so I won't look like an idiot."

I pushed myself from my chair and tucked it away. "Sure, unless Seamus needs me."

Vivi snorted and headed down the spiral staircase to the street. "Going by what Aiden and Joey have said, Seamus is going to need a lot of things tonight, primarily painkillers and alcohol. I don't think he's going to be in a position to complain if you duck out to say a few words." She pushed open the outer door, and I followed her into a perfect British summer, the kind one ordinarily sees for perhaps three days a year. "I'll give you the tour while we're here," she offered, leading me down the strangely carless street. "Let you see some idea of what direction we're heading. Come on, I'll show you the school," she said, and linked her arm around mine. "Take a look at the houses on the way, see what strikes your fancy. Robbie *loves* to do custom work."

Seeing as I was without a change of clothes, there was no point in returning to Eleanor's mansion to freshen up before the meeting that night. After taking Vivi's grand tour of the Fringe settlement—which, I had to admit, was wonderfully planned on short notice—I made camp on a park bench and kept my mobile close, hoping for a word from Seamus. But after an hour with no calls—or at least my mobile thought it had been an hour, though I didn't know how well the realms synchronized their respective watches—I took a walk.

Lured by the smell of warm gingerbread, I stopped outside one of the shops and drooled until the middle-aged proprietress beckoned me inside and gestured to the glass display case. "What'll you have?" she asked with a smile.

"I, erm," I stuttered, "that is, I don't have any money at the moment—"

She laughed at that. "You must be the new coordinator. *No one* has any money. I run a bakery because I enjoy it and want something to do. Nothing to buy, so there's no point in trying to make money."

I looked behind her at the bags of flour and sugar stacked by the wall. "But where do you get—"

"It's as easy as calling a Stowe boy. There's always at least a handful of them around," she explained. "They kind of adopted this place. Builders, provisioners, security—if not for them, I don't know what we'd be doing now." She shrugged and slid on a pair of plastic gloves. "The queen and king have been generous, but I think they turned the day-to-day operations over to that clan. Here, give this a taste and tell me what you think," she said, passing me a piece of gingerbread.

It was warm and slightly chewy, heavily spiced, and just

sweet enough to make my taste buds pay attention. "Perfect. And the arrangement works?"

"It seems to. It's adorable, really," she added in a smiling murmur. "They take their marching orders from Vivi. There's power in being the baby sister, isn't there?"

"I wouldn't know, but I'll take your word for it." I nibbled another bite, then grinned sheepishly at the baker. "As long as they're free, any chance of getting one for the road?"

The afternoon passed in a pleasant hum. As I made my rounds, familiarizing myself with the layout of the town, strangers stopped me to say hello or offer their welcome. "We knew you had to be the coordinator," an old man explained as his wife bobbed her head. "Not too many strangers around here, and…well, not to be rude, but we didn't think you looked fae."

"*Heinrich*," his mortified wife snapped, then looked at me and began to babble. "Forgive my husband, he is terrible in polite company—"

"He's honest," I said, and patted her arm. "I've earned the crow's feet."

He had a point, I thought, walking on through the sunshine. In a world of perpetual youth, surely I stuck out like an unpleasant curiosity—any Fringer over thirty would be an obvious outsider. Then again, I had yet to see a faerie in town, with the exception of one of Vivi's many brothers, who'd taken on the task of educating the older teenagers while the school committee figured out a game plan. This was a world within a world, a little island of quiet where the Fringe could regroup. So what if half of us were a touch wrinkly?

A low brick wall, only waist-high, marked the edge of town—a decorative border more than a defensive measure, I surmised, and took a seat atop it while I finished my snack. Past a rolling field and what appeared to be an expansive orchard rose a great stone castle, and if I squinted, I could pick out smaller structures dwindling toward the horizon. Seamie was somewhere out there, but I had no idea where Val might have taken him—hell, I had no idea of how to get back to Eleanor's mansion.

As I mulled this over, I looked to my right at the sound of footsteps and found a brown-haired man strolling my way. "Badger, I presume," he said by way of greeting. "Did Vivi release you, then?"

His accent was definitely English, but I couldn't place it. "Some time ago. Thought I'd clear my head."

"The view's not bad here. May I?" I gestured to the spot of wall beside mine, and he hopped onto the ledge. "Ned Stowe."

The name rang a bell, and I recalled what I'd seen in the database. Small wonder I couldn't pinpoint his accent: Vivi's eldest brother was somewhere north of five hundred years old. "*Ah*. You were in Montana, yes?"

"I was. Ghastly installation they have."

"Never seen it in person, but I hear that Arcanum 1 lacks a certain ambiance."

He nodded and pointed to the castle. "That's Lord Coileán's. You're staying with my lady, aren't you? Do you need a lift? It's not easily walkable."

"Thanks, no. If you're looking for your sister, I left her back at the command center."

But Ned brushed it off. "Just taking a tour of the wall. Security." Seeing my expression shift, he explained, "You're safe here, more or less. Better than back *there*, anyway. But the boys and I aren't keen on leaving Vivi completely unattended, if you follow me."

"You're…worried about problems in the Fringe?"

"Problems out there," he replied, gesturing toward the distance. "There's been enough trouble here of late—no sense in making this place an easy target. It's mostly sorted for now, but…" He shrugged. "Faeries."

"I hear that."

He watched me for a brief moment, then cleared his throat and stared at the orchard. "It'll feel more like home before long. Bit of a transition, to be sure, but it's not so bad."

"It's lovely," I replied, watching a flock of birds pass over the castle.

"Vivi said you hadn't come alone."

I cut my eyes to him and found Ned watching me again. "He's been whisked off for basic training. I keep waiting for a buzz," I added, pulling my mobile from my pocket, "but nothing yet."

"How old is he?"

"Forty-seven last March. We're three weeks apart."

Ned whistled low. "*Forty-seven*? Our Harry's fifty. To have no training at that age…" He made a face and shook his head. "Boy's in the best place for him to be right now. His tutors will see to him."

"I don't even know where he is," I mumbled.

"Don't worry, I'm sure he'll come round before long."

"Maybe." Seeing Ned's bemusement, I sighed and rubbed my healing wrist. "We haven't been close of late, and I dragged him into this, so I suspect he'll have a few choice words for me when we next meet."

"Be that as it may, you're the one person he knows here, right? I'd say he'll get over it. A familiar face goes a long way. Or name," he added with a knowing look. "Word's been spreading today that Badger's come over."

"What more could I do for them than Vivi's already done? You've all done marvelous work—all you're missing is a bingo hall and a hospital."

"Can't speak to the bingo situation, but there's little need of a hospital. We can fix minor injuries—you're ahead of me on that," he added, pointing to the enchantment around my wrist, "and I've yet to hear of so much as a sniffle. This realm seems to be disease-free."

I shook my head. "Maybe so, but people break down. It's part of the whole 'mortal' package, you understand."

"Well, yes and no." Ned grinned. "No one's told you the little secret about aging here, have they?"

"I know *you* don't, but we—"

"Also don't. There's enough magic here to keep you as you are. We can't turn back the clock, but no one will grow old while they're here. Apparently, you get it back all at once when you leave the realm, though, but that's a matter for another time. For now...well, I hope forty-seven suits."

I stared at him, momentarily dumbstruck. "So...wait, I'm—"

"Not going to age while you're here. In other words, I should think you'll have time to get things sorted with your friend." With that, he stood and stretched. "I'll leave you to it. You'll be at the meeting tonight, yeah?"

"Yeah," I mumbled. "See you."

As Ned walked off, I tried to come to terms with the information he'd dropped in my lap. Seamus was exactly where he needed to be. I could stay here, in this lovely little town with picture-perfect weather, and continue on indefinitely. There was nothing preventing Seamie from coming over to see me once he had himself straightened out, and maybe...

Sure, twenty-two years was a long time, and I was no cover girl, but *maybe*...

I bit into my cooled gingerbread and stared at the world around me, seeing everything and nothing, until the light began to redden and I forced myself to walk back through town.

By the time I strolled in the rear doors of the community center, most of the rows of seats had been filled, and Vivi stood behind a spot-lit podium on the stage at the front. Seeing my entrance, she beckoned for me to join her, and I felt the crowd's eyes follow me as I mounted the steps to the stage.

As the room quieted, Vivi made quick opening remarks, thanking the assembled for coming out on short notice and presenting half a dozen announcements. "But the reason you're all here, of course," she continued after mentioned a planning committee for the new playground, "is the lady to my left. Badger, would you like to say a few words?"

I've never liked audiences, let alone situations that call for microphones, but Vivi was smiling hopefully, and the room was waiting. With a deep breath, I took her spot at the podium and nodded to the crowd. "Ehm…good evening," I began, squinting at the room through the spotlight's glare. "I'm Hannah Parsons, call sign Badger. I'm sure you can't imagine where I got that name," I said, brushing my white forelock from my eyes.

The crowd chuckled, and I pressed on. "For those of you who don't know me, I'm the coordinator for northern England, the borders, and Scotland. Or, ehm…well, I was. Don't suppose I'm coordinating much at the moment. To be honest, I've been in hiding most of the last few weeks. But it's lovely to see that so many Fringers are safe, and I can't tell you how nice it is to not be looking over my shoulder tonight." I paused to sort through my snatches of thought, but no words of wisdom were forthcoming. "Those are all the prepared remarks I have. If you've got questions, I'll do my best."

A hand went up near the front, and when I pointed that way, an older woman stood. "What about the others? The rest of the Fringe? What news?"

The crowd murmured, and I waited until it stilled to answer her. "I'm afraid I haven't got much to offer you. Elaine Davies and Marty Endicott are, unfortunately, among the deceased. Sunshine and Hornet, if you've spent much time in the UK corners of the network. Their daughters came over with me, and I assume they'll be living with their grandmother for now. Ehm…" I hesitated, then said, "Gerri Tidwell—Iris—threw her lot in with the Arcanum. When I last saw her, she was injured but alive. That's all I can report…"

The murmuring resumed with new vigor, and I held up my hand for quiet. "For now. I'm going back to find the rest of us, one way or another."

Vivi began to sputter, but I shook my head. "You showed me the names," I told her. "The missing. It's my job to find anyone on the run and bring them here to safety."

"It's *suicide!*"

"Maybe, maybe not. But someone's got to try. I'm a coordinator, Vivi—"

"Which is why we need you here." She gripped my uninjured wrist and looked into my eyes. "Stay, Badger. The Fringe here needs a coordinator."

I held her gaze. "How old are you?"

"Twenty-five. Twenty-six in August. Why?"

"I have to ask for form's sake." Gently pulling free of Vivi's grip, I stepped away from the podium and guided her to a clear spot on the stage. "Kneel."

Her blue eyes widened in comprehension. "*Badger—*"

"Kneel." She dropped to one knee, and I put my hands on her shoulders, trying to remember the words my father spoke to me a dozen years before. "Vivian Stowe—"

"Perryman."

"Vivian Stowe Perryman," I amended, "I find you loyal to the Fringe and capable of leadership. Do you accept the responsibility I offer you?"

"Yes," she whispered, looking at the floor.

"Then by the power vested in me by my office, I name you coordinator of the Fringe in exile, with all rights and duties attendant thereunto." I helped her to her feet and spun her to face the crowd. "These are your people now. Serve them well."

The town broke into loud applause and whistles, and Vivi blushed under the stage lights. "I, um…I'll do my best."

It wasn't the usual coordinator script, but it sufficed. "I have utter confidence in you," I murmured, bending to her ear. "Keep up the good work."

She turned and called my name before I could step off the stage. "*Stay*, Badger. You don't have to do this."

I smiled as reassuringly as I could. "The Fringe here has a coordinator. Don't you think the ones at home need someone, too?"

CHAPTER 7

I shook a few dozen hands and exchanged small talk with people I'd previously known online, listening to their escape stories and accepting their condolences for my own loss. As the crowd thinned, I made my way back toward the door, hoping to slip out without being asked for nonexistent details about my grand plan. Ned had to be lurking about, I decided—I'd find him and ask for a gate back to my borrowed bed, and tomorrow, I would try to put a plan together that didn't end in my immediate assassination.

But before I could leave the building, a firm hand grabbed my upper arm to stay me, and I turned to find Val in the shadows. "A word?" he asked.

I nodded and followed him through an inner door and down a tiled hallway to the community center's breakroom. A pair of coffeemakers offered regular and decaf, and a plastic water heater sat on the counter beside them next to white and pastel packets of sweetener. Val considered the door for a second, and with a twitch of his finger, the window turned to wood. An accompanying sound of metal on metal told me the door was locked.

"For privacy," he explained, and indicated one of the empty tables. "Please sit."

He was keeping the conversation in English, I noticed, though whether that was also for privacy or to put me at ease, I couldn't say. "Where's Seamus?" I asked as I pulled out a chair.

"At Eleanor's home, resting. He needs to sleep off his

injuries, let them heal."

"*Injuries?*"

Val held up his hands in placation as my voice shrilled. "Nothing serious, a few bruises. We had a...*difficult* day." He rested his elbow on the table and began to massage his head. "I need your help."

"What can *I* do?"

"I need information. An understanding." He straightened, then cut his eyes to the counter. "Is that supposed to be coffee?"

"Drip, I think."

With a shudder of distaste, he produced a pair of white espresso cups on our table and nudged one toward me. I sipped, grateful for something to do with my hands, and waited while Val collected his thoughts. After a long moment, he sighed and pushed his empty cup away. "The boy is half fae, this much is clear. Untrained, but that shouldn't present a physical problem. He has everything he needs in order to learn."

"But?"

"But. There is something preventing him from using his power—not even direct attacks provoked it. He's not bound, which makes me think it's something *here*." Val tapped his forehead. "He has used magic before, yes? When? How?"

I thought back, feeling the unpleasant knot in my gut when my mind's eye flashed on memories I wished I could forget. "Three times," I muttered. "Twice when we were younger, and the third time was a few days ago."

"Mm. How was he raised?"

"It's kind of a long story..."

"I have time."

"Right," I muttered, then let out a long breath. "I've known Seamus all my life. Our families lived in two sides of a semi-detached house, and we shared a garden. There was a big tree in the back, and our dads built us a little house up there to play in—kept us out from underfoot."

"Seamus said your father was a witch."

I nodded. "A decent one. His parents pushed him to leave Glastonbury, and he went to uni at Durham. Met my mother there—an exchange student from the States. They fell in love, she changed her plans and decided that Durham was preferable to west Texas, and that was that. She was a librarian, and he opened a shop dealing in esoterica." I smiled at the memory of the place, a jumble sale of candles, tarot cards, and bric-a-brac that always smelled like patchouli. "It was the sixties, you see, and there were enough people who thought it was risqué to have their cards done or their palm read to keep him in business—crystals, incense, all of that rubbish. He did a bit of real work for customers in the know, but he mostly hid in plain sight, as it were.

"Well, the Malones—Seamie's parents—they weren't thrilled at first to have them for neighbors. They were a little older, and Tom's a doctor, and suddenly, there was Dad and his weird store and his American wife. But Mama and Mary were fast friends, and everything was fine."

"Your father never told them about his talent?" Val asked.

"Eventually." I sipped my espresso. "Tom was cleaning the gutters one day, and his ladder broke, and he ended up hanging from the roof. Dad just happened to be in the garden, and he whipped out his wand and caught him before Tom could hurt himself. *That*, apparently, took some explanation, but then again, since Dad had just saved Tom from cracking his head open, they gave him the benefit of the doubt." I paused and swirled my coffee. "Mama never cared that Dad was a witch. She thought it was useful, and she never had a kind word for his parents for ignoring us. I mean, she didn't tell *her* family about it— I don't know how much you know about Texas, but it wouldn't have gone over well had she told her Southern Baptist kin about her husband and his magic wand."

Val smirked in reply. "There's a priest here. We have

had conversations."

"Catholic?" He nodded, and I said, "The reaction in Texas might have been worse than even he could anticipate. So anyway, long story short, the Malones came round to the idea that it wasn't horrible having a witch next door, and Dad always did for them what he could. Any chance of a refill?" My cup topped up, and I slugged it back. "Cheers. Long day here, too. So, I was born in March of '69, and Tom found Seamie at the door on April Fool's Day. Some joke," I muttered. "He decided Seamie was two days old, so we're three weeks apart."

"Why did they keep him? Surely they noticed—"

"Not at first. It's…you know, mundanes don't look at a child with a weird metal allergy and think 'Aha! Faerie!' You only see that sort of paranoia among the Fringe." Val chuckled, and I resumed. "They kept him because they couldn't have kids. Mary was sick as a child, see. And then, out of nowhere, there was a healthy baby, and since there were no leads about his birth parents, the Malones were able to adopt him. But once the papers were finalized, Dad figured him out."

"Fringe intuition?"

"No, a silver teething ring. My parents brought over a gift basket that night, and little silver things are traditional—spoons, rattles, stuff the baby will probably never use. Mary gave Seamie the ring to hold, and, according to Dad, he burned like they'd put his hand on the range.

"My parents apologized, of course, and they took the ring back with them. But Tom knew something was up—Dad was always a terrible liar. His face gave him away," I explained. "Tom cornered him and said he needed to know what was wrong with his son—he'd never seen an allergic reaction like that, and he wanted to help Seamie, so he was desperate enough to look for a magical explanation. Dad told him he'd never believe the truth, but Tom was a little more open-minded then than he'd been when my parents first moved in, and he insisted. So Dad told him that he thought Seamie was fae. Said he needed to keep him away from iron and silver, but that the baby wouldn't need his vaccinations. And he said the best thing they could do for him would be to expose him to as little magic as possible and hope that he never caught on."

"Foolish," Val muttered.

"Desperate," I countered. "No one could have controlled him, had he come into his power as a child. And what do you suppose the Arcanum would have done if they'd heard about him?"

"Nothing good," he admitted. "But you're a witch, yes? If they were trying to isolate him, why did they let you interact?"

"We shared a bedroom wall and a garden—they didn't have much choice. Seamie and I did *everything* together when we were small. And then my talent really started to develop." I paused as my cup refilled again, then smiled and sipped. "It came on quickly…too quickly, I suppose. I sort of burnt out."

"Meaning?"

"I was a decently strong witch when I was seven or eight, relatively speaking. But it faded. My grandparents sent me a dragonscale wand when I was nine, and my parents thought it was more than I needed, but I suppose my grandparents were the prescient ones. I can't do anything without it now, but then…" I swallowed hard at the taste of bile. "*Star Wars* came out during Christmas when we were eight, and Seamie and I must have watched it half a dozen times. Do you, ehm…"

"I've seen it."

"Oh, good. Nice to be on the same page," I muttered. "So yes, we were enormous fans, and our parents bought us all the action figures, you know, the plastic figurines of the characters and the ships and whatnot." I felt my cheeks begin to flush. "That summer, we were playing up in the treehouse, and I…I told Seamie I had something like the

Force, and I made the ships fly around. I shouldn't have, but I knew he would like it," I said in a rush, "and he was my best friend—"

Val raised a hand to stop me. "You were a child."

"I should have known better," I mumbled into my cup. "But Seamie was properly impressed, and I swore him to secrecy. As far as I know, he's never told a soul. And then we went back to school…"

My companion watched while I collected myself. "There was a new boy in our class, Doug Stewart," I continued. "Right bastard, that one. I think he did a stint in prison, come to mention it. But he gave Seamie and me grief because we were always together. Called me Seamie's girlfriend, and then he said Seamie was a girl for playing with me, and when that didn't work, he started picking on me. My hair, mostly."

"The, uh…"

"The white bit isn't dye," I said, trying not to be defensive. "It grew in like this—poliosis, if you want to be technical. Children are little beasts, so I was teased on occasion, but not like it was with Doug. He just wouldn't *stop*. And one day, he'd been poking at me all morning, calling me a freak and everything else, and by lunch, I couldn't take it anymore. I started crying, and Seamie…he saw me."

Val waited through my silence, then prompted, "And?"

"And Doug flew across the yard into a brick wall, face-first. Broke his arm, cracked a few ribs, took out his two front teeth. Seamie didn't touch him, but we both knew he did it. He was so scared that *he* started crying, and Mary, who was working in the infirmary by then, sent us home sick when the paramedics came for Doug."

My hand clenched around my cup. "It was my fault. If I hadn't started showing off around him, Seamie would never have…have had his accident." Val made no reply, and I pressed on. "So we camped out in the treehouse that night. We'd always had this thing—if you were worried or upset or whatever, you took the other's hand, no questions asked. I remember waking up in the night, and our hands were together. Must have done it in our sleep. But, ehm…anyway, I slipped inside for a drink of water, and I found my parents and the Malones talking in the den. So, naturally, I eavesdropped."

"Naturally."

"I was *nine*, and they sounded upset. They were talking about Seamie and what he'd done, and Dad…Dad said he couldn't help him. His gift wasn't like Seamie's, he said, and he told them the best thing to do was to encourage Seamie to control his temper and try not to do anything like…*that*…again."

I forced my hand to loosen its painful grip. "So I sneaked back to the treehouse, and I thought I'd got away with it, but Dad talked to me the next morning at breakfast, when we were alone. He said Seamie was probably fae, and for his safety, we couldn't tell him. If Seamie didn't know, then whatever had flared up in him might die down.

"I never told Dad about the action figures, and I never did anything like that around Seamie again—not while we were children. And he didn't have any more accidents."

"Until he did," Val murmured.

I sighed and rubbed my temples. "We couldn't keep everything from him. He knew I was a witch, and he'd been in Dad's shop loads of times. But I barely did anything around him—it was too hard, anyway, once my power dropped off. I think I fixed a wobbly table leg and a lightbulb when we were at uni, but that was all." Val watched impassively, and I said, "I *knew* what he was, okay? But Dad said it was for the best, and he was a coordinator, and I…I wanted everything to be all right for Seamie."

He nodded to himself. "When did you fall in love?"

There was no point in lying to someone who could poke around inside my head. "Secondary school, I think.

We dated during uni, and we were firmly an item before we started police training. We both found jobs in Durham, and a year later, after we'd had a few paychecks, he put together a candlelight picnic in our old treehouse—terrible idea in retrospect, but at least we didn't set the tree on fire. And he proposed."

"You accepted?"

I hesitated, feeling suddenly exposed, then reached under my shirt and drew out my necklace, a gold chain on which I'd hung my little engagement ring. The diamond was tiny, and the other guys had laughed at Seamus for being so cheap, but to me, sitting in a treehouse at twenty-four while the love of my life slid it over my knuckle, that ring was perfection.

"Yeah," I told Val. "I accepted. We were colleagues in the Constabulary, and we were going to marry and be partners in life. And then it all went to hell."

He watched me as I tucked the necklace away. "How so?"

"Seamie had his second accident. We'd only been engaged about a month, and I came outside at work one afternoon to find him and one of our coworkers in an argument. I don't even know what they were fighting about. But I tried to break it up before they could start punching each other, and so I stepped between them. The other guy, Northwood, shoved me. It may have been accidental, for all I know. But I saw the look in Seamie's eyes when I caught my balance, and the next thing I remember is picking myself up off the pavement. I had glass in my hair, and Northwood's car was a flaming wreck."

"And Northwood?"

"Thrown by the blast, but otherwise unharmed. The bomb squad had a look, but they never found anything. They wouldn't—Seamie and I both knew he had done it."

My throat began to tighten, but I swallowed and pressed on. "Dad told me later that Seamie went to him a few days after and begged for help. He knew he could have killed Northwood, you see, and he didn't want that to happen. But Dad said he couldn't do anything for him, and all Seamie could do was try to be calm. That…wasn't good enough."

I looked away to collect myself, refusing to cry in front of a virtual stranger, but the memory smarted as if it were fresh. "He put in a transfer to Belfast. Didn't tell me. Didn't tell anyone until everything was final, and he gave two weeks' notice." I blinked through my pricking eyes and scowled at the floor. "I found out with the rest of the Constabulary, when our supervisor made the announcement. And then I dragged Seamie's arse outside and demanded to know what was going on, and he…he said he knew he was cursed, and he wasn't willing to put me at risk because of it. I *begged* him to reconsider for those two weeks, and I begged him all the way to the airport, but he took my hand at the last and said, 'This is me protecting you. Don't follow me, Badger. I'll ring you when I can.' I remember every word…"

The exhaustion of the last weeks and the roller coaster of the last days worked against me then, and I tried to swipe the tears away as quickly as they escaped. "I'm sorry," I mumbled, "just…give me a minute."

Val waited as I dragged myself under control, then cleared his throat. "You didn't follow him?"

"Not to Belfast. This was '94—the Troubles, see? He knew that only an idiot would have followed him, and I decided that if he wanted to get himself killed, he could bloody well do it without me. But I kept asking him to come home. Twenty-two years of calls and texts and e-mails, and he never darkened my door again until he had another accident."

"Tell me what happened."

I glanced into my cup, found it empty, and pushed it aside. "Lost his temper with a suspect. Child rapist. Bastard mouthed off once too often and pushed him over the edge."

"Mm. What about this suspect so infuriated him?"

"How should I know?" I muttered. "I wasn't there—"

"This wasn't the worst case he's ever seen, was it? What was different with this man?"

I thought back over the few details Seamus had let slip. "Little girl, football league, he's her coach…" My eyes widened as the pertinent information surfaced. "And she's got a streak like mine. Poliosis again."

"And there it is," said Val, leaning back in his chair. "The connection. You see it, yes? Every time he loses control, he thinks you are in danger. The boy who made you cry," he said over my sputtering protests, "the man who pushed you, and now this man who hurt a child who resembles you. *You* are the trigger, Badger. Help me reach him."

I stared back at him, momentarily lost for words. "I…I don't know how, I didn't mean to—"

Val sighed and folded his arms. "The problem is in his thinking. Every time he uses magic, it's accidental, violent, and 'bad.' He fears it. Until he's willing to face it, I can do nothing. So why don't we provoke him? Force him to face himself?"

"How?"

His head tilted as he considered my expression. "How far are you willing to go to help him?"

"Tell me what you need. This is all my fault—"

He huffed in exasperation. "Stop saying that. No one is to blame for his talent. That's the root of the problem— you've treated him like he has a terrible secret. Of course he's unwilling to experiment when he thinks it's evil."

"Okay, then *that's* my fault!"

"Not you—*you*," he replied, tracing a circle with one finger. "All of you. This language is not precise…" He studied me again, more carefully. "You are very angry with Seamus."

"I'm fine."

The look he shot me said it all. "Because he left?" Reluctantly, I nodded, and Val shook his head. "Surely you understand why he did it. He cares for you—that much is obvious. If leaving meant that he could protect you—"

"*Stop.*"

He obeyed, but one eyebrow slowly rose.

The last of my tears dried as my temper flared. "I knew better than Seamus himself what he is. I *love* him. And he walked out without so much as asking me how I felt about his grand plan."

"Only to protect—"

"That wasn't supposed to be a unilateral decision! That was *us*!"

"And we both know what you would have said," he countered. "You would have objected, and he would have continued to live in fear of losing control and killing you. He left to protect you, don't you see? How do you think he could have forgiven himself if he'd let you come to harm?"

I glared at Val, too infuriated to formulate a response, until a thought popped into my mind like a searchlight in the fog. "What was her name?"

"Whose?"

"The woman you abandoned to protect," I said with forced calm. "What was her name?"

He stiffened in his seat, and I was beginning to rethink the wisdom of provoking a faerie when he murmured, "Caecilia."

"You didn't give her a choice either, did you? Thought it would be easier to walk out, never mind what she thinks."

Val stared into the distance for a moment, then met my eyes. "I went off to fight," he said quietly, "barely a season after we married. And then I had an 'accident' of my own. My comrades chased me off. If I had returned to her, to my father and his wife, to my brothers and their wives and children, how long do you think they would have lived?

How long before someone who had seen what I could do murdered them in their beds as monsters? Yes," he said, leaning toward me, "I abandoned Caecilia. I abandoned my family and my life, and I swore my sword to Titania. There was no alternative that would keep them safe." He withdrew and shook his head. "I hope they were told I died in battle. Something honorable. Not that I ran like a coward and never looked back."

With that, he stood and waved our cups into oblivion. "I'll return you to Eleanor. Tomorrow, will you help me?"

"Yeah," I muttered, equally angry and embarrassed. "Yeah. Whatever you need."

I didn't hear a peep from Seamus all night, and he was gone by the time one of Eleanor's staff brought me a tray of breakfast. "The captain starts early," she explained as I fixed my tea. "Your companion left at dawn."

"How was he?"

"Perhaps a little stiff. Starving, but sore."

Fearing I was already behind, I ate and dressed quickly, tucked my wand into my jeans, and asked the aide to take me to the training site when she came to collect my tray. "I don't know where they are," she replied, "but my lady would."

Five minutes and a quick word with Eleanor later, I found myself standing outside a building that seemed a cross between a barn and a commercial aircraft hangar. Turning in a circle once the gate closed, I spied Coileán's palace nearby, then noticed the fenced pasture full of sheep. "Is this the right place?" I asked Eleanor.

Someone cried out in sudden pain, a voice I recognized all too well, and the queen nodded. "There's a practice yard in front of the barn. No worries, now, I'm sure Georgie is keeping everyone in line."

When we rounded the corner, I saw what she meant. The barn opened onto a massive square of trampled dirt, where I found Val standing with his arms crossed and Seamus scrambling to find his feet. The tip of the black dragon's snout peeked out from the barn, and Joey and Aiden had taken up seats on hay bales beside her like spectators at a wrestling match.

"Looking for someone?" Eleanor called, and Val quickly crossed the yard.

"Thank you," he said, nodding to her, then sized me up and frowned. "You have no other clothing?"

"Did you see any luggage when I dropped in?" I retorted.

"Good point. Drink water, boy," he said over his shoulder as Seamus picked himself out of the dirt.

He was filthy, streaked brown from head to toe, and his clothes were ripped at the elbows and knees. A wicked-looked cut traced a bloody path across his forehead, and he swayed as he regained his footing. "*Badger*?" he said. "What are you doing here?"

"She is going to be of assistance. Water," Val ordered, pointing to a pile of bottles beside Aiden's feet. "Drink before you faint."

He did as he was told, but he kept his eyes on me as Eleanor took her leave. "What's the plan, then?" I asked Val when Seamus was out of earshot.

"Patience."

A few minutes later, he deemed Seamus properly hydrated, and my partner limped back to the center of the yard. "Here is what will happen," said Val, taking a few steps away from me. "On the count of three, I will throw Badger across the yard and into the pasture. Hopefully, she'll clear the fence."

Seamus's eyes went wide with alarm. "You can't, she can't defend herself, that's not—"

"I'm well aware of her limitations. So you have until the count of three to defend her. Shield her. Do what you need to do to protect her...if you can."

"No, please don't do this," he begged, "I can't control

it, please don't hurt her…"

While Seamus continued to plead with him, Val looked at me, then made a show of cracking his knuckles. "Is this about last night?" I asked. "I might have phrased certain questions better."

He grinned. "Apology accepted, but no. And don't worry—I should be able to put you back together." He raised his hand and took up his stance. "It's time, Seamus."

"Goddammit, *no!*" he cried. "I can't, I don't know how—"

"One."

"Don't hurt her—"

"Two."

The busted wand in my waistband was useless—but then again, it would have been useless even if it had been whole. I couldn't fight a faerie and win, not even with the best dragonscale wand ever made. My heart thudded in anticipation of the blow to come.

"Val, *don't!*"

He locked eyes with me and nodded. "Three."

I saw the wave of force leave his palm, a bright ripple against the background magic, and gasped. Flying on instinct as time slowed, I took a step back and extended my hand as if I could somehow absorb the blow that was coming to throw me a bone-crushing distance.

"Shield," I whispered, and cried out as the bolt neared in my vision.

With a flare like an explosion, it collided with something beyond my hand and dissipated. My arm shook with the impact, and I screamed at the anticipated hit, but an instant later, I looked through the haze of the shield beyond my hand and saw wonderment on Val's face.

"Interesting," he said, and shot again.

The shield held, but the second bolt was stronger than the first had been, and it was rapidly followed by a third and a fourth, each slightly more powerful than the last. I cried in terror and focused on the shield that had come from nowhere, praying wordlessly that whatever power had put it before me continued to think I deserved a fighting chance.

The eighth bolt was bad, but the ninth made me yelp in pain, and the tenth sent me to my knees. "*Seamie!*" I screamed. "Seamie, help me!"

I barely had time to blink before *Val* was sailing over the fence and tumbling into the sheep's drinking pond. He splashed down in an awkward belly flop, and I rose on trembling legs, tracing his trajectory back across the yard to Seamus, who stood stock-still with one hand raised. An instant later, he was running to my side. "Badge! Shit, Badger, are you all right?"

I threw my arms around him and broke into hysterical sobs, and he pulled me close and murmured reassurance, both of us shaking.

And then, in the distance, I heard laughter.

Whipping around, I saw Val climb out of the pond, dripping and cackling. As we watched, he squelched his way through the sheep and over the fence, then willed himself dry and beamed at us both. "Cheap, but effective," he told Seamus. "I should have watched my flank. As for you—"

Seamus yanked me out of the way and stood between Val and me. "There will be no more shooting the unarmed witch, got it?" he snapped.

"Witch?" he echoed, and shook his head. "No witch could have done that. You're a wizard, Badger," he said, leaning around Seamus to see me. "A *strong* one. What are you doing in the Fringe?"

It takes a few minutes to calm down after a near-death encounter, imagined or not, and Seamus kept his arm around me as I sat on a bale and drank. Georgie snuffled like a blast furnace beside us, and the others watched with concern as I alternately hydrated and hiccupped.

"I'm no wizard," I finally managed, once my heartbeat had slowed to a tempo under a sprinter's pace. "My wand is rowan and dragonscale—"

I glanced to my left as soon as I'd said that, but the dragon seemed unfazed.

"And it's broken right now," I continued when I was sure that I wasn't about to see the inside of Georgie's mouth. "Leaking core. I can barely put a ward together."

"But you shielded," said Val. "Very well, I should say. Empty-handed."

"That's impossible."

"Look around," he replied, gesturing to the other men. "No one here shielded you. *Georgie* certainly didn't. That leaves only one possibility."

"You two can argue later. First things first, let's see how bad the wand is," Aiden interjected, and held out his hand. "There's a good crafter among the refugees, but she's young. If the break is bad—oh, no, that's...that's ugly," he muttered as I pulled my tape-wrapped wand out of its hiding place. "*Ooh*...I mean, I'm no expert, but that one may be a total loss."

"May I?" asked Val.

I shrugged and put the wand in his hand, but the instant it touched his skin, he jerked and let it fall. "What's wrong? There's no iron in that."

"No...something else," he muttered, and crouched beside my wand. He passed one hand back and forth over its length as if he were trying to determine whether he'd left a curling iron on. "There is something bad about this wand," he finally announced. "I've held a few. None of them felt like this."

"It's strong," I protested. "You're feeling a strong wand, that's all."

"I sincerely doubt that. Boys, call Toula," he said to Joey and Aiden. "We need a wizard."

One short phone call later, a gate blazed open, and Toula, wearing ratty yoga pants and a long-sleeved T-shirt, stormed onto the yard. The only indication that she'd not just rolled out of bed was her head of perfectly gelled black spikes. "Let me get this straight," she said, heading for her brother. "You did *what* to Badger?"

"She's unharmed!" he protested, backing up as Toula bore down on him.

"I don't care. Did you shoot at her, yes or no?"

"She volunteered!"

Toula stomped her foot, which might have been more threatening if she'd been wearing anything but flip-flops. "Are you out of your damn *mind*? You shot at a witch? What the hell is wrong with you?"

"*Wizard*! She's a wizard! Test her!"

She gave him the sort of look that would have sent a lesser man running. "Wizard or not, you had no idea when you opened fire. Tell me if I'm mistaken."

He seemed to deflate as she glared at him. "She was assisting me with Seamus's training."

"Yeah, I've seen what 'training' entails around here," she muttered, and turned to me. "Badger, I am *so* sorry. Are you all right?"

"Fine," I lied, trying to smile. "Just, ehm, shaken."

"I don't blame you." With a final glower for Val, Toula held out her hand and began to whisper, and as my skin tingled, a white sphere manifested in front of me. In a matter of seconds, it had coalesced into a lattice of vibrant green. "Well, now," she said, considering it as it rotated, "*that's* interesting."

"I told you," Val muttered, slinking back to the pack.

"Witches show up as dull green," Toula explained to me, ignoring her brother. "Now, I've looked at my fair share of wizard orbs, and that..." She paused it in its rotation with a fingertip. "That's the kind of color I'd expect to see in a magus. You may be many things, Badger, but you're sure as hell not a witch." She split my orb in two with a slight gesture, and the color changed: my father's orb to dull green, my mundane mother's to blue.

"Yeah, I see what you came from, but it can happen."

"But...my wand," I protested, thrusting it toward her. "Dragonscale, my grandparents bought it for me."

"Your grandparents...the Glastonbury Parsons?" she asked, and grasped my wand. "*Whoa*. That ain't normal."

"You feel it, too?" Val asked her.

"I don't know what I feel, but that isn't a proper wand. What's with the tape?"

"I broke it a few weeks ago. Been trying to keep it together until I could find a crafter," I explained. "It's been weakening as I lose core material."

"Mm. May I try something?" I nodded, and Toula extended my wand. "Lorem."

The tip of the wand sparked, and a little puff of smoke rose from the burst of flame.

"I've held a dragonscale wand," she told me, passing back the useless tool. "They don't feel anything like that. Come on," she said, and waved open a gate as carelessly as if she were shooing a fly. "We need a crafter. If you idiots will promise not to shoot any witches," she added, glaring at the men, "you're welcome to come along."

CHAPTER 8

The crafter in question had a modest storefront between the bakery and a café, an unmarked door next to a red-tinted window that colored everything inside, including the crafter, a disturbing shade of blood. But if the lighting bothered her, the young blonde at the bench gave no indication. "Hi!" she called when we trooped into the workshop, and pushed a magnifying visor onto her head. "Come on in, be right with y'all."

We filled the two rows of chairs against the walls in the vestibule, and Toula leaned close to me to keep her voice low. "Amy's not a master crafter, but she's the best we've got right now. Her mother was Amelia Levey—you know, out of Charleston?"

"She didn't make it?"

"Nope. Neither did her father. But Amy's the product of two witch-bloods, so if anyone can figure this crafting thing out, she can. The kid's only sixteen, and she's *solid*."

I paused to consider the slim creature in the other room, who had slipped the visor back into position and was busily completing a wand. "Double witch-blood? Does she have court ties?"

"None that I know of, and she hasn't wanted to find out. I can't exactly blame her."

A few minutes later, Amy jogged into the vestibule and flashed a megawatt smile. "Hey, Miss Toula, how're you doing?" she drawled. "All y'all need wands?"

"Just one," said Toula, taking the lead. When she stood, she towered over Amy, who was barely more than a meter and a half. "Amy, honey, have you met Badger?"

Though I'd not have thought it possible, Amy's grin widened. "I *thought* you looked familiar!" she said, and pumped the hand I extended. "Nice to meet you, Miss...uh..."

"Hannah Parsons," I offered.

"Miss Hannah." She turned her large hazel eyes on the others and smiled apologetically. "Sorry, y'all, I'm *terrible* at names."

"I'm Joey," he said, stepping into the breach, then went down the line. "That's Toula's brother Val, the sweaty guy is Seamus, and the dork over there is Aid."

I expected a retort from Aiden, but from the look on the boy's face, he had other matters on his mind. Cutting my eyes to Seamus, I saw that he'd drawn the same conclusion. High lord or not, Aiden was in the presence of a pretty girl of about his age, and he seemed to be having some difficulty forming coherent syllables. "I've managed to break my wand," I told Amy, hoping to distract her from contemplating the sheer number of faeries in her waiting room. "It may be a total loss, but I was hoping you'd take a look anyway."

"Sure thing," she said, and motioned me into the workshop. "Y'all can come if you want," she added to the others, "just don't touch anything. Sorry, it's kind of a mess in here."

I'd never had occasion to see a crafter at work, and the chaotic clutter of Amy's workbench surprised me. Over the smells of sawdust and varnish rose bitter hints of other compounds, assumedly ingredients in her cores. While all good crafters knew the basic wand combinations that worked, the excellent ones experimented and created new wands as well, and I could only imagine what was lurking in the jars scattered about the room.

Amy plopped down in her chair and held out her hand. "Okay, let's see the damage."

I pulled the wand out but hesitated before surrendering

it. "Sorry about the tape. Oh, and Toula and Val think there's something odd about my wand…"

"That's fine, I like a challenge." Her fingers curled in invitation, and I dropped the wand into her palm. Amy twitched, then held the wand between her index fingers and frowned at the wrapping. "All right…this one could be a doozy. Let me get this tape off, and we'll see what we're working with."

It took her five minutes of picking and peeling before she extricated the wand from the melted tape, and she nodded knowingly at the adhesive-streaked wood she'd revealed. "Yep. Thought so."

"Can it be fixed?" I asked.

"No, and you wouldn't want to. Let me guess, you were told your wand was rowan and dragonscale, right?"

"Yes…"

"Come here, have a look at this," she offered, and handed me her magnifying visor. I slipped the headset into position, and Amy pressed an unfinished piece of wood into my hand. "That's rowan. Look at the grain, see how it runs? That's a good piece right there, and it'll make a solid wand. Now, let's compare yours." Before I could protest, she dumped out my wand's contents and gave me half the shaft to examine. "Look at that beside the rowan. What do you notice?"

I've never been a botanist, but I couldn't miss the dark rings within my wand. "They're different."

"Uh-huh. What you've been trying to cast through is a type of cured wood taken from a rare species of tree that grows only in the Gray Lands. Shadow alder—it's not related to the alders here, but someone thought they looked similar. It doesn't conduct magic at all. In fact, it's an excellent inhibitor."

I stared at the wand stump in my hand. "What about the core?"

"Mostly sawdust, but there's powdered merrow mixed in," said Amy. "Just strong enough to give you a little charge, even with the wand body, but not enough to make the wand useful." She looked up at me and made a face. "I really hope you're not in the market for a new merrow wand. Working with that stuff gives me the willies."

Stunned, I dropped the wand and returned the visor to Amy. "But…but my grandparents bought that for me…"

Amy and Toula exchanged a look. "How connected?" asked the girl.

"The Glastonbury Parsons."

"*Ugh*. Figures." Catching my confusion, Amy explained, "There are a few crafters who will make certain special wands if the price is right. Shadow alder is highly illegal, so someone paid dearly for that wand. Maybe someone who didn't want a witch hanging around, embarrassing the rest of the family."

Seeing my confusion, Toula intervened. "It's a nasty practice, but it's a known…*solution*, if you will, for well-placed old-blooded families. Let me guess, your dad was a witch?" I nodded, and she shrugged. "A witch out of the old Parsons line had to be an embarrassment. Was your mom a witch, too?"

"Completely mundane."

"Even better. The Parsons' dirty little secret married a mundane and had a child of his own. You think they wanted you hanging around, reminding everyone that witches happen even to the best families? A wand like the one they gave you must have seemed generous. I mean, nine times out of ten, if you cross a witch and a mundane, their kids aren't going to be *stronger*. Of course your dad would have been thrilled to get an expensive wand like that to help you along. Why would he have suspected sabotage from his own parents?"

My guts twisted as I looked at the remnants of my beloved gift. *You must be careful with that*, Dad had warned me. *It's extremely valuable. I know they don't come to see us, but your grandparents love you very much. That's the best wand in all the world for you.*

"Giving you that wand ensured that you'd never be able to do much in the way of magic, so you'd never come around Glastonbury," said Toula as I fought down my nausea. "You'd probably marry mundane, too, and in time, your whole branch of the family would forget that magic ever existed. End of problem." She picked up the broken stump of my wand and grimaced. "This stuff isn't just an inhibitor while you're casting—it can have residual effects. Short-term contact is harmless, but a child doing daily practice, trying desperately to learn to use a wand...well, once you started, your talent in general would have seemed to fade. Honestly," she added, dropping it to the table with a flicker of distaste, "breaking that wand may have been the best thing you ever did. The tape probably lessened its effect on you. Insulation, as it were."

I sat on the edge of Amy's table and stared into space. "But they didn't *know* I would be weak," I protested. "I could have been like Dad..."

"Or you could have been as you are," she replied. "Imagine your extended family's joy at seeing you come for lessons in Glastonbury, no better than a new-blooded wizard. Your father diluted the bloodline, and there you'd be, a living reminder of the Parsons' black sheep. You couldn't expect them to sit back and let that happen, right?"

As I tried to process everything Toula was telling me, she sat beside me and clasped my hands. "They told me my wand was a dragonscale, too. It was nothing but pine and filler because I don't *need* one. You may not—plenty of magi have them only on principle. But at least my handlers had enough sense not to give me a wand like yours. Like Amy said, shadow alder is illegal—imagine the fuss if someone caught the Council dealing with it," she muttered. "Giving a kid your sort of wand is reprehensible, but that's all past now. Let's get you something you can use, and I'll give you the crash course in what you should have been taught."

By then, Amy had risen and was on her way to a shelf half-stocked with skinny blue wand boxes. "I'm starting with the demo models," she explained as she pulled an extra-wide case off the bottom. "See what feels good, and we'll go from there."

She unlatched the case on the workbench and popped the top, showing me the standard six wands set into depressions in the black velvet. "Like I said, I'd rather not work with merrow, and I don't have it in stock," she explained, pointing to the fourth, "but the others are all available. There's not much call for wizard wands around here, anyway. Take your time, there's no rush."

Hesitantly, I pulled the one on the far left free—the rowan wand I'd believed I'd always had. A sharp tingle raced up my arm as I gripped the wand, and a brilliant white flash exploded from the tip. "*Way* too much wand," said Amy, prying it from me before I could set her workshop on fire. "You're overloading it without even casting." She peered at my face, then patted my shoulder. "It's okay, Miss Hannah, just relax. They're not gonna bite you."

Torn and uncertain, I looked over the other options— the oak and unicorn, or maybe the maple and amber—and my hand stretched over the case and moved back and forth as I tried to decide what to do. Suddenly, I smelled the familiar scent of sweat, and then Seamus had one arm around my shoulders and was checking out the wands beside me. "It's okay," he whispered, bending to my ear. "You can do this, Badge."

I glanced at his grime-streaked face, and he smiled in reassurance. "If there's anyone in this world that I'd trust with a pointy stick of doom, it's you," he murmured.

"I just…I don't know," I mumbled as my eyes fell back to the spread. "I've always been useless at this, and—"

"You're not useless. You've never *been* useless. And I promise you this: if your bloody stupid grandparents are still around and I ever meet them, I'll give them the beating of their lives for doing this to you."

He wasn't kidding—I knew his voice as well as I knew my own. "I like to think I can handle a couple of pensioners."

"Then at least let me get a few good punches in. I haven't properly bloodied a nose in a few years." Seamus began to grin in earnest. "We could tag-team this—you take the one with the cane, I'll tackle the one in the wheelchair, and we'll make quick work of it."

"You're *horrid*, Malone," I replied, but I couldn't help smiling back at him.

"No, they are. So pick a damn stick already. Show them what you're made of."

Throwing caution to the wind, I reached for the wand on the far right, a pine shaft set with a tiny piece of rose quartz in the tip. There was no shock that time, but the wand felt inert, like just another dowel. "I think this one might be too weak," I said to Amy. "Not feeling anything."

"Give it a try," she coaxed, stepping clear of my blast radius. "Something non-destructive, if you don't mind."

Fearing I was about to make a fool of myself, I stretched out the wand, tried to ignore the eyes that followed me, and whispered, "Shield."

Like water through a pipe, the translucent bubble of magic shot from the wand and expanded in front of me, growing until it stretched at least a meter in all directions. As I gaped in shock, Amy moved back into range and waggled her eyebrows. "Too weak, huh? I don't know, that one looks pretty good to me."

Toula examined my shield, squinting at my admittedly sloppy handiwork. "Good effort, but the execution needs help," she declared. "It's solid, but it could be better if you had a little more control over the spell. That comes with practice," she added before I could deflate too far. "If you're fae and enchanting, you can do whatever the hell you want ninety percent of the time"—Val nodded in agreement—"but spellcraft calls for greater finesse. We'll work on it. And believe me, my teaching methods involve a lot less of...*that*," she said, waving one hand at Seamus's filthy clothes. "There's no need to beat this into you."

Amy gave Seamus a critical glance and made a face. "Yeah, I don't want to know. But as for wands...I've got an idea, if you're willing to try it," she told me. I nodded, and she climbed a stepladder to pull a wand box from a high shelf. "My own design," she said sheepishly. "Same principle as the standard pine, but it might give you a little boost while you're learning."

The wand was stained nut-brown, and when I lifted it from its box, it felt pleasantly warm in my hand, like brick on a sunny spring afternoon. "Giant sequoia," said Amy. "Old-growth and cured. The core's a composite, but I think it'll work for you."

I gave the wand a test flick for weight and balance, then held it out and summoned a shield again. The spell was more quickly accomplished that time, the shield larger and thicker, and Toula nodded her approval. "I think we have a winner," she said. "What's the core?"

"Striations of ground hematite, pyrite, magnetite, and a layer of heliotrope. Iron compounds are surprisingly helpful for spellcraft—and I store my supplies carefully," she added for the benefit of the suddenly uneasy men. "Just don't break open that wand."

"I'm sure they'll be careful. Badger? Satisfied?"

I stared at the shield in front of me for a long moment, then broke the spell and nodded to Amy. "Kid, you're brilliant."

"Shoot, no, just lucky. Glad it works," she said, handing me the empty box after I slid the new wand into my waistband. "And enjoy. It's not every day I craft for a coordinator."

The others filed out of the workshop, but I lingered for a moment on the vestibule threshold and watched Amy tidy up. "I'm sorry about your parents," I said as she carried her sample crate back to the shelves.

She paused and nodded at me. "Thanks. Did your family make it?"

"No."

Amy slid the box into its hole and straightened. "That was my mom's tester kit. She said I'd be ready to craft when I could make my own standard set, but...you know..."

"Desperate times." I tapped the wand box under my arm and smiled. "She'd be proud of you, Amy. You're doing the people here a great service."

"At least I'm not the only crafter around. There's two a couple of blocks over. They're not as good as Mama was, but..." After a brief hesitation, she seemed to screw up her courage and hurried across the workshop toward me. "I heard what you said last night. About going back, I mean."

"Amy—"

"Let me go with you," she said, speeding over my protestation. "I want to help."

"That's brave of you, but absolutely not."

"But what if your wand breaks? What if you need a new one? You need someone like me," she insisted, crossing her arms. "I'm good on trips, and I'm not picky, and I've got my conditional license—I just can't drive between midnight and six. Please let me come. *Please*."

"You're already doing your bit," I told her once she came up for air. "Right here, where you're safe."

"I can shoot straight. Daddy used to take me hunting. I'm pretty good with a shotgun, and I'm better than some with a compound bow. I could help you," she insisted, and I noted the first sheen of threatening tears. "Really, I wouldn't get in the way."

I put my box on the table to clasp her shoulders. "I appreciate the offer more than you know," I said slowly, "but you're young, and you've got a lot left to live for. This isn't your responsibility, and I can't in good conscience take you back into danger. Your parents would be horrified—"

"If they weren't dead." Her wet eyes bored into mine as she stared up at me. "I *found* them." That took me aback, and Amy pressed her advantage. "I was home from school for the holiday. Easter Monday, Catholic school, you know? I slept in and went for a run when I got up, and when I came back, they were dead. Blast holes in their chests. Guess the wizard who came for them forgot about me. So let me go with you, Miss Hannah. I want to help you beat them."

Her sunny demeanor had masked a current of pain and anger that I was beginning to fathom, and I knew too well what she was feeling. "I won't be beating anyone. Hiding, for the most part. Trying to find missing Fringers and get them to safety. If you thought I was planning to take on the Arcanum by myself, then I'm sorry to disappoint—"

"Anything. I'll do anything if it'll ruin those...those b-words' day."

"B-words?" I echoed.

"You know, *bastards*," she mumbled. "Sorry. Mama always said it's not ladylike to cuss, but sometimes..."

I considered the slip of a girl for a moment longer, watching her blush over her profanity, and felt my resolve crumble. "If you come with me," I murmured, "you're going to be hearing a lot worse than that."

Her face lit up. "I can come? You mean it?"

"Desperate times." Releasing her, I picked up my wand box again and stepped back as she squealed in excitement. "Pack only what you can carry. I'm not leaving tonight, but...let's say two days. Will that give you enough time?"

Amy's face-splitting grin was only slightly worrisome. "Just let me get my ammo and a toothbrush, and I'll be good to go."

"So," said Toula as she closed the door to our makeshift practice room, "what sort of training does the Fringe do for wand work?"

I looked around the stone-walled dungeon cell to which Coileán had directed us and tried to control my nerves. The cell seemed to be an empty storage room, larger than my first flat had been, and lit only by a slit of a window near the vaulted ceiling. Toula had *tsk*ed when she saw it and called forth a quartet of glowing orbs to light the room, but that did little to make the space seem any friendlier or to put me at ease. I'd seen what Val's idea of training entailed—against Toula's better judgment, I'd stuck around the barn for an hour in case Seamus needed another reminder of how to tap into his power, but to my relief, whatever we'd triggered that morning seemed to have done the trick. By the time Toula shepherded me to the castle for my own tutoring session, Seamus had finally figured out how to put up a shield.

He couldn't keep it together once Val started shooting at him, mind, but it was a beginning.

"Well," I said, trying to remember my father's lessons, "Dad taught me about proper stance, focus, triggering words…that's about it, I suppose."

Her eyebrows rose. "Crisis focus techniques? Tandem casting? Spell repair?"

"I figured a bit of that last one out on my own—"

She closed her eyes and groaned. "Oh, boy, we're starting with the basics. It's not your fault," she quickly added, "you were trained by a witch, and we *know* what sort of education the Arcanum gives them. But until you get some techniques solidified, you won't be able to fully use what you've got."

"I *did* manage to shield twice empty-handed," I mumbled. "That's something, isn't it?"

"Mostly instinct. It's my job to help you learn to do that on command." She waved a couple of chairs into existence and sat. "Be honest with me, Badger: how long do you plan to stay here?"

I took the other chair and tucked my wand into my waistband. "Couple of days. What can we do between now and then?"

Toula rolled her eyes to the ceiling and considered my answer. "Not a ton, to be honest, but I think I can put together a short course. Hope you weren't planning on getting much sleep."

Late that night, tired and sore from the physical strain of hours of holding dynamic spells together, I sent Seamus a text message, hoped for the best, and grabbed a quiet two-top in the settlement's little Italian restaurant. As the chef's chatty husband brought garlic bread, the over-the-door bell jangled, and Seamus limped in, clean but splotched with purpling bruises. A network of enchantment surrounded him like a second skin, healing him while he rested.

I waved him over and watched while he eased himself into the booth. "You look like shit, Seamie."

"Better than I feel." He glanced up as our lone waiter circled by and pulled out a notepad. "What do you have in the way of spirits?"

The man took one good look at Seamus and put the pad away. "Just tell me how drunk you want to be by the end of dinner."

"Numb, if you can swing it."

He winked and slipped off to the long bar, where a few diners were laughing over mussels and chianti. A moment later, he pulled an unmarked bottle from beneath the counter, and I met Seamus's weary eyes. "Sure about this?"

"He said the enchantment would heal and numb. It may be healing, but it still hurts like the dickens."

"What hurts?"

"*Everything.* Cheers," he sighed as the waiter returned with a lowball glass half-full of clear liquid. He held it to the light, then gave it a test sniff, which ended in a coughing fit. "How about giving me a hint," he wheezed, wiping tears away, "before I destroy my liver?"

The waiter grinned and crouched beside our booth. "Shine," he whispered. "Family recipe. It'll either cure what ails you or make it so you don't care. Better let your lady friend do the driving tonight," he added, and stood again. "So, who's in the mood for pasta?"

We put in our order, and Seamus, with a worried grimace, knocked back half the glass in a quick gulp. When he slammed it onto the table, he gasped and reddened, and I handed him my napkin as his eyes streamed. "Okay," he muttered when he could finally speak again, "he wasn't messing around. In case I do get completely pissed, do you remember where we're sleeping?"

"I've got Toula programmed," I replied, holding up my mobile, and handed him my water. "Don't make yourself sick, love."

"Do my best." He took a swig of water, then passed back my drink. "How brutal is your boot camp? You've seen mine."

"I've had better days, but I'm intact. Ehm...I shouldn't ask, should I?"

He shook his head and sipped the moonshine.

"I'm so sorry. I thought this was the best thing for you, and—"

"It is, don't apologize. Val's teaching me how to control myself, so, you know, minimal risk of spontaneous combustion going forward. That's good." He rotated one shoulder and winced. "His methods are killer, but I'm learning. Oh, and if you're interested, I've been invited back to the barn tonight so that some of his former victims can ply me with alcohol. Medicinal purposes, of course."

"Of course." I smirked and raised my glass. "To surviving."

"Hear, hear." He clinked and sipped again, grimacing as the liquid went down. "That really is vile, but I think it might be working. Still..." Pushing the glass away, he folded his arms on the table and regarded me over the laden breadbasket. "We need to talk."

"Yeah," I muttered. "Seamie, I'm sorry, I should have said something sooner—"

But he waved my apology aside even as I tried to get it out. "Forget that. What's this I hear about you going back two days from now?"

I shrugged. "Time's being wasted. The sooner I'm home, the sooner I can get back to hunting people down."

"Badger—"

"Stop," I interrupted, and took his hand across the table. "You're not changing my mind on this. And now that I have everyone's contact information, I should be able to phone someone with access to a gate in case of emergency."

"You're not going alone."

"You're right, I'm not. Amy Levey's going with me."

He sputtered incredulously. "The *crafter*? She's all of what, ten?"

"Sixteen. We'll be fine. She's got a gun, I've got a wand—"

"Forget it. If you're taking a *teenager* with you, then you're damn well taking me."

I squeezed his hand, praying for patience. "Seamie...you're exactly where you need to be right now. Work with Val, figure yourself out. I'll be fine."

"Like hell you will!"

The look I gave him was usually sufficient to make my underlings stand down, but it wasn't having the desired effect that evening. "You know, I've made it perfectly well on my own for the last, oh, twenty-two years. I think I can handle this without your supervision."

"What supervision? Damn it, Badger..." Flushing, he looked away until his breathing slowed and his jaw stopped clenching. "Look," he muttered, "I know bugger all about the Fringe, yeah? This is your case. Tell me what to do, and I'll do it. But if you're going back to face the murder wizards again, you're not going without me. No lone rangers, remember?"

"Amy—"

"Doesn't fucking count. Nice kid, but I'm not trusting her with your life."

"And since when do you get a say in that?" I snapped, dropping his hand. "You're right, it's my case. Get out of the way and let me do my job."

Seamus started to respond, then shut his mouth and stared at the bar in silence, fuming. Just as I thought he was about to walk away from the table, he looked back at me and murmured, "I'm sorry, okay? I'm sorry about Belfast. I'm sorry you found out like you did. It was a shite move, and I..." He paused, searching for the words. "I just wanted you to be okay. Forget about me—I wanted you to be all right. But I shouldn't have gone about it like I did."

He reached for my hand that time, and I didn't pull away.

"Be angry with me if you like. If you never forgive me, I'll deal with it. But Badger, please, don't do this alone. They want you dead, love. Take me with you. Even if it's only to watch the door at night, take me with you."

As I saw his fear, I realized why Toula's blue eyes had seemed so oddly familiar.

"You understand," I said softly, "that should you come along, you'd have to share space with a sixteen-year-old girl."

He squeezed my hand and smiled, then released me as our dinner arrived.

"Pretty sure I could inhale this," he said once the waiter had dropped an oversized plate of spaghetti in front of him. "You're not marking off for manners, I hope?"

"At least try to be tidy," I replied, attacking my ravioli.

Seamus unrolled his napkin, then groaned at the glint of atmospheric candlelight on the stainless-steel cutlery inside. "Damn it. My kit's back in the car."

I put down my knife, pulled my wand from behind my back, and whispered at the table. An instant later, the active magic solidified into the forms in my mind, and I grinned as Seamus picked up the plastic fork. "Yeah?"

"I *knew* there was a reason I liked you," he said, then carefully nudged the offending silverware away and tucked in.

CHAPTER 9

Dawn came far too quickly for my taste, though Seamus had the worse time of it. I'd only had a couple of drinks at the commiseration party, but we'd been out at the barn until the wee hours, and I'd had to help him stagger to bed when the walls wouldn't stop spinning. Joey and Aiden had been generous hosts—"We know your pain," Joey had explained as he'd passed the beers for a fifth time—and by the end of the night, at least half of Coileán's guards had stopped by to swap horror stories.

"Don't misunderstand me, Val's great," said Mina, his second in command, as she nursed a double of bourbon. "Couldn't ask for a better captain. But until he thinks you're up to standard, working with him is *hell.*"

Apparently, our late-night carousing was no secret, as the first thing Val had done on finding Seamus hunched over the breakfast table with a cup of black coffee was fix his hangover. "A useful trick," he'd explained, smirking as Seamus blinked in surprise at finding his headache gone. "Coileán has more experience with it, but it's not difficult to master. You can learn later," he'd added, hustling Seamus out of the dining room and on to another day of being thrown into unforgiving objects.

But unlike her brother, Toula appeared to be in no hurry to resume our lessons. A few minutes after I'd been abandoned with my eggs and potatoes, she rang to say we'd reconvene after lunch. "Meeting's come up," she explained. "We think we might have a way of getting you back over without immediately surrendering you to the

Arcanum, but there are a few kinks to work out." She offered no further details, and so, alone and restless, I asked one of Eleanor's aides for a lift back to the Fringe village.

I made a beeline for Vivi's command post, thinking I could at least get a copy of her data before I left the realm. After all, if I was going to find the missing, I decided it would be helpful to have a list of their names and last locations. When I reached the top of the stairs, however, I found Aiden alone in the room, crouching behind the humming servers in a flannel work shirt, jeans, and a knit cap. "Hi," he said, raising a gloved hand. "Vivi's gone to a committee meeting, but come in. Hungover?"

"No, I'm fine." I closed the door and waited until he slid out and began stripping off his protective gear. "You know, you could probably find someone to actually connect the fiddly bits for you."

"See, that's the problem—you don't know which 'fiddly bits' go where," he replied, plopping into a wooden swivel chair. "Vivi and I built this system together, so no one knows it like we do."

"Why not wait for her, then?"

"Meh." He slapped the gloves onto the counter and shrugged. "If I waited on Vivi every time this baby had a hiccup, I'd never get anything done. Besides, she can't patch the enchantment that's keeping the computers from self-destructing."

I folded my arms, puzzled. "There's not that much active magic here—"

"Too much to keep the servers happy, especially whenever Robbie decides to throw up a new building or six. Phones seem to last, and small appliances are okay, but get something large and sensitive assembled around here, and it'll do everything it can to blow itself up." He turned to face a monitor, which was filled with unreadable lines of text that I vaguely recognized as code. "So I've got a buffer enchantment going around the perimeter of the room, but it degrades. Not much I can do but patch it. Help you with something?"

"Actually, yes. Have you got a copy of the Fringe dataset? At least for the missing Fringers, I mean."

"Oh, sure. Pull up," he offered, patting the chair beside him, and I took a seat while he slipped a glove back on. Reaching beneath the counter, he extracted a plastic box of odds and ends, then lifted the lid and dug around he found a flash drive among the detritus. "Bingo," he said, inspecting it in the light. "Let me clean this little guy off, and I'll transfer the files for you." Leaning over to load the drive, he asked, "Do you have a computer handy?"

"I...well, I *had* one," I replied, suddenly recalling that my laptop was back on Skye. "Left it behind with the rest of my things."

"No worries, I can build you something in the next day. Okay with a PC?"

"That would be fantastic, actually."

"Sweet. Here we go...let me reformat this..."

He was interrupted by the sound of knocking, and I spun around in my chair as the door opened, revealing Amy on the threshold. "Morning, Miss Hannah," she said, beaming. "I didn't know you'd be around today! Is Miss Vivi—"

"At a meeting, I'm afraid," I replied, and cut my eyes to my suddenly frozen companion, who stared at Amy in panicked silence. "Just Aiden and me right now. Do you need her?"

"Nah, I was going to see if she had any last-minute wand requests. And speaking of wands..."

I smiled to dispel the worry in her eyes. "It's perfect, love."

"Good," she sighed, visibly relieved. "Well, I don't want to bother y'all. See you later, Miss Hannah." She glanced askance at the slack-jawed boy. "Uh...bye, Aiden."

The door was already closing behind her when Aiden blurted, "Hair!"

Amy turned back, perplexed. "Hair?"

"It's pretty."

"Oh, uh...thanks." She smiled, flipped it over her shoulder, and headed down the stairs.

When the door closed, I stood and patted his shoulder. "I'd better have a word with her. One moment," I said, and followed Amy into the sunshine.

Catching up to her was no real chore—Amy was young, but her legs were proportionally short, and she seemed to be in no hurry. "Any second thoughts?" I asked as I jogged beside her.

She looked up at me and grinned. "Nope. You?"

"No. Seamus is coming, too."

Her brows briefly lowered in thought, then relaxed as she connected the name with a face. "Your friend from yesterday, yeah? The other Brit?"

"Exactly. We're both detectives, so I hope it's not going to drive you bananas if we talk shop."

"Shoot, no, that's great. Most of my parents' DVR backlog was *Law & Order*, so I know the lingo," she added, flashing her thumb. "Hey, do you think there's any chance of getting into a shootout?"

"Let's hope not," I replied, slightly unnerved by her excitement. "I'll, ehm, tell Vivi you stopped by."

Amy walked on, and I thought again over the many ways my new mission could go horribly wrong as I climbed to the computer room. But when I neared the top, I heard agitated muttering, and so I paused with my ear to the door before letting myself in.

"Hi," said a voice I recognized as Aiden's, albeit with forced confidence. "Great to see you again. That's a fantastic color on you. Hey, I'm going to the bakery—want to come with?"

Easing the door open, I found him slumped at his monitor, talking to the wall. "She's not going to bite you, you know," I said, chuckling as he jumped in embarrassed surprise. "Amy's pretty harmless."

Aiden covered his face and groaned. "Please, *please* don't tell anyone you saw that."

"What, your monologue or your attempt at sweet talk?"

He put his head on the counter, but with his hair pulled into a ponytail, I could see the scarlet blotch racing up his neck. "Cheer up, I won't tell a soul," I said, and pulled my mobile out. "Besides, you're going to have another chance."

He looked up in alarm, but Amy's phone was already ringing. "Hello, Hannah again," I told her as Aiden frantically shook his head. "I was wondering if you'd had breakfast."

Through a combination of coaxing and threats, I made Aiden leave the safety of the command center and join us at a nearby café. "Blueberry pancakes, definitely," said Amy as the menus passed around. "Get extra syrup, it's life changing."

"I've eaten, so I'll take your word for it," I replied, and nudged Aiden's foot under the table. "How about you, any thoughts?"

He hid behind his menu and stared intently at the omelet offerings. "Uh…"

"Seriously, pancakes." Amy reached across the table and pulled his menu down, then grinned at Aiden's awkwardness. "Trust me, dude. Hey, you're working with Miss Vivi on the network rebuild, right?"

He managed to nod, though he looked like he wanted to bolt from the table and be sick.

"Awesome. She said I could help with the beta testing, but I didn't know how far along in the project y'all had gotten."

"Still, um, uh, building."

"Aww, too bad." Amy leaned back against the vinyl booth and shrugged. "I offered to help with the coding, but she said y'all had it covered."

At that, I detected the tiniest shift in Aiden's expression, which to then had most closely resembled a deer in the middle of the motorway. "You code?"

"Proficient in Python, passable in C++ and Java, and I've played with a couple iterations of Perl, but I wouldn't trust myself yet without a manual. Good to have goals," she replied, then laughed at his surprise. "What, you thought I hid in a room all day with my wands? I have to get out occasionally—that varnish has *got* to kill brain cells."

Slowly, hesitantly, as if afraid he might trigger her theretofore unseen wrath, Aiden said, "I've been working on a little problem this morning. Think I have a solution, but it could be more elegant. Would you, uh…I mean, if you're not busy…"

Her face lit up. "Sure! But pancakes first. I don't troubleshoot well when I'm hangry."

As she turned to wave at our waitress, I sneaked a peek at Aiden, whose face reflected an odd mixture of shock, joy, and nausea. "Suave," I murmured, and flipped my mug over for tea.

With the teenagers fed, I retreated to a quiet corner of the command room and began reading the salvaged notes on the missing. Across the room, Amy and Aiden stood by a whiteboard, markers in hand, debating the solution to a problem I couldn't begin to follow and correcting each other's scribbles. Their bickering was genial, at least, and by the time Vivi returned, Amy had squeezed into the space beside Aiden at his preferred monitor and was pointing out other ways to improve his work.

Once I'd slipped off to grab lunch, Vivi shot me a text message: *OMG. He's in full puppy mode. Adorbs.*

Much as I wanted to stop by and check on their progress, I had an appointment to keep with Toula, who brought me back to the dungeon and made me practice holding shields until my wand arm felt like jelly. During a water break, she casually said, "So, I had a word with Vivi before I picked you up. How do you think Aid's going to take the news that his crush is heading out with you? Or is this some nefarious plot to convince Amy to stick around as the Fringe's newest code monkey?"

I smirked and toweled off my face. "I'm not saying it is or it isn't. I just thought she could do with options in her life."

"Sneaky. I like it."

"Opportunistic. She's of an age, and he's cute enough. Older man, ponytail…aside from the crippling anxiety, what's not to like?"

Toula chuckled. "Yeah, I've never seen him quite so shy, and that's saying something. Kid's got it bad. I mean, you'd think that having ruled Faerie, he could talk to girls, but then again, he's not exactly experienced in the field. Colin is going to give him *such* a hard time when he finds out about this," she said, grinning. "Might be kinder if Amy went with you, but then I'm sure I'd find Aid moping around, listening to emo and locking himself in Vivi's office all night." She conjured up a fireball and tossed it from hand to hand in contemplation until it fizzled out. "Then again, having her here could do him good. He's been so worried about his sister—this could be a good time for a distraction. Okay, enough chit-chat, take your position."

As we geared up for another round, I stalled for time. "Where are you dropping us, anyway?"

"Virginia. Shield," she replied, and shot a bolt my way that almost knocked me off my feet. I blocked and slid to the right, looking for an opening as Toula calmly watched me scramble. "You're going to be a foursome, as it turns out. Guy named Stuart Purcell is joining you."

"Fringer?" I panted, deflecting another blast.

"Not exactly." She paused to send a rain of fireballs my way, and I dropped to roll out the flames after one grazed my shoulder. "He considers himself a wizard because he's been *certified* by something called the Mid-Atlantic Circle. Lots of chanting and incense, no actual talent. You okay, champ?"

I dusted the charred bits off my sleeve and stood. "Let's hope that doesn't blister. So is he or isn't he a wizard?"

"Hell, no, but I bet he does a mean palm reading. Come here, let me patch that."

I waited while Toula worked on my raw skin. Her healing construction was neater than Val's, a hybridized product leaning heavily toward spellcraft. "What am I to do with this Stuart, then?"

"Not much. He's going to make the introductions for you." Seeing my bemusement, she explained, "You have no support network in place. The wizard wannabes can't do jack shit in the way of magic, but if they think you're working for the 'Light' or whatever, they'll probably be willing to lend a hand. Couldn't hurt to have a bed, eh?"

"Or funding," I muttered.

"We've got you covered on that front. I'm sure you'll work out how to produce your own money in time, but we'll load you up with cash before you leave. Val and I probably owe Seamus a few years of birthday money," she added with a smile. "Though something tells me he isn't going to be eager to spend any time with us after all the fun he's having. Okay, en garde."

I ran back to position and cast a shield just before Toula could immolate me. "Is this how you learned, then? This is the Arcanum's preferred teaching method, trial and error?"

"Of course not. This is the quick and dirty crunch course. I'd be happy to sit down and do several months' worth of casting theory with you, but since you're leaving tomorrow, I figured you'd prefer practical instruction." She flicked a finger, and several slabs rose from the floor, floating boulders that I'd have to deflect or destroy. "Your previous limitations are actually helping you now—you're a much more technical caster than you realize. I had to do something similar when I was bound, and it's helped in the long run. So yeah, I'm pleased with your progress."

The slabs flew at my face, and I dropped the shield to call forth a shock wave that shattered them into gravel.

"Good choice," said Toula as I massaged my tingling wrist. "See, you know what to do, and you finally have the power to do it. Your biggest hurdle right now is convincing yourself that you can cast...well, and a little technique," she added as her latest fireball narrowly missed my hip. "But I think you'll figure a lot of this out as you go along. There's no teacher like experience, right?"

I grunted and reinforced my shield. "And Seamus?"

Toula shrugged. "Val says he's improving, but he's still a head case. Congrats, you've got a new project."

Perhaps feeling a tiny bit bad that Seamus and I were being pummeled on his turf, Coileán invited us to dinner that night, and Toula and Val tagged along. I couldn't help but notice that Seamus kept a healthy buffer zone between himself and his uncle, though Val seemed nothing if not chipper.

Shortly before the soup, Aiden joined us at the table and stared morosely into his wine glass as it filled. "Problem?" Coileán asked, leaning around a flower arrangement to better examine the boy.

Aiden drank up, then sighed. "Nothing."

"He's upset because his crush is leaving with those two," said Toula, forking her fingers at Seamus and me.

Aiden glared daggers down the table, but Coileán covered his mouth and coughed to hide his mirth. "Crush?" he asked Toula. "What crush is this?"

"Little Amy Levey," she replied, ignoring Aiden as he purpled. "You know, sixteen, blonde, maybe five foot two if she stretches, kind of elfin..."

"The crafter, right?" He cut his eyes to his mortified brother and grinned. "Not bad. Ran her off, did you?"

Reluctantly, he mumbled, "They killed her parents, and she's going to help Badger. What was I supposed to say?"

"That 'become Batman' isn't a particularly wise career path, especially for a witch-blood? Other than that, you're out of luck." He flinched, then looked at the ceiling and grimaced. "She's being vocal again," he muttered, rubbing his temples. "Seamus, I'm sure you're perfectly fine as cops go, but I'm not going to be sorry to see your back, kid."

"But he *could* stay, yes?"

The table turned to Val, who had fixed his eyes on the king. "You said he could stay, my lord," he continued, his voice soft but intense. "He needs more training than I can provide in such a short time…"

The two held each other's gaze, and Coileán nodded. "Yes, of course, whatever he wishes, but since he is, apparently, determined to go, I won't miss these little headaches."

Val sat back, mollified, and Seamus squeezed my hand under the table. "He's right," I whispered, leaning close to Seamus when the others had returned to poking Aiden's soft spot. "You could stay, keep working. Join me in a month or so."

But Seamus shook his head. "If I stay here another month, there'll be nothing left of me. Just one big enchantment, holding all the loose pieces together." Absently, he ran his free hand over his opposite elbow, which was a mass of green and violet bruises. "He may mean well, but I've discovered too many breakable parts in the last three days. Honestly, at this point, I think I'm safer with the Arcanum."

Since the local time was approximately synchronized with the American east coast, we decided to leave after lunch and give everyone with actual belongings a chance to pack.

Val spirited Seamus off that morning for one last session, and Toula stopped by with a backpack full of twenty-dollar bills and a pair of duffel bags stuffed with clothing and camping gear. "I think I got the sizing right," she said as I thanked her for the offerings. "If not, well, it'll be good practice for you. And here, let me show you how to get the healing matrices off."

Shortly before lunch, Aiden rapped on my door and handed me a custom-built laptop in a reinforced bag. "The Fringe files are preloaded, and I've put in a link to the old network, just in case you get desperate," he explained. "We check it, you know." He scuffed one toe against the rug. "Um...if Amy wants to come back, you'll help her, right?"

"Of course," I replied, and patted his arm. "I'm not going to put her on the front lines, love."

Aiden hesitated, then pulled what appeared to be a pink iPhone clone from his back pocket and thrust it toward me. "She said it's her favorite color," he mumbled in a rush, "and if she gets in trouble or anything, I've programmed numbers—"

"I'm sure she'll like it," I soothed, and gently shooed him on his way.

Shortly before lunchtime, I hauled our new gear down to the main dining room, where I found a painfully angular man waiting beside a meowing stack of pet carriers. Noticing my arrival, he pushed his limp brown hair from his eyes and strode toward me, long hand outstretched. "Stuart Purcell," he said in an annoyingly nasal voice that, unfortunately, coordinated with the rest of him. "Badger, I presume?"

To my pleasant surprise, his hand wasn't damp when I shook it. "I also answer to Hannah Parsons," I replied with a professionally polite smile. "You're the, ehm, wizard?"

His dark, slightly frog-like eyes narrowed. "I see they've told you about me."

"Just the basics. So...what's this Mid-Atlantic Circle,

then?"

He stepped over to the crate stack for a moment in an unsuccessful attempt to calm the cats. "The MAC's the preeminent organization for practicing wizards between the Carolinas and southern New England," he explained as he poked a finger through the top crate's door. "Training, certification, support, products, you know the drill."

"I suppose…"

"Laugh it up all you want, but it's a respectable professional association." He straightened and patted the crate, and the cat protested more vociferously. "I'm sworn to the Light, and my path lies back there. But since I'm going anyway, I told Colin that I could introduce you to some of our higher-ups. People who know people. Might get you started." Stuart gave me a once-over, then asked, "Witch?"

"Technically, wizard." I pulled my wand out of the back of my waistband and shrugged. "Got the shiny new stick and everything."

I let him take it from me and give it an experimental flick, and he passed it back with a look of mild distaste. "Should be heavier. And it's pretty plain, isn't it?"

"Functionality trumps design, and since the crafter who made it is joining us momentarily, I'll thank you not to criticize—"

That was as far as I got before the door opened and Amy marched in, nearly unrecognizable in camouflage and face paint. The girl looked as if she'd prepared for a long stint in a hostile jungle—military-surplus convertible duffel buckled in place, hair hidden under a forest-green ski cap, and sheathed hunting knife strapped to her right thigh. Around her waist were a crossed pair of nylon belts bearing loaded holsters. She carried a case slung over each shoulder, which she dropped with a little *oof* by the scared cats. "Hi, Miss Hannah!" she said, and stuck out her gloved hand toward Stuart. "Amy Levey, nice to meet you."

Stuart shook it, though he looked as though he'd have preferred to be on the other side of the wide room. "Stuart, uh, Purcell. Wizard. Um…you have a lot of bags…"

"Shotgun and rifle, compound bow," she said, nodding to each bag in turn. "Be prepared, that's what my daddy always said."

"And the face paint?" I asked.

Amy shrugged. "Just in case. I didn't know y'all's plans, so I didn't want to be the last one ready for action." She considered our distinctly civilian attire and frowned. "Guess I may have overdone it, huh?"

"Just a touch," I said, and looked behind her as the door opened again.

I could see that the newcomer was male, but I didn't recognize him until he was almost upon us. "Seamie!" I called, hurrying to meet him. "What did you do to your *hair*?"

He grinned and pulled my hand up to feel it. "Goes to the roots. Does it pass inspection?"

I ran my fingers over his silvered temples, noting the gray that spread in a natural progression through the rest of his dark locks. He'd picked up crow's feet since breakfast, and the veining in his hands was more pronounced, the knuckles more prominent than they'd been before. I laughed in surprise and touched his face, feeling the rough sprinkle of salt-and-pepper stubble on his jaw—he'd never needed to shave, and the sudden growth could only mean one thing. "Glamour?"

"It's actually easy to hold together. What do you think, Badge? I mean," he said, suddenly unsure, "I can drop it, if you want, but I thought, you know, fewer questions this way…"

"It's perfect." I stepped back to take in the full effect. Seamus looked his age, early wrinkles and all, and I couldn't stop smiling. "You didn't want anyone to think I'm your sugar mama," I teased. "That's all this is about."

"Saving you from rumors of cougarhood," he countered, and finally noticed the others. "Good God, Amy, we're going to Virginia, not Vietnam. And, ehm…Stuart, yes?"

The would-be wizard inched closer to his distraught cats. "Charmed."

Before we had time for more than pleasantries, the others arrived in a little clump—Coileán and Eleanor, Toula and Val, Vivi and Joey, and, morosely bringing up the rear, Aiden. "Georgie sends her regards," said Joey, breaking from the herd, "but getting her through the door would be a challenge. Do you have everything you nee—" He froze at the sight of Amy, then said, "Think you've got enough gear, hon?"

"I'm *prepared*," she protested. "Since some of us can't just pull weapons out of thin air."

"Fair enough. Need more ammo?"

Amy shifted her backpack and shook her head. "Not for a while. Might take you up on that later." She hesitated, then asked, "You're married to the grand magus, yeah?" He nodded, and she said, "I'm really sorry. We'll try to find her—she's got to be out there somewhere."

Joey cleared his throat. "Helen's tough. You worry about the Fringers first, okay? But, uh…if you hear anything…"

"We'll be in touch," I said, and gestured to the rest of our quartet. "So, lunch and goodbyes?"

"Lunch, definitely," Eleanor replied, "but…" She and Toula exchanged glances. "There's a *tiny* hitch involving Stuart that we need to address before you go."

Stuart's brows lowered in sudden consternation. "I told you, I'm not going to try to fight a wizard using my spells—"

"No, not that. It's come to our attention that…well…"

"You're in the Fringe database," Vivi interrupted. "I did another search last night to be sure. You're not mentioned much, but you're mentioned—and that means you're compromised."

"Compromised?" he echoed.

"We have to assume that anyone listed in our records is now known to the Arcanum," she explained. "By name *and* face. In other words, you can't safely get anywhere near the silo."

His dismay deepened as she spoke. "There's no way they know what I look like! I'll use an alias. Maybe Mulder and Scully here can fix something up."

"Dibs on Scully," Seamus muttered, and I elbowed him in the ribs.

"Actually," said Vivi, "they could know your face. We have no idea what sort of surveillance they may have conducted in recent months. Sending you guys to Rigby is already taking a risk."

Stuart started to protest again, but Toula beat him to the opening. "If you're going, you're going transformed. End of discussion. Think about how you'd like to look while we eat."

She headed for the table, and Stuart hurried after her, jabbing his finger at the rest of our group. "What about them? You can't tell me *they* aren't known!"

"One," she said, rounding on him, "they're a wizard, a faerie, and Rambo Barbie. Two, you're the only one insane enough to volunteer for Montana. Let's not be stupid, Stu," she muttered, sinking into her chair. "We're trying to keep you alive out there. Better bone structure is an added perk."

I couldn't fault Stuart for sulking throughout the meal. The notion of transformation was disturbing to me, and I had the background to at least understand the concept. Glamour is pure illusion—solid, convincing illusion that fools even cameras, but still illusion. Transformation is a more intensive process, a binding into another form, and I knew as well as anyone that Stuart would be unable to break that bind on his own.

Once he resigned himself to his fate, Stuart came up with several suggestions, most of which would have allowed him to pursue a lucrative career in male modelling. "The point," said Toula, finally exasperated with his doodles, "is to make you nondescript. Unmemorable. The kind of guy no one would think twice about."

"And making you too young would be a bad idea," Coileán added, "especially if you plan to stay for any length of time. If you don't age, you end up like Mr. Bad Dye Job here…well, pre-glamour." He gestured at Seamus, who shrugged. "You need a look that lets you fly under the radar. Something bland and durable."

Eleanor, who had been rubbing her chin and squinting at Stuart's mockups, murmured, "What if we skewed older? If we go gray and put some wrinkles in, then he should be able to pass for a decent while."

Though Stuart vehemently disagreed, he didn't get a vote in the matter. By the time we congregated with our bags in Coileán's office for departure, the man was unrecognizable, taller but slightly dumpy, gray and softening with middle age. Toula had mellowed his voice toward a pleasing baritone, but Stuart seemed anything but happy about the situation. "And just how am I supposed to convince anyone in the MAC that it's me?" he whinged, poking at his new face in the mirror.

"Come, now," said Coileán with a smug little grin, looking up from his last-minute work on our mobiles, "you *are* a wizard, are you not? Tell them it's magic." His smile only widened as Stuart glared at him in the glass.

From a technical standpoint, I admired Toula's handiwork. The transformation bind was fine and neat, so close to his skin that it blended into his background aura. Unless I'd known what to look for, I'd have missed it. I also knew there was no way in hell that I could replicate or repair what she'd done, so I hoped for Stuart's sake that he didn't discover latent talent and experiment with freeing himself.

When Coileán finished, he handed our phones back and walked to the wall shelving. "Decide what sort of identity you want," he said as he began moving books around, "and I assume that someone in your party will figure out how to make the necessary fake papers. Yes?" he added, giving me a look.

"Yes," I nodded. "If I can find the appropriate models."

"Shouldn't be too much trouble. He'll need a driver's license, Social Security card, birth certificate…maybe a library card, if you're feeling generous. Think you can put your professional scruples aside for now and do a little light counterfeiting?"

I turned slightly to show off my loaded backpack. "If I had moral qualms, I wouldn't be carrying all of this lovely new money."

"Mm. Glad to see we can work together, Detective."

With the books shifted elsewhere, I spotted a tiny hole in the back of the bookcase, no larger than a fifty pence piece. Coileán stepped back and gestured, and the shelves folded out of the way as the hole widened, forming a gate perhaps a meter in diameter. Something appeared to be blocking the way, and he moved it with an irritated grunt, revealing a sofa and a dusty coffee table in a dimly lit room. Cautiously, he poked his head and torso through the gate and listened, but all was silent on the other side, and he beckoned us forward. "Looks like your apartment's untouched, at least," he told Stuart. "The power's probably been turned off by now. Glad we got the Internet enchantment synched up with the cellular one before you stopped paying the bills, eh?"

"So we're roughing it tonight, I guess," Stuart replied.

"I wouldn't stay past sundown, if you can avoid it. They know my old stomping grounds—they may very well keep an eye on Rigby." He moved aside to let us pass. "Good luck. Stay in touch. Don't be a hero."

Stuart picked up the first two of his cat carriers and trudged toward the gate with as much dignity as he could muster. "And as you know, a wizard doesn't run."

"Wouldn't be so sure of that," I said, grabbing another cat with the rest of my gear. "It's kept me alive thus far. Underrated skill, running."

Even with all her baggage, Amy managed to snag the last of the cats. I glanced back to see Seamus lingering on the threshold, perhaps still—and rationally—wary about traversing holes in the fabric of the universe. Coileán gripped his shoulder, and I heard him murmur, "Forget my headaches. Val's right—you have a place here if you want it."

"Thanks," said Seamus, then met my eyes across the gate. "But my place is elsewhere right now."

"Figured you'd say that. Out with you, then," he replied, and nudged Seamus on his way.

CHAPTER 10

As quickly as it had opened, the gate contracted to its usual peephole, and we dropped our bags into piles on the living room floor. "Better cover our tracks," I said. "Seamie, grab the other end of the entertainment unit."

With the room reassembled and the gate hidden behind the television, I took stock of our situation. Seamus loitered awkwardly by the couch, awaiting instructions, Amy had taken her makeup bag down the hall to find a bathroom where she could remove her face paint, and Stuart had disappeared down a staircase into what appeared to be a shop on the ground floor. "Okay there?" I called from the top landing.

"More or less," he yelled back as he righted a toppled display of hanging wind chimes, which snarled around themselves in an atonal cacophony. "Someone chained the front doors. Doesn't look like there's been any looting."

Descending, I scanned the shop, saw cluttered displays of the sort of "magical" rubbish my father used to sell to dabbling mundanes, and decided to keep my opinion of Stuart's wares to myself. "There's not much point in tidying, yeah? We're meant to get out of town."

He picked up a few fallen staves—in function, nothing but intricately carved walking sticks—and tucked them neatly into their corner. "If I'm calling in the heads of the Mid-Atlantic Circle, then I'm not going to have them walk into a pigsty when they get here. You people may not care," he said with a pointed sniff, "but these are practitioners who take magic seriously. There's a degree of decorum—"

"Oh, come off it," said Seamus, who'd followed our voices downstairs. "And stop wasting time with…whatever this is," he muttered, plucking a bulbous figurine off a table.

Stuart barely spared him a glance. "Fertility totem."

"Of course it is," he muttered, dropping it back into place, and wiped his hand on his trousers. "You heard what Coileán said—we need to leave town."

He rolled his eyes and continued to straighten the mess. "I have standards, people. Once this place is presentable, I'll call my contacts at the MAC and try to convince someone that I'm still myself. *Faeries*," he grunted, making adjustments to a tray of ceremonial knives. "Think they know everything. Think they can just come in and—"

"Mid-Atlantic Circle, was it?" asked Seamus, heading toward the back of the shop—which, I noticed, featured a long counter with a darkened monitor squatting atop it. "Have you got a website?"

"For informational purposes," he replied, suddenly suspicious. "For the uninitiated. But you won't find anything sensitive on there."

Seamus punched the buttons, then scowled as he recalled the building's current lack of electricity and pulled out his mobile. "I don't need anything sensitive. All I need is a contact number, or at least a name. Shouldn't be that difficult to track someone down. And look here," he said with mock surprise, "Coileán tweaked the SIM card! We've got Internet access after all."

"If you're trying to hurry me, it's not working," Stuart snipped.

"No? Well, if I can't find what I need, we've got a teenager at our disposal upstairs. What do you say, Badge, give her five minutes online before she finds it?"

Stuart began to sputter, but by then, I'd had enough. "Look here, you little twat," I said, grabbing him by the anorak, "I'm not going to give the Arcanum a sitting target for long. Either phone your people and get us moving, or I'm splitting with the others—and if I go, you can figure out your papers for yourself."

"You can't—"

"I can, and I will. I've been shot at too many damn times in the last month already." Releasing him, I gave him a bit of space and folded my arms. "I'm not going to die because your shelves are dusty. Get to work."

"I'm in," said Seamus. "Ooh…that background MIDI is a nice touch. And these sparkly graphics are circa what, 2000?"

Though he glowered at us both, Stuart yanked his mobile from his pocket and began to dial.

As a Fringe coordinator, the greatest complaint I ever heard from our members was that our security system was too complex. Our network had existed in one form or another since the early days of the Internet, and the Fringers who'd built it had taken every precaution. One password wasn't enough—gaining access required half a dozen sequential passwords, none of them simple, and one wrong keystroke would send you back to the beginning. Too many failed attempts sent an alert to the closest coordinator, who would make a courtesy call to the hapless Fringer who'd locked himself out. Yes, it was a royal pain to navigate, but until Greg Harrison opened wide the gates, our network had remained unbreached.

But the Fringe's security protocols were nothing compared to the gibberish I heard on Stuart's end of the conversation. Whereas we had passwords and the occasional passphrase, he had to recite complex, nonsensical litanies, some in poorly pronounced Latin, and concluded with what seemed to be a list of every popular wizard in history, starting with Merlin. I was worried that he would continue all the way to Gandalf and Dumbledore when he fell silent, his contact on the other end apparently satisfied.

"Yes, Your Eminence, it's Stuart Purcell," he finally managed. "I've, uh…well, I've been ensorcelled, actually." He sounded embarrassed at the admission. "By someone with skill beyond mine. But that's not why I've disturbed you, Your Eminence—the Darkness has risen against the Light, and we are called to arms…"

"Bloody hell," Seamus muttered to me five minutes later as Stuart's impassioned blathering wore on, "someone needs to put a cork in that one. You're sure he's our best option?"

"No, but I haven't got anything better at the mo." I listened for a few seconds, heard nothing new, and shrugged. "If he's this bad, wonder what his boss is going to be like."

Suddenly, Stuart fell silent for a brief pause, then gushed, "Thank you, Your Eminence, I'm honored by— hello? Hello, are you…damn it," he muttered, putting the phone away, "connection broke." Seeing us still standing nearby, Stuart ran one hand through his artificially thinning hair and looked around the shop, shaking his head. "She's leaving Richmond now. I won't have time to do a real cleaning."

"Who is this *she*?" Seamus asked.

"Lady Francesca, the Potentate. If I only had a few more hours—"

"The what?"

Stuart rolled his eyes and huffed impatiently. "The head of the MAC. Try to keep up, huh?"

"And how am I supposed to keep up when you say nonsense like that? I can't be expected to know the names of all your grand poohbahs, or whatever you call them," Seamus griped. "Honestly, you lot sound like a bunch of nerds playing D&D."

"Says the faerie," Stuart retorted, stomping upstairs.

"Says the *one* of us who's ever been laid," Seamus

countered.

"Shut it, both of you," I interjected before they could come to blows on the staircase, "or so help me, I'll whip out the wand and try a little target practice."

Seamus looked back with a knowing smirk, and I arched an eyebrow, hoping he could read the unspoken in my expression: *Provoking him isn't helpful.*

Sorry, love, he mouthed, and I pushed him onto the landing.

Two hours later, Stuart made our quartet assemble at the foot of the flat's back staircase—the only entrance that hadn't been chained shut in his absence—and wait in the warm afternoon sun until a rusting blue Honda pulled down the alley and into his driveway. As the driver's door opened, he executed a sweeping bow that ended on one knee. "Your Eminence, welcome to my humble home. Thank you for coming."

The middle-aged woman who unfolded herself like a shaky gazelle from behind the wheel was, to be kind, gawky. She'd pulled her mousy hair into a lopsided bun, and a pair of thick, smudged glasses perched at the tip of her freckled nose. Her jeans stopped above her ankles— less a fashion statement than a case of poor tailoring, I imagined—and seemed out of place with her red velvet corset top and coordinating pentacle choker, which also clashed with her sensible black Birkenstocks. All in all, the potentate was one lanyard away from looking like she'd executed a halfhearted attempt at convention cosplay.

She shifted uncertainly, watching the top of his head as Stuart continued his welcoming remarks, then finally blurted, "What the hell *happened* to you?"

Before he could launch into a ten-minute explanation, I leapt in. "Hi, Francesca?" I said, extending my hand as I pushed past Stuart. "Hannah Parsons, pleased to meet you."

Her fingers were delicate, but she had a respectable grip. "Franky Booth. Um...what, exactly—"

"He's been ensorcelled for his own good. Long story short, he may be on the hit list of the most powerful wizards in the world. I know *I* am, and my friends here are likely targets as well," I said, nodding to Amy and Seamus. "He's undercover, as it were. We need your help."

She gawked as Stuart stood and brushed off his knees, giving him a silent once-over, then turned back to me with an unmistakable look on her face—a look I'd seen countless times before from the officers I'd trained when they were presented with an unexpected hitch in the investigation. "That...he's Stuart Purcell? You're *sure* that's Stuart?"

"I saw him transformed with my own eyes. We all witnessed it. I know this may be difficult to believe, but—"

"*How?* I've never made a spell work like that! How is that even possible?"

I took a deep breath, trying to quickly think of the best explanation, then settled on, "I don't mean to be rude, love, but you've been play-acting at magic. That's the real thing," I said, inclining my head toward Stuart, then pulled out my wand. "I'm a real wizard. And I'm asking for your help."

Franky seemed to struggle with the notion of the unornamented stick in my hand. "You're...*you're*..."

"Demonstration," Amy muttered.

My stomach clenched in momentary panic—*You can't do anything,* my gut whispered, *you're just a witch, you have no business with that wand*—but then I caught Seamus's eyes and his barely perceptible nod. With a sigh, I cleared my thoughts and willed myself not to be sick, then pointed the wand at the potentate's car and whispered, "Rise."

Franky wheeled about in alarm at the sound of shifting gravel, then squeaked as the car floated a meter into the air and held its position. As she backed away, I gently lowered the car and examined her ashen face. "Could we go inside and talk, please? Or, ehm…do you need a glass of water?"

"Uh, yeah, water," she mumbled, and passed out in the weeds.

By the time Franky came to, Seamus and I had lugged her into the flat and plopped her on the couch. Her purple-lined eyelids fluttered as she gazed at the ceiling, and then she caught sight of me and gasped.

"Easy, now," I said, showing her my empty hands. "You're all right, you just had a fall. Water?"

Carefully, she sat up and took the glass from Amy. "How did you do that? With…with that—"

"Wand?" I pulled it out again and held it in my palms, letting Franky take a closer look. "If you want a scientific explanation, you're out of luck. I've got a talent for magic, this helps channel it, and the result is what you saw. No cauldrons, no bonfires, no potions…this is spellcraft."

Her watery eyes widened behind their lenses. "How did you learn? Can you—"

"It's inborn. You've either got it or you haven't. I'm sorry," I said, picking up speed, "I don't mean to, ehm, denigrate what you do, but your ideas of magic and mine are rather different to each other."

"Ours actually works," Amy added.

I shot her a look and shook my head. "But let's put that aside for now," I told Franky, taking a seat on the coffee table while she sipped her water. "The fact is, we're in a lot of trouble. The biggest magical organization in the world is trying to pick off practitioners with lesser talent. A few hundred witches are unaccounted for, possibly hiding, possibly dead. We're trying to find them and bring them to safety."

Franky listened without interruption as I gave her the condensed version of the last three months, simplifying as much as I could, and Stuart's head bobbed in the appropriate places. "I don't know what this 'Light' and

'Dark' entail," I concluded, "but as far as I'm concerned, anyone who would set children on fire needs to be stopped. Will you help us?"

She put her glass aside and tugged her mostly empty corset back into place. "What can I do against *that*?" she asked, pointing to my wand. "I don't know any sort of magic stronger than what you've shown me…"

"That's quite all right, I understand. We need a roof. A place with electricity, perhaps, somewhere that isn't this town. Transportation would be nice."

She pursed her lips in thought, then nodded to herself and rose from the couch. "I'm honor-bound to assist a sister witch if I can. Let me make some calls. I'll share your story with a few members of the MAC—those who understand discretion, of course. We may have something for you. Tonight, y'all can stay at my house, and…well, we'll work something out. Do you have a car?"

"Mine's downstairs," Stuart offered.

But Franky shook her head. "You've been hiding for weeks. If your car suddenly goes missing, the cops might get involved. Y'all can squeeze in my Civic, right?"

We looked at each other, our piles of bags, and Stuart's crated cats.

Amy raised one finger and grinned. "Shotgun."

The notion of violating the rules of vehicular seat assignments deeply offended Amy's sense of justice, though I did suggest that perhaps someone taller than a child would be better served in the front. But as no one was in the mood for a quarrel, Stuart and Seamus each took a window, and I scrunched between them as a living buffer. The classical music playing on the public radio station almost drowned out the yowling cats, which had been stowed in the boot.

Stuart offered his troubled potentate her pick of his wares as recompense, and I insisted on buying her a tank of petrol on the way out of town. By the time she'd topped up, Seamus had made the conversions on his mobile and was gawking at the posted prices. "That's forty-five pence a liter. How do they *do* that?"

Amy, who had settled back into the front seat with a blue slushie and a family-sized bag of barbeque crisps, turned and winked at him. "Magic."

"Seriously, do you realize how cheap that is?"

She shrugged and slurped. "It's cheaper in South Carolina."

"*Really*?"

"Welcome to 'Murica. Chips?"

By the time we pulled into Franky's quiet subdivision outside Richmond, the light was fading in the east, the snacks were long gone, and the car smelled faintly of artificial smoke flavoring. I stretched my cramped legs by the side of the vehicle as Stuart rescued his angry pets, and when the cats were away, Seamus began hoisting our gear free. "All right?" he asked as I massaged my knees.

"I think so." With a sigh, I straightened and took my bags from him, still silently marveling at his altered appearance. "For now. Tomorrow? After that?"

He dropped his bag and pulled me into a tight hug. "We're going to be okay, Badge," he mumbled into my hair. "And we'll find them. I promise you, we'll figure it out."

I didn't need to say anything. Seamus's shoulder was warm, and his familiar scent was a comfort in itself. One of his hands held me at the waist, while the other rubbed up and down my back, and I could feel myself melting into him. *This* was home, safety, a port into which I'd thought I would never sail again. I wanted nothing more than to rest my cheek against his shirt and pretend that he had never let me go, that we were standing by our wobble-legged kitchen table in our little flat, two kids holding on to each other as the world opened up before us.

But then then I heard Franky clear her throat and lock

the car. "My husband's making burgers," she said as I reluctantly slid out of Seamus's arms. "Is that okay?"

"Perfect," I replied with a forced smile. "Do you need any help? I'm rubbish in the kitchen, but I'm halfway competent with a grill."

"Nah, it's under control." She took up one of our bags and headed for the screen door, but paused and glanced back at us as we brought up the rear. "Uh…one thing, if you could."

"What's that?" said Seamus.

Franky lowered her voice. "Try to keep Stuart away from the fire, huh? I'd rather not have a repeat of what happened out in Sacramento."

"Sacramento?" I asked.

She shook her head. "I'm sure he didn't mean to trip into that brazier, but my insurance isn't that great. So let's let Larry do the grilling, if you know what I mean."

The grill master was perhaps the most happily mundane person I'd ever met. Tending his crowd-sized chrome monstrosity with a pair of tongs in hand, sporting a red and white apron over a polo and chinos, Larry chatted about his work in sales and the merit of Virginia Tech's various teams for the upcoming school year. After ascertaining that we were friends of his wife's, he asked us about nothing even vaguely related to magic, instead keeping the conversation light and the ice chest stocked. "Hope y'all don't mind cold beer," he said, pressing bottled Coronas into our hands, and hesitated only once he reached Amy. "You look a little young, sweetheart. Cokes are in the fridge."

"You wouldn't like it, anyway," Seamus called after her as she muttered off to the kitchen.

That evening, we gorged ourselves on burgers and oven-baked chips—or fries, as the Americans insisted. It was a filling meal, if not the most healthful. Afterwards,

Franky announced that she and Stuart had a meeting to attend, leaving the rest of us to our own devices. "Don't feel bad," said Larry as he scraped the burnt drippings from the grill plates. "She never lets me come to her meetings, either."

"You're not a witch, then?" Seamus asked.

Larry gave him a look of incredulity, then slugged back his latest beer. "Hell, *she* ain't a witch. But if it makes her happy, I'm not going to raise a fuss. She goes to her witch things, and I go fishing, and we meet back for dinner." He peered at Seamus again. "Are you supposed to be some kind of wizard or whatever?"

"Who, *me*?" He snorted. "Hardly."

They clinked their bottles and drank, enjoying the cooling quiet of the back yard.

"Tourists?" Larry ventured once they'd slaked their thirst.

I could see his wheels turning when Seamus looked my way. "Not exactly," he told Larry. "Work."

"Aw, too bad. What'd you say you do, again?"

Seamus's glance that time was more pointed, and I picked up the thread of the tapestry he'd begun to weave. "Mr. Booth," I said, leaning on the deck railing beside him, "what did your wife tell you about us?"

"Nothing, really," he replied, puzzled. "I mean, I kind of guessed y'all were some of her MAC friends, but…"

When he left the question dangling, I ran with it. "I'm trying to think of what, exactly, I can tell you," I said after a pregnant pause. "You should have been properly briefed, but since you weren't—"

A note of alarm crept into his voice. "Briefed about what?"

I made a show of looking to Amy and Seamus, who nodded me onward. "Franky…does excellent work," I murmured. "High-level work. *Classified* work. Do you follow me?"

Larry frowned and shook his head.

"Your wife is a true patriot, Mr. Booth. And in this particular instance, the interests of your government and ours...intersect, shall we say?"

"Government?" he whispered.

It was Seamus's turn to ad lib. "The less you know, the safer you'll be. In fact, should anyone make enquiries, it would be best if you'd never met us and we'd never been here. Understood?"

Larry glanced back and forth at us as we flanked him, his beer forgotten. "Who *are* y'all?"

Seamus sighed, then reached into his back pocket and extracted a slim black wallet—the kind in which we kept our credentials. "I'm going to show you something," he told Larry, "and perhaps this will make it clear to you why your silence is so important." With that, he flipped the wallet open, revealing his PSNI identification.

Our host stared at the card in silence for a moment, then looked up at Seamus with eyes round as saucers. "MI6?" he squeaked.

Seamus nodded and put the wallet away. "As my colleague said, for the time being"—he cocked his thumb toward Amy, who loitered on a sun-bleached chaise— "your government and ours are working cooperatively."

Taking her cue, the girl nodded vigorously and joined us at the railing. "Lives and assets have been lost already, Mr. Booth. It's a matter of international security that this evening never happened."

Larry's jaw dropped, and he goggled at us for a moment before taking another long draught of beer.

"I'm afraid that's all we can tell you," Seamus continued. "For your own safety, you understand. But rest assured that your wife is doing important work for your government and ours, and your...*tact*...about this evening is of paramount importance."

"Of course," he rushed. "Sure thing. Not a word, but, uh...can I ask one question?"

"Go ahead."

"What about that Stuart fellow? Is he—"

"Company man," Amy interjected. "That meeting tonight is to help Franky keep up appearances."

Larry's head bobbed, and I smiled at Amy when he turned back to his beer. The girl was young, but something told me she just might be teachable.

I stirred on my couch bed that night when the screen door squealed open in the wee hours, announcing Franky and Stuart's return. "All right?" I asked as they shuffled past me in the dark.

"All right," Stuart replied, and left me to catch a few more precious hours of sleep before Seamus nudged me awake at dawn.

"Breakfast's ready," he murmured, brushing my mussed hair from my face. "I think she wants us out of here. And the next time you sleep on a decorative pillow, maybe choose one without so much texture," he teased.

I patted my cheek, feeling the impression of the corduroy on my skin, and swung myself upright. "Sod off."

To my surprise, he kissed my forehead before pulling me from the couch. "I don't know, red welts become you. Now hurry—I saw Amy lurking near the bacon."

"She needs it more than you do. Girl's skin and bones."

I slung my duffel over my shoulder and headed for the guest bath to brush my teeth and make the best of my dirty hair. As I glowered at my dark circles, Seamus rapped on the door and held up his new toiletry bag. "Borrow the other sink?"

He unpacked as I brushed and spat, but I stopped him before he could open his toothpaste. "How'd you do that?" I muttered, sliding closer to him to keep my voice low. "With the creds last night, I mean. The card said PSNI."

Seamus frowned at his reflection in thought. "Honestly,

I'm not sure," he finally replied. "I'd hoped it would work, but I wasn't sure it would until he saw it."

"You mean…"

"Like glamour. He saw what I wanted him to see. I *might* have borrowed that move from *Doctor Who*," he admitted with a sheepish grin, "and I have no idea what MI6 hands out by way of credentials—"

"But neither does Larry," I finished, and nudged him in the shoulder. "Well done, you. Is it coming more easily?" I asked, packing my toothbrush away.

"Maybe. I don't know." He sighed, then stuck his tongue out at the mirror. "At least I haven't flambéed anyone lately. Progress, I suppose."

Before I could respond, Amy darted into the bathroom with a look of horror on her face. "Y'all. *Y'all*," she insisted, "you *gotta* see the van."

"Van?" I asked.

She groaned and motioned for us to follow.

We left our belongings and trailed Amy through the house to the garage door, where she paused and grimaced. "Stuart said the MAC's loaning us wheels to get to a safe house in New Mexico."

Seamus frowned. "How far away is that?"

"At least two days' drive. Far side of Texas. Something about a sister organization, I didn't pay attention to the details. The van was too distressing. I mean…well, see for yourself," she said, and stepped aside.

I pushed open the screen door and stopped in my tracks. "Bloody hell," Seamus muttered behind me. "That's…unique."

"Awful," Amy groaned.

I had to agree with her. The panel van parked in the Booths' garage was huge and angular, probably mid-sixties in vintage. That alone wouldn't have bothered me—I'd driven plenty of questionable vehicles prior to that morning—but the paint job was appalling. On top of the matte black undercoat was a DayGlo scene straight from an acid trip: a badly drawn white-haired wizard in blue and purple robes, sparking wand outstretched, conjuring down lightning upon an army of sword-wielding skeletons. The crude artwork was too weird to be anything but a police magnet.

"One of the local wizards had a band back in the day," said Stuart, emerging from the kitchen with a bacon sandwich. "They broke up, but he kept the van. She still runs, but the interior smells a little, uh…funky."

"We can't drive this," I told him. "There's no way in hell."

"I know it's big, but I got it here—"

"Never mind the size—it's practically a cop beacon!" He began to protest, but I spoke over him. "The first time we're pulled over and questioned, how should we explain ourselves? Two Brits, an American girl, and you, heading west in a *'funky'*-smelling van?" I shook my head and huffed, then pulled out my wand. "Well, I hope your friend won't be too upset if I give this thing a new coat of paint."

Stuart sounded doubtful. "He painted it himself. It matched their first album cover."

"I don't care if it was painted by Leonardo da fucking Vinci," I said, and took aim. A blast of channeled force shot through my arm as I envisioned the spell, and in a matter of seconds, the van was white and glossy, and the tires were no longer bald. "Better," I muttered. "Let's see about the inside. Stuart, keys."

He gaped at the repainted van. "Okay, it was ugly, but you didn't have to—"

"*Keys*, Stuart."

With a grunt, he lobbed a nondescript keyring into my hands, and I unlocked the back door to a wave of old marijuana. "Reasonable grounds on wheels," I said, and beckoned to Seamus. "Help me with the interior. Amy, Stuart, eat up. We'll leave as soon as we're finished."

Amy slid past me to peek into the van, then recoiled

with a grimace. "Is that—"

"Exactly what you think it is," said Seamus, pulling her away. "Go inside before you get high." As she headed for the house, he climbed into the back of the van and coughed. "Shit, this place is foul. And Badger?"

"Yeah?" I said, joining him by the van door.

"Ten to one the band wrote at least one terrible song about elves. We're gutting this junker on principle, if nothing else."

Seamus was still reluctant to do much with his newfound abilities—which I could appreciate, given the proximity of highly flammable petrol—but I had enough control to strip out the van's lone bench seat and ancient carpeting, which I replaced with a pair of captain's chairs, a tiny bed, and an interior that didn't smell like a uni dorm. Working together, we stowed the baggage, and then we crammed down the remnants of breakfast as Stuart tearfully said his goodbyes to his apathetic cats. "A life on the run isn't fair to them," he explained as he sniffled, "and there are people in the MAC who can...can foster..."

I returned to the van, giving him a chance to sob in peace, and honked fifteen minutes later when there was still no sign of him. Stuart finally emerged, red-eyed and splotchy, and climbed into the back with Amy. "We have an address?" I asked as he buckled in.

He handed me a slip of paper, and I tapped it into my mobile. "Thirty hours," I muttered as the route appeared. "And they're expecting us?"

I saw Stuart nod in the rearview mirror. "The Circle of the Sun has a place you can hide, at least for a while. They said to give them a day to prepare."

"No worries there." The van sputtered to life, and I waved back at the Booths as I guided us onto the road heading west. I felt a twinge of guilt at the story we'd fed Larry, but I decided the lie was worth his silence.

Besides, convincing a mundane that we were spies was a hell of a lot easier than delving into the truth.

CHAPTER 11

There was no point in stopping. We raised enough eyebrows when we took breaks for fuel and food—quick breaks, all of them, since Seamus and I could easily imagine a well-meaning officer thinking we'd kidnapped Amy. Had it been my call, *I* would have stopped us for questioning, and so we pressed on before any good Samaritans could get the wrong idea. Besides, I'd left my wallet and credentials back in the car on Skye. Getting pulled over without identification was low on my list of things to experience in our drive across America.

After we left Richmond, Stuart and Seamus slept through the morning while Amy took the wheel and I "supervised," by which I mean I tensed and gasped whenever she drove too close to the vehicles around us. By the time we'd crossed the mountains and met I-81, I insisted that she take a break—mostly for my sanity—and steered us southwest, following the Appalachians toward Tennessee. Or so my GPS informed me—having never been to the States, I had little concept of the geography beyond a vague notion that New York and Los Angeles were on opposite ends and my mother's relatives lived somewhere in the middle. The country was huge in comparison to mine, that I knew, but after the fourth hour of unremarkable Interstate driving, I almost longed for the chaos around London to break up the monotony.

Not until late morning did I turn on the radio, find a news station, and hear about the so-called Brexit vote, the results of which had come in overnight. The prime minister was resigning, Scotland was vowing another referendum…and, I realized with a jolt, I didn't care. By then, my world had constricted to the walls of the van and the rolling green countryside, the oversized SUVs and the roadside churches, and the constant, irrational fear that there'd be an Arcanum roadblock over the next hill. Survival was all that mattered; the political-economic future of the UK was someone else's problem.

I glanced in the mirror to locate Seamus, who stared out the window with his chin on his fist. If the radio report troubled him, he gave no sign.

Seamus relieved me after a lunch stop near Knoxville, but I kept my front seat to guide him and, if necessary, remind him of which lane was his. Fortunately for the British drivers in the van, the Interstate barriers kept us from drifting left on instinct, and Seamus guided us west on I-40 across the long afternoon. We found a McDonald's just over the Arkansas border for dinner, and Stuart groggily slid behind the wheel for the first night shift while I crashed in the back.

Amy had offered to drive again at dawn, but that left me with the unenviable task of steering us through the wee hours. Around three the next morning, I passed a sign welcoming us to Texas, and for an instant, I reconsidered our journey. We could veer south, deep into the state that Mama had fled, and look for strangers who bore a passing resemblance to me. Or we could backtrack to Norman— I'd seen signs for the turnoff—and find my cousins there. Would they remember my mother, Kathy McAdams, who'd flown away to England and never come home? Would they have even heard of her death? Before I went on the run, I'd called the Malones and asked them to see to my parents' arrangements—had anyone sent word to Mama's tiny hometown newspaper, alerting them that their expat daughter had been murdered in her own house? And if her distant family knew of her passing, would they want anything to do with me?

Hello, I'm Hannah. Lovely to meet you. Just so you're aware, a bunch of wizards have been trying to kill me since Easter—could my friends and I camp in your spare room?

Putting that fancy aside, I drove on until the horizon glowed behind me and Seamus insisted that I surrender the wheel.

We took our breakfast break east of Albuquerque, and then we pressed on for the last leg, following I-25 south along the Rio Grande and the narrow band of settlements on its banks. Around us spread a wasteland of brown soil and scruffy green shrubs, distant rocky hills and endless powerlines, all under a bright, stiflingly hot blue sky. Late June had been unpleasant thus far in our trip, but the mugginess of Virginia and Tennessee had given way to an arid heat, a far cry from the summers I knew. Then again, we were driving through a state that seemed to be mostly desert. The van chugged along, but I kept an eye on the engine's temperature gauge, just in case.

Stuart's suggestions concerning lunch had become more vocal when we crossed the town line of San Angelo, another wide, verdant oasis off the Interstate. The GPS directed us to the outskirts of the settlement and along a gravel path through the scrubland to a pink adobe mansion that appeared to have come straight from a resort brochure, down to the cacti in front and the umbrellas behind that gave away the pool's location. Even the postbox was perfect, a stylized flowering cactus planted by the side of the road.

Seamus cut the ignition, then handed me the keys, took off his gloves, and let himself out. I followed suit, wincing as my long-cramped legs stretched, and squinted in the noon glare. A high cinderblock fence extended from the driveway around the back of the house, blocking the view of the garden, but before I could explore, the front door opened, and a tanned blonde my age emerged. "Hello!" she called, wiggling her perfectly manicured fingers, and hurried down to meet us, her white tennis skirt gleaming in the sunlight. She was barefoot, oddly enough, but was otherwise the picture of moneyed health. "I'm Julia Wiggins," she said, pumping our hands in turn. "Welcome to Rancho Escondido! Come on in, we're making lunch. Is everyone cool with enchiladas?"

"Ooh, *yes*," said Amy, blazing a trail after her while we sorted through our bags. "Your house has a name? That's awesome!"

Julia smiled. "Well, we use it as a guest house. Small groups, you know—a bed and breakfast. But we're empty right now, so there's plenty of room for you. And don't worry," she added as we neared, "this place is *totally* private. You'll be safe."

She jogged up the flagstone steps, then held open the door while we filed through into the airy foyer. "Just put your things anywhere, we'll figure rooms out later," she instructed, then called, "Tony! They're here!"

I dropped my duffel and turned at the sound of footsteps on the tile, extending my hand to meet my host…and then I froze and desperately tried not to gawk.

A man had appeared from the kitchen, a smiling, tanned, bald man with taut muscles, perfect teeth, and a pair of deep dimples.

And aside from the sauce-stained white apron he sported, he was completely naked.

He beamed and shook my hand as I desperately searched for something polite to say. "Hi, I'm Tony. You guys must be exhausted—did you drive through the night? We weren't expecting to see you until at least dinner," he said, clasping Seamus's hand. "No problem, there's plenty for lunch. How hot do you like your salsa?"

As Tony moved on to greet Stuart, my partner reached out and slapped his palm over Amy's bulging eyes.

"No one told you we're naturalists?" Julia passed the steaming dish of enchiladas to Stuart and clucked her tongue. "Wow…I'm sorry, that must have been a shock."

Tony, now sporting running shorts as a concession to our discomfort, nodded beside her. "Yeah, they could have shared that before sending you on your way."

"We've *warned* the high priestess," she added. "You're not the first to see more than you were expecting, but normally it's someone in the Circle."

"Or the UPS guy."

They grimaced in unison. "Roderigo is such a nice man, but if I don't throw a shirt on, he gets flustered," said Julia. "Backed into a cactus once. We try to keep property damage to a minimum around here, so we've got a stash of emergency clothes. But anyway, Rancho Escondido is a naturalist retreat—and before you ask, yes, towels are mandatory. The furniture's safe."

Seamus ceased his sudden squirming.

"You're welcome to go nude or not," said Tony, smiling at us over a bowl of quinoa salad. "Give it a try, if you like, but if it's not your cup of tea, we'll understand." He passed the bowl to Amy, who had been unusually quiet and red-cheeked throughout the meal. "But enough about us. What do you folks do?"

"Detective," Seamus mumbled.

"Detective inspector, actually," I said. "Both of us. Ehm…"

The Wigginses shared a look, and Julia took a helping of quinoa. "Little straight-laced, are we?"

"A wee bit," I admitted.

She patted my hand. "Then think of this as a vacation, huh? You're perfectly safe here. We were up early this morning casting spells of protection around the property."

"Oh, ehm…thanks," said Seamus, who was concentrating on his enchilada. The silverware on the table was steel with enamel handles, and he was handling his set as if he'd been given a pair of uranium rods.

"Of course," Julia replied. "The high priestess told us what the potentate had said—well, at least some of it. You have enemies? Black magick at work?"

"Something like that," I replied, and stared across the table at Seamus until he looked up at me. Concentrating, I whispered under my breath and focused, and the tines of his fork quickly grew a protective coating of clear plastic. *Thanks*, he mouthed, and tucked in with slightly more vigor.

Julia turned to Stuart, who had nearly cleaned his plate. "You're Stuart Purcell, aren't you? From California?" He nodded, and she beamed. "Tony and I read some of your work. *Fascinating* stuff. You really are quite the scholar."

He perked up and dabbed the sauce off his lips. "You're too kind. Uh...if I may ask..."

She began to count off on her fingers. "*Intention and Meditation, Simplifying Spellcraft, Potent Potions...*"

"Love that one," Tony cut in. "Great reference manual. I use it all the time."

"We both do," said Julia, then leaned conspiratorially toward Stuart. "You know, I'd heard a rumor that you had another book in the pipeline. Something about fairies?"

At that, Seamus choked on his enchilada, and Amy thumped him between the shoulders until his coughing fit subsided.

"Really?" I said to Stuart while Seamus wiped his watering eyes. "I didn't know that. How's it coming along?"

His face reddened to scarlet as he dug into the quinoa. "It's, uh...on the back burner. Got sidetracked."

"Oh, that's too bad," said Tony. "I'd heard you'd found a colony of them in Virginia."

His head bobbed. "Yeah. A few."

Julia's dark eyes widened, and she grabbed Stuart's arm. "You did? You really *did*? Well, don't hold out on us, silly! What did you find?"

"Yes," I said, staring him down, "what *did* you find?"

He looked up from his plate, found no quarter with me, and licked his lips. "Um...well, I spotted maybe half a dozen on the coast. Tiny people with beautiful wings. They glow in the most brilliant colors. I…I could never get close enough to do a thorough examination, but I did see them."

"That's funny," Seamus muttered, "I didn't know you'd legalized LSD in the States. Or were you using hallucinogenic mushrooms at the time? Licking toads? I don't know, what do wankers like you use to get high around here?"

Tony cut his eyes back and forth between Stuart and Seamus. "You know, there's room for friendly disagreement in the community—"

"What I saw were technically pixies," Stuart interrupted, glaring back at Seamus. "Which *do* exist. Ask your aunt and uncle if you don't believe me."

"Pixies are a type of fairy," Julia added with forced cheer.

But Stuart shook his head. "Only in the sense that they originate outside this realm. They're not magically adept—long-lived, but not talented. So that project is on permanent hiatus," he continued, turning to the Wigginses. "Now, about these protective spells—what did you use? Something of mine?"

"Not this time. We thought about trying a few of yours," said Julia, "but we went for something stronger."

"Stronger?" Amy echoed. "Like…what, exactly?"

Again, the Wigginses looked at each other, and Tony took the lead. "I don't know what discipline all of you follow, but Julia and I have done extensive tantric work."

The girl put down her fork. "As in—"

"Sex magick," Julia clarified, as matter-of-fact as if she were discussing the train timetable. "There's something so powerful about two people unifying their life forces and intentions. It's…*pure*. Beautiful, really."

"I'm sure," I cut in before Seamus could make the situation worse. "But all the same, I'd like to ward your property. Can't be too careful, right? Seamie, why don't you give me a hand?"

"Sure, that's a great idea," Tony nodded. "Want us to help—"

"*No.* Thanks, ehm...you've done so much already," I replied, and pushed back from the table. "We'll just be in the garden, then. Thank you for lunch, it was...nice."

"I really don't know what I'm doing," Seamus murmured as I faced the garden wall and wove the strands of the ward system together. "I mean, I see what you're doing, but I don't know how to do it."

"I realize that. You're out here to keep you away from Stuart."

"Oh." He paused while I grunted and dragged a stubborn channel into position. "Sorry, Badge. I don't mean to be an ass, but—"

"He pushes my buttons, too, but he's our problem for now."

"Understood." Seamus watched me work for a moment in silence. "*Can* I help?"

I lowered my wand and found him staring at me, his expression by turns hopeful and nervous. Even with the heat, he'd stuffed his hands in his pockets as if subconsciously trying to sheath a weapon, and my heart ached to see him so uncertain. "I don't know, but we can try," I said, and tucked my wand in my belt. "Come here, feel what I've done."

Tentatively, he approached the wards and stroked two fingers over the glowing filaments of active magic. "Tingles."

"It's supposed to. Walk through them and come back."

"Through the *wall?*"

"You could always use the gate." I grinned, and Seamus sheepishly did as instructed. As soon as he crossed into the garden, the existing wards flashed red in time with a deafening klaxon blast. "See?" I yelled over the noise, then gestured to reset the wards. "An alarm system. Before I finish, I'll build in exceptions for the six of us here, but first, I've got to construct the rest of the wards."

He chewed his lip as he considered the partial fence. "Is there any way to make a solid barrier? Not just an alarm, but, like…a fence?"

"Technically?" I sighed. "Yes. But it's a more involved process, and I've never attempted something so complex. Alarms are fairly easy—actually keeping people out takes skill."

Seamus draped his arm over my shoulders. "You're a wizard, love. I have faith."

Under ordinary circumstances, having another body that close to mine in the summer heat would have been miserable, but something in me relished our contact. "The vote of confidence is appreciated, but really, I don't know the first thing about building barrier wards. Toula couldn't cram in an Arcanum education that quickly."

I reached up and took his dangling hand, and we examined my work in the hush of the hot afternoon.

"The truth of the matter is that I'm a lousy wizard," I muttered. "Talent aside, wand aside, I don't have the training I need to pull off complex spells. It took me three years to get warding basics down, but Dad couldn't teach me more than that."

"You lifted a car," Seamus pointed out. "That's impressive."

"That's child's play. The spell is elementary—whether you lift a feather or an elephant, you put together the same spell, then add the appropriate *oomph*. And shielding's basic enough that I can defend myself to a point. But complex wards, or that aural stuff Toula did…*far* out of my wheelhouse."

"You're talking to the bloke who sets accidental fires, remember. I'm still impressed."

I looked up at him and squeezed his hand. "It'll come, Seamie. Even if Val has to beat it into you, it'll come."

He rolled his eyes. "Old boy actually texted me last

night. Wanted to be sure we weren't dead yet."

"Yeah? What'd you tell him?"

"That we were heading west, and Stuart had dumped the bloody cats." Seamus's mouth twitched in the ghost of a smirk. "I meant to tell him that he didn't need to use full punctuation and wouldn't lose points for contractions, but I thought that might be a bit much. I mean, he's fucking ancient. At least he knows how to use a phone."

"Nice that he cares."

"Yeah," he muttered. "And I think he *likes* me, which is concerning. How badly do you think he beats the people he hates?"

I chuckled and unwrapped myself from Seamus's arm. "Let's hope we don't find out. But how about it, want to give warding a go?" He stepped back, hesitant once more, and I caught his wrist before he could escape. "Come on, you can do this."

"If I lose control—"

"You won't. Relax." After pivoting him to face the wards and moving to stand behind him, I pulled out my wand and held it in front of us both. "What you're going to do is focus on creating a single channel. Think of it as a piece of wire in a chain-link fence. You're not powering it, you're just creating it and attaching it to the pieces that are already there. Watch." I called the construction to mind, then felt the pulse flow through my wand and produce the filament of active magic, a channel as long as my arm. With a twitch of my index finger on the wand, the glowing strand affixed itself to two of the other strands, melding into a solid matrix. "See? A little piece like that is all we need. Your turn."

Seamus took a deep breath, then extended his hand and whispered, "Please..."

The background magic flashed, then coalesced into a jumble of tangled coils several meters long and high, a construction with all the internal order of a mat of hair in the shower drain. Seamus tensed in shock, and I slipped around him with my wand out in case his creation suddenly decided to explode. But his ward seemed stable—unpowered and detached from mine, but in no imminent danger of turning the garden into a crater—and I allowed myself to breathe a sigh of relief.

"Perhaps a tad over the top, but you're getting the idea," I told him. "Let me see if I can attach your wards to mine…"

"I *really* wouldn't do that, Miss Hannah," Amy called as she hurried through the sliding glass door. "Put the wand down and step away from the enchantment."

"It's inert wardwork," I protested as she crossed the artificial turf and skirted the pool. "That's not proper enchantment."

"What else would it be?" she replied with a snort.

"It's not active, for one thing."

"It's *enchantment*. If you attach that to your wards—if you *can* attach that to your wards, I mean—and fire it up, you're going to blow the whole system. Want to explain the fireworks to the naked mundies?"

"Shit, are they naked again?" Seamus muttered.

"Why do you think I've been watching y'all work?" Amy made a face and shuddered. "Look, I can't do diddly-squat with magic, but my folks were big on teaching me theory. Comes with the territory if you're crafting. And I'm telling you that trying to cast an enchantment into your ward system is going to end in tears."

"But…" I mumbled, "but it's not *active* enchantment…"

"Doesn't matter, Mr. Seamus made it. Those two constructions are oil and water on their own, Mentos and Diet Coke when you turn on the juice." She scowled at me and folded her arms. "Man, they really don't teach witches much, do they?"

"Unfortunately. Seamie, ehm…I hate to ask…"

He closed his hand into a fist, and the enchantment dissolved. "I'll get our bags out of the foyer," he said, and headed back toward the house.

"Wait, Seamie—"

"I'm in the way out here, and someone has to keep an eye on Stuart." With a small, wistful smile, he carefully maneuvered around the door's steel handle and disappeared into the shade.

By nightfall, as the first stars blazed and Mars rose overhead, I was able to put the finishing touches on the ward system and gingerly let myself back into the house. Sun cream hadn't been part of my kit, and my face, neck, and bare forearms were red and raw. Even my part hurt when I finger-combed my hair, and I could only imagine how lovely the peeling would be in a few days' time.

While I stood at the bathroom mirror and poked my cheeks to assess the extent of the damage, Stuart knocked on the doorframe, then whistled when I looked up. "Good grief, that's bad," he muttered, taking in my new crimson complexion. "Want some aloe? I'm sure they keep a bottle around."

"In a bit." I pressed a wet flannel against my face and winced. "Need something?"

"ID, if you're not too crispy. I'm hitting the road in the morning."

I dropped the flannel in the basin and frowned at him. "Already? We just got here!"

"Yeah, and I'm wasting time. I've done all I can for you—it's time I head on to Montana."

"And do what, exactly?" I asked as I resumed my careful cooldown. "Spy on the silo from the bushes? You won't be able to get in there."

"Actually, I was planning on trying a more roundabout method."

That piqued my interest, and I began to sponge off my neck in order to watch him. "I'm listening."

Stuart leaned against the wall and folded his arms. "The

silo's in the middle of nowhere, but they're not entirely alone. Aiden says all the silo kids go to the county schools with the locals. They're in walking distance."

"And you…what, plan to teach?"

"I haven't taught before, but it can't be that hard, right?"

My eyebrows rose. "You don't know many teachers, do you, Stuart?"

He ignored the jab. "Little school systems are always looking for volunteers. Librarians, coaches, whatever. What about a volunteer art teacher?"

"What do you know about art?"

"Enough to teach grade schoolers how to finger-paint," he said, smirking. "Back in California, I used to make my own vessels—blew glass, threw pots, even wove a couple of baskets. Let's say an aging hippie artist decided to move into the country to clear his head and work in peace, and the local school just so happened to have an opening. Not a bad plan, huh?"

I shrugged and regretted it when my collar rubbed against my burnt neck. "Could do. But why bother with the school? Set up a studio and get to know the locals. Consider it a long stakeout."

"But how many Arcanum wizards do you think would be interested in pottery classes?" He shook his head and straightened. "If I get into the school, I can watch the silo kids—and you know the little rugrats say the darndest things." He lowered his voice and added, "The grand magus was pregnant when she was taken. Joey says she's due in September. If the kid doesn't show up in kindergarten in a few years, that might be a sign that something's happened to Helen."

"How would you—"

"Know?" His smirk returned full-force. "These people are brash enough to stage a coup and take hostages against the courts. You think they'd try to hide the kid? Unlikely. Smug people make stupid mistakes."

Personal experience? was on the tip of my tongue, but I bit it back and dried off. "Find pictures of the documents you need, and I'll work them up tonight."

"Before or after the meeting?"

"What meeting?"

"Right," he mumbled, "I knew I forgot to tell someone. The Circle's meeting for dinner—well, the locals and a few out-of-town dignitaries," he amended. "The Wigginses thought you'd want to say hello and ask the other witches and wizards for help."

I couldn't stop the glower that followed the announcement, and Stuart held up his hands. "I know, I *know*, but try to be nice, will you? These are good people. Well-studied people. Maybe their sort of magic isn't the most effective, but they mean well. They believe in what they're doing."

"Which is next to nothing," I retorted.

"Be that as it may, they're willing to help you. Can't hurt, right? Or do you have a better option?"

I turned back to the mirror with a sigh. "Think I'd be here if I did?"

"Exactly. And keep in mind that not everyone in the magical community has taken an extended field trip into Faerie."

I opened my toiletry bag and fished for my lipstick, which was just pink enough to make my lips blend into the rest of my face that night. "Your friends aren't *in* the community."

"They think they are. Seriously, Hannah, just be nice, okay?"

Glancing at his reflection, I saw that Stuart had lost some of his customary self-assurance. His arms had tightened across his chest, and he watched me with a flicker of worry. "I'll behave," I muttered.

"They've been good to me," he said softly. "All of the practitioners I've ever known have been kind. And I..." His mouth drew down to a thin line. "Sometimes, I seem to rub people the wrong way. You may have noticed."

There was no point in lying to him, so I continued to freshen up.

"The community has always accepted me," Stuart continued. "I tried to impress to the high priestess how much danger they're putting themselves in by harboring you three, but I don't think the message got through. And even if it did, the Circle of the Sun probably doesn't care. Wizards don't run in the face of danger."

"This one does." My hand paused over the bag, and I opted to forgo foundation in favor of lotion. My face was unsalvageable that night, anyway. "This one runs and hides as necessary. They're going to *love* me."

Stuart grunted and took a seat on the edge of the clawfoot tub. "You know, I don't see eye to eye with Colin on everything, but he's shown me that there's a difference between running and *running*. Remember when Rigby got trashed a couple of years back? Or did that not make it onto the Fringe's radar in your neck of the woods?"

"Oh, I remember. Great big bloody disaster, and those giant bug-wolf things...we never did settle on a proper name for them..."

"I was at ground zero," he murmured, and I turned from the mirror, lotion in hand. "And I'd probably be dead right now if Colin hadn't been there. I got to blast a couple of those things, but we didn't just sit still and wait for them to find us. We—well, Colin and Toula and Slim," he admitted—"were strategic about it. And if he hadn't yanked me along for the ride, I'd have tried to take the monsters on as they came down the street, counting on my finest homemade wand and some *powerful* protective spells to save me."

"Dear God," I muttered. "What sort of spells—"

"The kind you people laugh at. Perhaps rightly so," he said, and shrugged. "Maybe some of them work—maybe they make you a little luckier in love or give you a better night's rest or clearer skin. It's not like we do controlled studies. But anyway, they were nothing compared to a loaded Dud Defender. Ever fired one of those?"

"Once or twice." Remembering the lotion in my palm, I slathered my face before I dripped it onto the bathmat. "They've got a kick to them."

"Is that so? I barely remember. I was scared out of my mind and on the verge of soiling myself, but I know it worked."

"Giant monsters tend to have that effect on people."

"Forget the monsters. Until that day, I was a *wizard*. Educated, respected as a scholar, sworn to the Light. I had the utmost confidence in my ability to change the world through my skill with magic. Ran my shop. Went to meetings and gatherings and conclaves and whatnot. I had summer and winter sets of custom-tailored ceremonial robes, I'll have you know." Stuart grimaced and shook his head. "And then Colin barged into my shop and...well, he went full Coileán on me. The dull, perfectly mundane skeptic at whom I'd been looking down my nose for months turned out to have power like I'd never *imagined*. And he told me it was time to run. So don't beat yourself up," he said as he pushed himself off the tub. "You ran to stay alive—but you came back, didn't you?"

"To a completely different continent," I replied.

"Yeah, you chose the one with the wizard silo. I wouldn't call that running." He straightened his polo and stepped into the hall. "We're heading over in half an hour. Hope you don't mind driving the van."

CHAPTER 12

With its walled garden and spacious, well-appointed den, Rancho Escondido would have been an ideal meeting place for a modest group like the Circle. Then again, perhaps the rest of the Circle shared our doubts about the enforcement of the Wigginses' towel rule, as we ended up across town in a shag-carpeted basement rumpus room that stank of old cigarettes, stale beer, and too much "cleansing" incense.

The witches and wizards of the Circle—even our naturalist hosts—had attired themselves in their finest polyester and velvet robes for the event. Stuart sported an overly long crimson number, assumedly a loaner from Tony, and Amy, Seamus, and I looked underdressed by comparison as we clumped against the wood paneling. While the so-called practitioners moved folding chairs into a rough circle under the antler chandelier, I pressed my back to the wall, feeling the comforting jab of my wand against my spine. As if sensing my disquietude, Seamus reached for my hand, and I smiled at him as our fingers touched.

"You look nice," he whispered.

"I look like a hairy tomato."

He grinned and squeezed my hand, and I rolled my eyes. Glancing at Amy, I found her focused on her new mobile, rapidly tapping with both thumbs. "Taking notes?" I murmured, nudging her in the arm to draw her attention.

She looked almost guilty when her head jerked up. "Huh? Sorry, uh…"

"I asked if you were taking notes. Advancing your magical education."

"Very funny, Miss Hannah."

Her screen showed the unmistakable back-and-forth bubbles of a text conversation. "Who're you chatting up, then?"

"Oh, um…Aiden," she said. "I'm sorry, I thought we had time—"

"*Aiden?*" Seamus cut in with an evil grin. "Now, that's surprising. I'm sure you two have loads to talk about."

I couldn't be certain in the dim golden glow of the horrible chandelier, but I thought I saw Amy redden. "Just a coding question," she mumbled. "He's working on the Fringe network, you know, and he's trying to build a new security protocol, and—"

Seamus held up his hands and shook his head. "Stop. For the love of all that's holy, girl, *stop*. What's the matter with you?"

"With me?" she asked, befuddled.

"And him! What sort of stupid—"

"What Seamie's trying to say," I interrupted, "is that he's disappointed in your flirting game."

"*Flirting?*" Now I was sure that Amy was blushing. "I'm not flirting with him, I'm talking about the network!" she managed after a moment of furious stammering. "Why would you think we're flirting?"

"Becau—*ow!*" Seamus yelped as I stomped his foot.

"Because he's being silly," I replied. "Carry on."

She bent back to her mobile, then looked at me again with a pensive frown. "You don't think Aiden is flirting with *me*, do you?"

"Over network architecture? I doubt it. Excuse us," I said, and dragged Seamus into a shadowy corner of the basement.

"Liar," he murmured once we were out of earshot.

"Are you trying to jinx them?"

"No, but for two clever people—"

"Exactly. Two young, inexperienced, clever people who haven't the faintest idea what they're doing. Let them flirt in peace."

Before Seamus could argue with me, the woman in the purple robes, whom I'd taken to be the high priestess due to her abundance of silver and gold necklaces, called the meeting to order. "If you could find your seats, please," she said, raising her arms with a clatter of bangles and bracelets, "we'll open with an invocation, and then we'll turn to the business portion of the evening."

The other members, many of them still holding paper plates of hamburgers and baked beans, made their way to the folding chairs. One even carried a bag of Doritos and a jar of salsa with him, which he began passing to his neighbors. Stuart took the last of the chairs, sitting between the high priestess and Julia, which left the three of us to skulk outside the ring and cast uncertain glances at the musty couch.

I half-listened while the Circle did its chanting bit, feeling rather foolish to be in the midst of the meeting, but as the invocation wrapped up, the door above us slammed open, and light footsteps ran down the staircase. "Sorry I'm late," the newcomer panted, straightening his utilitarian black robe. "Work emergency. What'd I miss?"

The high priestess beckoned him toward the circle, and he pulled a chair from the wall and squeezed between two elderly witches. "What sort of emergency could you possibly have on a Saturday night?" one of the women asked. "Did someone exchange your records for good ones?"

"Ha," he muttered, and looked up at us. The tardy wizard was young, maybe twenty-five, with a black ponytail and a deep tan—perhaps Native American, I mused. "Hey, Jim Wheeler," he said, raising one hand. "Have we done names yet?"

The high priestess rubbed her forehead. "I was getting there. Uh...well, okay, this is Jim, our local celebrity," she told us. "DJs one of the morning radio shows."

The young man flashed a brilliant smile and held up his thumb. "Jim Dandy on Hot Country 104.7," he added, dropping into a polished twang. "Weekday mornings, five to ten—"

"They get it," she interrupted. "I'm Lisa Rodriguez, and if we could continue to my right…"

When the others had said their names, Lisa motioned us forward. "Lady Francesca told us a little about you, and Stuart has been filling me in," she continued, nodding to him in recognition. "They say you have powerful enemies. That black magick is in play."

Seamus and Amy looked at me, and I took the lead. "I don't know about black or white," I replied, stepping into the middle of the circle. "The kind of magic I was taught didn't use those labels. Magic is magic—any spell can be used for good or ill." I caught a few of the members nodding and pushed on. "My, ehm…colleagues and I are here now because some very talented wizards have attacked the weakest of our kind. They killed my parents. They killed Amy's," I said, pointing to her as Seamus put his hand on her shoulder. "And they would have killed us, had we not run.

"We're here because we're the lucky ones. The ones who were too quick to be caught. Many have been evacuated to—to a safe place," I said, stopping myself before I could invite a barrage of questions. "But many others are still missing. We're trying to find them. Alive or dead, hiding or captured, we don't know, but we're trying to locate the lost."

I turned to take in the circle. "We need a place to stay. Perhaps a car, if you have a spare—I assume Stuart will be taking our van when he heads on. But you should know that harboring us would put you at risk. If our pursuers find us here, they won't just kill us. They'll come after you, too."

The Circle was silent for a moment, and then Jim raised

his hand. "Who, exactly, is after you?"

"They're called the Arcanum," I replied. "The most powerful magical organization in the world. And they—"

"Never heard of them," one of the old witches interrupted. "They don't come to the national conclave, do they?"

"No."

"Hmm." She sniffed and adjusted her bifocals. "Think they're too good for us, eh?"

"Undoubtedly."

"And what's your affiliation, dear?" Jim's other neighbor chimed in. "Order of the Seventh Star?"

Stuart shrugged helplessly, and I shifted in place as the eyes followed me. "Ehm…no. I'm a coordinator for the Fringe. It's an organization for the less magically inclined. The Arcanum—"

But the biddies wouldn't drop it. "Never heard of that one, either," the first one said. "Are you're *sure* you're a witch? You don't look like one."

I breathed deeply, praying for patience. "I'm not a witch. I'm a wizard. There's a difference."

The second old woman frowned over her pince-nez. "You're…a man?"

With a sigh, I pulled out my wand, held it above my head, and whispered, "*Light.*"

The chandelier bulbs exploded, each burning with a brilliant white flame, and the Circle members shrieked and covered their heads as the glass fell to the carpet. "A wizard," I said over their cries, "is a person gifted with a certain ability to manipulate magic to his—or *her*—own ends. A witch is a wizard who isn't very good at it. And while I'm sure you think you're using magic, I can almost guarantee that you aren't." I lowered my wand and spun in a slow circle, and each chair rose and fell on an invisible wave. "I'm Fringe because my father was a witch," I continued while they stared at me, ashen-faced. "The rest of my family is Arcanum. And no, we don't go to your conclaves." I gestured at the buffet table, and a hamburger flew across the room to land in my outstretched hand. Taking a bite, I chewed and waited until the Circle straightened themselves out and fell silent. "You play at magic," I said, waving over a plate on which to put my dinner. "We live and die by it. Now, will you help us?"

The others turned as one to the high priestess, who found her shaky legs and stood. "That…uh…you…"

I put the plate on the coffee table beside the ceremonial candles and stuffed my wand back into my trousers, then showed her my empty hands. "Look, I'm not here to intimidate you, but I am what I say I am. We generally do without the robes and chanting, that's all, so sorry for any confusion. Ehm…" I started to rub my neck, then remembered the sunburn and yanked my hand away at the twinge of pain. "Stuart speaks highly of you," I said, attempting to placate them through flattery. "Our idea of magic is different to yours, but in this case, I think we're on the same side. You'd agree with me that genocide is a problem, yes?"

She blinked slowly, then seemed to remember how her voice worked. "You…you need to go."

"Come again?"

"Go. You. We can't help you."

I stared at her, as shocked as she'd been moments before. "But…Franky said—"

"*Go!*" she screeched, then began waving her hands in front of her and shouting in high, mispronounced Latin.

Stuart rose and pushed past her. "That's a protective spell," he muttered as he joined me in the middle of the room. "One of mine, actually. I think this may be our cue."

We sat in the Wigginses' driveway until their SUV pulled up beside our van. "We'll go," I told them before they could do anything that would necessitate a loss of clothing.

"Just let us get our things, and we'll be off."

But Julia shook her head. "I don't know what's gotten into the high priestess, but we told you that you could stay here, and that offer's at least good for the night. Come on in."

We trooped after her, letting Tony bring up the rear. When we'd gathered in the warm kitchen, which still smelled like enchiladas, I took in the Wiginses' stiff posture and moved a few steps away from them. "We didn't come to hurt you," I said. "And we won't stay where we're not wanted, especially if it's going to cause problems for you. Tomorrow morning, we'll leave with Stuart. Will that work?"

Julia nodded, but Tony cleared his throat. "That…what you did tonight, with your wand, that…how…"

"It's a talent, and I can't teach you to do that. You're welcome to try," I added, pulling my wand free, and extended the handle to Tony. "Give it a go. You won't hurt anything."

Tentatively, his fingers curled around the wand, and he gave it a proper flick. When nothing happened, he frowned and tried again, making a more exaggerated motion that time. "Nothing," he muttered, and passed it back to me.

I held the wand still and whispered a few words to focus my thoughts. When I felt power begin to flow, I aimed at the stove and lifted the kettle from the range. The Wiginses backed away in fright, but I floated the kettle to the tap, filled it, returned it to its burner, and turned on the gas. As the flame blossomed, I lowered the wand and turned to them. "Where do you keep your tea?" Julia pointed to a cupboard, and I walked over and pulled out the box by hand, my point having been made. "I could do with a cuppa. Anyone else?"

I nursed my third cup of tea while Amy hunted online for

pictures of the various documents Stuart would need for his new life. While Tony offered up his Social Security card as a model, I also had to fabricate a birth certificate and driver's license. Stuart, who was born in California and theoretically knew what his papers should look like, was able to choose the proper images among the pictures Amy provided, and I whipped up the forgeries by midnight, plus a faked high school transcript. The fact that the man had no real educational credentials, no bank account, and no credit couldn't be helped. I gave Stuart half of the faerie-made cash, and I carefully copied a few thousand dollars to replenish our stores while Julia looked on with faint disapproval.

With our meager packing completed, we crashed in the guest rooms, none of us eager for another long day in the van. I snuggled between the crisp sheets and sighed, trying to relax myself to sleep. Just as my thoughts began to drift toward the surreal, the wards outside blared to life, and I jumped up with a shriek.

Weeks on the run had taught me to sleep in sweats, so at least I was decent when I slammed open the front door and ran out with my wand sparking. Around the property, the ward system flashed crimson against the black desert night, a strobing fence with a correspondingly loud alarm. As I squinted into the darkness, I spotted the cause: Jim the DJ, who stood just inside the ward line with his empty hands raised. "Nice work!" he yelled over the siren. "Would you mind cutting it off?"

I waited until the others had joined me on the porch before silencing the wards, though I gave them a static glow to illuminate the yard. "What are you doing here?" Tony asked, pushing his way to the front. "It's two in the freaking morning, man, what's going on?"

I said a silent prayer of gratitude that our hosts had the presence of mind to throw on silk kimonos before coming out to face the intruder.

With his hands spread, Jim slowly crunched up the

driveway. "I need help. Thought I should ask your guests before you run them out of town."

"What sort of help?" said Seamus.

"The sort that needs a real wizard's touch. No offense, guys," he added, glancing at the Wiginses. "A gate into the Gray Lands opened three days ago, not far from here. I can't close it by myself. Not really my forte. Anyone want to pitch in, help a brother out?"

My eyebrows rose. "*You're* a wizard?"

He smirked in the wards' light. "Got the wand and everything. Here, want to—"

I caught a bright flash out of the corner of my eye, and Jim's thought ended in a squeak. Turning, I saw that Seamus held a ball of blue fire in each palm, which he bounced up and down as he slid in front of me. "Keep your hands where we can see them, mate, that's it. Bring them back in front of you, nice and slow." Jim did as he was told, and Seamus nodded. "All right, now, on your knees."

"What?" he protested. "Why?"

"Because nothing good ever came from anyone caught sneaking into a place in the middle of the night," I said, stepping out from behind Seamus. "And I don't trust you. On your knees."

To my right, I heard the unmistakable sound of a shotgun racking, and I wheeled about to find Amy with the weapon raised and trained on Jim.

If magical threats didn't do the trick, the mundane approach seemed to convince him. He knelt and locked his hands behind his head, and I hurried down the drive to disarm him. The wand I found in his waistband was thick and heavily carved, more akin to a rod than a typical wand, and set with thin bands of quartz. I held it toward the porch and nodded, and Seamus's fireballs disappeared.

"You can get up," I told Jim, who trembled as he found his footing. "Now, you're going to tell us who you're working for and why you're here, or you're not going to see the sunrise. Your choice."

He swallowed hard and brushed off his jeans. "I could ask you the same thing. There aren't any wizards in the Fringe, and what the *hell* was that?" he demanded, pointing at Seamus.

"Well, *this* wizard happens to be Fringe, and Seamus is with me. Talk."

Jim hesitated, saw that Amy's gun was still pointed at his head, and decided to cooperate. "Ever heard of the Minor Arcanum?"

"No."

"Good. That's the way we like it. The less those assholes in Montana know about us, the better." He paused to consider my expression. "So...okay if I come in?"

I didn't know who was twitchiest: Seamus, whose new nervous tic was calling fireballs into existence, Jim, who sat across the room and watched him, or the Wigginses, who stood in the corner and gawked. Only Amy seemed serene as she perched on the recliner in her pink nightgown, cradling her loaded shotgun in her lap.

"We're separatists, more or less," said Jim. "There's been talk of getting together with the Fringe, but in all honesty, we don't want to deal with the bureaucracy. You find a lot of loners out here." He looked around the room, saw that death wasn't imminent, and continued. "Know much about the Arcanum's demographics?"

"In what sense?" I asked.

"Racial breakdown. Wizards pop up at a fairly consistent rate across the board—have you ever taken a good look at the Arcanum's makeup?" I shook my head, and he shrugged. "Well, whatever, you're British. I imagine it's pretty white in your neck of the woods. But anyway, if you actually run the numbers, you'll see that the percentage of Native wizards in there is low. Most of us want nothing to do with the Arcanum."

Seamus frowned and extinguished his latest fireball. "You're…"

"Diné. Navajo. Three-quarters, I mean—my dad's mom was white." Jim shifted in his chair and turned to me. "Long story short, the Minor Arcanum is an independent group. More like a confederacy, really. We don't want trouble with the Arcanum, so we try to fly under their radar."

Even as a Fringer, I'd inherited some of my father's Arcanum sensibilities, and the notion of ungoverned wizards made me anxious. One purpose of the organization was to keep rogues from messing up the system—after all, no one wanted to be the idiot who inadvertently revealed real magic to the mundane world. A self-governing "confederacy" of wizards, presumably wizards without proper educations, would raise the Arcanum's hackles, and rightly so. But if the Arcanum's new leaders were murdering witches, what would they do to wizards who told them to kindly bugger off?

"Understood," I replied. "What were you saying about a gate?"

Jim grimaced. "I've got a dark magic detection system—it's an antique, but it works. Went off three days ago, and I tracked the anomaly out into the desert. You can ride to it, but you need four-wheel drive," he explained. "It's a new gate into the Gray Lands, maybe twenty miles west of here. I've been keeping tabs on it as much as I can, and I don't think anything's come through yet, but it needs patching, pronto. Can you help me?"

I shook my head. "You won't have to worry for long. The Arcanum monitors the gate situation—"

"*Monitored.* Past tense."

"I'm sorry?"

"Yup. We track them, too, at least around here. When one opens, the Montana crew's always out in a couple of days, but not lately. There've been two other gates since

April, and we had to patch both of them. Of course," he muttered, "if what I heard tonight is accurate, the Arcanum's priorities may have changed. I guess stopping the monster invasion falls somewhere below burning the witches now, huh?"

"Wouldn't surprise me." I mulled this over, trying to calculate the odds of seeing unfriendly wizards in town in the near future. "You really don't think they're coming?"

"Not if recent history's any indication." Jim spread his hands and shrugged. "Look, I know you've got your own problems, but a gate's bad news for us all, especially if the bulk of the folks with firepower aren't going to lift a finger. I can't do this alone, and I can't exactly go to the Circle for help."

I cut my eyes to our silent hosts. "Dare I ask why you're wasting your time in the Circle, anyway?"

"Reconnaissance," he said with an embarrassed smile at the Wigginses. "Trying to keep the mundies out of trouble. I didn't think it would ever actually *help* me, but hey, it brought you out here." He paused. "You believe me, right? I'm not Arcanum, I'm not here to hurt you, I just need help with the gate."

I gave him a long, hard look, then turned to Seamus, who barely nodded.

"Amy, love, point the gun elsewhere," I said with a sigh, then tossed Jim's wand back to him. "I believe you when you say you're not Arcanum because no self-respecting member would carry *that*. What's with the flourishes?"

He caught the wand one-handed and rotated it for our inspection. "Arcanum buries the active bits in the core. We put them on the outside and add the channels to boost."

At that, Amy cocked her head and rose, leaving her shotgun on the rug. "Can I see?" Jim handed her the wand, and she held it to the light as she examined the construction. "Sure, it's functional," she concluded, passing it back to him, "but a core would be more stable and less likely to get damaged."

He smirked. "Arcanum rhetoric."

"Thaumaturgics 101, plus common sense," she retorted. "What crafter thought that was a good idea?"

Jim stiffened and stuffed the wand back into his waistband. "*This* crafter. I made it myself five years ago—"

"But you're a wizard, right? Shoot, no wonder the wand's crappy. Sorry," she quickly added, seeing his expression change, "that was rude of me. It's not *crappy*, but it could be so much better."

"Sure," he muttered. "If you're Arcanum and you've got crafters everywhere, then you can be picky and do core work. But for the rest of us, you make do with what you have."

"You need a crafter?"

He snorted. "Who doesn't? Know of one?"

"Hi." Amy raised her hand and grinned as his jaw dropped. "Witch-blood here. My kit's in my bedroom— want to try a few wands? I brought some spares with me."

Before Jim could jump out of his seat, I raised my hand to stop him. "I have a proposition. We help you with your wand situation, and you give us a place to crash for a few days. Fair?"

Jim made a face. "You can stay with me, but I live in a two-bedroom apartment. It'll be tight."

"Still better than the van," said Seamus, and made a shooing motion at Amy. "Go on, get your sticks. Let's see the fireworks."

Twenty minutes later, Jim was lovingly flicking a proper phoenix blood wand, one of two that Amy had brought along, and the Wigginses were sitting in the kitchen in front of the twin shots of tequila Stuart had poured them. "Believe me, I know it's a lot to take in," said Stuart, putting the bottle back in its cupboard. "It'll all be a little better if you slug that."

I joined Amy in her bedroom as she repacked her wares. "Beautiful work on that one," I said, handing her a bundle of hollowed shafts.

"One of my mom's," she replied with a sad smile. "I don't have the materials for another core like that, so if you run across any phoenixes, let me know." She slotted the last bags and bottles into a padded suitcase, latched it, and slid it back into her duffel. "He's definitely a wizard, but he's not as strong as you. Could have used a unicorn— maybe not a full unicorn, but at least a composite—but he seemed so opposed to trying one that I didn't push him."

"No one likes to be told he's below average."

"Sure, but let's not let pride stand in the way of survival." With a trio of clicks, Amy fastened the bag's reinforcing straps and put it back on the floor. "Here's the thing, Miss Hannah: I know what I am, and I deal with it. He shouldn't be so reluctant to admit that he might need a little extra help."

"You—"

"I'm a witch-blood of witch-bloods." She hopped onto the edge of the bed and looked up at me. "Good at magical arts and crafts, crummy at actual magic. All my life, I've been around witches and wizards and faeries, and I've seen what y'all can do. I can't, so I find strength elsewhere."

"What do you mean?"

Amy's mouth twitched. "My dad didn't just teach me to shoot straight so we could take hunting trips. He taught my mom, too. Didn't save them in the end, but at least it let them sleep better thinking they could defend themselves."

I slid onto the bed beside her and gave Amy a hug. "You have a rare gift," I said, patting her back. "It's valuable, love. Maybe it doesn't let you throw lightning, but it's a precious thing."

"Easy for y'all to say," she murmured, but she didn't pull away from me. "Aiden and I talked about it.

Everything about it sucks. He's witch-blooded, too, you know?"

"Maybe on a technicality…"

"Yeah, but he *gets* it." She sat up and squeezed my hand when I released her. "I know that what Stuart and his friends do is nonsense, but I also kind of know why they do it. If there were any chance at all that the chanting and potions and stuff worked, I'd be right there with them."

"I'm sorry, Amy."

She nodded, but before she could continue, Jim appeared in the doorway and knocked for attention. "Hey…about that gate…"

"Right," I sighed, and rose to follow him into the den. "I've not done this before, so if you could give me a few pointers before we drive out, that would be great."

Jim turned to me with a strange look on his face, a blend of guilt and panic. "I haven't, either. A few of our guys did the other two patches, but I'm closest this time, and—"

"And you've no idea what you're doing," I finished, motioning Seamus into our huddle. "This will be tricky. Seamie, any ideas?"

He stared at me incredulously. "There was nothing about gates in Val's crash course."

"Crash course?" Jim asked.

We ignored him. "Toula didn't cover it, either," I said. "Think we should ring them?"

"Rather than get ourselves killed? Probably not a bad idea." He jogged to his bedroom and quickly returned with his mobile. "What time do you suppose it is over there? We were basically synchronized when we were in Virginia, so…"

I tried to recall how many time zones we had crossed. "They're probably a couple of hours ahead, but I think it's still early. May as well try—all they can do is tell us to phone later, right?"

Seamus raised an eyebrow. "I imagine they could do

more than *that*, but let's try them anyway. Maybe they're early risers."

He scrolled through the preloaded contacts list, found one, and flipped the phone's speaker on. After a few rings, the line clicked, and I heard Val's slightly groggy voice: "Seamus?"

"I'm sorry to bother you—"

"It's no bother. What's wrong?"

He held the mobile out in the middle of our little circle. "I'm here with Badger and this wizard called Jim. He's trying to close a gate."

"Gate?" Val asked, perking. "What sort of gate?"

Seamus looked at me and shrugged, and I picked up the conversation. "He says he's found a new gate into the Gray Lands, and he needs to patch it because the Arcanum has dropped the ball. None of us knows what we're doing. Any tips?"

I couldn't be certain, but from the sudden tenor of his muttering, I assume Val's speech had veered toward the profane. "This may be beyond your skill," he finally said, "and I do not have any particular advice for *you*, Badger. I have never closed one of those gates—"

"Colin has."

We turned to Stuart, who had left the Wigginses in the kitchen with their Mexican nightcaps and was hurrying to join us. "Val? It's Stuart," he said, raising his voice for clarity. "I've seen Colin do it. That mess in Rigby—"

"Yes, of course," Val interrupted. "Forgive me, I had just gone to bed. Night shift…"

Having come home from work one too many times at dawn, Seamus and I flinched in sympathy. "Really sorry about this," he said. "Should we call back?"

"No, no, boy." I heard shuffling, then the sound of a door opening and slamming shut. "Coileán can be roused. A moment."

Jim's brow creased as we listened to the ambient noise on the other end of the line. "Who's that?" he whispered.

"My uncle," said Seamus.

"Oh. Fringe?"

"Not exactly."

Two minutes later, I heard muffled voices, and then Coileán came on. "Okay, *who* is trying to close a gate?" he said, sounding froggy with sleep.

"Sorry for the wakeup call," Seamus began, "but—"

"Never mind that. Details, kid. And Val, could you get Toula, please?"

"It's Seamus, me, and this other wizard we've just met," I explained. "He's young, but Amy's fit him with a decent wand—"

"Where'd you find another wizard?"

"He says he's part of something called the Minor Arcanum. Ever heard of it?"

"No, I thought that was the point of the Great War. Shit, that puts a wrinkle into things, doesn't it? Is he close?"

"He's listening," I replied.

"Ah. All right, wizard kid," said Coileán, "got a name?"

"Uh…Jim," he mumbled uncertainly. "Who are—"

"They can explain later. Why are you in charge of this gate project? Do you have any idea how to close one?"

"Well, um…not exactly. That's why I asked them for help."

Coileán sighed. "Patching gates is high-level work. Anyone can throw a patch together and slap it on, but making it stick is another matter entirely. You're trying to mend a hole in the realm itself, and holes like that don't want to close prematurely. Particularly not stabilized gates."

"I watched all of you open and close gates," Seamus interjected. "Didn't look that difficult."

"One," said Coileán, "those were intra-realm gates of short duration, and they're inherently unstable. Two, if I opened a gate to you right now and then tried to close it, I'd be enchanting a patch in a magic-heavy environment, and it would stick. The hole would heal quickly because that patch would be saturated by magic on one side. What you're trying to do is harder by several magnitudes of difficulty."

Seamus looked at me blankly, then back at the phone in his hand. "Could you possibly dumb that down?"

"Sorry," he said through a yawn. "Let's take this to basics. Enchantment and spellcraft are built off of magic, yes?"

"Yes."

"Did you notice that the concentration of magic over here is much greater than it is on your end?"

"Yeah…"

"It's inherently easier to do anything involving magic here because magic is so abundant. When you open a gate from Faerie, there's an outflow of magic—it diffuses down a gradient, I suppose."

From the corner of my eye, I saw Jim take a slow step away from the circle.

"So when you construct a patch between the realms," Coileán continued, unaware of Jim's sudden trepidation, "it's constantly being fed by that magic outflow, and the hole closes in a matter of seconds. The area might be a little weak for a while, but the hole itself is gone. Do you follow?"

Seamus nodded along. "Sure, but—"

"Hold that thought," I interrupted. "Stuart, get Jim a chair, won't you?"

"Everything all right?" Coileán asked as a door slammed in the background. "Hey, Toula. The fuzz are trying to close a Gray Lands gate, and I'm explaining why they're probably going to fail."

"The hell?" Toula muttered. "Badger, I thought the goal was to stay alive over there."

"Working on it," I replied. "Though apparently, no one has any faith in us…"

"It's nothing personal," said Coileán. "You're trying to

push a boulder uphill. As I was saying, when you close a gate into Faerie, you've got magic on your side. But when you do that with a gate into the Gray Lands, you're trying to enchant—"

"Or cast," said Toula.

"*Or cast* against an outflow of dark magic. You do know what that is, yes?"

"Of course," I said. Seamus shook his head, and I covered the phone to quickly whisper, "Easiest way to think of it is anti-magic. If you've got a lot of dark magic, you *haven't* got a lot of the useable stuff, and spells fall apart."

"Oh," he muttered as I unblocked the phone. "So if we try to plug that gate—"

"The patch will degrade before the hole closes, probably sooner rather than later," Coileán finished. "I tried it once when I was quite a bit older than you and actually had a handle on what I was doing, and it still fell apart. But look, this may not be so bad. Gates *happen*. The borders between the realms fluctuate, and there are weak points. I mean, there's almost always a gate into the Gray Lands somewhere in the Bermuda Triangle, no matter how quickly the Arcanum finds the holes. It's a thin spot, like the elbow on a sweater. But a gate here and there isn't the end of the world."

"Yes, but we're talking about a gate twenty miles from civilization," I countered. "We're in New Mexico, and it's not particularly populated out here, but still. Correct me if I'm wrong, but isn't this the kind of thing the Arcanum usually handles?"

"She's right," said Toula. "That's way too short a radius to leave it alone. Acceptable safe range is fifty miles in all directions."

"How do they do it, then?" Coileán asked. "I only made a patch hold by opening another gate into Faerie and letting the streams butt against each other."

"I know, I was there. And if you have massive amounts

of power *and* magic at your disposal—*ahem*—then you can be wasteful with it. For the rest of us, the trick is to trap magic within the spell itself. You construct the matrix to plug the hole, but you build in little pockets of raw magic. It takes a practiced wizard to pull off, and a big enough spell will drain all of the magic in the area for a few days, but a patch like that can close a gate within an hour."

"If we work together," I began, "maybe come up with a hybrid construction…"

Toula laughed in disbelief. "*Hybrid?* Badger, do you have any idea how much work it takes to make spellcraft and enchantment play together without going *boom?* You have to know what you're doing, and that's not something I can teach you over the phone. I'm sorry, guys, I don't mean to be a downer, but I don't see this working."

"Damn it," Seamus muttered, and held his mobile closer. "What would you suggest, then?"

"Avoidance?" said Coileán. "You're not ready to rumble, kid. And by the way, what are you doing in New Mexico? Aiden said something about a meeting?"

"The situation is still in flux, and…ehm…" He glanced at Jim, who had paled and appeared to be on the verge of wetting himself. "We've got a slight problem here. Explain later?"

"Sure. Bye. Don't be stupid," he replied, and the line went dead.

Seamus slid the phone into the pocket of his sweatpants and frowned at Jim. "Okay there, mate?"

The DJ swallowed hard and cut his eyes to me as he pointed at my partner. "That…*that's*…"

I let him stammer for a moment, then nodded and crossed my arms. "That's Detective Inspector Malone, and if you know what's good for you, you'll get over it."

"But that's—"

"Part of this package deal."

"That's a faerie!"

From the kitchen came the sudden sound of chairs

scraping against the tile. "Fairy? *Where?*" Julia cried as she ran into the den, clutching her kimono closed and looking about wildly. "Did the little thing fly away? Stuart, did you see it? I could get some sugar water…"

Seamus covered his face and sighed. "Was there any more tequila?"

CHAPTER 13

"If it helps, remember that I'm just a cop with a metal allergy."

Jim shot a glance at the rearview mirror. "Right. And those harmless little fireballs you've been making all morning?"

"Okay, a metal allergy and a party trick. I'm no threat to you. There's a reason Badger's the one sitting up front."

Jim's well-worn Expedition bounced along over the rutted dirt track, heading through the scrublands and into the mountains. Gripping the wheel and gritting his teeth, Jim stared out at the headlights' path. "Yeah. She's up here so I can keep an eye on you."

Seamus grunted and tucked himself against the door as Jim hit another pothole. "What, you think I can't incinerate you from back here? It's the one thing I can do reliably well."

"No one is incinerating anyone," I interjected, and turned to scowl at Seamus. "Can't we get along, boys?"

"Yeah, seriously," said Amy, who rode behind me with three of her favorite firearms. "Give him a break, Mr. Jim."

"You expect me to overlook the fact that I was just sitting in on a conference call to friggin' *Faerie*?" he demanded.

"If it helps," I said, "Toula was an assistant to the grand magus until recently."

"I don't care if she's the queen of England. That was the Ironhand on the phone, wasn't it?"

I didn't deny it. "They're sheltering the Fringe right now, and he's relatively pleasant in person."

"So who's *he*, then?" said Jim, jabbing his thumb toward the second row. "Muscle? Babysitter?"

"My partner. Slow down, you're losing the Wigginses."

The following SUV, a city model whose shocks had surely never seen such abuse, was dragging, and Jim braked to give Tony time to close the distance. We'd encouraged the mundanes to remain at the house—there was no sense in dragging all seven of us out into the desert in the middle of the night—but our hosts wouldn't be dissuaded. I sent Stuart with them to keep them in check and out of the line of fire, but we couldn't very well leave them behind in the wilderness.

"What do you mean, 'partner'?" Jim asked. "You're *working* with one of them?"

"I was working with Seamus when you were still in nappies," I snapped, "and you can drop that tone any time now."

"We both started in the Durham Constabulary," Seamus offered. "Went through training together."

Beside me, Jim was still struggling. "But…why the hell would a faerie become a *cop*? That doesn't make sense."

"Let me put it like this," said Seamus. "I've been with one police department or another since I was twenty-one. I've known about this 'faerie' thing for a week. So can we all move past this and focus on the hole in the fabric of reality instead?"

Jim frowned as he considered that. "A week?"

"A week. Maybe eight or nine days by now, but no longer." He clung to the door handle as the vehicle hit another rough patch. "I'm sure this is all a massive letdown to Tony and Julia. They've had a bad evening."

While Seamus had knocked back a quick shot of Patrón, Stuart had taken the overly excited Wigginses aside and explained why his fairy book would never see the light of day. I felt for them—it must have been difficult to spend your life hoping to spot magical, intelligent butterflies and end up with a sleep-deprived cop in sweatpants—but their disappointment couldn't be helped. They were seeing real magic for the first time, no matter how non-sparkly it was. Given that they'd been subjected to this unexpected reeducation all night, I wasn't surprised that they'd insisted on accompanying us to the gate.

Even with Toula and Coileán predicting utter failure, Seamus and I decided that we couldn't very well look away and pretend the gate didn't exist. Neither could Jim...but that didn't mean he had to be happy about the seating arrangements in his Ford.

"I just don't see what you're doing here, though," said Jim, looking back at Seamus in the mirror. "She's a wizard—"

"She's the best friend I've ever had, and the entire fucking Arcanum wants her dead. What would you do? Promise to write?" Seamus shook his head in disgust. "I may not have this magic thing perfected, but I can bloody well shoot straight. Speaking of which," he said, turning to Amy, "could you spare a loaner? I still need ammo for mine."

"Oh, sure," she chirped. "Want the Remington or the Glock?"

"Pistol, please." He took it with gloved hands, turned on the reading light, and examined the weapon. "Fairly new? How many rounds?"

"Ten, and it was my fifteenth birthday present. Daddy thought I was ready for a semi-automatic."

"I'll take care of it," he promised, and Amy passed him a box of cartridges.

Jim tracked their movements with occasional glances away from the road. "How's that better than fireballs, again?"

"Never said it was," Seamus murmured. "But I've qualified on pistol for some time. You did hear me when I said I've known about the other thing for a week, right?"

"Oh, yes, that other little *thing*, meaning—"

"Exactly. Drop it."

Even in the near darkness of the car, I could see Jim's eyes narrow. "What are you so—"

"If you woke tomorrow and someone told you that the reason you throw people into walls and set them on fire when you're angry is that you're some sort of superpowered immortal with an uncontrolled trigger, how would you handle it?"

"I still don't get how you didn't *know*."

"Because I didn't tell him, okay?" I cut in. "Now can we talk about something else, please? Like what we're going to do about this gate?"

Jim, imbued with the wisdom of youth, wouldn't take the hint. "You had to know something was wrong—"

"Of course I knew something was fucking wrong!" Seamus exploded. "I even ran out on my family and my fiancée because I didn't want to kill them. All right? Any other burning questions?"

When I turned around, I found him with teeth clenched, glowering at the back of Jim's headrest. "Hey. Hey, Seamie, look at me," I said, and took his hand. He squeezed back hard enough to make me wince, but at least he wasn't casting death glares in our driver's direction anymore. "You're here now," I soothed. "That's what counts."

"I still don't know how to control it—"

"You're doing fine, love. Just fine. Worry about the gun and leave the fireworks to me, okay?"

He stared at me, and as the rage faded, it revealed something raw and scabrous that made his face twitch. "I'm so sorry, Badge..."

"I'm sorry, too," I said, clinging to him as we bounced over the rough terrain. "Put it aside. We'll look at the damn gate, and then we'll get a few more hours of sleep. Yeah? Sound like a plan?"

He hesitated, poised to speak, then nodded and

released me. I turned back to the front, cut my eyes to Jim, and muttered, "Not another word until we get there."

"Short trip. It's around that corner." He smirked and pointed to the bend in the trail.

"Then let's have a moment of silence."

It might have been dark, but Jim saw the look in my eyes and shut his mouth.

As we approached the turn, he slowed and pulled onto the side of the road, then cut his lights and waited while the Wigginses caught up. "We should go on foot from here," he said, turning off the ignition.

"Element of surprise?" Seamus asked, sliding out of the back. "Going to sneak up on the hole, are we?"

Jim disembarked with a grunt. "One, genius, concentrated dark magic has the same effect as concentrated magic on delicate electronics, and I don't want to risk frying the onboard computer in this baby. She's out of warranty. And two, we have no way of knowing what's lurking near the gate. No reason to announce ourselves."

"Granted, but you're also abandoning your getaway vehicle." With a shrug, Seamus filled his pockets with ammunition and left the box in the second row. "Right, this is your circus. Lead on."

The following SUV arrived and disgorged its passengers, and Jim waited until they'd joined our clump. "Okay, then," he said, giving Amy and her assorted weaponry a wide berth. "We do this silently. Stay close until we can see that it's clear. I'm going to at least try to patch it—you in, Hannah?" I nodded, and he pulled his wand out of his waistband. "Julia, Tony, Stuart…stay out of the way. Let's go."

We followed him, keeping off the gravel road in favor of the quieter dirt. Though the wand in my hand was a comfort, the night unnerved me—the wilderness was too quiet, the sky too clear, and the temperature had fallen to an uncomfortable chill. Seamus, too, seemed to be on edge, and though he carried his borrowed pistol with the barrel aimed at the ground, his arms were tense, and his eyes darted about.

Jim paused in front of a stony hillock, then pointed to the road, which curved around and seemed to begin a descent. "In the valley," he whispered. "A few hundred yards that—"

A scream rent the night—high and piercing, and far too close to human to be ignored. Jim froze in his tracks, but Seamus and I ran in wordless agreement, sprinting around the bend to take in the valley below. By the time we rounded the hillock, he'd raised his gun, and I had thrown together a fairly solid shield ahead of us both, a defense against whatever might be waiting below.

We came to a halt and stared down at the valley, and the hairs on the back of my neck rose. There was the gate—a hole darker than its surroundings, perhaps a few meters in diameter, hovering just above the valley floor. A flood of dark magic spewed forth from the opening, black against the ambient background magic, pooling near the gate and dissipating into the wilderness. And *there*, just on our side of the border, was a roaring campfire.

I squinted into the distance, trying to make sense of the figures moving around it. A couple seemed to be standing, and perhaps another few were squatting nearby. "How many do you count?"

"Four," said Seamus. "Something big on the ground by the fire, but I can't make it out. And there's something standing back there…horses?"

Jim panted behind us, then swore when he got a look at the scene. "The fuck are those?" he muttered.

"Bipedal," I replied, and glanced over my shoulder at the sound of footsteps to see Amy approach with her favorite rifle primed. "I think. But without light, at this distance…"

Seamus lowered his gun and extended one hand. "I've got an idea. Don't know if this will work, but it might scare them away."

"Wait—" Jim began, but it was too late.

Like a rocket, a ball of white light flew from Seamus's palm, rising high above the valley. One of the figures around the fire looked up and pointed, and the others stared at the sky as the ball climbed to the top of its parabola.

"Shield your eyes," Seamus cautioned just before the ball detonated.

A makeshift flash grenade, I realized, covering my ears as the bang echoed through the night. The bright light lingered long enough to illuminate the things around the fire below—definitely four, all wearing black robes or cloaks, plus four animals that looked somewhat like emaciated black horses. "The devil *are* they?" I said as their angry cries rose from the valley.

Jim's dark eyes were wide. "I don't know, man, but they look kind of like Nazgûl…"

As their shouts crescendoed, the creatures ran for their mounts and flung themselves upon their thin backs, then turned in our direction and began to gallop toward the road.

"Aw, shit," Jim yelled, "you pissed them off!"

Amy raised her rifle to her shoulder, and I readied my wand. "Seamie, flash-bang them again, closer to them if you can. Get it in their faces. Jim, if you're going to panic, go stand with the mundies."

Seamus did as I asked, and the second blast exploded a few meters in front of the oncoming pack. The mounts reared with screeching cries, and as their masters struggled to control them, I took my wand in both hands, scrunched my eyes closed, and summoned all the focus I could muster as I whispered, "*Boom.*"

My wand jerked with the force of the spell, and I opened my eyes in time to see a bolt of lightning arcing from the tip toward the riders. A breath later, it slammed into the first, then jumped to the second rider's horse.

Before it could hit the third, the rider jerked and fell, and I recognized the clap behind me as the sound of a rifle firing. Amy had taken a knee to my right and was lining up a second shot. "Two down, plus a horse," she said. "Keep shooting or let them retreat?"

"Shoot them, *shoot them!*" Jim cried, and finally remembering his wand, he sent a blast of fire after my lightning, which caught the fourth rider's robe.

I shot lightning again, but there was no need for a third bolt. By the time the smoke of Jim's conflagration cleared, Amy and Seamus had finished off the riders and their mounts, and we hurried into the valley for a closer look. Shaking and feeling slightly strung-out, I forwent the wand in favor of my mobile's built-in torch for safety reasons—I didn't trust myself to hold an illumination spell together at that moment.

Two of the riders were charred beyond recognition, and the third had taken a round through the face. The fourth, however, had been shot in the gut, giving me a decent idea of what we'd just killed. The creature was vaguely humanoid in a mummified sense, pale and painfully thin, its skin stretched just over the bones beneath. Its pronounced brow ridge intersected the short, knobby crest that bisected its hairless skull, running from the spine to the nose. The cheeks and forehead were streaked with blue and green lines, though whether they were its natural colors or tattoos, I couldn't tell. But in its death grimace, I could see a mouth of interlocking fangs— and the fresh blood on its chin wasn't from its own wounds.

Its hands were long and bony, four-fingered and tipped with bloodstained, claw-like nails. One held a wicked-looking hunting knife, while the other still clung to the reins of the twitching mount, which was, in fact, horse-like, if one overlooked the extra set of eyes, nearly fleshless body, black scales, and sharp teeth. Though burnt, the creature still struggled to rise, and Seamus dispatched it with a mercy shot to the head.

"Bloody hell," he whispered as we took in the corpses. "What do we do?"

A camera flash caught our attention, and we found Amy squatting beside the nearest rider with her mobile out. "I'm documenting them for research purposes," she explained, seeing our incredulous expressions. "For the database, if nothing else. I mean, you weren't planning on dragging these guys around with us until we get back to Faerie, were you?"

"No," I mumbled, and looked away. "Take your pictures, and we'll burn the corpses. Let's put the fire out—"

A moan from the campfire silenced me, and Seamus readied his pistol. I nodded and raised my wand, and together, we crossed the scrub until the dark shapes by the fire came into focus.

Even with my Fringe training, I hardly believed my eyes, and Seamus whistled as he stopped beside me. "Is that..."

"Centaur," I said, nodding to the nearer lump, which appeared to be a corpse. The rope-bound body was still, and the ragged chunks missing from the equine bits showed me all too clearly how it—well, *he*—had met his end. But the other captive was moving against its bonds, writhing in the dirt and groaning in pain, and I put my wand away. "What's that saying about my enemy's enemy?"

"Are you sure?" Seamus muttered.

"Not at all, but we can't just leave...*him*, yes," I said, circling the downed centaur. Definitely male."

Each pair of legs had been tied together, and the pairs had been locked in a tight hobble around a pole, rendering him unable to stand or run. His arms were bound behind his bloodied torso, wrapped with thick ropes to the elbow, and his torso was tied down to his front legs. His captors had knotted one rag over his eyes and gagged him with another. Avoiding the hooves, which looked sharp enough to do damage, I moved to his head and knelt beside him. "It's all right," I murmured. "I'm going to cut you loose. Be still."

His back bowed to escape my touch when I put my hand on his shoulder, and I retreated. "Slight complication," I said as Seamus joined me. "He can't understand us. If we free him, what do you suppose he'll do?"

He squatted by the centaur, whose double chests had begun to heave with his panicked gasps. "Val was able to put another language in my head. Can you do that?"

"I wouldn't know where to begin to construct a spell like that. What about you?"

"*Me?* I'm the novice here!"

"You've got a better chance of succeeding with that sort of enchantment than I do."

"But I don't know—"

"Seamie," I interrupted, "I'm no expert, but I can tell you that enchantment is a hell of a lot easier to intuit than spellcraft. We see both in the Fringe. Pit an untrained quarter-blood with some talent against an untrained witch, and the faerie's going to figure it out first. So think about how it felt when Val zapped you and try to replicate it."

He frowned with worry, but he reached for the centaur's head...then paused. "What if I screw this up and incinerate him?"

"I'm right here. Give it a try."

He hesitated a moment longer, swore under his breath, then mumbled, "Hold him steady, if you can." I braced my hands against the centaur's forehead and neck, and as he strained to shake me off, Seamus touched the creature's temple, closed his eyes, and whispered, "If this hurts, I'm really sorry."

The centaur cried out, then went limp under me and panted. Seamus and I withdrew a few paces, giving him room to breathe. When he seemed to calm to his previous level of terrified agitation, I approached again and cleared my throat. "Ehm...hello?"

He froze, and his head tilted toward me.

"Can you understand? Nod if you understand me." His head scraped against the dirt, and Seamus sighed in relief. "Fantastic," I said, and crouched beside the captive. "Listen, we're going to help you. Be still. Those things that were with you are dead. You've got nothing to fear from us."

"Were you going to try to magic the ropes off," said Amy as she joined us, "or would you like this?"

She offered me one of the riders' long knives, and I took it gratefully. "You should have stayed back," I chided.

"Eh, Stuart has it under control. Jim's hyperventilating, and the Wigginses threw up, so I figured I'd mosey this way. And *wow*, is that what I think it is?" she said, taking a closer look at the centaur. "I thought they were just a myth!"

"Another update for the database," I replied, and cut the ropes holding his torso and arms. He groaned in pain as he unbent and slowly pulled his arms apart, revealing the stripe of red hair down his spine, and I wondered how long he'd been bound. "It's all right, let me do the work," I told him, and cut off his blindfold and gag. He squinted at me as I pulled away the rags, and I smiled. "There, now. Worst is over. Let's see about the legs, eh?"

"Broken," he croaked. "The front, they hit..."

"Amy, love, see if there's any water in the cars," I said, and she ran back up the hill as I turned my attention to the hobble. The front-right leg *was* bent at an odd angle and caked with dried blood, and I grimaced as I began sawing through the ropes. "We'll splint it," I told him. "After we clean you up. Give me a moment—"

"My brother?"

"Sorry?"

"Brother," he rasped. "He...I heard him scream..."

"He's gone," said Seamus, kneeling beside us. "I'm so

sorry, but they got him before we could get them."

He closed his eyes and seemed to slump, and I worked as quickly as I could to cut the remaining bonds. "You're alive, and you're safe, and that's the important thing right now," I said. "But we need to see about your injuries, and we can't do that here." I severed the last rope and stood, then cupped my hands around my mouth and bellowed, "Jim! Get off your arse and get the truck down here!"

"Where are we taking him?" Seamus asked.

"Back to the ranch, and if the Wigginses know what's best, they won't put up a fuss. Be a dear and burn the bodies, won't you?"

While Seamus jogged away to cover up the evidence, I pulled the ropes off the centaur and watched him struggle to rise. "Weak," he mumbled after another failed attempt left him gasping in the dirt. "Arms are stiff."

"Rest. We're going to help you." When he looked up at me, I saw the fear lingering in his face. "I'm Hannah," I said, sitting cross-legged beside him. "Seamus is the one on body disposal, and the others should be here soon. We're going to take you to a safe place. Can you trust me?"

His eyes held mine for a long moment, and he sighed. "I have no choice, it seems." Gritting his teeth, he managed to raise his torso, but his attempt to put weight on the bad leg ended in an agonized yelp. Still, his eyes had adjusted to the firelight, and he turned as well as he could to see his surroundings. "Where am I? And what is *that*?" he asked pointing to the gate.

"Short answer, New Mexico. You've crossed out of the Gray Lands."

His expression clouded. "The what?"

"The Gray Lands. Back through that hole." When that generated no flicker of recognition, I said, "The world in which you live—what do you call it?"

"The world," he replied with a one-shouldered shrug. "There...is another?"

"At least two, actually. Ehm...your queen *is* Nath,

correct?"

He snarled at the name. "She calls herself a queen. She is not *ours*. We have no queen—"

"Easy, now," I said, coaxing him down as he tried yet again to stand. "Right, duly noted. No queen. But your people live in the same realm as Nath, yes?"

"Yes. Far from her kind, but..." He looked up at the starry night and blinked in surprise. "What are those lights above us?"

I looked over his head through the gate, but I saw nothing but an unmarred black sky on the other side. "I'll explain later. Do you know where your family might be? Someone who could take care of you while you heal?"

He shook his head so violently that his long hair whipped his face. "The raiders killed my family. All but my brother and me. They carried us on poles..." He gestured toward the fire, where I could make out a long stick among the flames. "Upside-down for days, blind. Hib and me, and all the rest—our mother and father, our sisters, their mates, Hib's mate, his son..." He paused, struggling as his eyes filled. "We heard the raiders devour them. One by one. We were the last ones left."

"My God," I murmured, "I'm so sorry."

He swiped his arm across his eyes, leaving a dirty streak on his cheek. "You will burn Hib, yes? He should not be eaten by scavengers."

"Of course. But is there no one left for you? Friends, neighbors, no one?"

His jaw tightened. "When a raiding pack comes, it does not come alone. Four took my family. I do not know how many others in our village were killed, but I heard screams, and I smelled blood."

We looked up as Seamus returned. "All right, then?" he asked.

"All right. Please burn the last body."

He cut his eyes to the centaur, who nodded, then flicked his fingers toward the corpse, turning it into a blue bonfire. "How's the patient?"

"Dehydrated, at the very least. He's been trying to stand, but with that leg…"

Seamus frowned in thought, then held out both hands to the centaur, who shied back and covered his face. "What's—"

"He's not going to burn you," I hastily explained.

"What? Oh, no, that's…no. Fuck. I'm sorry," Seamus mumbled. "No fire, promise. Let's get you off the ground."

Hesitantly, the centaur gripped Seamus's hands. "You are smaller than I am."

"I'm stronger than you think," he replied, digging in his heels. "Badger, can you roll him?"

"Badger?" he asked.

"I answer to a lot of things," I replied, and knelt by the middle of his back. "There's no way in hell that I can make you budge without magic, so hold on. This may feel strange."

I didn't need to use the wand to merely apply force. Tucking my fingers in the dirt underneath him, I flipped my palms upright and focused, channeling magic through my fingertips. With the amount of dark magic in the area, I struggled to start the spell, but it coalesced after a moment, and the centaur began to rise. He scrambled for the ground, letting Seamus hold him steady, then got his back legs under him and found his feet. When I brushed myself off, he was standing with his hands on Seamus's shoulders, balancing himself on three legs, and I saw just how badly he'd been beaten and scraped—and how painfully thin he was. "Well, you're not going anywhere in a hurry," I said, "but let's see if we can get you into the Expedition."

He watched with concern as the SUV neared in a cloud of dust. "What is—"

"Our ride," said Seamus, "nothing to worry about. And there's the other one," he added as the Wigginses' vehicle rounded the bend. "I hope everyone's stopped puking by now."

"You and me both," I muttered, and conjured up a smothering blanket of dirt for the campfire.

The Expedition pulled up beside us, and Jim jumped out, looking rather disheveled. "Is that a—"

"He needs medical attention," I interrupted. "Do your seats fold flat?"

"The third row…"

"Get it down. Ehm…" I looked up at the centaur, who still clung to Seamus as his weak legs wobbled. "This will be a very tight squeeze, and I'm sorry, but it's the best we can do for now. You'll have to curl up in there."

Jim hurriedly expanded the cargo bay, and the centaur made a face. "It will suffice. Can you—"

"Sure," said Seamus. Slowly, he starting walking backwards toward the waiting vehicle, and the centaur shakily followed in an awkward dance.

"You know, I *could* just float him," I offered after a few steps.

"Yeah, but where's the fun in that? Come on, you've got it," said Seamus, wincing as he took his partner's weight. "That's it, just a bit more, almost there…"

But the centaur's legs were wobbling badly, and I whipped out my wand as he began to list. A quick spell caught him before he could tumble, and Seamus released him while I levitated him into the SUV. He tucked his legs as well as he could, flicked his tail, and nodded when I broke the spell, settling his weight onto the rear axle. "It's not a long trip, I promise," I said as I reached for the back door. "And we'll ride with you."

He nodded, then seemed to reach a decision. "Kippit."

"Sorry?"

"I am Kippit. Kip," he offered. "And I will trust you, Hannah-Badger."

Before I could close the door, the Wigginses pulled up, and Julia leapt from their vehicle before it came to a full stop. "Oh, my *God*," she cried, catching sight of Kip, "is that—"

"This is your newest houseguest," I replied. "Hope you don't mind. You did say your home was rather private, did you not?"

Her jaw flapped open and closed for a few seconds, but she managed to nod.

"Wonderful." I slammed the back door and opened one to the second row. "We'll meet you there. Ah, Amy, splendid," I said as she darted out of the other SUV with a plastic water bottle. "Come with us, love. He must be parched."

The wards flared again as we drove back onto the property, and I waved them off with a groan. "Sorry, people, I'll fix those when it's properly light out. Still with us, Kip?"

He'd contorted his torso to face the front and clung to the second row's headrests to stabilize himself, but the centaur had seemed a bit green for the last few minutes. "Fine," he mumbled, though his face said otherwise.

"Right. Jim, park as close to the fence as you can. Amy, see to the gate, there's a dear." She jumped out while Jim cut the ignition, and I patted Kip's filthy arm. "We'll go into the garden. You need a scrubbing, but I don't know if you'll fit in the showers inside, and anyway, stairs sound like a bad idea. Okay?"

He nodded, and Seamus slipped out to open the back hatch. When everything was unlatched and the Wigginses were pulling in, I carefully maneuvered Kip out of the SUV and floated him into the garden, and Jim closed the gate behind us. Kip's eyes lit at the sight of the pool, and as I laid him on the artificial grass, I hastily warned him, "Don't drink that, it's salt water. Right," I said, looking around for a garden hose, "hydration. Could someone fill a bottle in the kitchen?"

"Wait," said Jim, "there's a sterilizer in my car. Use that

first."

"The water here is fine," Seamus protested.

But Jim shook his head. "Fine for *us*. We have no idea how our bacteria's going to affect him. It's a UV sterilizer, I take it camping all the time," he explained. "Easy. Amy, get a gallon or so, and I'll get the hardware."

While the befuddled Wigginses stood by, hopelessly at sea, Stuart found the switch for the patio lights, Seamus located the hose, and I pulled half a dozen beach towels from the linen closet and a bottle of cheap shampoo from the master bath. Kip seemed uncertain as I approached with my arms full, and he looked even less pleased as Seamus filled the first bucket. "I'm sorry, I know you're exhausted," I told him, "but you're cut to pieces, and we need to clean the wounds. The water's going to be cold, and there's no help for it without considerable magic, and I'm sure this will sting a little—"

"I will trust you," he said, and closed his eyes as he braced for the shock of the water.

Having never been a horse girl, I was uncertain of the best way to go about bathing Kip, but Seamus leapt straight in with the hose, and Kip bore the assault without complaint. While Amy worked on his drinking water, Seamus handed him a flannel and the shampoo, then pulled a bench over and stood on it to let Kip shower under the spray. Kip moved stiffly with his injuries, and I ended up scrubbing the dirt and blood from his matted hair while he prodded at the lacerations across his arms and chest. When the wet ordeal was over, he slung a towel around his shoulders and gulped down three bottles of water while suffering the indignity of letting Seamus and me pat the rest of him dry and apply antibacterial spray.

The sun was rising by the time we finished, and Tony wordlessly made tea and toast as Seamus, Jim, and I puzzled over Kip's broken leg. We immobilized it with packing tape and scrap wood from the garage workshop, but that wouldn't guarantee a clean mend, and we all knew it. Finally, Jim sighed, retrieved his mobile from his car, and scrolled for a number. "She's going to kill me," he muttered, "but we're out of good options."

Kip jerked and turned to him in alarm. "Who is going to kill you? Why?"

"No one. Figure of speech." He held the phone up and waited until it connected. "Hi, Carey, it's...Yeah, I know, I'm sorry. Emergency situation. I went out with the Humane Society tonight on a horse rescue, and this guy's in bad shape. Banged up all to hell, underfed, and I think he's got a broken leg. Is there any way you...Yeah? You do? Oh, that would be great. They're stabilizing him here, but I could load him and have him up to you by lunch, if that would work...Yep. Thanks, sis. Owe ya."

He dropped the phone into his pocket and cracked his knuckles. "My big sister is one heck of a wizard *and* a large-animal vet," he told us. "She and her husband have a ranch northeast of Albuquerque. They rehab abused horses all the time."

Kip frowned. "What is a horse?"

"You'll see when we get there. She'll be able to fix that leg," he replied, and snatched another piece of toast from the platter Julia carried out. "So now I've got to find a trailer on short notice. There's a rental place north of town, but it's Sunday, so I've got to call in a favor. Be back as soon as I've got something."

Jim let himself out, while Kip, his thirst momentarily slaked, finally noticed the bread. Half a loaf later, exhausted, he stretched out by the pool and slept in the warming sun, and the rest of us stumbled inside for a nap. "Thank you," I told Julia as I headed for my room. "Are you going to be okay?"

Her face was drawn, and the shadows beneath her eyes spoke of the long night, but she nodded. "There's a centaur in my backyard and a faerie in my guest room, and Amy's got more guns than a militiaman. And you killed some monsters in the mountains tonight. I...haven't really processed this yet, but…for now…"

I patted her shoulder. "Save the processing for this afternoon, and we'll all be better for it."

CHAPTER 14

Having seen what was truly out there, our hosts begged Stuart not to go, but he wouldn't be dissuaded. "Your high priestess can do as she likes," he told them while he loaded the last of his belongings into the van. "I serve the Light. And if all I can do is watch and wait in Montana, then that's what I'll do." He slid the door closed and nodded to the rest of us, who had come to see him off. "Take care. Safe travels to you, and I...hope to see you again."

Seamus shook his hand. "Don't be a hero, mate."

I followed suit, and Amy gave him a tight hug. "You be careful, okay, Mr. Stuart? You've got my number, right?"

Stuart gave her a lopsided grin and patted his pocket. "I'll be in touch. And the name's Quentin Galloway, remember? No more Stuart."

She hesitated, then threw herself at him again, squeezing so hard that he sucked for air, and came away with moist cheeks. "Please be careful."

He wiped off the worst of her tears with his thumb, then climbed into the van and rumbled off, heading north. We watched until he disappeared, me with my arm around Amy, who continued to wave until the last.

As she sniffled her way back to her room to prepare for departure, Tony caught my elbow and pulled me aside. "Is she okay? I didn't know they were close."

I waited until Amy's door latched, then murmured, "I think I may have mentioned that the Arcanum murdered her parents not three months ago. Stuart's master plan is to spy on them from their own backyard, and he's as much a wizard as you are. If she *didn't* have issues right now, I'd be concerned."

Tony stared at her bedroom door. "Then do you think it's wise to let her have all those guns?"

"No, but I'm not 'letting' her have anything. And considering what's in the mountains, you'd be wise to pick up a pistol or two. Don't they sell them at the grocery store or the chemist or something around here?"

"It's not *quite* that unregulated, but there's a pawn shop off of I-25 that keeps a decent stock. I'll, uh…I'll take Julia by after you leave. Maybe see if someone can give us a quick lesson."

"Keep it clean," said Seamus, who had overheard us as he passed by. "Hold it with both hands, and don't point it at anyone unless you mean to kill him. Simple." He frowned, bemused. "I thought you people learned this sort of thing in primary school."

"We're pacifists," Tony explained.

"Mm. Well, whatever else might come through that gate probably isn't, so do yourself a favor and avoid it."

"We'll be back as soon as we can to try to close it," I added, and Seamus nodded. "Maybe Jim's sister knows what she's doing. But in the meantime, give it a wide berth, yeah?"

Tony shuddered. "No problem there."

Leaving the others to finish their packing, I went into the garden to dismantle my wards—a far easier task than building them—and check on Kip. He slept soundly in a patch of bright sunlight, resting with his head on his crooked arm, and one hoof twitched as he dreamed. In full daylight, I could better appreciate the extent of his wounds, leaving me wishing I'd been taught a few decent healing techniques. And the centaur was *young*, I realized— his darkly tanned face was unlined under all the grime and gore. I estimated he was perhaps twenty, somewhere between Amy and Jim, but then again, there was no way of knowing for sure without asking him. After all, Seamus didn't look his years, and my knowledge of Gray Lands natives was next to nil.

As I turned to go back inside, Jim drove up to the house and opened the gate. The rattling sound I'd heard over the engine of his Expedition was a single-horse trailer, a rusty box on wheels with a pair of barred windows for ventilation. "Well done," I said as he jumped out. "How long is this drive?"

"About four hours. Take 25 up past Las Vegas—not the one with the casinos, the one on the Gallinas, not nearly as exciting—and then it's a short drive on the back roads. Decent pastureland comes at a premium in this state." He shrugged. "But hey, it's home."

"Is it in a…ehm…" I hesitated, suddenly unsure of the propriety of my enquiry.

But Jim seemed to divine where I was going. "On a reservation? No. Wrong end of the state. We've never lived in the Navajo Nation."

"Oh. Sorry, I…I wasn't…"

He patted my shoulder. "If you want to ask dumb questions about Native issues, just ask me, okay? I can't speak for everyone, but I'll do my best. Better to ask than to piss off the wrong people."

"I don't want to cause offense…"

"Unless you're bringing a war bonnet to Coachella, we'll probably be fine. Bilagáana morons." He snorted, rolling his eyes. "But no, my family's been in the Albuquerque area for a while. I know, like, a dozen words of Navajo. My mom was fluent," he added as we headed into the house, "but she thought Spanish would be more useful to me in the long run."

I paused, hearing the implications of that offhanded statement. "I'm sorry, did you lose your mother—"

"And my dad. I was nine." Jim closed the door and shrugged. "They owned a jewelry store. Robbed at gunpoint one night when they stayed late to do inventory. Their wands were in the back room. You can probably see why I don't go anywhere without mine."

"Good God," I muttered. "You and your sister—"

"Oh, Carey's seventeen years older. She and Zeb practically raised me." He folded his arms self-consciously. "You, uh…are you close to your parents?"

"I was. Arcanum murdered them at Easter."

"*Shit*, I forgot, I'm sorry—"

"No worries." I looked out into the garden, where Kip continued to doze, then back at Jim. "Well, I suppose we can have a little group bereavement session in the car, and Seamus can nod along in the proper places. Shall we load up?"

The trailer wasn't glamorous, but if that bothered Kip, he didn't let on. Jim had put straw down to pad the metal floor, and Kip let me levitate him into the box after a moment's protest. "I can walk with help," he said when my wand came out. "You do not need to exert yourself."

"But Jim's loading bags, and I *really* don't want to get too close to the trailer," said Seamus, "so let's do this Badger's way."

Kip mulled this over while I floated him through the garden gate. "Are you afraid of it?" he finally asked Seamus as I steered him inside, trying not to bump his bad leg against the walls.

"Iron. I've got a nasty allergy to the metal," he explained. "Burns on contact. Best to avoid it if possible."

The centaur touched the inside wall without incident, then turned his attention to me, puzzled. "And you? Are you also affected?"

"No." I leaned against the trailer to demonstrate. "Most of us aren't. I'm native to this realm—one of the few with some magical ability, but I'm human. So is Jim," I said, pointing to him as he and Amy emerged with her bagged arsenal. "Seamus…"

"Go on," Seamus said when I hesitated, and shrugged.

"I don't think *he's* Arcanum."

"True. One of Seamus's parents was fae," I explained to Kip. "From a third realm—"

"And I'm rubbish with everyday objects," he concluded. "You don't have any sort of, ehm…talent, do you?"

"Like that?" said Kip, pointing to my wand. "No, none. There are some with the gift—the ones who follow Nath—but not among my people."

"Ah. How old are you, anyway? You're grown?"

"Nineteen seasons. I will be a man at the next."

Seamus's brow furrowed. "Seasons?"

Kip thought for a moment. "This speech, it is strange…imperfect. The season is when the villages gather. The young are born, the ones who have come of age choose mates…there is a festival to celebrate the"—he paused, reddening—"the *getting* of children. This is not your custom, I presume?"

"Not at all, but I get the picture. Your people are mortal, then?"

"Aren't most?"

"You know, until recently, I thought all of them were." He glanced away as Jim slammed the back door. "Ready?"

"Ready," said Jim, dusting off his hands as he came around the trailer. "I'll do my best to keep it smooth," he told Kip, "and the road shouldn't be bad once we hit the Interstate, but if you start feeling sick back here…uh…"

"I'll call," said Amy, slipping past me with her backpack. "Hi! Got a little extra room in there?" Kip slid himself closer to the back, and she tucked herself into the corner by the door. "All set," she said, smiling up at me. "Close us in, Miss Hannah."

"Whoa, now, wait a second," said Jim, "that's not safe—"

"I'll be *fine*. Sheesh, I grew up in the back of a pickup truck," Amy scoffed. "And you want Kip to ride the whole way by himself? That's no fun." She cut her eyes to him and grinned. "You don't mind sharing space with a girl, do you? I brought snacks."

The SUV was quiet until we reached I-25, at which point Jim flipped off the pop station and said, "Is it just me, or are we at all concerned about leaving Annie Oakley back there?"

I opened my eyes—the morning sun was a marvelous sedative with the front seat reclined—and yawned. "No, I shouldn't think so. If you brake hard, she'll slam into Kip first."

"Kip was what I was concerned about. We don't know the guy—"

"We don't know you, either," Seamus pointed out from the second row, which he'd taken for his new bed.

"At least I'm *human*."

"So? Loads of humans are shite. I've arrested my share."

Jim grunted and glared in the mirror. "Look, this is going to sound nerdy, but I had a real thing for mythology as a kid. You know the kind of stuff centaurs got up to?"

He sighed. "Enlighten me."

"They were wild. Tried to kidnap women all over the place."

"Are we talking about the same body of myths that gave us Zeus seducing someone as a swan? Because we all know how plausible that is."

"I'm just suggesting that there might be a grain of truth to the stories," said Jim. "And if so, we've left Amy alone with him in a locked trailer."

"He's got a broken leg—"

"He's hung like a *horse*, man!"

While my companions bickered, I rang up Amy's mobile and relaxed at her cheery greeting. "Hello, love," I said, shushing the men. "Everything okay back there?"

"Oh, sure," she replied, pleasant as ever. "I was telling

Kip about the Arcanum mess."

"*That's* a delightful conversation. Call us if you need anything."

"Will do. Bye!"

I hung up and looked at Jim. "She sounds fine. Let's proceed on the assumption that he's not a raving sex maniac, shall we?"

Jim appeared to be unconvinced, but he dropped the matter.

"Anyway," I said, tucking one hand behind my neck as I made myself more comfortable, "we have more important things to discuss."

"Such as?"

"Well, for starters, why the Minor Arcanum?"

"Why not? It's helpful to know a few other wizards in times of trouble—"

"No, that's not what I meant. Why not just merge with the Arcanum? Seems like it would be simpler in the long run—assuming you don't mind slaughtering witches, but that's been a more recent development."

Jim focused on the road, which was ours but for a few speeding cars. "I realize you're British, Hannah, but you have some notion of how well Natives have gotten along with whites over the years, don't you? Trail of Tears? The Indian Wars? The BIA? It hasn't exactly been smooth."

"The Minor Arcanum is entirely Native, then?"

"No, but many of us have opted to trust that group over the grand magus and his cronies."

"Probably wise, all things considered," Seamus quipped from behind us.

"We've got a few in the Arcanum, but they're a minority," Jim continued. "The rest of us want nothing to do with that group. No need to get involved in Arcanum politics."

"Who teaches you, then?" I asked. "If you're not getting a formal Arcanum education…"

"We learn the same way we always have: one on one.

Carey taught me, and our parents taught her. And Zeb pitched in," he allowed. "He's not a great wizard, but he taught me a lot. There's more to life than magic, yeah?"

"What about medicine men?" asked Seamus.

Jim cut his eyes to the mirror. "What about them?"

"They're all wizards, then? Or are they more like your illustrious Circle of the Sun?"

He sighed deeply. "Okay, one, no. And two, be glad you asked me that and not my sister. Zeb's cousin is a hataalii, and they'd take a question like that *really* personally."

Seamus sat up, perplexed. "Sorry, I just thought—"

"Magic and medicine are entirely different. Medicine…it's spiritual, see. Hataalii train and learn chants, they learn herbs, they learn sandpainting and the ceremonies. They heal people. Fight witchcraft."

"But—"

"Not our sort of magic," he explained. "Curses." Jim hesitated, frowning at a passing Greyhound, then quietly said, "Like, the things the yee naaldlooshii do. It's bad and it's powerful, but there's a spiritual dimension that's absent from our magic." He drummed his fingers on the steering wheel as he thought. "Saying magic and medicine are one and the same would be like…I don't know, like saying all Catholic priests are wizards because they turn wine and crackers into flesh. Get it?"

"I…think so," said Seamus.

"Medicine is good. It's natural," Jim continued. "It *heals*. What we do with wands and shit…that's not normal. It's not medicine, but it's not really witchcraft—it's both and neither, you know? Which is all a long way of saying that Zeb's cousin has no idea what we can do, and that's for the best. Guess that's one thing we have in common with you guys," he added with a weak laugh. "Mundanes are mundanes, no matter their skin color."

Second Chance Ranch wasn't huge, as Jim had informed us, but at nearly five hundred acres of rolling grassland, it was large enough to impress me. A paved access road led us through a tidy wooden fence and down to a cluster of buildings, a modest two-story brick house and what appeared to my untrained eye to be a pair of barns. The road terminated in a wide asphalt circle, and Jim parked beside a similar SUV and a pair of battered white pickup trucks. Radiating from the apparent car park were rutted dirt paths leading into the fenced pastures and toward the metal shed that protected a trio of horse trailers.

Our driver, who'd seemed to become increasingly nervous as we neared the property, took a deep breath. "All right, here we go," he said, and rolled down the window as he honked the horn. "Carey!" he called toward the barns. "It's Jim! Got the patient!"

A woman's voice floated back from the nearer barn: "Hey, Goober! Offload him and bring him on back! I'm setting up the X-ray gear!"

"Okay, then," he muttered, and climbed down. Seamus and I followed suit, gratefully stretching our legs after the long drive, and Jim unlatched the trailer door. "Everyone okay in here?" he asked the occupants.

Kip looked slightly guilty as he handed Amy her pink mobile. "Fine. Have we arrived?"

"Oh yeah, all's well. I've been kicking his butt at Yahtzee for the last hour," said Amy as she unfolded herself and stood. "Could use a Coke, if you've got one."

"Carey keeps the barn fridge stocked. Uh…" He watched as Kip struggled to find his footing. "How far can you walk, do you think? We could do this with wands…"

But Seamus nudged him aside and stepped into the trailer. "Come on," he said, holding out his hands. "It's not far. I'll help you."

Kip's brow creased. "You said you cannot—"

"As long as I don't touch anything, I'll be okay. Here, now, on your feet."

Jim and I moved back as Seamus slowly guided Kip onto the ground. "It's really no trouble to levitate—" I began, but Seamus shook his head.

"That's all a bit much, isn't it?" Kip nodded vehemently, and Seamus met my eyes. "We'll do this the old-fashioned way. Make everyone happy." Turning to look over his shoulder at the path, he waited as Kip hobbled into position, then started walking backwards toward the barn. "You're doing fine, mate. Nice and easy, that's the trick. I'm not going to let you fall…"

As they shuffled toward the barn, Jim and I took up positions on either side of Kip as reinforcements, while Amy closed the car and trailer, then caught up with us. "Oh, look!" she exclaimed, pointing to the trampled dirt in front of the barn. "A calico! My neighbors used to have one of those. Hi, sweetie…"

She ran off to make friends with the cat, and Seamus paused and glanced at Jim. "What, ehm…what does your sister keep around here in terms of animals?"

"Twenty-odd horses, last I checked," he replied. "Maybe half a dozen cats, and she had a border collie until last winter. Why—aww, *shit*," he muttered as the cat bowed up and began hissing at our nearing party. "Faerie. Forgot about that…"

From inside the barn came the sound of snorting and frantic neighing, and Seamus rolled his eyes. "Terrific. Haven't been here five minutes, and I've already traumatized your sister's menagerie."

"It's not just you," I said. "Anything out of Faerie *or* the Gray Lands sets them off, remember?"

He looked back at Kip and shrugged. "Well, then, I guess we're fucked, aren't we?"

As the cacophony escalated, a short woman with a dark, stylish bob emerged from the barn—Jim's sister, I had to assume, given the facial resemblance. She couldn't have been much taller than Amy, but while the girl was waiflike, Carey had a more athletic build. She'd rolled the sleeves of her oversized chambray work shirt past her elbows, and something told me that not all of the splotches on her black boots were mere mud. "Is everything okay out there?" she called, squinting into the sun as she shaded her eyes. "Sorry about the noise, something's spooked—*the hell?*"

Jim ran to the front of the pack and held up his hands. "I can explain—"

Her mouth hung slack for an instant before she shook her head and focused on her little brother. "You said you had an injured *horse!*"

"He's...half..."

"*That* is not a horse!" She jabbed her finger at Kip, who had paused in the middle of the path. "That's...that's a..."

"Hello," I said in my best police voice as she sputtered, and extended my hand. "Hannah Parsons, I'm with the Fringe."

Even if her mind was spinning, her manners kicked in, and she shook my hand with a firm grip. "Carey Jones. Uh..."

"Dr. Jones, a gate into the Gray Lands has opened near Jim. We went there early this morning to try to close it, and we found a group of...ehm..."

"Raiders," Amy offered.

"Raiders, thank you. They'd kidnapped Kip here and were going to eat him. The gate's still open, unfortunately, but we couldn't just leave the poor fellow in the desert to die. We think his leg's broken—he can't put any weight on it. Your brother says you're a veterinarian?"

"Uh..." She goggled at Kip, who looked back at her uncertainly, then seemed to remember herself. "Yes. Yes...I specialize in equine rehabilitation, but..."

"Could you at least check our splint? I'm rubbish at anything more complicated than a plaster."

Hesitantly, she slid past us to take a look at our handiwork, then pursed her lips and strode toward Kip. "The splint looks solid, but there's too much tape to see clearly. Is the break in the upper or lower leg, do you think?"

"Upper," said Kip, briefly releasing Seamus to point to a spot on the splint. "They hit it with a rock."

She stopped in her tracks, wide-eyed, and stared up at him. "You understand me?"

He nodded, then dipped his head toward Seamus. "He did something. I do not know how, but yes, I understand."

Carey edged forward to take a look at Seamus's face. "And you…are *also* Fringe?"

"I'm with her," he replied, glancing toward me.

"He's Fringe," Jim interjected before Carey could probe. "So's Blondie over there with…uh…" He pointed to the roof of the barn, where the calico had sought shelter, then at Amy, who stood below making kissy noises to lure it off of the shingles. "It's been a long day already," he said apologetically. "I would have warned you, Carey, but I didn't want to take a chance on you saying no…"

She waved it off and scowled at Kip's leg. "All right," she said after a moment's contemplation, "here's how we're going to do this. Jim, get Zeb—he's making chili— and you two empty this barn. You're going to have to harness them all and lead them one by one since we've got a centaur and a faerie out here."

Seamus stiffened. "How—"

"The few Fringers I've encountered are upfront about it, and I've yet to meet a lesser blood who can transmit language. That's straight-up enchantment. But I'll deal with you later. *Go*," she ordered, shooing Jim toward the house. "I can't get him X-rayed until the barn's clear. Move it!"

Jim jogged toward the house, and Carey shook her head. "Now, as for you," she continued, turning to me, "what's your story?"

"I'm a coordinator. My father was a witch—turns out I'm a wizard after all," I replied, and showed her my wand. "Amy over there made this. We understand that you may be in need of a crafter."

The vet's face lit up. "Are you kidding? We haven't had a real one in our ranks in twenty years—"

"Tend to Kip and let us camp here for a couple of days, and Amy will do whatever you need."

She gave me a hard look, then muttered, "I heard a nasty little rumor that the Arcanum had killed half the Fringe."

"They may have. We're here to find the survivors."

"*Are* there any?"

"I don't know, but someone has to search for them." Carey's expression softened, and I pressed my advantage. "Jim told us a little about the Minor Arcanum. I wouldn't ask for your help if I didn't need it. Faerie has done all they can, but their hands are tied here. Our entire search party is the three of us—"

"Four."

Startled, I looked at Kip, who nodded. "Four," he repeated. "Amy told me of your mission. I will help you."

"No, that's not—"

"You saved my life. A life debt cannot go unanswered. When this useless thing has healed," he said, shifting his broken leg, "I will help you. Amy has extra weapons, and my aim is true."

"Well, then, there you have it," I told Carey. "The rescue team for the Fringe is up to one undertrained wizard, one *severely* undertrained faerie, a crafter who's doing well for being all of sixteen, and one lame centaur."

"That's pathetic," she muttered.

"Yeah. So how about it?"

Before she could answer, the front door to the house slammed open, and a tall, muscular man in jeans and a ratty Garth Brooks T-shirt ran onto the porch. "Holy *hell*," he exclaimed, "is that what I think it is?"

Seamus and Kip exchanged a look, and Kip raised one hand. "Hello. You are Zeb?"

"Just get the horses, dear," Carey called back to him, then sighed and rubbed her shoulder. "Let's take this one thing at a time, okay? He needs doctoring."

Within half an hour, Jim and Zeb had managed to coax the terrified horses out of their stalls and into the second barn. "We mostly use that one for foaling," Carey explained while we waited. "Bigger stalls. But if we make a few of the mares double up for today, it won't be the end of the world."

It was Kip's turn to gawk as he watched the transfers being led up the trail between the barns. "What *are* they?" he finally asked Carey.

"Horses," she replied. "Zeb and I rescue and rehabilitate."

"But…" He shook his head in horrified bewilderment. "What happened to them?"

"That, uh…that's the way they come around here. Good for riding, liable to throw you and bolt if a plastic bag blows the wrong way. Or maybe those are just mine," she said, folding her arms. "We don't exactly breed champions. Most of the pregnant mares we get are either too old to be safely pregnant or they're abuse cases, and those aren't mutually exclusive categories. So I know a thing or two about broken bones," she told Kip, "and with sufficient rest and a solid healing spell, you should be back on all four feet in a day or two. Clear?" she called across the yard, and Zeb flashed his thumb. "Great. Okay, this way, watch your step."

As Seamus led Kip toward the barn, Kip asked, "Where might I find your latrine?"

Carey looked back at him, perplexed. "Latrine?"

"Is that the wrong word? Where do you, um…"

"Oh. *Oh,*" she mumbled. "Well…uh…the horses normally go wherever they want in the stalls. We muck them out, and I'll get the boys to clean one up for you while we do X-rays, but…"

Kip's face twisted in disgust. "There is no latrine,

then?"

"None like you're thinking of," Seamus interjected, "and nothing you'll be able to reach without walking. Would a bucket do you for now?"

"I suppose." He stumbled on a loose clod, and Seamus grunted as he took his weight. "Sorry, I did not see—"

"Don't worry, you're almost there," said Carey from the barn door. She stood to one side while Seamus and Kip wobbled in, then directed them to a spot in the middle of the barn, where she had placed an apparatus on a hay bale to give it height. "Have a seat, then put your foot here," she told Kip, patting another bale. He lowered his back legs and propped the injured one as directed, and Carey set to work with a knife, peeling the tape away. "*Ouch*," she said when she saw the damage. "That's got to be painful."

"It is not pleasant."

"I bet not. This'll help." Reaching under her shirt, she pulled a pyrite-banded wand free and began muttering as she aimed it at Kip's leg.

Within a minute, the spell was complete, and he marveled as he twitched his injured limb. "The pain is gone."

"Good. Now hold still unless you want to make it worse." With practiced motions, she began rearranging her setup to accommodate Kip. "Pain's useful in that it tells us something's wrong. I dulled yours, but I haven't fixed the problem. Here, you're going to hold this over your front," she said, handing him a lead apron. "Anyone else who's staying here needs to suit up, too."

A few minutes later, as Jim crafted a spell to clean out the largest of the abandoned stalls, Carey put the X-rays on a folding light-up board and showed us the damage. "The good news is that what I'm seeing here is remarkably close to equine anatomy," she began. "The bad is that a broken leg is a *beast* to fix. This break looks pretty clean, but there's a good deal of swelling, and I'm going to reclean and sew up a few of those lacerations. You'll barely feel it," she assured Kip. "And once I've done that and splinted the leg, then *you*, buddy, are going on bed rest."

He looked into the stall, which was now empty but for warped pine floorboards. "In...there?"

"I'm sorry, but it's the best I can do. There's no way you'll fit comfortably in the house."

While Carey readied her equipment for the splinting and sewing, I took a glance in the stall, grimaced, and grabbed my wand. "Describe your preferred bedding, Kip."

"Low, not more than knee-high," he replied. "Long and wide enough to lie on the side. We stuff the beds with dried grass, typically."

"Mm. Let's see how you like memory foam." I called the construction to the front of my thoughts, envisioning it as well as I could, and focused. When the surge left my wand, a puffy mattress filled half the stall, and I tapped the wand against my knuckles. "Blankets? Pillows?"

He seemed relieved by my work. "Please."

I made the bed, then produced an antique-style wash basin and pitcher, a stack of flannels and towels, an oversized ceiling fan, and, at a loss for a better idea, a covered bucket. Throwing some sheers around the barred windows of the stall and a sturdy rug on the floor, I stepped back, examined the result, and turned to Carey. "Have you got an extra television?"

"Tack room. There's a dorm fridge in there, too—take the power strip and the extension cord on the workbench. I don't have cable out here, but at least it's something to look at."

Kip twitched as she splinted his leg. "I appreciate this, Carey..."

"No problem. I'm not used to having a patient actually cooperate. Or tell me where it hurts," she added, chuckling. "I think I could get used to this. All right, that's the brace. Hold tight, and I'll get the disinfectant and a razor."

"Razor?" he echoed.

"Some of that hair's got to come off. I need to see just how deep those cuts go."

As Carey set about her work, Zeb corralled Seamus, Amy, and me and led us to the house. "We don't have a ton of space," he said, showing us two adjacent guest rooms, "and since Jim's here, that's one room down. Can you make do with these?"

The three of us looked at each other, appraising the situation and the pair of queen-sized beds, and I finally broke the silence. "This is lovely, thank you. Amy, why don't you take that one? It's closer to the bath. Seamie, ehm…"

He hesitated. "I could probably camp with Kip, if you—"

"Don't be ridiculous. There's loads of room."

Amy's expression was all too knowing for my taste, but she said not a word as she headed outside to retrieve her bags.

By the time Carey had finished stitching Kip back together and casting an intricate healing spell around his broken leg, Zeb deemed the chili passable, and we decided to picnic in the barn. Kip had no previous conception of chili, but he downed three bowls and half a tray of cornbread by the end of lunch, drank a liter of purified water, and settled in on his new bed, full, comfortable, and unfazed by the fact that he was sporting the patchiest shave of his life.

Carey handed him the remote control and a bottle of water, fresh from Jim's equipment. "You need to sleep," she said, casting a bedside table and lamp into existence as a last touch. "The more you can rest, the better that spell will work. Tomorrow, depending on how you're feeling, we'll see about getting you a bath."

"I bathed this morning," he replied, collapsing onto his

side.

She turned the fan up and drew a blanket over him, then thickened the curtains until they blocked the afternoon sun. "Your tail's nothing but mats, you've got dried mud in your hooves, and that mop could use at least a trim," she said, ruffling his hair. He swatted her hand away but smiled, and she laughed to herself. "You're as bad as my brother. Be glad you chose radio, Goober," she said, and shooed Jim out of the barn. As Kip's eyes began to close, she put a walkie-talkie on the side table and pointed to a button. "If you need anything, press that. We'll be around."

Kip was already breathing slowly when I followed Carey out into the midday heat. "Thank you," I murmured. "I mean it."

"You saw what came out of that barn, right? I don't turn away patients," she replied, then pointed to the house. "Come with me, Hannah. If you want to find your missing Fringers, I have an idea."

CHAPTER 15

Carey led me through the house, past the rooms where Jim, Amy, and Seamus had crashed for a much-needed post-lunch nap, and down into her furnished basement. The room was warm and comfortable, filled with overstuffed couches and decorated with woven hangings, and the massive television mounted on one wall gave me a good idea of the basement's purpose. "This is Zeb's man-cave," said Carey, answering my unspoken question, "except when I need it. We have a time-sharing agreement, I guess you'd say," she added with a grin. "Have a seat."

I fell onto one of the couches, sinking deep into the cushion, and Carey plopped down beside me. "When you said 'undertrained wizard,' what exactly did you mean?" she began.

Mulling over my education, I replied, "My father was a witch, and he did what he could, but he wasn't Arcanum-trained. I, ehm…" My stomach clenched, and I paused until I'd calmed. "I never showed much promise because my dear grandparents tricked me into using a shadow alder wand."

Carey covered her mouth. "*Seriously?*"

"You've heard of it?"

She snorted. "You know how a measles blanket works, yeah?"

"Sure…"

"Well, wands have never been big in the Native wizard communities. We use them now, but wandless casting is the standard—you're not really a wizard if you can't do it without the stick." She folded her arms and shifted against the throw pillows. "European wizards, on the other hand, have been on a wand kick for centuries. So around the time of the Civil War, some of the white wizards with whom they'd been trading sold a group of Native wizards shadow alder wands on the promise that they would make them more powerful. Gave them to the children as a goodwill gesture." Carey smiled bitterly. "It took a few years for the Natives to figure out why magic was failing them—they'd seen how well wands worked for the whites, right?—but someone experimented with a wand long enough to realize the wood was the problem. That shit's poison."

There didn't seem to be a proper response to that story. "I'm...so sorry—"

"Not your fault." She shrugged. "And if you grew up on a shadow alder, then it's not you who needs to be apologizing. So you were stunted and no one ever thought to train you, is that about it?"

"More or less. Dad taught me wand basics...I can ward, and I had a bit of a crash course last week, but I'm not magus material by any means." I chuckled to cover my embarrassment. "Any teenager in the silo could probably hand me my arse right now."

Carey studied me in silence, cocking her head while I tried not to squirm. I knew the trick too well from my line of work—people abhor uncomfortable silences, and if you wait long enough, almost any suspect will start filling the void. After a long moment, she said, "If you really have the talent, then your ignorance is curable. May I see something?"

I'd barely mumbled in agreement when she clasped her hands together, closed her eyes, whispered a word, and then pressed her palms toward me. Before I had time to shield, I was enveloped in a bright blue light, while a sound like a hundred wind chimes in a hurricane echoed around the room. Carey nodded and smiled, then twitched her finger to break the spell.

"What…" I began, rubbing my ears.

She seemed unfazed by the sonic attack. "Aural analysis. Yeah, you're a wizard—a strong one, too. I can work with that."

"Oh. That spell was much quieter when Toula did it," I muttered.

"Toula Pavli? She's Arcanum-trained, right?" I nodded, and Carey spread her hands. "They have their techniques, we have ours. Different spells. I know the one they prefer, but mine's easier."

"How do you know Toula?"

"I don't. I know *of* her," said Carey. "Just as I know of some of the local Fringe brass. We pay for information."

That surprised me. "Dark Company?"

"Bingo. There are only so many ways to stay on top of the competition while staying unnoticed, and occasionally, we go to the spymasters. But enough about that. You're trainable—not quite a blank slate, but close enough. I may be able to help you help yourself. Teach you how to find your missing comrades."

"I don't have the samples for a blood trace, and even if I did, traces are complicated—"

"Who said anything about a trace? Those things are gross, anyway." She stood and unkinked her back. "I've never liked casting around bodily fluids."

I frowned up at her. "If not a trace, then what?"

Carey began to pace in front of the darkened television. "Patience, Hannah. First, answer me this: what are the great magics?"

The last person to have asked me that question was my father, right around the time that I began wand training, and I heard an echo of his voice in my mind: *There are three great magics, love. Three things any top wizard can do…*

"Wandless casting," I recited, counting on my fingers, "gate creation, and transformation. The three great magics."

"That's an excellent Arcanum answer," she replied, pausing in her circuit to look at me. "And it's wrong. There are *four* great magics."

"Four?" I echoed, bemused. "I've only heard of three…"

"Because I would bet that everyone around you with any real training has gotten it from the Arcanum, right?" She shook her head and smirked. "There's a fourth, but it's difficult to master. And since the Arcanum would rather pretend that it doesn't exist than acknowledge that they don't have a lock on all things magical, it's not discussed in Arcanum circles." Pushing a stack of *Rolling Stone* back issues to one side, she took a seat on the coffee table in front of me. "Sleepwalking, we call it. Dreaming to locate. It takes focus and practice, and the techniques you use to learn it run counter to the Arcanum's preferred methods. Honestly, it takes a level of discipline that most wizards never attempt."

"Dreaming? As in…"

"You may need to actually sleep at first, but eventually, you figure out how to trance. Much quicker." She paused, considering my expression, then quietly said, "Sleepwalking started here in the Americas. It brought our people together, and then it almost destroyed us."

"How?"

Carey sighed and stared into space as she collected her thoughts. "Wizards have existed all over the world as far back as anyone knows. Maybe someone's got different intel over in Faerie, but until proven otherwise, we'll just say 'dawn of civilization' and be done with it. Anyway, the information we have shows that until the European expansion, most wizards lived among mundanes." Her mouth quirked into a half-smile. "Europeans started segregating themselves early. We don't know if it was for safety or convenience, but the practice took root there and spread. But as I was saying, wizards existed worldwide— they just weren't as concentrated, so we don't have the early records that Europe has. Our tradition goes back to around 400 or so, and most of that passed orally for centuries."

"No writing," I remarked.

"Exactly. Then again, the accounts across tribes are remarkably similar, so it looks like oral preservation worked. There are variations, of course—at least two dozen tribes can make plausible claims about the Mother—but the basic story remains the same."

"The Mother?"

"Her true name hasn't survived. She was the spiritual mother of American wizardry, but she's nameless. What else is new?" she said with a shrug. "As the story goes, she was the only wizard in her tribe—the only one for miles around—and she set out to find others of her kind. Going on foot wasn't an option since she didn't have any idea where she was headed, but she meditated about it until she made the breakthrough into sleepwalking. It's almost like lucid dreaming," Carey explained, "but she was able to expand her consciousness. And she found others out there in that liminal place.

"Language doesn't matter when you sleepwalk, so all of these scattered wizards, separated by distance and tribe and tongue, began to communicate. They shared a dream space in which they could tell each other of techniques, discoveries, threats, whatever. I mean, it wasn't perfect—sometimes they warned each other of impending attacks, and sometimes they kept their mouths shut—but more and more wizards taught each other how to sleepwalk. One would reach out to a sleeping novice, teach him how to do it while he dreamed, then wait until he learned how to do it for himself."

"How far did she reach?" I asked.

Carey smiled. "I don't know how far it went in the Mother's lifetime, but it's said the sleepwalkers eventually spread from coast to coast, Alaska to Argentina."

"Goodness."

"I mean, not everyone was on at once. I know wizards who can only sleepwalk from sleep, even with training, and expecting people on both sides of the continent to synchronize their sleep schedules was probably asking too much. But they did manage to communicate." Her mouth tightened. "And then they started reaching out. You know, if you sleep late enough on the West Coast, you can overlap with Hawai'i, Australia, the Pacific islands...Japan, if you're lucky. And if you sleep early enough on the East Coast, you can reach Europe and Africa.

"So suddenly, you had wizards worldwide who were sleepwalking and communicating, learning from each other, building a community beyond their communities. Then 1014 rolled around. Know what happened?"

Any witch with the most basic grasp of magical history had that date imprinted on his brain. "The Great War."

"Uh-huh. Europe's little foray into consolidation. Simon Magus and the Arcanum beat down the rival arcana within their hemisphere, then they moved south and east."

"Yeah, I know. Dad showed me the maps. Africa by 1060, Asia by 1062."

Carey's smile was icy. "Ever think about how they conquered the rest of the world?"

I flashed through the color-coded arrows of domination in my memory but drew a blank. "No, actually," I mumbled. "I suppose I'd assumed there wasn't an arcanum to quash over here."

"There wasn't," said Carey. "Remember, we didn't segregate ourselves in the Americas. Tribal loyalties were a hell of a lot more important than loyalty to some wizard half a world away. But Simon Magus was on a conquering spree, and when he'd done all the damage he could do in Eurasia and Africa, he turned his attention to Oceania and to us."

"He didn't come over—"

"Oh no, he didn't actually make the trip. He did it by sleepwalking." Carey paused and drummed her fingers on the tabletop while she thought. "There's no denying that Simon Magus was one of the greatest wizards who's ever lived. A genocidal conqueror, sure, but incredibly talented. Someone taught him to sleepwalk. And when he told all of the thousands of distant wizards here about the brave new world of Arcanum oversight, they declined to join his club. Big mistake. He was able to cast *within* the dream space— only wizard to have ever managed that—and one night, as wizards began coming in, he wiped them out in waves. They couldn't defend themselves, and he slaughtered them in their sleep."

"Jesus," I whispered, aghast.

Carey's smirk said it all. "Yeah. I wasn't entirely surprised to hear about recent events concerning the Fringe."

"I never even *heard* about—"

"You wouldn't have. It goes against the Arcanum's tidy narrative—'Here we are, the mighty champions of justice and order, bringing civilization to a chaotic world.' But Simon Magus didn't conquer us through might and justice—he murdered innocents to win a pissing contest against his own ego. But anyway, over the next few nights, as the survivors sleepwalked and realized what had happened, he was waiting for them. And faced with annihilation, they agreed to recognize the Arcanum as the supreme magical authority. In practice, a lot of that was lip service," she added, "but not all. They didn't have a choice."

"So once European expansion began…"

She chuckled drily. "Once they had boots on the ground, they had allegedly loyal wizards already in place. The Native wizards couldn't repel the colonists because the Arcanum forbade it. They also kept at least a few wizards in the dream space at all times, monitoring the Native wizards who tried to maintain contact with each other. We were helpless.

"So perhaps you can see why there aren't many of us in

the Arcanum. Our numbers rebounded after the Great War—it's just that the Arcanum leaves a bad taste in our mouths."

I nodded. "The Minor Arcanum, then—"

"Is a support network for wizards who don't give a fuck about what the silo thinks. No grand magus, no enforcers, just each other. And while the Arcanum has apparently gotten lazy and forgotten how to sleepwalk, we keep the tradition alive. Want to see a real wizard? Look for someone who's mastered all four of the great magics."

"Ah. And I'm to assume that I'm in the presence of a master, I suppose?"

"Well," said Carey, dusting invisible lint from her sleeve, "I don't like to brag…"

"You could teach me to sleepwalk, then?" I asked, leaning toward her. "If I did it properly, would I be able to find witches?"

"Witches, faeries, and everything in between," she replied. "It picks up on all practitioners if done correctly. You can narrow it, but for your purposes…yeah, it would work."

For the first time in days, I felt real hope bloom within me. "Hell, why not cut out the middleman? If you can sleepwalk and find our missing people, we could track them down!"

At that, however, Carey stiffened and shook her head. "I won't do it for you. I *can't*. If the Arcanum caught on and found me…I've got people to think about, too. I'm sorry, Hannah," she said, clasping my hands, "I can't take that risk. But I'll teach you to do it, if you're willing."

There was fear hiding under her surface, palpable fear, and I decided not to press my luck. "Whatever it takes," I told Carey, squeezing into her grip. "When do we begin?"

Regardless of whether one is a wizard or witch, training in the Arcanum mode begins with the same basics.

Somewhere between the time a child discovers that she has talent and the time that a wand is first put in her hand (and aimed in a forgiving direction), she starts to intuit focus, the ability to blank her thoughts, concentrate inward, and envision a clear picture of what she wants to make manifest. Depending on the spell at issue, this can go one of two ways: either she calls to mind what she wants to create or, when she's had practice, she imagines channels through which magic can flow and learns to link them into wards. Shielding is somewhere between the two, as a shield is basically a massive piece of active magic, often sloppy as a result of being built in the heat of the moment.

Carey's lessons took a different tack. This time, I wasn't focusing inward—I was to expand my focus and seek out other consciousnesses around me, a trick far easier said than done. I sat on the cushy couch as she directed, closed my eyes, stilled my breathing, and tried to meditate my way to success, but within moments, I was supremely aware of how noisy my breathing was, or of how my ankle itched, or of a hair that had fallen into my face.

And that, she explained when I continued to fail after a frustrating hour, was why novices were only able to sleepwalk after having first *slept*. "Have you ever tried to dream lucidly?" she asked while I walked about the basement to uncramp my legs. "You're dreaming, but you're aware that everything's a dream, and you can manipulate it. Yeah?"

"No," I muttered, stretching my hamstrings. "I've never bothered with dreams, to be honest."

"Well, then, I guess we have a starting place," she replied, and pointed to the staircase. "Come on, let's do some laps first."

"Laps?" I wilted immediately at the thought of the midday summer heat. "You...have a pool?"

"Nope. Head out back, and you'll see the training ring. It's fenced, you can't miss it. I'm going to lunge a horse, and you're going to run in circles, and you'll both be good and tired by dinner." She gave my ensemble a second glance and frowned. "You didn't pack shorts, did you?"

"Haven't got any," I said, following her upstairs.

"Make a pair, then. Running sneakers, too, and a shirt you don't mind soaking. It's been in the nineties all weekend." Carey waited as I shut the door behind us. "You aren't prone to heatstroke, are you?"

Even if one's primary role in the Job is to sit at the desk and take complaints, one is expected to maintain a certain level of fitness. For obvious reasons, British policing involves far fewer shootouts than its American counterpart, and the two best skills in one's arsenal are often the ability to diffuse a situation through talking and, that failing, the ability to take and throw a punch. In my prime, I could scrap with the best of them, and I was still fit for a woman on the downward slide to fifty—after all, a bloke on a bender who thinks you're the problem isn't going to cut you any slack for being a girl.

That said, Carey's outdoor cardio session was one of the worst afternoons I'd passed in years. As I plodded around the ring with sweat-plastered hair, dripping, panting, and wincing as my shirt chafed against my fading sunburn, she kept her attention on the young horse on the other end of her long line, who trotted in circles around her at her command. When the horse behaved, Carey would engage in a one-sided conversation with me, since I was often too exhausted to keep up my end. "He's just a yearling," she explained as the horse broke into a canter. "We rescued his mama, and she was pregnant when we got her. Should be able to sell him off in a few months, but he needs training before then. Sweet boy, though—hey. *Hey*, I'm over here, bud."

I'd learned the basics of riding—there were occasions in my line of work that called for the odd horse—but I'd never had to deal with one so young. "Going to breed him?" I managed.

"Nah. He's been gelded. I've already got a decent stallion on the property, and there's no sense in provoking—*left*, now, come on—provoking him, especially since I don't have papers on either of this guy's parents. But he's pretty, isn't he? And full of himself," she muttered, giving the line a tug. "Hey, do me a favor and remind me to keep my stallion out in the pasture, huh? I know the herd's going to avoid the barn anyway with Kip around, but I don't want to risk a territorial challenge from a confused horse. I've got a couple of mares in heat, and Dan is *mighty* particular about his ladies."

Apparently, Carey's master plan was to work the horse and me until we were both ready to drop. By four, the little horse was in a lather, and Carey allowed me to limp into the house for a shower. Seamus and Amy were still asleep, and so I bathed in peace, even taking care to rinse the sweat and grime from my necklace.

When I emerged, still red-faced but less odiferous, I found Jim lurking in the hall. "Heading back," he whispered as I straightened my towel turban. "Morning show hours are brutal. I'll keep an eye on the gate, but I wouldn't raise a stink if someone wanted to close it."

"Thank you for everything," I said, and shook his hand. "If you have time to check on the Wigginses…"

"I'll make time. Be in touch," he replied, and took his leave.

Carey was waiting at the door to give her brother a hug on his way out. When his SUV was speeding toward the road, she gestured to her sweat-dampened clothes, then pointed toward the master suite. "Give me ten minutes, then meet me in the basement."

I descended and sat alone under the humming ceiling fan, feeling the couch mold to my aching legs as I stretched out to rest. All too soon, Carey appeared in clean sweats. I had only a moment to look for her over the back of the couch before she turned off the fan's light, plunging the room into instant darkness.

She landed on the couch adjacent to mine and sighed as she made herself comfortable. "You'll like this part," she said. "Naptime. With all that exercise, it shouldn't take you too long to fall asleep, right?"

I murmured in reply and closed my eyes.

A black plain, featureless in all directions, stretched around me to meet an equally unremarkable sky. At least the dome above had a shading gradient, black fading to dark blue around the zenith, but there were no stars, nothing to give me any sense of location. As I squinted at the emptiness ahead, I came to a strange realization: I was dreaming.

And I *knew* it.

"Don't worry, I'm right here," said a voice behind me, and I turned to find Carey standing a few meters away with her arms folded. To my shock, she was glowing with a soft yellow light, which seemed to radiate from within her head and chest. She laughed at my surprise and came closer. "You're seeing the halo, right? Just an effect of the dream space. Makes it simple to find people, though."

I raised my hand to reach for her, then froze, seeing a glow emanating from my own skin.

"Signifies talent," Carey explained as I turned my hand this way and that to marvel at the change. "Come here."

I closed the gap between us, though I continued to look around at the landscape. "Are we the only two wizards dreaming?"

"Far from it. You can't see them, but there are at least a dozen in the distance...East Coast folk, I'd assume, or maybe someone needed an afternoon siesta. It's a form of protection built into this place—if you don't come here on your own steam, you only see the wizard who dragged you in. Once you're able to take yourself here without me, you'll see the others."

I looked down into her glowing face. "How do I do

that?"

Carey reached up and placed her palms on either side of my head. "I'm going to teach you the quick way. This will show you what you need to do, but it'll be up to you to figure out how."

Her fingertips seemed to warm against my skin, and suddenly, a rapid stream of images flickered through my field of vision—not just images, but sounds, smells, sensations, a burst of information unlike any I'd ever experienced. I would have reeled if Carey hadn't been holding my head steady. As I struggled to process what was happening, I realized I was seeing the way into the dream space—a sleepwalking tutorial played at fast forward. A few seconds later, the vision ended, and Carey stepped back while I rubbed my temples. "It's a lot," she said, sounding more matter-of-fact than apologetic, "but that will guide you."

Feeling dizzy, I sat on the smooth floor and cradled my head in my luminous hands. "I...I'm not sure I caught all the important bits..."

"You did, you just don't know it yet. Trust your intuition while you learn." She squatted in front of me and waited until I looked up again. "I've shown you the way, and I'll try to help you along it. But what comes next is up to you, Hannah."

I woke a few minutes later, feeling like I'd spent the night in an epic pub crawl, and groaned when Carey turned on the light. "The first time's always the worst," she said as she returned to our couches. "How're you feeling?"

"Like something crawled into my head, made a nest, and invited all of its friends for a party," I muttered.

She nodded. "Par for the course. Ready to try again?"

"*What?*"

"You're not going to learn how to sleepwalk if you lay there and whine."

I forced myself to sit up and blink the nearest wall hanging into focus. "This isn't *whinging*. My head really hurts—"

"All part of the process, I'm afraid. Want some Tylenol?"

With a pang, I thought of Mama, who'd insisted on referring to paracetamol by its American trade name even after years in the UK. I nodded to Carey, who left me to my fuzzy-brained misery for a moment. When she returned, she carried a glass of water and a plastic bottle. "Take two and quit griping."

Parched, I finished the water, then collapsed again and handed her the glass. "Anything stronger on hand?

Carey chuckled and put the bottle away. "Not for human consumption. Now close your eyes, you big baby."

And thus, my fate was sealed for the rest of the afternoon and evening, with only a quick dinner break (and Zeb's spicy chili mac) to clear my head. Fortunately, I was tired enough to go to sleep over and over again, thanks to Carey's workout schedule, but when we broke around ten that night, I'd made almost no progress toward sleepwalking on my own. Sure, I could fall asleep, and once I even managed to catch myself dreaming, but Carey inevitably shook me awake a few minutes later when she'd tranced into the dream space and I was nowhere to be found.

Weary, I stumbled upstairs to bed and collapsed into the space Seamus had left me on our shared mattress. He was already asleep—a full stomach, a few beers, and what must have been a pleasant evening had relaxed him—and so I made as little movement as I could, trying not to wake him. I rolled onto my side to face the wall, and I'd just closed my eyes when I felt him shift behind me. He slid toward me in his sleep and draped his arm over my side, and I held my breath for fear that I would start to bawl.

The bed wasn't ours, and we were several time zones and a couple of decades away from our old flat, but my Seamie was holding me again, pressed against my back like a softly breathing security blanket. I could have shaken him off—perhaps I should have done, considering how we'd ended it—but his touch felt like home, and that night, I needed a familiar anchor to give me strength. I closed my eyes, relaxing into his embrace, and prepared for sleep.

Twenty minutes later, still wide awake, I ruminated on the downside to Carey's instructional schedule and realized sleep wasn't coming. Carefully, I disengaged myself from Seamus's hold, pulled the blankets back over him, and padded into the hall of the quiet house. The only sounds were my foot on the squeaky floorboard and the ticking of the antique grandfather clock in the dining room, and I sighed, anticipating a lonely night.

Feeling momentarily maternal, I cracked open Amy's door to check on her, only to find the bed mussed but empty. Her weapons and wands appeared to still be in their cases, I saw after a quick search, and her personal effects were scattered across the dresser—she hadn't run away, then. A moment's deduction led me back to my room for my sweat-damp trainers, then out into the night.

It's difficult to be sneaky in the dark when one is still uncertain of one's surroundings. The light of the waning moon helped to a degree, but still, I stopped every few paces to listen to the sounds of the nighttime ranch and let my eyes adjust. In the distance, I heard the soft snorting and nickering of the horses in the far barn, followed by responses from the ones left out to pasture. A pair of bats clicked and swooped overhead, and something buzzed by my ear—though whether it was a fly, mosquito, or creeping horror, I couldn't say. The most innocent of sounds took on a sinister dimension when one was alone in a strange place in the dark, and I reminded myself that this was a *ranch*, not an enclave of evil, and I was too bloody old to be jumping at shadows.

Concentrating, I listened to the rustling of the breeze through the grass, and then I heard low voices coming from the nearer barn. My hunch was on target, and with a flicker of satisfaction, I tiptoed down the path and peeked inside.

The lamp was lit in Kip's makeshift sickroom, and though the curtains were still drawn, the stall door was cracked just enough to show me a sliver of his bed. Through the gap, I could see Kip where we'd last left him, awake and sitting up, and Amy on the bed facing him. She'd tucked one leg beneath her, and the other one, which was bare under her nightgown, swung over the side and trailed along the rug.

My first instinct was to "casually" interrupt them—species aside, they were two teenagers alone on a bed, and one of them was naked—but then I heard a loud sniffle and hesitated.

"Why us?" said Kip, his voice cracking. "We never hurt them. We were *farmers*. And they...*they*..."

With that, his fragile composure shattered, and he covered his face as he sobbed. Amy, comically petite beside him, stood on the mattress and wrapped her arms around him, pulling his head against her shoulder. She rubbed his shaking back for a moment, letting him weep, and then she murmured, "It's not okay. They tell you that it's all going to be okay, but it's not. It's *never* going to be okay." There was brittle steel in her voice. "I went to four or five sessions with a grief counselor after I got to Faerie. She's a nice lady, Brazilian. Really sweet. But I got all I could out of it."

When they pulled apart, still holding each other's arms, his eyes were red and puffy. I didn't need to see hers to hear the tears that threatened.

"We're in the same boat, Kip," she continued. "Mama and Daddy were the only family I had. I'm alone, too."

"At least you have Seamus and Hannah—"

"That's not the same. They're nice enough, but we're

all here to do a job." She took a deep, hitching breath, but she managed to steady herself. "I want one more hug from my mama. I want my daddy to help me line up one more shot. And I'm *always* going to be wanting that because they're…" With difficulty, she stopped her voice from breaking. "They're gone. Nothing I ever do is going to bring them back, and I miss them so *damn* much…"

They held each other again in the quiet barn, Kip sniffing and Amy angrily crying against his chest. Deciding that there was no point in shattering their illusion of privacy, I began to ease away, but I paused when Amy spoke again through her tears.

"You know what I want? I want to find the one who did it. The one who shot them. I want someone to bind him so he can't fight back. And I'd lock him in a room where he'd never be heard. Never see daylight."

"Why not kill him?" asked Kip. "Cut his throat, stab him in the hearts…" He paused, frowning in sudden thought. "Or heart? Do you only have the small one?"

"Too quick, too clean. I'd make him suffer." She straightened to look Kip in the eye. "I'd shoot him, but only where it wouldn't kill him," she said softly. "Every day, a new shot. Give him something to look forward to. And then I'd cut off all the non-essential bits, one at a time."

I held my breath and strained to listen. Amy sounded as unbothered as if she were discussing her weekly shop.

"I'd start with the fingers and toes. Maybe one a day, maybe only a knuckle at a time. Then the rest of his hands and feet. I'd leave him with stumps. And I'd take his ears. His nose. His tongue. His…*bits*."

Kip grimaced in involuntary sympathy.

"I'd take his eyes last. And then I'd force him to eat everything I'd cut off," she continued in that eerily calm tone. "Give him a hearty meal. Then I'd sew his mouth closed, chain him to the wall, and leave him there to starve to death, alone and in the dark." She looked away, collecting herself. "I know that's a really bad thought," she murmured, "but it...makes me feel better sometimes. On nights like this. Even if I got him, it wouldn't bring my family back, but some part of me can't help but think it would be wonderful to make him beg for death." She laughed to herself, but there was no mirth in the sound. "I guess that's the faerie in me talking. I'm sorry, that was a horrible thing to say—"

He eased her back into their embrace and bent close to her head. "You forgot something. Salt. Every day, when you take a new piece, you cure the wound with salt."

Amy laughed again, a sound suspiciously close to a sob.

"The raiders who slaughtered my family are dead," he continued, holding her close. "I am the only one left to avenge them, and I never struck a blow. So I will help you. Find out who killed your parents, and I will hold him down while you stab him as much as you like."

She sniffled and wiped her nose on her fist. "I'm better with a gun."

"You have yet to show me this gun of yours."

"Tomorrow. If Miss Hannah catches me sneaking out of the house with my guns in the middle of the night, she won't be happy." Amy looked at Kip again, then reached up to wipe his face dry. "It's not okay," she said with a small half-smile, "but we'll figure something out, right?"

I sneaked back to the house without being detected, then took off my shoes and eased into the space beside Seamus. Without fully realizing what was about to happen, I felt the tears welling up and cried as quietly as I could, hoping to go undetected.

But Seamus had always had a sixth sense for my moods, and he stirred as I curled up to muffle the noise. "Badger?" he whispered, sitting up beside me. "What is it, love? What's the matter?"

I felt him stroking my hair, pulling it away from my wet

face. "I'm so tired, Seamie," I mumbled. "I'm tired, and I hurt, and I don't know what to do, I can't sleepwalk, and how am I going to save anyone? I couldn't even save Dad and Mama…"

He said nothing, but he spooned beside me in the darkness with his arm around me, holding me until I cried myself to sleep.

CHAPTER 16

I awoke to sunlight on my eyelids—strong sunlight, the kind that only hits when one has had a long lie-in. I shifted against the glare, cracked my crusted eyes open, and realized I was in the middle of the big bed, tangled in the sheets and buried beneath the duvet against the air conditioning. The room was quiet, and Seamus was nowhere to be found. Sitting up, I picked at the crud on my lashes, yawned, and squinted at the nightstand until the glowing numbers on the bedside clock came into focus.

Half *ten*?

I scrambled out of bed, threw on yesterday's clothes, grimaced at my still-prominent sunburn, and patted my hair flat, then hurried into the hallway, looking for a sign of life. The house seemed to be empty after a cursory search, but I spied a loaf of bread and a jar of jam in the kitchen, along with a note: *Emergency this morning. Eat up, Hannah. –CJ.* Wondering what had called Carey away, I made myself two pieces of toast, found a plate, and carried breakfast outside in search of the rest of my party.

The morning heat hit me like a furnace blast, but I soldiered on until I spotted Seamus and Kip, who were leaning on a rail fence near the back of the barn, watching the distant training ring, where Zeb was walking a horse on a line. "There she is," said Seamus as I joined them. "Get some rest?"

"Enough. How are you feeling, Kip?"

He turned slightly, revealing his missing splint and brand-new crutch. "Much better," he replied, smiling.

"There is little pain, and the leg is stronger. Seamus made this for me."

"Practice," Seamus explained, coloring slightly. "Doc said the bone's set, but it's still a bit soft. I thought that might help him get around without putting too much weight on it."

"Good call," I replied. Kip did look healthier in the sunlight—thin and still oddly shorn in places, but his cuts had closed to scabbed lines. "Wish I could cobble together a spell like that. She's quite the wizard."

"Well, thank you," said Carey, emerging from the barn with dripping arms. "Healing magic's a specialty of mine since I'm shit at the offensive stuff." A towel manifested in her hands, and she began to scrub herself dry. "Morning, sunshine. Ready to work?"

I crammed half a piece of toast in my mouth and chewed as quickly as I could. "Everything all right?"

"Better now. Been a long morning." Carey slung the damp towel over her shoulder and propped one foot on the lowest rail. "I've got a friend twenty miles down the road with a breeding operation, and he had *three* mares go into labor at once. The first two came like dominoes, but the third was carrying twins—*surprise* twins, I should add, and I'm going to have a strong word with his regular vet."

I looked at Kip in time to see his eyes widen to saucers.

"Frankly, it's a miracle that both babies made it," she continued. "One's a little runty. They're both standing and nursing, but the little guy's probably going to need bottle feeding—mom's young, and I'm not sure she knows what to do with the pair of them running around." Noticing Kip's expression, she asked, "Know something about twins, do you?"

He nodded. "They are death. Always death."

"Yeah, horses aren't designed to carry multiples, either. If Reggie's normal vet weren't, like, ninety and blind, he'd have seen the second fetus in the scan and removed it. But what's done is done, and we got lucky this time. And I may have gotten a new client," she added with a weary grin. "Anyway, just had to give my arms a good scrub-down when I got back—I've been inside *way* too many mares this morning. There's a lingering funk, if you know what I mean." She looked toward the training ring for a moment, shading her eyes against the glare, and grunted. "How long have they been at it?"

I took another glance at the ring and realized that there was now a rider atop the horse—Amy, who clung to the reins as Zeb slowly led her around in a circle.

"Since eight or so," said Seamus. "She said she was going to work on the wands this morning, but Zeb caught her at breakfast and asked if she wanted a quick lesson. There's nothing on the telly, so Kip and I have been watching the show."

Carey frowned. "Has she been falling much?"

"Nah, but she's nervous. Mounting and dismounting took a little time. And *someone* has been enjoying the view," he added, nudging Kip in the side.

Even with his coloring, I could tell the centaur was blushing. "She is well-built. That was all I said," he protested.

I leaned around Seamus and smiled at him. "Amy *is* a cute little thing. Don't worry about it."

My partner grinned wickedly. "He was talking about Felicia."

"Who?"

"That would be the mare," said Carey, who seemed to be stifling a laugh. "And yes, I think she's lovely. You've got good taste, kid."

Kip's face burned. "She has, uh...very nice legs."

"That she does. I'm not sure she's the best choice for a newbie rider," she added, changing the subject, "but as long as Zeb's out there, they should be fine. She was half-starved when we got her last year," Carey explained. "Sad case. She's been Zeb's pet project for a few months—he had to halter break her, and she should have learned that *years* ago—but she's a pretty gentle girl. If Amy would loosen up a tad, she'd have an easier time of it."

Our crafter sat ramrod straight in the saddle, staring down at Zeb, who seemed to be chatting with her as he walked the mare around the ring.

"She said she's not done this before," Seamus replied.

"Yeah, that's obvious. But I'm glad he's got her out there," said Carey, watching them make another circuit. "Zeb has a gift for broken things."

"Magic?" I asked.

"No. More of a heightened awareness of other creatures. This ranch was his idea, you know. We married when I was in college, and when I started vet school in Texas, he bought this place from an uncle and ran it to keep himself busy. Ranching family," she added. "He's got it in his blood. And since he kept horses around, I thought I'd go for the large animal end of the spectrum. He bred a few to pay the bills, and he started rehabilitating and rehoming neglected horses…" Carey's face twitched. "Then my parents died, right before our fourth anniversary, so suddenly it was the two of us doing the long-distance thing, half a dozen neurotic horses, and Jimmy. While I took a month off to have my come-apart, he stepped up and raised my brother—did it almost solo for two years while I finished school. I know Jim remembers Mom and Dad, but Zeb's been a second father to him." She flashed a brief, wistful smile. "But that's his gift, my Zeb. Always tries to fix the broken."

"Sounds like you got a good one," I replied.

She nodded. "The best. I'd have settled for a good mundane, but Zeb's the total package. Now," she said, turning her attention back to Kip, "let me have another look at that leg. You may be able to come off that crutch after lunch—"

Before Carey could lay a hand on him, the ring exploded.

A diamondback, Zeb told us later, a small one hiding in

the grass near the edge of the ring. If it had only stayed on its side of the fence, Felicia might never have noticed. But it came into the ring and curled up near a post, and when she walked too close, it began to rattle.

The mare was no fool, and she reared, whinnying in fear as the snake coiled to strike. As the panicked horse stomped, Amy screamed and tightened her grip, digging her shoes into the mare's sides. And with that, the terrified Felicia bolted across the ring, dragging Zeb off his feet before yanking the line from his hands. I watched in horror as she sailed over the ring's fence, thinking that Amy would land on her unprotected head at any moment, but the girl managed to stay in the saddle as the horse galloped for the far pasture.

"What the *hell*—" Seamus began.

"Zeb!" Carey cried, running for the ring. "Oh, my God, Zeb, are you okay?"

Felicia was shrinking in the distance, and I held my breath as she jumped yet another fence in her mad dash for the safety of the herd. Amy wouldn't be able to coax the horse back on her own, that much was clear, and I looked around for a convenient mount to go after her, all the while trying to convince myself that I remembered saddle basics. But before I realized what was happening, Kip threw his crutch aside and thundered after the escaping mare.

"*Fuck*," I muttered as he vaulted the first fence. "He's just going to drive her away—"

"Dan's out there!" Carey yelled at us as she knelt beside Zeb and pointed at the herd. "Stop him, he's heading straight for Dan!"

"Who?" Seamus asked.

"The stallion," I replied, dropping my breakfast plate into the grass. "We've got to go."

Taking my wand in hand, I sprinted after them, though I knew there was no way I'd beat Kip to the herd. He was running at full gallop, and I'd never been a track champion. From the corner of my eye, I saw Seamus close the distance to join me, and we ran together, matching strides.

"Kip!" I shouted after him with the little breath I could spare. "Stop, you're going to spook them! Don't fight the stallion, he's *shod*!"

If Kip could hear me, he paid me no heed. Amy was still shrieking on her runaway horse, and he picked up his pace. He cleared the next fence with ease, though he stumbled slightly on landing, and I worried about the integrity of his healing leg.

In the distance, I saw Felicia slow as she reached the outer edge of the nervous herd, and the other mares moved aside to admit her. From their noisy midst stepped a white horse—a beautiful, muscular, white horse—who snorted and called a challenge.

"Dan?" Seamus panted.

"Think so."

Seamus barely had time to swear before Kip was upon the stallion, who reared and kicked at the air. Without hesitation, Kip engaged, striking Dan with both sets of hooves as the two ran and spun in search of openings. But after receiving a few good blows, Dan seemed to take his opponent's measure and went on the offensive, furiously kicking and biting.

"*Kip!*" I called across the distance as Dan's steel-shod hooves landed on his flank. "Get out of there!"

"No time," Seamus huffed, then grabbed my wrist. "Hold on—"

The world blurred and swam, and I vaguely recognized the sound I was hearing as my own scream once reality stopped spinning. I saw we were within a meter of the fight only a second before Seamus tackled me out of the way, knocking the air from my taxed lungs.

"Sorry," he gasped as I sucked for breath. "Didn't know if it would work. Val showed me."

I didn't have time to argue with him about the necessity

of warning me before using me as a guinea pig for untested enchantment. As I pushed myself out of the grass, I extended my wand and yelled for a shield. The spell coalesced almost instantly, forming a protective barrier around the two of us, but I forced it outward, letting it flow into the shifting space between the fighters. Summoning all of the willpower I could muster, I concentrated on the shield until it began to solidify, a protection not only against magic but also against Dan's hooves and teeth.

Kip stepped back, puzzled at the sudden wall in front of him, then turned and noticed us. "What are you—"

Seamus's hand shot out, and a second shield formed as Dan ran around the side of mine, looking for an opening. "Get away from here!" he yelled. "We'll get Amy, go back to the barn!"

Before Kip could argue, I heard hoofbeats behind us, and then Carey and Zeb rode up, each sitting bareback on a wild-eyed horse, holding a coil of rope. As they passed, they readied their lassoes and turned to flank Dan, who continued to kick at the shield and scream his frustration. Within seconds, Zeb's rope had circled the stallion's neck, and Carey managed to catch his back legs when he kicked at her. The ropes cinched, and Dan fell, foaming and struggling in the grass.

I was about to breathe a sigh of relief when the frightened herd, seeing the stallion fall, decided to run for safety—including Felicia, to whom Amy still clung, too petrified to slide down. In the next second, Kip, who was again limping and bleeding, turned and took off after the mares. They scattered as he sprinted through the pack, and he quickly closed on Felicia. "Jump!" he called to Amy. "I will catch you!"

Amy's response was swallowed by the distance, but I could see her holding on to the mare like a barnacle.

Kip picked up his speed, drawing almost level with the screaming horse, and grabbed Amy's arm. His touch seemed to break her paralysis, and she turned to take his other hand. Keeping his strides in tandem with Felicia's, he leaned closer, then yanked Amy out of the saddle and slowed, letting the mare escape. With a fluid motion, he swung Amy onto his back, dipping as she accidentally kicked him, then turned and limped toward us.

"Holy shit," Carey sighed. She and Zeb had released their mounts in the chaos, and Zeb was already halfway back to the barn, leading Dan, who was suddenly willing to cooperate. Joining Seamus and me in our winded clump, she watched with us as Kip neared, bloodied and grimacing. Of Amy there was no sign but for the pair of thin arms locked in a death grip around his chest and the dirty trainers flung awkwardly to either side. "He's too big for her," Carey muttered. "Especially sitting on his shoulders like that—she'd have an easier ride if she moved down his back."

"I think she's more concerned with staying on than with comfort," Seamus replied.

"Mm. And I'm more concerned that he's hurt himself *again*." She stepped forward and cupped her hands around her mouth. "What did I say about keeping your weight off that leg?" she bellowed across the field. "You're not ready for stunts like that!"

Kip continued his slow plodding, occasionally patting Amy's arms as if trying to reassure her that she wasn't about to be flung off. When he finally reached us, I winced to see the extent of his fresh wounds—horseshoes at speed are unforgiving—but if we thought we were removing Amy from his back, we were sorely mistaken. She'd pressed her face against his spine and squeezed her eyes closed, and Kip stepped away as Seamus reached toward him to pull her down. "She weighs nothing," he mumbled, wearied by his exertions. "I will carry her."

"You're *hurt*," Seamus protested, but Kip wouldn't hear it.

"I will carry her," he insisted, and headed for the barn.

As he patted her arms again, I heard him murmur, "You are safe. Everything is all right now. You are safe, Amy."

When we finally pried Amy off of Kip, she lurched around the barn on jelly legs, and I coaxed her into the house before she could fall. After planting her in a kitchen chair, I put on the kettle and hunted through the Joneses' cabinets until I found teabags—Lipton, unfortunately, but there was nothing for it. "Here," I told Amy, pressing the warm mug into her hands. "Be a good girl, sit there, and sip this until your legs stop shaking."

She seemed surprised when she noticed the tremor. "I'm fine. Kip—"

"Is in good hands. Drink it down, now."

Too rattled to fight me, Amy did as she was bidden, and I'd risen to make her a second cup when Seamus walked in. His shirt was drenched with sweat—mine was no better, I realized after a quick inspection—and he collapsed into the chair beside Amy as I added water to the kettle. "I've been kicked out of the barn," he explained. "Doc's orders. Zeb said the horses are spooked enough having Kip in proximity, and I'm making a bad situation worse."

"Mm. Cuppa?"

He sighed. "Cheers."

I scrounged another clean mug from the cabinet, pulled out the milk, and delivered the goods to the table. "You'll have to take it from here," I told him. "I'm going to check on Carey, see if she needs a hand."

Amy perked at the news. "I'll go—"

"No, little miss, you're going to sit here and take it easy," Seamus interrupted, nudging her fresh mug toward her. "You had quite a ride."

"I'm fine now…"

He leaned closer and peered at her face. "Yeah, no, I've had too many people who look like you do right now tell me that, then fall out on me. Drink your tea."

She scowled but took a sip. "This is just a placebo, you know."

"Oh, really? You won't say that when it's the only thing keeping you going at the end of a double shift. It's medicinal at the very least."

Leaving them to bicker, I headed back for the barn, keeping well clear of the trails Zeb was using to coax a few of the anxious mares in from the pasture. When I stepped inside and my eyes adjusted to the shade, I found Kip sitting by the hay bales again, looking thoroughly chastised as Carey splinted his bad leg. "Because they're a herd species," I overheard her telling him. "One male to a bunch of females. Dan either saw you as a threat to the mares or thought you were coming to steal them." She tightened a strap, then nodded and stood. "I imagine he's a little confused. Pretty boy, but high-strung and not always the brightest. Wiggle that."

Kip moved his leg around for her inspection. "How long?"

"Until tonight at the *earliest*, mister. Ten to one you've got at least a new hairline fracture. Let's get you cleaned and patched up, and then it's back to bed with you."

He rolled his eyes. "I bathed yesterday…"

"You barely got a good hosing," she countered. "I need to take a look at your feet, and were you trying to grow your tail into dreadlocks, or did that just happen?"

"Dreadlocks?"

"You've got nothing but mats," she explained, glancing at his back end. "When's the last time you brushed it out?"

"You sound like my mother," he mumbled.

"Hey, I raised a boy—the nagging comes with the job." Carey beckoned me closer with two fingers. "Bottom line, you've still got dirt caked in all over you. I know you've been through hell," she said, softening, "and I'm sure you're still sore. Let me clean you up, okay? I don't know about you, but I always feel better after a bath." When he wavered, she added, "I go to the salon and let them wash and cut my hair, and Zeb lets me trim his. And *someone* has to scrub down all the girls in the pasture on occasion. What do you say, can we give you a hand?"

Though he still seemed displeased at the notion of cleanliness, he followed Carey to a concrete stall with a proper hose apparatus. "You set the temperature," she said, handing him the shower head, "and I'll start brushing. Hannah, have you done this before?"

I watched her as she pulled a selection of brushes and combs from the wall. "Ehm…"

"I'll take that as a 'no,' then. Brush with the hair, leave the tail to me. You're trying to loosen the dirt before shampooing. Speaking of which"—she grabbed a plastic bottle from its shelf and handed it to Kip—"lather up your head. Try to get the cuts clean, if you can—antibacterial soap is right there," she instructed, pointing to another bottle. "And I realize this is a little awkward for all of us, but try not to kick anyone, eh? Hey, *no*," she said, catching my elbow and dragging me toward her, "do *not* stand directly back there. Work from the sides. Amateurs," she grumbled.

While Carey repositioned me, Kip started shampooing and turned to see what the fuss was about. "I would not kick you," he protested.

"And I appreciate that," said Carey, "but I've been on the wrong end of too many hooves to take stupid chances. Ever broken a rib? Not pleasant, let me tell you. Heck, I've got stories…"

Carey kept up a steady stream of talk, and after a few minutes, Kip began to relax. I'd been assigned to rinse duty, and I duly followed Carey around, dodging the occasional splash when Kip's tail flicked. After half an hour, she deemed him passable—"You can handle the undercarriage yourself when you're less banged up," she told him—and Kip watched warily as she approached with a pair of scissors. "I like a man with long hair," she said, climbing onto her stepstool at his shoulders, "but there's a difference between *good* long and 'I'm too lazy to trim this' long, and you, my friend, are looking shaggy." She held out her empty palm. "Hannah, comb."

Kip endured the haircut without complaint, even letting Carey push his hair to one side to take a closer look at the short mane growing down his spine. She trimmed until she was satisfied, then climbed down, cleaned his hooves, and turned her attention to the real problem. "Okay," she said, lifting his knotted tail, "this is going to take some doing, and I don't know how much I can salvage."

Worried, he turned and watched her finger-comb what little she could. "You…want to cut off my *tail?*"

"Oh, no, the tail itself isn't going anywhere," she assured him. "But I think the best option would be to cut your hair short and let it grow back. This is a disaster, Kip." She held his tail up by its matted middle and shook her head. "I can't clean it thoroughly, and it's just going to get nastier as stuff gets stuck in it. Trim it?"

He looked unhappy about it, but he nodded and turned away. "Tell me when you are finished."

"Big baby," she replied, but she smiled as she began to shove her scissors through the tangles. "You should see some of the haircuts we've had to give our rescues when they get here. This is *nothing.*"

Carey made quick work of the job, leaving Kip with a sad, patchy stump of a tail. "It's not much to look at," she said apologetically, "but it's for the best." His face fell even further when he turned to see the damage, and she patted his shoulder. "Cheer up, it's just hair. You should see some of my pictures from the eighties. I was an absolute disaster."

We toweled him off, and Carey used a quick spell to dry him the rest of the way. "Now, back to bed," she ordered as he hobbled out of the shower stall. "Zeb will bring you lunch in a little while. And as for you," she continued, poking her finger into my chest, "it's naptime."

Not since I was six and convinced that some unspeakable abomination was living in my wardrobe had I so dreaded the idea of falling asleep. I spent the afternoon locked in a frustrating cycle of drifting off and being shaken awake when I once again failed to sleepwalk. Each time, Carey offered a pointer or word of encouragement, but by dinner, I was still no closer to mastering the elusive technique.

While Carey freshened up, I helped Zeb schlep the spaghetti and its accessories out to the barn, where Seamus and Amy were already waiting. I spied one of her kits on Kip's rug beside a pile of sawdust, and she showed me her latest work as I set up the table. "Just a few rods, but I left most of my good ones in Faerie," she explained, fanning out the selection of hollowed dowels. "Zeb said he'd take me out to look for new wood tomorrow," she added, beaming at our chef. "I want to play with ponderosa pine and desert willow. Hard to get back east."

She returned to the stall to clean up, and Seamus helped me organize the dishes. "Since I'm being useless right now, I thought I might as well be a useless chaperone," he murmured. "Yeah?"

"Sounds wise," I told him. "Any problems?"

"Not at all, we just kept the telly on. Daytime programming around here is *special*."

"How so?"

He lifted the napkin from the wicker silverware basket, saw what was inside, and quickly passed it to me for safekeeping. "There's a program with this old guy and all of these horrible people, kind of like *Jeremy Kyle*—you know, the talk show?—except he never tells them they're horrible, and he seems to mostly do paternity tests. I may have missed something," he admitted, "since I could really do with subtitles, but that was my impression. Anyway, there was that one, and one with a judge, and the news…oh, and Amy found *Cops*."

"Your afternoon was off the chain, then?"

"Completely epic." He grinned and nudged me in the arm. "Missed you, Badge."

"Missed you, too, Seamie."

He hesitated as I unpacked the warm garlic bread. "I, ehm...I'd ask if you fancied a drink later tonight, but seeing as we're in the middle of nowhere and don't have a car..."

Before I could reply, Zeb slung his arm around my shoulders. "Friend of ours runs a bar about ten miles down the road. Nothing fancy, but the beer's cold. You two want to double-date with us?"

Seamus looked panicky at the word *date*, but after a moment's pause, I nodded at him across the table. "Thanks, Zeb. We'd like that very much."

The promised bar had little in common with my old local in Durham, a cozy tavern with the requisite scratched pint glasses and dartboard, populated mostly by pensioners who'd slipped away from the missus to have a nip with the boys. Instead of brick and plaster, the walls at the desert watering hole were adobe and tin, the tables collapsible and mismatched, the lights mostly of the colored string variety. But the modest crowd was welcoming, and Zeb's friend kept a surprising variety of microbrews in stock. After asking Seamus and me a few questions about our preferences, he popped a couple of bottles onto the counter, added a pair of Corona-branded glasses, and told us to come back if he'd guessed wrong. He hadn't, and the beer went down like a welcome, if over-chilled, friend.

The Joneses allowed us to buy the first round, but that was all. They insisted that the next was their shout, and our offers to pay them for their hospitality were rebuffed. "We don't often have guests," said Carey, "not since Jim got out of high school. It's kind of nice having people around the place."

After assessing the proximity of our nearest neighbors,

I lowered my voice and leaned across the table. "As long as we stay with you, we're putting you in danger. We're not any old houseguests."

She shrugged. "I realize that. But if what you've told me is accurate, the Arcanum has no idea that you're back in this realm."

I'd been careful to keep off the Fringe network in the last days, lest there be someone in the silo who could pinpoint my IP address, but that wasn't the only concern on my mind. "I don't know if they'd think to trace Amy, but it's possible that they could find me if they looked. My dad's parents are still living."

Zeb's eyebrows rose. "Blood trace?"

"Easy way to hunt me down. Run it, see where all his family is, then start narrowing the field. The clan's based in Glastonbury—how many of us do you suppose would be wandering around in New Mexico?"

"Fair enough," said Carey, "but we'll cross that bridge if we come to it. Until we hear otherwise, let's assume they aren't actively looking for you." She sipped her ale and smirked. "And if they come knocking, they'll have a nasty surprise."

"You said you were rubbish at combat," I pointed out.

"Zeb ain't." He lifted his glass in salute, and his wife patted his muscular arm. "Told you I got the complete package when I snagged this one."

"But what happens if I ever figure out this sleepwalking thing?" I pressed, whispering. "What if I'm out there and some Arcanum goon catches me? Tracks me back to you?"

The Joneses looked at each other for a long moment. "We had a talk last night," said Zeb. "And as far as Carey and I are concerned, the right thing to do here is to help you. To a point, at least," he amended. "You obviously have nowhere to go. Stay with us, figure yourself out, and try to find your people. I'm sure sleepwalking will come in time—maybe it'll come someday for me, too," he added with a lopsided smile. "And if you do make contact with an Arcanum member out there…well, we hope you'd be honest with us and get out of town ASAP. Sound fair?"

"Sounds incredibly generous," I replied, and Seamus nodded beside me. "In terms of payment—"

Carey covered my hand and whispered, "Wizards. No biggie."

"We can't mooch indefinitely," Seamus protested.

"You're not," said Zeb. "Amy's agreed to do some crafting for us, maybe half a dozen wands. Shit," he told Seamus, "do you have any idea what a good wand goes for, *if* you can find a crafter willing to work outside the Arcanum?"

"Not really…"

"Thousands. The stronger the wand, the higher the price. Start looking for unicorn horn or dragonscale, and you're talking about a solid used car."

I frowned. "It's not nearly that high in the Fringe—"

"Yeah, because you've got crafters of your own, and I'm betting the Arcanum's willing to let it slide. But everything done for us is under-the-table freelance, and it's not cheap."

"Hell," said Carey, "do you think we'd be using homemade wands if we had a reasonably priced crafter available? We can either buy them or pay the bills, not both."

"You…*could* just make money," Seamus offered. "We've been able to pass off the homemade dollars so far."

"Sure, because you're living off the grid," said Zeb. "But settle down, get established, and suddenly, the wrong people are going to ask questions if you always have cash on hand. Can't take it to a bank—anyone who looked into it would think you're cooking meth or something."

"And crafters generally insist on being paid by check," Carey added. "Or a direct transfer. The ones who work for us want proof that their money isn't going to vanish."

"So the fact that Amy's willing to work for room and

board? I mean, we're getting the better end of the deal, here," Zeb concluded. "That's your bed and breakfast taken care of, man. Now, we don't have an extra vehicle lying around, but if you think your money's passable, I'll take you to the lot this week, let you find something that runs. Better than hoofing it everywhere around here."

Seamus put down his beer and crossed his arms on the table. "Speaking of hooves…"

"What the hell are we going to do about Kip?" Carey finished. She paused while Zeb rose from the table to chat with another pair of patrons in the far corner of the bar, then said, "I have no idea. He's healing up nicely, and I know he wants to help you, but…"

"But what can he do?" I said when her voice trailed off. "He can't go anywhere, we can't let anyone see him—"

"We're not forcing him back through the gate," Seamus interjected. "You saw what those things did to his brother, Badge."

"No one's forcing him anywhere," I replied, and lowered my voice. "Carey, I haven't broached this with him, and I certainly don't know enough to do it myself, but have you had any experience with transformation?"

Her lips narrowed, and she emphatically shook her head. "Nope. No way. We don't do binds, and we don't do transformations. Put that out of your mind."

"If he were willing—"

"*No*, Hannah." Catching Seamus's confusion, she explained, "Those two spells put limits on other people. If you bind someone, you render him powerless, and transformation…" She shuddered. "No."

Seamus patted his crow's feet. "This isn't exactly natural."

"That's glamour, and you did it to yourself. Transformation is something you do to someone who's not powerful enough to stop you."

"But what's the plan, then?" I asked. "Leave him in that barn for the rest of his life?"

Carey chuckled to herself as she raised her glass. "You know, we could set up a workshop space for Amy out there, and I think the two of them would be just dandy."

"Oh, sure," said Seamus, "until Aiden got wind of it."

"Who's Aiden?"

"The teenage faerie lord who's become her texting pal."

She considered this information. "Good looking?"

"Not bad," I said. "Tall, blond, computer programmer with a ponytail—little awkward, but his brother *is* the king, so there are certain perks."

"Huh." Carey sipped slowly, squinting at the wall over my head, then shrugged. "Since I'm assuming this Aiden has the right number of legs, I'm putting my money on him in the long run. But if all else were equal?"

Seamus's brows knit. "You don't actually think—"

"I'm a wizard, bub," she said, giving his cheek a pat. "I never say never to *anything*."

We lingered at our cozy table until eleven, breathing again after a couple of long days and swapping war stories. For every sloppy inebriate Seamus and I could recall, the Joneses had an equally bad incident with an animal, often involving far too many bodily fluids, and we laughed until we ached and the pints ran dry. We knew the evening was drawing to a close by the time Zeb was out in the aisle, doing his best impression of the well-endowed blonde on the local news who couldn't get a Spanish name right in the first five attempts, but we couldn't slip away until he'd done the rest of the small-time celebrities for the howling patrons. After all, everything, even bad acting, can be funny with enough hoppy lubrication. At least Carey stayed sober enough to drive us home.

Once we'd pulled up to the house, Zeb and Carey went inside to crash, and Seamus trailed at their heels. "I'm just going to check on the kids," I told him, and slipped out to the barn to see if anyone was still awake.

The barn was empty, but peeking through at the training ring beyond it, I spied the two of them at the fence, Kip with his bad foot propped on the bottom rung and Amy sitting on the top rail. The quarter-moon had yet to rise, and the brilliant swath of the Milky Way glittered across the southern sky. Amy held her mobile heavenward in one hand and braced her other hand against Kip's shoulder, steading herself as she twisted on her perch. "That bright one right there is Saturn, I think," I heard her tell him, pointing with the phone. "And the reddish one down a bit and to the right is Mars."

"And that one?" he asked, pointing in turn.

She consulted her screen. "Arcturus. I like this app—I suck at constellations, and there are *so many* stars out here. My dad was always good at naming them, but then he also knew how to navigate." She lowered the phone and looked up at Kip. "You've really never seen stars?"

He shook his head. "At home, the sky is gray. My father says...he *said*," he amended after a pause, "that one night, when he was very small, the gray parted, and he could see black beyond. And there were lights in the sky then, in the cracks. But this..."

"Beautiful, isn't it?"

"Yes." His sad, stubby tail twitched. "What are they?"

"What, stars? Um...well, most of them are like the sun, you know, just far away."

"*Truly?*" Kip sounded shocked. "How far?"

"Farther than we can go," said Amy, playing with her mobile again. "But those two—see them there, Mars and Saturn?" she asked, holding the screen between his face and the sky. "They're a lot closer. Other worlds. Mars is about our size, and Saturn's a lot bigger."

"You have been there, then?"

She giggled. "Uh, *no*. But here, I can show you some pictures..."

I left the amateur astronomers undisturbed and quietly

let myself into our room, where Seamus, who'd kept a light on, was already curled up under the duvet. "They're alive," I told him, kicking off my trainers. "Good enough for me."

"All right, then," he replied, and slapped one hand over his eyes. "I'm not peeking."

"You're not missing anything." I slid out of my clothes and into pajamas, taking care to tuck in my necklace, and climbed into bed beside him. "Okay, show's over."

He turned off the bedside lamp and rolled over to face me in the dark. "Is this weird? Say the word, and I'll camp on a couch."

"It's weird, but I kind of like it," I murmured, running my hand over his glamoured stubble.

Seamus caught my hand and held it, then pulled me closer. "I've missed this, Badger. I've missed *you*."

I closed my eyes and tucked my head against his T-shirt. "Missed you, too."

"Got to say, though, that I have *not* missed your snoring."

He grunted when I kicked his shin, but by the time my weary brain had thought up an appropriate retort, he was already unconscious. "Love you, Seamie," I whispered to the dark, then let sleep take me again.

CHAPTER 17

The next three days followed a punishing pattern: I woke, ate, ran until I ached, rinsed off the sweat, and retreated to the basement to meditate on my inability to sleepwalk until nightfall, when Carey gave me a few hours' reprieve from my continued failure.

The rest of our band had it marginally better. As promised, Zeb took Seamus to the used car lot on Tuesday morning, and they returned with a black, late-nineties Suburban. "The interior's rough," Seamus told me over pizza at lunch. "Looks like the previous owner might have been breeding panthers in the back seat. But the tires are good, and Zeb says the engine's clean—probably a rebuild. I didn't get close enough to check," he admitted as he reached for the breadsticks. "That's a *lot* of steel in one place, you know?"

To help assuage his boredom, I gave Seamus the laptop Aiden had built for me, and with Carey's encouragement, I finally logged in to the Fringe network. "This is set in 'ghost' mode," I told him as I handed him the computer. "It's a coordinator perk. You can see everyone, no one can see you. Keep an eye out for activity, and don't engage with anyone. If you see anyone else log in, get off and let me know. Let's hope no one can trace this."

But Seamus's vigil was a lonely one, as no one else logged in all day. When Zeb sent me out to the barn to round up the others for dinner, I found my three huddled around Kip's borrowed telly, cheering on an overweight patrol officer in foot pursuit of a suspect as *Cops* went to commercial break. The laptop sat open but unattended on the rug beside Seamus, while Amy's afternoon haul from her tree-hunting excursion with Zeb remained in a pile outside the stall door. Kip, once again freed from the leg brace, lay on the floor with his legs tucked to save space, and Amy leaned against him while they watched the show, passing a bowl of popcorn.

The following morning, while Carey saw a patient in the next town and I resumed my slow run through hell, I was startled from the contemplation of my weeping blisters by the sound of gunfire. Sprinting around the far barn, I found everyone gathered in an empty pasture, where Zeb had set up paper targets and tins. Amy's bags of weaponry lay in the grass, unzipped and emptied, and she waved at me in greeting as she reloaded her rifle. The shooting continued until lunch, then resumed mid-afternoon, occasionally waking me from my ineffective naps. "Kip's good, but Amy's a marksman," Seamus told me that night when I dragged myself into the bed. "And they're both becoming a bit too invested in *Days of Our Lives*, if you ask me."

Thursday brought a brief respite, as Carey was called out to deal with sick heifers all morning. I lay in bed alone and tried to will myself to sleep, but I was too well-rested to succeed, and the morning light only served to remind me that I should be outside, sweating. Wearying of running in circles, I laced up for a cross-country jog of my own routing, which ended with me limping into the barn shortly before lunchtime. Amy, who had been watching a game show while she varnished a wand, looked up at the sound of my panting and made a face. "You okay, Miss Hannah?" she asked as she put the wand aside, perhaps out of fear that I was about to collapse onto her work.

"Fine," I managed, leaning against the stall while I caught my breath.

Kip frowned and rose from his bed. "You are burned."

"Just hot."

"No," said Amy, pressing two fingers against my skin, "that's a sunburn. *Another* one," she chided. "Don't you have any sunscreen?"

"Fresh out, I'm afraid. It's...very bright here."

"*Yeah.* It's almost July," she replied with a look of incredulity. "Why do you think we're hiding out in the barn?"

My guess as to that answer had nothing to do with the weather, but I held my tongue and let Seamus rub lotion into my shoulders before I descended to the basement for another afternoon of miserable failure.

Having started late in the day, Carey kept me long past my bedtime, and so I found myself lying on the duvet at midnight, staring at the ceiling while Seamus slept beside me. Awake and bored, I glanced in Amy's empty room, then headed outside to find the kids.

As I sneaked through the dark, I heard Amy's voice, then spotted the two of them at the fenced ring. "It's *terrifying*," she was telling Kip, sitting awkwardly on the top rail to face him. "You're up there, you're barely hanging on, and then the darn thing bolts on you..."

"But you stayed on. Very well, I think. I was not sure I would be able to pry you off her back," he said, chuckling.

"I was holding on for dear life," she replied, and I could hear the pout in her voice. "She kept rearing, and she was so fast...it was scary, okay?"

"I believe you." Kip folded his arms and considered her for a moment, then sidled closer to her perch. "You were afraid because you did not trust her. That was a new experience for you, yes?"

"Sure, I guess."

"Do you trust me?"

"Yeah..."

He stepped beside her and held out one hand. "Come with me. I can carry you."

"*Kip*," she protested, "I can't—"

"You can. I will not let you fall." He paused and

cocked his head. "*Won't?* Is that the word?"

"That's right, but—"

"But what? Learn how it is supposed to feel, build your confidence, and the next time, you will have an easier job with Felicia."

"But…I mean…you know," Amy stammered, "I'm heavy, I can't ask you—"

At that, Kip laughed in earnest. "*Heavy?* You are tiny! You weigh nothing. And you"—he hesitated as he mulled over the words—"you didn't break me last time. Come on." He patted his wide back in invitation. "Trust me, Amy."

Though I moved behind the barn wall to avoid detection, I watched through a chink in the boards as she hesitantly slid from the fence onto Kip. "Steady?" he asked, checking over his shoulder.

Amy sat stiffly, holding her arms out for balance. "No. There were stirrups and stuff before, I had something to hold on to…"

He waited, standing stock-still as she found her uneasy center, then started to slowly walk down the fence. "You are tense," he said, casting a glance back to gauge her response.

"Just trying not to fall off."

Kip twisted his torso slightly and reached toward her. "If you feel unsettled, grab my arm. You are safe, Amy."

She latched on to him, then whimpered as he turned to retrace his steps.

"No faster than this," he soothed. "Not until you are ready." He stopped and looked at her again. "Relax. I can feel you at least as well as you feel yourself—if you slide, I will know it. You are like *this*." He swiveled far enough to show her his other hand, which he tightened like a claw. "Rigid. You are scared, and you are fighting me. Loosen up, move with me. For this to work, we must move together."

Amy's voice sounded strained. "Like…dancing?"

"Exactly. Let me lead." I could just see him grin in the dim light from the barn. "You will have your turn with Felicia later."

Kip started to walk again, letting Amy clutch his arm. As I watched, her posture gradually began to shift, and she lost some of the tension in her shoulders and back. She swayed slightly with his steps, anticipating the movement, and gradually started to compensate.

"Better," he told her. "Mind your knees, you are squeezing my ribs."

"*You're* squeezing."

"Picky," he sighed. "What I said was not incorrect."

"*Wasn't* incorrect."

He turned to give her a look, and Amy smiled wickedly. "Remember which of us actually has his feet on the ground, hmm?" said Kip.

"You wouldn't."

"Keep that up and find out."

He made another slow circuit, and Amy finally released her iron grip on his arm. "Hey, Kip?"

"Yes?"

"Seamus said you thought Felicia was cute."

He shrugged and looked back at Amy. "I said she had good legs. That was all. Her face is another matter," he muttered. "Probably not much of a talker—"

"Nope."

"Mm. And since she runs in terror whenever I get close, I will have to appreciate her from a distance."

"Okay," she said, inching closer to his shoulders, "so, like…ideal girl, drop-dead gorgeous. What are we talking about?"

Kip snorted, but I saw him smile. "I…have not given the matter much thought."

"Yeah, right. Come on, out with it."

That earned a quiet chuckle. "Felicia has some, uh…excellent qualities. To a point."

"And that point would be right about here?" she asked,

leaning forward to poke the side of his torso.

He startled at the touch, then looked back at her and nodded. "Approximately."

"So we have a reverse mermaid situation, then."

"A what?"

"Hang on, let me get down. Leg cramp." Kip stepped closer to the fence, and Amy managed to make her ungainly dismount onto the top rail. "Reverse mermaid," she told him, massaging one calf. "There's a race called the merrow, yeah? Kind of freaky looking most of the time, but they can shapeshift. Anyway, mundanes think they're just a myth, and they're confused about them—they think they're human up top and fish down below. Mermaids."

"Fish?" he asked bemusedly.

"What do you mean, *fish*? You've never seen a fish?"

"Not that I recall…"

"Man," Amy muttered, "we have *got* to do more research on the Gray Lands. So, uh…fish live in water, and they're scaly. They have a tail instead of legs. Here, I'll get a picture."

Kip leaned over to watch as Amy swiped at her mobile. "That…no, I know nothing of your fish."

"Okay, well, imagine one as big as me, then stick my top on its bottom end, and voila, mermaid. Look here, I found some drawings."

"*Ah*." He nodded at the screen.

"So…you know, you get stories, guy falls for a mermaid or whatever, and now he's got a problem. She's pretty from the waist up, but once you get below that…"

"Yes. Yes, I see. Felicia is a reverse mermaid." He stepped back a few paces, then hesitated as Amy looked up from her screen. "You…realize what that makes you, yes?"

"Confusing, I assume."

Kip opened his mouth, but he seemed to rethink whatever he intended to say and coughed instead. "Your cramp is better? Want to try something faster?"

I watched her slip onto his back again, this time with

less hesitation, and then she scooted forward until she could wrap her arms around him. "Barnacle position assumed. I'm ready."

"That cannot be comfortable," he protested.

"*Can't* be comfortable, and aside from your hair in my mouth—"

"For that, you are getting a lap, picky girl," he interrupted, then let himself into the ring and broke into a full gallop. Amy shrieked as he ran, but there was laughter in the sound.

When I sneaked back into the house, I was surprised to find Zeb at the kitchen window with a cup of tea, watching the training ring—or at least the sliver visible from his position. "Looks like they're having fun," he whispered as I took off my dusty trainers. "Tea? There's plenty of water."

"Caffeine is the last thing I need." I joined him at the window and tapped the glass. "He's trying to help her figure out riding."

"He seems like a good kid. And this is chamomile," he added, nudging a box of teabags my way. "Go on, it can't hurt."

I don't take much convincing in matters of tea, and I made myself a mug in short order. "What do you think? Seriously?"

"About that?" asked Zeb, pointing to the ring. "I think we've got two orphaned teenagers who found a kindred spirit in a time of crisis. Wouldn't worry, Mom."

"I'm not *worried*, but you don't think…"

I left that unfinished, and Zeb shrugged. "I think they've got something platonic that could theoretically become something more if they didn't have to work around that *teeny* compatibility problem."

The water was the perfect temperature, and I sipped for a moment while Kip and Amy ran into and out of our view. "She's his mermaid," I murmured when they'd disappeared again into the shadows.

"Not a bad way of putting it," he replied, then frowned. "Just checking, but she's only a witch-blood, right? No shifter in that mix?"

"As far as I know. Besides, have you ever heard of an equine shifter?"

"No, but they wouldn't get far in the Dark Company, would they? Neither sneaky nor deadly…'Oh, no problem, I'll just morph into a horse and mosey on over there to eavesdrop. No one will ever notice me!'" He chuckled into his mug. "Yeah, horseshoes sound like a terrible idea for espionage. Speaking of which, assuming Kip's going to stick around, we might want to broach that idea with him."

I cut my eyes to Zeb and grunted. "Would *you* like to explain to him why you want to nail a piece of metal to his feet?"

"It doesn't hurt the horses," he countered. "Anyway, we may be able to avoid that conversation—Carey wants to go back to San Angelo tomorrow night. Jim called and said the gate's still open, and since we're the closest wizards with any real chance of getting the job done, we might as well do the responsible thing and make the drive."

"If Kip wanted to go home—"

"We've got horse trailers for *days*. He's back in one piece, and we could load him up with enough food and gear to get him to civilization…probably. I mean, I don't know jack about the Gray Lands," he admitted, "but there has to be a village like Kip's somewhere near that gate, right?"

I nodded and drank my tea. "We should at least make the offer. Amy…well, surely she'll understand."

To my surprise, however, Kip was vehemently opposed to the suggestion that he go home. "I owe a life debt," he protested over breakfast in the barn. "I cannot—*can't*— leave that unpaid."

"You saved me from Felicia," Amy pointed out. "That's something."

"That was hardly a life-or-death situation—"

"There's nothing to repay, Kip," I interrupted. "Whatever debt you think you owe...we forgive it." Seamus nodded beside me. "We want what's best for you. If you'd like to go home, there's an open gate, and—"

"What home?" he murmured. "My home is gone, my family is *dead*, I have nothing left..." His eyes sought Amy's, then turned back to mine, begging. "Let me help you, I will do anything, but do not send me away—"

"Whoa, *whoa*," Carey interjected, holding up her hands to stop his accelerating plea. "No one's kicking you out. We just thought you might want to go back, that's all. You can stay here."

As relief washed over Kip's face, I noticed Zeb watching Amy, quietly studying her as she hugged Kip around the waist. "In that case," I said, "maybe it would be best if you kids stayed here tonight. Guard the ranch. Surely the four of us can close a gate, right?" I asked the others.

Seamus grimaced. "Seeing how well that worked last time..."

"We didn't actually try to close it, you know. With Carey and Zeb along—"

"I'll still be in the way. You plus me equals *boom*, right?"

"Oh, no," said Zeb, throwing his arm around Seamus's shoulders, "you're coming, bucko. In case of eldritch horrors, it can't hurt to have a faerie on hand."

"I...*have* mentioned my lack of training, haven't I?" he muttered.

Zeb grinned. "No problem. I'm sure we can find you some practice."

We grabbed an early dinner that afternoon, then loaded into the Joneses' Jeep and made the long trek back to the southwest, catching naps as we could. Zeb offered to drive the whole way, but Carey insisted on taking the second leg. "I want you in fighting form," she explained as he climbed into the passenger seat. "Rest up. It's going to be a long night."

"Aren't you the one with the seven a.m. patient tomorrow?" he countered.

"Thanks for the reminder, and you can drive back. Buckle up."

Around nine, as we followed the Rio Grande down the last dark stretch to San Angelo, Jim called his sister to coordinate. "I'm at the Shell at the exit ramp," he said over the car's speakers, "parked in the back. It's dead here."

"Excellent," said Carey. "We'll be there in ten." She glanced in the mirror at Seamus and me, then said, "You want to just squeeze in here with us? No sense in taking both cars out."

Jim hesitated. "Uh…thanks, but I'm not alone."

"Huh?"

"They're harmless," he rushed, "they just want to help, and they've been out to the gate—"

"Bloody hell," Seamus interrupted, "did you bring the nudists along?"

"Naturalists," came Tony's muffled reply.

"Mundanes," I offered for the Joneses' benefit. "Tony and Julia Wiggins, they're in the Circle of the Sun."

Carey swore softly and clenched her hands around the wheel. "What the hell, Jimmy? This is no place for gawkers!"

"They brought guns. Come on, they want to help us," he wheedled. "Can't hurt, right?"

"Unless they get caught in the crossfire."

"We'll stay out of the way!" Julia called in the background.

With a sigh, Carey looked at the rest of us and

whispered, "Thoughts?"

"They did let us bring Kip to their home," I replied. "And they let us stay even after their high priestess had a freak-out."

"Over *what*?"

"My terrifying display of magical prowess, but that's beside the point. They're already in on the secret."

"And they spent most of our last trip to the gate being sick on the side of the road," Seamus added, "so how much harm can they do?"

I could tell that she didn't like the situation, but Carey proceeded to the petrol station and found Jim's old Expedition parked outside the security light's radius. When she pulled alongside him, his windows rolled down, revealing the camouflage-clad Wigginses and what appeared to be a minor arsenal stacked around them. "Hi!" said Jim, and his passengers waved at us. "Follow me, and stay close, it's *dark* out there. Hey, is Kip not going home?"

"Not tonight. We left him with Amy back at the ranch," said Zeb, leaning over his wife to take a closer look at the mundanes. "Hi, there, folks. What, um…what did you say you do, again?"

"Oh, we're innkeepers," Julia chirped, and patted the rifle in her lap. "This is a relatively new hobby."

Seamus gawked at them through the lowered windows. "You said you were pacifists!"

"We are," said Tony, "but under the circumstances, we thought it would be best to have protection. I told you we were going to that pawn shop—"

"I thought you meant to get a pistol! *One*! Maybe one apiece!" He sputtered for a few seconds, then managed, "You can't possibly be competent on all of those guns."

"We've been out to the range—"

"It's only been *five days*."

"You know," Carey interrupted, "time's wasting, and we can talk about gun safety later. Head on, Jimmy, I'm right behind you…and, uh, maybe you guys should keep the guns in the car until we know what we're up against, okay?" she told the Wigginses.

As we pulled out of the lot, Zeb muttered, "He'd better hope he doesn't get stopped. Wonder how he'd explain those two to a cop?" He paused, then turned to scowl at Seamus. "Back up, man, *nudists*?"

Jim was right about the light situation: we were out hours before moonrise, and even when it came up, we'd have no more than a sliver. Carey stayed close to her brother's bumper, letting his high beams illuminate the track into the mountains, but she wasn't the only tense one in the vehicle. Zeb sat up straight beside her, scanning our surroundings, and I resisted the urge to tap my wand against my leg like a drumstick. A little flash caught my eye, and I glanced to my left in time to see Seamus extinguish the blue spark in his palm. He hadn't been quick enough, however, and Carey pointedly cleared her throat. "Let's not crisp my car, okay?"

"Sorry," he mumbled. "Nerves."

"You and me both, bub," she replied. "I've only worked on a couple of gates, and they're not a walk in the park with a solid team. Tonight…"

"You've got Jim," I offered.

She spared me a quick glance over her shoulder. "The fact that Jim took the two of you out to try to close a gate should show you exactly how inexperienced he is with these matters. Jimmy is a lot of things, but he's never going to set any records as a wizard."

I paused, trying to judge Carey's mood, then said, "Amy thinks he might need a stronger wand. He's using a phoenix blood, but she thought he could have gone with unicorn."

To my relief, she shrugged. "Wouldn't surprise me. Zeb and I snagged a couple of her ambers, and unless

Jim's changed a lot in the last few years, he wouldn't be able to use one."

"She said he's definitely a wizard—"

"Sure, but there's a lot of gray area at the wizard–witch border, and my brother's never been one to study what didn't immediately interest him."

"Chemistry," Zeb muttered.

"God, please don't remind me." Carey shook her head and sighed. "There are perks to an Arcanum education, don't get me wrong, and he'd be a much better wizard if he worked at it, but if he's happy and can feed himself, I'm not going to nag him. I've mothered that boy enough…"

Her voice faded as Jim tapped the brakes, and I recognized our parking spot above the valley. Carey followed him off the road and cut the engine, then unbuckled and pulled her wand out of her waistband. "So, who wants to perform in front of an audience? A couple of crazy mundanes makes everything better, am I right?"

"You're stalling, dear," said Zeb as he climbed out, and Seamus and I quickly followed suit.

By the time we reached Jim's car, the Wiginses had disembarked and were adjusting their handguns and rifles. "I thought you were going to keep those in the car," said Seamus, igniting his hand flame to examine the disturbing extent of the stockpile in the Expedition.

"They don't do any good if you don't have them with you, silly," said Julia, sliding a petite pistol into her pink hip holster.

"They also don't do any good if you can't *aim*—shit, not at me!" he yelped, darting to the side as Tony straightened and inadvertently raised his shotgun. "For fuck's sake, mate, point that thing at the ground!"

Tony mumbled an apology and adjusted his guns, and Carey, with a last roll of her eyes to the starry heavens, motioned us on. "Zeb, can you take point? Hannah—"

An inhuman howl rent the night, cutting her off, and my hackles rose with the instinctive knowledge that running would be the safest course of action. The Joneses froze with their wands out, but I found Seamus's eyes and nodded. In one smooth motion, he plucked Julia's pistol from her hip, then flung the Wigginses back into the dirt behind our vehicles. "Stay there," I barked over their surprised protestations, and Seamus and I jogged for the top of the rise with the real wizards in pursuit.

"Plan?" Zeb asked.

"If it moves, get ready to shoot it," I replied, readying my wand. "If it's howling, *definitely* shoot it."

"Do you have wolves here?" Seamus added, glancing back at the locals.

"Sure," said Carey, "but *that* ain't no wolf."

I reached the edge first and stared down at the dark valley. "What are those, then?"

As the others gathered around, I tried to make sense of the moving shapes below, which were still black on black as my eyes adjusted. There were multiple creatures down there, *large* creatures—the source of the howling, I assumed—and something in the middle...

Suddenly, a flash of lightning exploded in the middle of the shifting darkness, and the target howled in pain.

"Wizard," Carey muttered, jabbing her finger toward the lightning's source. "That's a wizard down there. Who the hell is that?"

"Not one of us," said Jim. "I checked again before we went out...did you see another car?"

"No," I replied, fighting my knotting stomach. "Which means whoever that is probably got in by gate. Arcanum."

"About damn time they showed up to patch that thing," said Carey. "Come on, I don't think he saw us—"

The wizard's wand flared again, but one of the injured beasts leapt onto his back even as he fired the shot. He screamed—human, that one, all too human—and my conscience reared over my self-preservation instinct. "He's outnumbered. We can't leave him."

I took off running into the valley, ignoring the shouts

behind me, and looked up at the whistle of one of Seamus's fireballs passing overhead. It arced over the valley floor and exploded into brilliant white light, and I almost turned around when I saw what I was running toward.

Carey was correct: the three bloodied beasts weren't wolves, if only because no wolf since the Pleistocene had been that massive. Flat-footed, they were taller than Great Danes and solidly built, two covered in shaggy black pelts and the third in a smoother brown coat. Several similar lumps lay motionless around them. Each of the living beasts bore singe marks and gashes...but then, the man in the middle of their narrowing circle hadn't fared well, either. I couldn't make out much about him in the limited light, but he seemed short and slim beside the monstrous wolves, gray-haired and sporting a blue anorak over dirty jeans.

If he'd worn black, I would have left him to fend for himself. But the wizard, whoever he was, wasn't wearing an assassin's uniform, and I couldn't just leave him to be mauled.

Seeing an opening, I shot a jet of fire at the nearest wolf, which cried with the pain and ran howling, its tail and hindquarters aflame. Another wolf was picked up and flung away from the wizard, and I saw Seamus running behind me with his hand raised. With a flick of his wrist, he flung the flying wolf at the ground, and the creature's neck snapped on impact. Seizing the opportunity, the wizard, though dazed and blinking in the afterglow of the fireball, electrocuted the third wolf, which collapsed at his feet.

I counted two corpses, and I was afraid I'd lost the first wolf when a stream of fire to my right showed me that Zeb had caught up and located the target. With the third wolf flambéed, we turned our attention to the injured wizard, who kept his wand high as we approached. "No closer, I'm warning you," I heard him say, and I barely had time to pick out the hint of public school in his voice before he collapsed.

"Always watch your flank," said Carey, lowering her wand as she appeared from behind the gate to my left.

Seamus tossed up another light, which he managed to stabilize before it could flare and die, and frowned at the motionless wizard. "What did you—"

"Stunned him. He'll be out for an hour or so. Not a bad little spell to have in the old arsenal, you know?"

"Not at all. And you're certain he's not one of yours?"

Zeb moved closer and nudged the wizard's leg with his toe. "Nope. We don't have but a handful of folks from your neck of the woods, and he's not one of them."

Seamus nodded, then offered me Julia's pistol. "Would you like to do the honors, Badge, or should I?"

"Whoa, now, wait," I sputtered, retreating from the proffered gun with my hands up. "We can't just *shoot* him—"

"Why not? He's Arcanum, he's armed, he must have some notion of what he's doing to be here…"

As Seamus rattled off the many reasons why it would be a good idea to kill the unconscious wizard, I stepped closer and took a good look at his face—a surprisingly young face, considering his mop of silver hair. "He's not an assassin," I interrupted, "and he's had a tough few days. Not all of these scratches are new, and his clothes…ugh," I groaned, getting a whiff of the funk. "I don't think he's on official business."

"So…what," said Carey, "he goes halfway around the world to close a gate on a lark?"

"I don't know, but I think *this* is premature," I replied, shaking the gun. "And he's in rough shape, Doc."

She sighed and came closer to give him her own inspection. "Why are you trying to make me feel bad for an Arcanum wizard?" she muttered.

"Because I think he might be more useful to us alive than dead. If he *is* Arcanum, then he might have intel."

"And if he's not?"

"Then we haven't murdered him without cause. Yeah?" I said, looking up as Seamus approached.

"Yeah," he mumbled, and took the gun back. "But assuming he's Arcanum, how do we keep him from killing us before we get back to the ranch?"

"Wait, who said anything about—oh, *damn it*," Carey muttered, and pointed to the top of the valley. "Fine. Put him in the car, and I'm going to work on the gate. Zeb, Hannah, get over here."

Jim, who'd been incinerating wolves while we dickered over the wizard's fate, raised his hand. "Want me to help with the gate?"

His sister shook her head. "No, I want you to get back up there and explain to your nudist buddies that we're not actually kidnapping anyone. Go on, shoo." She watched him jog off, then noticed my partner and groaned. "Seamus…no. *Magic*. Seriously, don't drag him."

My partner, who had grabbed the wizard under the arms and was pulling him backwards toward the dirt road, simply shrugged and continued on. "Less chance of accidental crisping or head trauma," he explained. "You do the gate your way, and I'll haul the bastard my way."

Carey considered the open gate, then cut her eyes to me. "You know, I think Zeb and I can take it from here. Why don't you—"

"Right," I said, and ran after Seamus to float the wizard to safety.

Working together, and with a minor assist from Jim and me, it still took Carey and Zeb nearly half an hour to construct the complex patch required to seal off the rift into the Gray Lands. After warning Jim to check the integrity of the patch in a few days and assuring the befuddled Wigginses that we were going to take good care of the battered wizard, we climbed into the Jeep and started the drive back to the ranch.

Of course, this left the minor problem of the unsecured wizard in the cargo bay, who was scheduled to wake before we reached the Interstate. With Zeb at the wheel, Carey angled herself to face the rear, wand at the ready. "I could strengthen his sleep," she said, holding on as we bumped over the rough track, "but anything stronger than that would require a bind, and—"

"You don't do binds, I know," I finished. "Can you at least pump up the juice? Buy us some time before we've got to explain the situation to him?"

As she cast the spell, I noticed Seamus fiddling with his mobile. "Who are you calling?" I asked.

"Val."

"Is he even awake?"

Seamus grimaced as he held out the phone and tapped the screen. "They were a few hours ahead of us, last we spoke, so hope for night shift, eh?"

Confused, Carey twisted closer to us and pointed her wand toward the phone. "*Who* are you calling?"

"My uncle," said Seamus, talking over the ringing speaker. "Who may or may not be—"

The line clicked open. "Seamus," said Val, who sounded closer to pleased than peeved. "Are you safe?"

"Ehm…more or less," he replied. "Sorry about the hour—"

"Forget the hour. What's wrong?"

I leaned toward Seamus's outstretched palm. "Long story short, the gate's closed, and we've picked up a wizard in the process. Our hosts are keeping him unconscious for now, but that's not a permanent fix—"

"Hosts?"

"Remember Jim? His sister and brother-in-law."

"Ah. Good. I'll have Toula call you back," Val replied, and the line went dead.

We looked at each other, then jostled in our seats as the Jeep hit another bad patch of terrain. "*So…*" Carey began, drawing out the word, "that was…"

"Turns out it's possible to make trans-realm phone calls when you put enough magic into play," I told her. "And Toula Pavli's going to ring us up, assuming she doesn't mind the time."

"*Arcanum* Toula Pavli? How does your uncle—"

"She's my aunt," Seamus interrupted as the phone began to chirp, then tapped the screen, which opened to Toula's sleep-weary face. "Hello, there. Didn't know this did video," he told her as she brushed her floppy spikes from her eyes.

"Surprise," she said through a yawn. "Who'd you pick up? Let me see."

He flipped on the reading light, then swiveled to face the rear and held up the phone. "Can you see him?"

"*Fuck.*"

"I'll take that as a yes." Seamus turned around and held the phone so that Toula could see Carey and me. "Talk to the ones who'd understand."

She squinted at us. "Uh…hi, I'm—"

"Toula Pavli, yeah?" said Carey. "Carey Jones, Minor Arcanum. What are we dealing with?"

"A potential disaster, actually. You've got Arnold Lowe knocked out back there."

"Who?"

"Oh, bloody hell," I muttered. "Lowe's one of the Glastonbury magi."

"A *magus*?" Carey snapped. "Fantastic. We've caught a magus. What the hell am I supposed to do with a magus?"

"It would be safest to kill him," said Val, leaning over Toula's shoulder. "Destroy the body, cover your tracks."

Toula gave her brother a side look. "Or, barring that, bind him. Make sure he can't fight you or go for help until you get to the bottom of this. Was he alone?"

"Yes," I told her, "which struck me as odd. I thought gate closure was a team effort."

"It is. He looks banged-up to me, too, and Arnold…I

mean, he didn't seem like the murderous type, but you never know. Still, better safe than sorry. Bind him until it's safe."

"Forget it," said Carey. "We don't do binds."

"But—"

"No. *Binds*. They're completely immoral."

Toula rolled her eyes and huffed. "Principles are lovely things to have, but when it's your ass on the line—"

"You keep them, because principles matter. What's the backup plan?"

"Aside from killing him and getting rid of the evidence?" She rubbed her neck as she thought. "How close are you to home?"

"About four hours," said Carey.

"Can you keep him asleep that long?"

"Probably, but—"

"No buts," Toula interrupted, holding the phone closer to her face. "Do whatever you have to do to keep him knocked out. Now, how are your knot-tying skills?"

CHAPTER 18

The magus groaned as he regained consciousness, waking little by little while Carey dismantled the spell holding him under. When the last of it dissolved, he tried to move his arms, then paused and frowned when he encountered resistance. Slowly, he opened his gummy eyes, squinted in the bright light of the barn's overhead lamps, and blinked. Perhaps unnerved to find himself the focus of three wands and a pair of guns, he looked down and contemplated the ropes binding him securely to a metal folding chair. And then, perhaps finally realizing the extent of the situation, he tried to shout—a futile effort, given the gag.

While the magus squirmed and snorted in his panic, Seamus stepped forward and conjured up a blue flame in his hand. "Hello," he said, casually tossing the fire like a tennis ball. "Sorry about the ropes, mate, but it was either this or kill you. We thought you'd prefer this option." He squatted to be on our prisoner's eye level and passed the fireball from hand to hand. "Now, here's what you need to know. I am currently the good cop. These fine folks behind me are the bad cops. You're going to answer my questions. If you choose not to cooperate, I'll let them have a turn at this interview. Nod if you understand."

He nodded frantically, and Seamus extinguished the fire, freeing his hands to remove the magus's gag. "Right, then. Let's start with the easy bit. What's your name?"

"Ar…" His voice cracked, and he cleared his throat. "Arnold Lowe. Arnold Edward Parsons Lowe, if that makes you happier. And am I imagining things, or is that a *centaur* with a *shotgun*?"

"Now, now," Seamus gently chided, "that's not how this works. Though yes, that's a centaur, he's rather cross at being awakened in the middle of the night, and he's not a bad shot—especially not at this range. Honestly, though, the one you want to worry about is *her*," he added, cocking his head toward Amy, whose filmy pink nightgown was somewhat incongruous with the rifle cradled against her shoulder. "So, Arnold...may I call you Arnold?"

The saucer-eyed magus nodded.

"That's quite a name, isn't it?" he said, making small talk in an effort to build rapport. "Couldn't stop with three?"

"F-family names," he managed.

"*You're* a Parsons?" I interrupted, and Arnold turned his fearful eyes on me as I advanced with my wand.

He swallowed hard, though whether from nerves or a dry throat, I couldn't say. "Yes, my mother is Esmerelda Parsons."

"Of the Glastonbury Parsons?"

"Yes, exactly," said Arnold, beginning to babble. "Ehm...she's the youngest of the family, and I was a bit of a late surprise—"

"Youngest?" I interrupted. "What do you mean, *youngest*?"

His blood-streaked forehead furrowed. "Youngest of her siblings. Alfred, Clarisse, Joshua, and Esmerelda. How do you know the family?"

"And Brian."

The magus's confusion deepened. "Who?"

"Brian," I murmured. "Alfie, Rissa, Josh, Essie, and Brian. The five Parsons children."

"I...believe you're mistaken, Miss—"

"*Parsons*," I spat as rage washed over me like an ice bath. "Hannah Parsons. And it's Detective Inspector, you fucking *twat*—"

Seamus grabbed me around the waist before I could

lunge at him and wrestled me away. "It's all right, Badger," he soothed, prying my wand from my tight fist. "Let's not kill the wanker yet."

"*Yet?*" Arnold squeaked.

Though I surrendered my wand, I broke from Seamus's hold and marched back to the chair, the better to glower down at the captive magus. "You've never heard of Brian Parsons?" I demanded, vaguely conscious that my arms were shaking.

He hesitated, then gave his head a quick shake. "No, Mi—Detective. No, I...my mother's never spoken of another brother."

I squeezed my eyes shut to stop the pricking. "My dad was Geoffrey and Charlotte Parsons' youngest. A witch."

"Oh. *Oh*," he muttered as the implications clicked home. "Your father—"

"Murdered at Easter with the rest of the Fringe. My mother, too, but I don't suppose you ever heard of her, did you? I mean, what does the Arcanum care about another dead mundane?"

"Christ," he whispered. "Detective, I...I had nothing to do with that madness, you must believe me—"

"Oh, a *magus* didn't know about the master plan? Sure, that's credible. And I was born yesterday, you—"

"I told you she's the bad cop," said Seamus, wrapping his arm around my trembling shoulders. "You *are* a magus, are you not?"

"Yes, but—"

Amy sighted down the barrel of her gun at him. "Good enough for me, Miss Hannah."

"I didn't know!" Arnold shouted, frantically straining at the ropes. "Not until the end of the day! I'm just a junior magus, I'm not on the Inner Council, and Mulligan is *insane*! Please, don't—"

Having tried to free himself a little too vigorously, he managed to topple his chair backwards, and he wheezed as he hit the floor and sucked for breath.

"Now, that's just pathetic," said Seamus as Zeb's wand waved Arnold upright. "Sounded painful, too. Are you going to be a good boy, Arnie, or should we drop you again?"

He nodded, though he winced when his head moved. "Don't shoot. I had nothing to do with the attack on the Fringe."

"Yeah?" said Carey, tucking her wand away as she approached. "Seems like you're hanging around awfully close to Hannah to be uninvolved. Look here, follow my finger with your eyes. The barn floor's unforgiving."

He did as instructed, and Carey stepped back, satisfied. "I'm here because of that blasted gate," he said. "She has nothing to do with it."

"Arcanum couldn't find a closer magus to deal with it, huh?" Carey asked.

"The Arcanum *isn't* dealing with it. I told you, Mulligan is mental," he muttered, scowling at us. "I'm on the lam. Once Mulligan took over and I got the real story…maybe it's a personal failing, but I'm opposed to genocide. Of course, with the Council backing Mulligan and the rest of the magi at least pretending to be on board, I couldn't very well tell him I thought his plan was abhorrent. So I skipped town."

"You're trying to get into the Gray Lands?" Zeb asked.

"No! I'm trying to do the job I swore to do." Arnold looked around, saw varying degrees of comprehension, and explained, "Part of the oath I took as a magus is to protect this realm from the Gray Lands. Mulligan's ignoring the gates—I think the plan is to blame any incursions on Faerie. It's worked thus far," he muttered.

"So what's the rest of the plan, then?" Seamus asked, holding me as I continued to shake with anger. "Kill Fringers and profit?"

He sighed. "No. Mulligan's told the rank-and-file that rogue faeries killed the grand magus, her husband, and part of the Fringe. After that business with the pack of werewolves, he seized control in the vacuum, and he's tightened everything up. Wizards who live outside an installation are being ordered to relocate into one for their own *protection*," he said with dripping sarcasm. "Faeries are dangerous, you know."

"And the Fringe?"

"They're being made useful," Arnold replied, his mouth tightening. "The ones that weren't killed are being hidden somewhere—I never learned where, but I suspect somewhere in the silo. Maybe Mulligan's hidden them wherever he put Helen. Hostages, you see. He's using them to control the courts." He paused to gauge his audience's reaction, then focused his attention on me. "Detective Parsons, I'm terribly sorry about your parents. Truly, I am. Had I known that you and your father existed, I'd have tried to reach out before now."

"Sure," I muttered.

"I mean it. Look, I heard about what the Fringe did for us when the silo was besieged. Everyone heard. It was probably the first time most of us had *ever* heard of the Fringe, to be honest, but the fact that you came to our help—all things considered, that was remarkable. And I know Helen was planning to meet with some of your people—"

"She did, in Faerie."

He snorted. "Safer than the silo, I bet. But I was excited about the Fringe initiative, you know? Connecting with you, working with you—it made sense. Had I known for a minute that I had a cousin in the Fringe, I'd have sought you out."

When I said nothing, Seamus murmured, "He's not lying, love."

"I know," I mumbled.

"Faerie intuition?" Zeb asked.

"Cop intuition. It's far better." He glanced around our semicircle and nodded. "Put them down."

Zeb, Carey, and Kip lowered their weapons, but Amy

shook her head and held her rifle steady. "He's Arcanum," she said, staring at the bound magus.

"And he's not the one to blame. Amy, listen to me. Put the gun down."

She tightened her grip in reply. "You don't know that."

I slipped out from under Seamus's arm and stepped between our prisoner and the rifle barrel. "No, we don't," I told her. "But I tend to believe him."

"Why?"

"I...I can't tell you exactly, but it's a feeling. This is experience talking. I've done thousands of interviews— Seamie has, too," I added as he nodded vigorously, "and sometimes—a lot of the time—you know when you're being lied to. He's scared as hell, but he's not lying."

Amy's jaw began to quiver, and I grasped the barrel. "Sweetie," I murmured, "if I thought for one second that he had anything to do with your parents' deaths, I'd happily stand back and watch you blow his head off. But I don't think he's the one you want."

After a long moment, she let me push the gun away, and I heard Arnold sigh in relief. Before he could get too comfortable, I turned back to him and poked my fingers into his chest. "Prove me wrong, and I'll kill you myself. I don't care if we're kin. Clear?"

"Crystal," he said. "Ehm...is there any chance of being untied tonight, or am I pushing my luck?"

I looked at the others for signs of protest, then turned back to him. "Depends. Here's the problem, Arnie: you know too much. What happens if you scamper out of here and run into another magus? Someone who might be forgiving if you told the assassin corps where to find us?"

He considered this briefly, took another long look at his well-armed captors, then nodded. "I don't suppose you're accepting recruits, are you?"

Fifteen minutes later, while Carey tried to catch a few

hours of sleep ahead of her morning appointment, Zeb made chamomile tea and passed mugs around the den. Kip, who had come into the house for the first time, stepped as gingerly as if he were walking on glass in his effort not to bump into the assorted end tables and hanging decoration, while Arnold sat on the overstuffed ottoman and held a bag of frozen lima beans to the back of his bruised head. "It took me a few days to figure it all out," he explained while the tea cooled. "One night, there are werewolves in the silo, and suddenly, the grand magus is dead and everyone's in a panic."

"*Dead?*" I interrupted. "I thought you said—"

"That's the official line. Mulligan called us all to the silo for a closed-door meeting and told us the truth. With Helen neutralized and a good number of Fringers taken hostage, Faerie wouldn't dare meddle in this realm."

"He's actually banking on that?"

Arnold smirked. "We know the king and queen are half fae. He thinks they're human enough to hold their fire if it means saving Fringers. Then again, seeing the company you're keeping, I don't know how well this plan of his is going to work in the long run. Which one sent you?" he asked, turning to Seamus.

"Neither," he replied. "I'm a free agent."

Arnold's eyes narrowed. "You...*don't* claim a court?"

"Nope. Got a problem with that?"

"I mean, it scares the shit out of me, but beyond that? No. You're Fringe, then?"

"I'm with her," said Seamus, nodding toward me. "Slap whatever label on that you like."

The magus shook his head, then peered at me. "You know," he mused, "you look like Grandfather—"

"The hair, I know, Dad told me. It's why I'm called Badger." I sipped my tea and stared back at Arnold, who'd won an entire head of early gray instead of a mere white stripe. "You're close to them? Our grandparents?"

He shrugged. "Not as close as some of us.

Grandfather's hard to read, and Grandmother's too formal to be fun. But they're not unkind," he rushed to assure me. "And my magus ceremony—they couldn't have been prouder. So glad to have another Magus Parsons around, you see. One of Grandfather's sisters made it, but she died young." He paused and considered my carefully blanked face. "Have you met them?"

"No." I sipped again, watching him squirm. "They never visited us. No one did. And assuming you're being honest with me, all of Dad's family have been pretending he never existed, so I suppose I shouldn't be surprised at the lack of contact. They gave me my wand, though," I continued, keeping my tone casual. "When I was little and just starting to learn. Told Dad it was a dragonscale. It was actually shadow alder."

Arnold's jaw dropped. "Shadow...but...but that...but *you*..."

"I used it constantly," I said over his sputtering. "Almost forty years on a shadow alder wand. And then Amy gave me this one," I said, tapping my new wand against my knee. "Want to guess the core?"

"I suppose...dragonscale? A proper one?"

"A mineral composite. Seems I'm not a witch after all."

He looked a little green at that. "I, ehm...I can see where you would be upset—"

"Toula peeked at my aura. Said I look like a magus to her. If I'd ever been trained..." I shrugged. "But that's neither here nor there, is it? And there's a magus out of the Parsons clan once more, so everyone's happy."

Arnold put his mug aside and flipped his makeshift cold pack. "What do you want me to say, Hannah? The whole situation is shite, but what do you want me to do about it?"

"Nothing. I just want you to understand why I'm going to slap our dear grandparents in the face if I ever have the opportunity."

"And we're going to tag-team this, right?" Seamus

added. "What's the point of a partner if you're going to insist on punching old people by yourself?"

My cousin stared at us for a moment like we were mad, then mumbled, "Knee."

"Come again?" said Seamus.

"Grandfather had his knee replaced five years ago. If you want to do real damage…go for the fake joint."

He flashed a timid smile, and I felt mine grow for a few seconds before a sobering thought hit me. "Are they running a blood trace on you? They didn't just let you sneak off, did they?"

"Oh, they may very well be running one, but it won't do them any good." Seeing our bemusement, Arnold grinned in earnest. "Let's say that while the Council was preoccupied in the first days after the grand magus's 'death,' I sneaked into their records and saw all the nasty little things they'd been up to. No one on the Council knows the first thing about e-mail security, I swear," he muttered, rolling his eyes. "They'd been collaborating with Lady Moyna, you know? Helping her out. That's where the werewolves came from. And someone had worked out a spell to hide her from blood traces."

"You…"

"Look closer," he said, beckoning me near. "See it?"

When I squinted at the area just above his skin, I noticed the pale sheen of an active spell, barely distinguishable from the background and his natural aura. "That's *brilliant*. Zeb, come here, you need to see this."

Zeb looked over my shoulder, then whistled his approval. "Okay, I'm impressed. That's some tight work."

"I don't have much of a social life," Arnold replied. "And speaking of work, what about that gate?"

"We closed it," said Zeb. "Maybe our patch isn't as pretty as the one you were planning to make, but—"

"If it's closed, it's closed, and you did save me from becoming a chew toy, so thank you. But back to the blood trace issue," he continued, looking at me. "Our grandparents are still alive, and even if they weren't, they surely have blood samples on file. Your father might even be in the Archives. If someone thinks to run a trace…"

"The last thing the Arcanum saw of me, I'd jumped off a cliff into Faerie," I replied. "And who'd be stupid enough to come back, eh?"

"That may well be," said Arnold, "but all the same, it couldn't hurt to have a block on you as well, could it? And what about you?" he asked Amy. "Were your parents witches?"

"Witch-bloods," she said. "Both of them. I've only met one wizard grandmother, and if either of them is still alive, it's news to me."

That took him aback. "A *double* witch-blood? Seriously?"

"The Fringe isn't as hung up on breeding," I interjected before he could further antagonize Amy. "But as long as you're blocking me, you may as well block her to be safe."

"Certainly. No sense in making it easy for the trackers." He finished his tea in a long slurp, then clutched the empty mug and cocked his head at Kip. "I don't mean to be rude, but what the devil are you doing with him?"

Kip, who'd been whispering with Amy while the wizards talked spellcraft, straightened. "I am here to assist. I owe a life debt—"

"Kip's honorary Fringe," I offered. "And right now, we'll take whomever we can get. Even you, Arnie."

"Ha." He began to stroke his chin but paused when his fingers hit dried blood. "I'm curious how you mean to put him to work."

"I am—*I'm* a good shot," Kip insisted. "Not as good as Amy, but with practice…"

"I don't doubt that," said Arnold, "but how do you plan to leave this ranch?"

He rubbed his bare arm as he thought. "When we left Julia and Tony, I had a place to ride behind the main vehicle."

"A trailer," said Amy.

But Arnold shook his head. "I'm not talking about the mechanics. If a mundane saw a bloody *centaur* walking down the street, there'd be panic."

Kip's forehead crinkled. "Why?"

"Because as far as the mundane world knows, you don't exist. And we'd very much like to keep it that way." He hesitated briefly, then scooted closer to Kip and held out his dirty hands. "Have you considered transformation?"

"We don't do that," Zeb cut in. "Carey and I don't do bind work."

"Could have fooled me," Arnold muttered. "And anyway, I'm not asking you to do it. I'm perfectly capable of pulling off a spell like that...assuming you're willing," he added, glancing at Kip.

The teenagers looked at each other with concern, and Kip frowned at Arnold. "What is transformation?"

He leaned toward them, warming to the subject. "To put it into layman's terms, it's the souped-up version of what *he's* doing," he explained, pointing to Seamus. "There's no way in hell he actually looks like that. Why don't you show them, prove my point?"

Seamus grunted, but his glamour fell away as Kip's eyes widened. "It's an enchantment that lets me look my age," he said. "Doesn't hurt. See?" In a blink, Seamus was graying once again. "Can't tell it's fake, can you?"

"Well...no," Kip admitted, "but *he* could..."

"Only because I know what faeries are supposed to look like, and he didn't make any secret of it. Half, I assume?" he asked Seamus, who nodded. "But as for you," he told Kip, "glamour might not be enough. Much safer to go full transformation, less chance of random illusion failure."

Seeing Kip's continued confusion, Amy said, "He can make you look like us. Pass for human."

"More or less," said Arnold. "I mean, I've never seen a

natural ginger with that much melanin. But I could get you down to the standard number of limbs. Oh, it's not permanent," he assured Kip, who looked less convinced by the second. "Any competent wizard could break it, or leaving this realm would do the trick. But at least you'd be able to get about without a horse trailer."

"You don't have to," Zeb quickly added. "No one is going to make you. But he does have a point—if you want to help with the Fringe effort, you're going to want to leave this ranch someday."

Kip sat in silence for a full minute, mulling this over, and finally turned to Amy. "What do you think?"

"I can't make that decision for you," she murmured. "Do what you think is best, Kip." She squeezed his shoulder, and he covered her hand with his as he looked back at Arnold.

"In the morning," he said softly. "I am tired, *you* are injured…sleep first, for my peace of mind. Treat your wounds."

With that, Kip rose to return to the barn, and Amy slipped out into the night beside him. I was standing at the back door to make sure they made it in the dark when I heard Arnold cry out behind me. "Bloody *hell*," he exclaimed, staring at himself in a mirror, "why did no one tell me I look like a chainsaw murderer on a spree?"

As we didn't make it to our beds until just after four in the morning—Arnold, at least, needed half an hour in the shower before collapsing in Jim's vacant bedroom—no one but poor Carey saw daylight until lunchtime. When I finally shuffled into the kitchen to consider provisions, I found her hunched over a cup of coffee at the table, too weary to glower. "No training today, okay?" she mumbled between long sips. "Gonna take a nap."

Stiff from the long ride the night before and still sore from my last forced run, I didn't protest.

Slowly, the others emerged, Seamus in his sleeping sweats, Zeb in a Taos T-shirt and plaid boxers, and then Arnold, who had conjured up a proper silk bathrobe, matching pajamas, and bedroom slippers. As a fresh pot of coffee percolated, Amy and Kip wandered in from the barn, both bleary-eyed and rumpled. "Sleep well?" I asked, willing the caffeine to work.

"Not really," said Amy as Kip shook his head.

I could guess the cause—the poor boy was giving Arnold as wide a berth as he could in the crowded kitchen, but considering Kip's size, there wasn't much he could do to avoid him. Seamus, who had taken on breakfast duty for the moment, worked around Kip as he scrambled eggs and kept a steady flow of bread going into and out of the toaster. I thought about stepping into the fray to help, but Seamus was surprisingly adept for a man wearing oven mitts and dancing around an equine back end with hot food, and besides, I'd found a comfortable stool on which to nurse my coffee.

Once we'd eaten and the worst of the grogginess had passed, Arnold rolled up his sleeves, pulled his wand out of his belt, and pointed to Amy and me. "Ladies, if it's all right with you, I'll put that blocking spell in place."

I pushed my empty mug aside. "Sure. Can you do it here, or do you need some quiet?"

He considered the rest of our lethargic pack and shrugged. "I've had worse. You first, eh?"

The casting didn't take long, only a couple of minutes, and I felt a pleasantly warm tingle race over my skin as the spell took effect. If I held my arm steady and squinted, I could just see the fine construction, and I nodded my satisfaction. "Tidy work."

"Should be—I *am* a magus. Didn't hurt?" he asked.

I sensed that the enquiry was more for Kip's benefit than mine. "Not a bit. Okay, Amy, your turn."

She closed her eyes and stood stock-still while Arnold muttered the protective spell into place, but she smiled at

Kip when the procedure was finished. "Miss Hannah's right, it doesn't hurt at all. But I swear, you don't have to do this if you don't want to…"

Kip took a deep breath and slowly exhaled. "It is for the best for now. I am ready, Arnie."

If the nickname bothered the magus, he didn't show it. "That's great," he replied, "but I don't think we should do it here. Your room is out in the barn, right? Let's do it there." He glanced around the table at our weary men. "Zeb, Seamus, come with us, if you will."

Seamus's eyebrow rose. "Correct me if I'm wrong, but I don't think you want me poking at your spell."

"Of course not. Kip is going to need, ehm…*instruction* in a few areas once everything's done. Three blokes are better than one for this, yeah?"

"Ah. *Right.*"

Once Zeb had topped up his coffee, the four of them headed for the door. Amy began to follow, but I caught her shoulder to hold her back. "He's going to be uncomfortable enough as it is," I murmured. "Let the boys handle the basics first, and then we'll go out when Kip's ready for company."

Her forehead furrowed. "It's not supposed to hurt—"

"It shouldn't, but a transformation like that will take some adjustment. Give them a little time, dear."

Though she stared wistfully out the kitchen window, Amy settled back at the kitchen table to wait. After a few minutes, I coaxed her into the shower, then helped myself to a refill and settled down beside Carey, who'd watched their departure with tight lips. "I know, I know, you're not on board with this," I said, raising my mug.

"Nope. But if Kip wants to do go through with it, I can't tell him no. I just won't have any part of it."

I drank in silence, considering her weary face, then decided to risk my luck. "How long were you bound?"

The question surprised her, and she hemmed and hawed for a moment before she accepted that I was on to her. "Thirty-two days," she muttered. "I was seven."

"Your parents grounded you, hmm?"

"No."

Carey said nothing further, and I was weighing the benefits of pressing her when she sighed and clutched her mug so hard that her fingers whitened. "My dad's mother had a bad stroke when I was four. When they finally took her to hospice, Mom and Dad thought I was too young to deal with it, so they left me with Mom's older sister, Susan, while they went to Santa Fe to take care of her. They didn't realize it then, but Susan...she wasn't quite right in the head. She'd always been a little different, but Mom didn't know how far she'd gone. They weren't super-close."

She stared at the empty chair across the table, avoiding my gaze. "School was out when they dropped me off, and Susan agreed to keep me as long as they needed. But she didn't like kids—I was noisy, underfoot...you know, *seven*. So as soon as my parents were out of the way, before I even had time to find my room, she...got me."

"Carey," I said, "you don't have to—"

She went on as if I'd never spoken. "Susan may have been nuts, but she was a talented wizard. Transformed me into a necklace, put me on, and went about her life."

I felt myself gape. "That...God, that goes against every rule in the book!"

"Susan was never overly concerned with the rules," Carey said dryly. "But here's the kicker: every night, she transformed me back, but she put a strict bind in place. When my parents called to check on me, I had to tell them about all the wonderful things Aunt Susan and I had done together and about how much fun I was having. And as soon as the call was over, she'd transform me again." She turned to me with the ghost of a smirk on her face. "I spent thirty-two days trapped in that hell, and when my parents came to get me, Aunt Susan left another bind on me so that I couldn't tell them the truth. I couldn't even tell them about the bind. They got me home, and my mom gave me a bath that night, and thankfully, she noticed. She knew me well enough to spot it. Once she broke it, I cried and told her everything, and she told Dad, and Dad…he went for a drive alone that night."

"And Susan?" I asked, though I suspected I already knew.

Carey smirked in earnest. "Dad didn't leave a body to find. She's still a missing person, as far as I know. But that's why I don't do binds, Hannah, and Zeb won't do them out of respect for my wishes. Honestly, I think they're evil." She shrugged and tossed her head toward the back door. "Unsurprisingly, the magus disagrees."

Before I had time to come up with a proper rebuttal, Zeb pushed open the door, and Seamus and Arnold followed him inside. "It's done," Zeb told us. "He wants a little time to himself. Maybe give him his space for an hour or so, huh?"

I glanced at the others for a clue to any subtext, but Arnold seemed unfazed. Only Seamus looked uneasy, but then again, he got that look about him whenever he witnessed any large-scale magic for the first time. "Right. I'll keep Amy occupied," I said, and headed for the bath to break the news.

Carey stayed awake that afternoon only long enough to patch up a few of Arnold's more troubling injuries. "I don't care what spells you have going, there's nothing like old-fashioned Bactine," she said, examining the cuts on his scalp. "And your healing spellwork's sloppy, anyway. Hold still, I'll fix it."

"It works," he protested.

"That may be, but it works better my way. Zip it."

Recognizing a lost battle, Arnold sat on his stool while Carey rewove the spell, then retired to Jim's bed to sleep off brunch and let the magic work. Her doctoring done,

Carey retreated to her room, and I found Amy passed out on her still-made bed, her wet hair splayed across the decorative pillows. With the pantry running bare, Zeb struck out for the grocery store, and Seamus tagged along with a fistful of our counterfeit bills to help the cause. At a loss for a better idea, and hearing no screams from the barn, I snuggled under the duvet and decided that cleanliness was overrated.

I knew nothing more until four, when I woke to a hand on my shoulder and found Amy's worried face hanging over me. "Kip hasn't come in yet," she said. "I'm going to check on him, okay?"

"Hold on, I'll go with you," I mumbled, and threw on trousers and trainers. While Amy tapped her foot, I woke Carey and relayed the situation, and she, too, groggily dressed to go outside. When we finally emerged, Amy ran in her impatience to get to the barn, and with a knowing look for each other, Carey and I jogged after her.

The barn was oddly dark and quiet when we arrived—Kip hadn't turned on so much as a lamp, and his borrowed television was silent. I paused on the threshold to take in my surroundings, but Amy barreled on, calling his name. "Kip? It's me! Are you okay?" she asked, hurrying to his stall, then opened the door and paused. "Hey, what are you doing in the dark? I'm sorry, were you asleep?" He mumbled something, to which she demanded, "What are you talking about? What's wrong?"

By then, Carey and I had reached the cracked stall door, and I saw what was bothering Amy. Something was curled up in the shaded recesses of the makeshift bedroom, a tight knot of limbs and denim at the back of the oversized bed. It had Kip's face, I could tell, and the rest of him seemed human enough, but he lay motionless in the shade, watching us with puffy eyes.

"Something went wrong," he told Amy. "I…"—he took a deep breath—"I am dying."

She flipped on the lamp. "*Dying*? You look fine to

me—are you hurting?"

He shook his head, then slowly sat up and clutched his new knees. "Do not be angry with Arnie, he tried, and this must have been a difficult task, but—"

"But what? What's the matter?" Sliding onto the bed beside him, she squeezed his shoulder and frowned. "Carey's right here if something's wrong…"

Kip watched the two of us slip into the stall, then rubbed his eyes in an ineffective attempt to disguise the fact that he'd been crying. "There is nothing to be done. Leave me, I will face this alone."

"Face *what?*" she said with rising panic. "Just tell me what the problem is!"

Suddenly, Carey smacked her forehead and groaned. "You can't walk, can you, Kip?"

"No," he mumbled. "I…I cannot stand…"

"Well, shoot, that's not surprising," said Amy. "You'll just have to learn to walk again. Gosh, you scared me—"

"Learn to walk?" he echoed, staring at her in disbelief. "How do you *learn* to walk?"

"I think I see the problem," said Carey as Amy's confusion waxed. "Kip, when your people are born, how soon do they walk?"

"Within the day, of course."

"Thought so." Turning to Amy, she explained, "A foal can stand in an hour and run in a day. They're practically born on their feet. And let me guess," she said, turning back to Kip, "if someone's suddenly too weak to stand, it's a good sign he's near death, isn't it?"

"Yes." He was beginning to look as confused as Amy. "If he cannot walk, cannot stand…death is near. Perhaps in the day, perhaps in two, but death always comes. This…is different for your people?"

"Oh, honey," she sighed, and sat beside him. "You're not dying, you just don't know how to manage without half your legs. It's damn difficult to walk like this—takes us months to learn."

"Months?"

"Seasons," she clarified. "Human babies...well, we're pretty floppy at first."

Kip nodded as he processed that. "Then...I am *not* dying? This is normal?"

"*None* of this is normal," she replied with a snort, "but this is expected. You're fine, and you'll figure it out eventually. Want to come inside?" she offered as she stood. "I'll make some dinner in a bit."

His face began to color. "Uh...no, thank you, I—"

That was as far as he made it before Amy punched his arm. "You big dork," she snapped, "you were going to die out here alone? What the heck?"

"I did not want to upset you—"

"You think I wouldn't be upset if I came out here and found you dead?" Amy turned away with a huff, but I saw the sheen in her eyes that she quickly blinked away. "Okay, here's what we're going to do," she said, and pointed to Carey and me. "Can one of you make Mr. Melodramatic here a good pair of stiff boots?"

"Sure," said Carey.

"Great. Kip, you're going to lace up, and I'm going to get you on your feet."

He looked doubtful at the notion. "You are smaller than me—"

"I'm tougher than you think I am. Come on, let's get you set up. A little ankle support wouldn't hurt right now, I bet."

As Carey whipped up socks and hiking boots, Amy helped Kip scoot to the edge of the bed and swing his legs over the side. "Let me know if anything pinches," she said, working the new footwear into place as Kip watched. She adjusted the hem of his jeans over the top of the boots— at least the boys had seen fit to give him trousers, if not a shirt—then stepped back, braced herself, and held out her hands. "Do you trust me, Kip?"

He hesitated before placing his hands in hers. "I do not

want to hurt you."

"I'll take that chance. Come on, up and at 'em," she said, and leaned backwards, pulling him to his feet.

Having latched on to Amy, Kip stood on his unsteady legs for a few seconds before the swaying grew too strong and he listed to the left. Amy pulled back, straining until he righted himself, then spread her legs to anchor herself and grinned. "See? Stronger than I—"

Swaying again, Kip fell back onto his bed, pulling Amy with him. "Sorry," he gasped, "I lost my balance. Are you all right?"

When she rolled off of him, she was laughing. "Fine. I'm fine. But boy, this is going to be a long night."

CHAPTER 19

No word came from the barn that afternoon and through the evening, though Carey had plenty to say to the men about leaving Kip without working legs. "He said he needed time to adjust!" Arnold protested, but she silenced him with a glare, and he meekly returned to his chicken and rice. Seamus and Zeb had little to say after dinner, but as I lay in bed that night, staring at the ceiling, Seamus mumbled, "The kid really thought he was *dying*?"

"He was pretty pathetic," I replied, rolling over to face him.

"Shit. I should have realized—"

"He's a teenager. They're all unfathomable at that age."

"Thanks," he muttered, "but I didn't mean to make the situation worse. He's been through hell…"

"He'll be fine, Seamie."

I knew his eyes well enough to tell that my partner was unconvinced. "Did they ever have dinner? I didn't see Amy sneak in."

"Probably not, then. Want to take food out?"

Seamus nodded and rolled out of bed, and I dressed enough for the hour. We took the leftovers from the fridge and pulled together plates and silverware, then headed to the barn to check on the kids. As we neared, I whispered, "Stay quiet and look in on them first. There are chinks all over the barn wall."

"Oh, are we surveilling now?" he asked with a teasing smirk.

"Two traumatized adolescents, at least one of whom

has access to a large cache of weapons?" I countered.

"Okay, right, we're surveilling. You take point."

Having by then figured out the quietest routes to the barn, I led Seamus through the grass and around the side of the building, then slid toward the open door and pointed to a gap in the boards at his eye level. Finding one of my own, I took a peek inside the barn and smiled to myself.

The overhead lights spilled a yellow glow onto the empty stalls and out toward the training ring. In the middle of the aisle, Amy and Kip moved in an ungainly tango down the wooden floor, him matching her slow backwards steps with a shuffle or lurch. Their pairing was comic for their size discrepancy—Amy was barely a meter and a half, while Kip was closer to two—but he gripped her shoulders and stared doggedly down at her, and she held his waist, coaxing him through their slow dance. "That's it, you're doing gr—oh, hang on, here's the raised board again," she said as they neared our hiding place. "We're not going to fall this time, right?"

"If you say so." Kip scowled as he carefully navigated the uneven ground.

Both of them were disheveled, sweaty, and streaked with grime. Amy's shorts and T-shirt hadn't protected her from acquiring a constellation of fresh cuts and bruises, and Kip's bare chest showed that he'd fared no better during the lesson. As Amy pivoted them, they made their way toward a low stack of hay bales against our wall, and finally, with a sigh of relief, Kip landed and released his hold on her. "I'll get some drinks," she said, and returned from his stall with a couple of Cokes. Passing one to Kip, she clinked her bottle against his and downed half before coming up for air. "You're getting steadier, I think. Yeah?"

"Perhaps." He squeezed and relaxed his fists, and I could only imagine that his hands had begun to cramp. "My feet hurt."

"No big surprise there—mine are tired, too. Let me

see." She patted the hay between them, and Kip maneuvered to sling one leg onto the bale. "I bet that spell didn't come with calluses," she said as she unlaced his boot. "You're probably going to be a little...oh. Oh, *Kip*."

His new sock was stained red where he'd rubbed his toes and heel raw, and Amy gingerly peeled it off of him to assess the damage. "Why didn't you tell me?" she said, turning his foot to see the extent of his blisters.

"You are hurt, too, and I thought...maybe this is what it is supposed to feel like."

"Okay, that's a big, fat no. Don't move, I think there's a first-aid kit in the tack room. Dr. Carey had *better* have band-aids," she muttered as she hurried down the barn.

Frowning, Seamus tapped my arm and pointed to the wall, but I shook my head to stay him.

Fortune was kind—the vet had liberally stashed her gear around the ranch—and Amy located a box of plasters and some antiseptic spray. "This is going to sting," she cautioned as she wiped down Kip's foot. "I'm sorry, but there's no better way to treat these. I ran cross-country last year at school. Did *awful* things to my feet, and my calluses were like horn by summer. Well, Mama took me to get a pedicure, and the poor lady didn't know where to begin with me."

Kip winced as the wet towel hit an open wound. "You realize I did not understand half of what you just said, Amy."

She looked up at him with a tired grin. "You'll get there. In other words, I know a good bit about doctoring blisters, and you've got a ways to go before your feet harden up." She kicked off one of her trainers and flung her bare foot onto the bale beside his propped leg. "See? Look at the tough bits around my toes and on the ball."

I knew a distraction when I saw one, and Amy continued her unpleasant work while Kip cautiously poked at her foot. "It is...odd," he said, earning a little smirk from Amy. "As if you have hands where your feet should be."

"That's it, more or less. There was this girl in my third-grade class, Natalie, who could write with her feet—she held a pen in her toes. It was so *weird*." Glancing up and finding him still examining her foot, Amy shook her head and unwrapped the first plaster. "I read somewhere that a hoof is basically one big toe. You're going to have to get used to striking differently. There's a lot of moving pieces to worry about, and they all get blistered if you aren't careful. Hang on, here comes the spray…"

His shoulders tightened with the sting, but Kip didn't complain. "You make it look easy."

"Well, I've been doing it for about fifteen years now, so I've had practice. It'll come," she said, shaking a handful of plasters out of the box. "We need to get you some better bandages in the morning. Something for blisters."

He sat quietly for a few minutes, drinking his Coke and watching Amy work, then put the bottle aside and cleared his throat. "You never answered my question last night."

She continued to wrap his toes. "Yeah? What's that?"

"Your ideal man. Who is he?"

"Jeez." She snorted. "I don't know."

"Come on," he replied with a mischievous grin, "you had enough to say about Felicia. Be fair."

Amy looked up and paused in her bandaging. "Seriously, I don't know. I've never given it much thought."

"No? You are of age, are you not?"

"Of age?"

Kip started to blush. "You know, to…take a mate."

Despite his embarrassment, Amy was unbothered, almost cool. "I'm close. You're not really legal until you're eighteen or twenty-one around here. Depends on what you want to do."

"Oh," he mumbled, and looked off toward the rafters while his face burned.

After an awkward silence, Amy lifted his foot onto her

knee and began tending to the blisters on his heel. "I haven't really thought about it because I'm not supposed to be with anyone," she said quietly. "Not much point in worrying about boys when you have no plans to go after them."

"Why not?"

She sighed and sprayed his foot again until Kip flinched. "Because it's not a good idea to make more witch-bloods."

"What is wrong with witch-bloods?"

"Just about everything," she muttered as she unwrapped an oversized plaster. "In the magical community, we're pretty much the lowest of the low. Whatever fae kin we have don't have anything to do with us, and the Arcanum keeps us around—*kept* us, I guess—only because we're useful to them. Okay, that's one," she said, patting his foot. "Unlace the other shoe and pop your foot up here."

Kip did as she bade. "I am sorry, Amy, but I do not understand you."

Seeing his bloodied sock, she made a face and began the extraction process. "So, typically, wizards and faeries don't mix. When you find a witch-blood, you can almost guarantee that his mom's a wizard and she wanted nothing to do with his dad. Yeah?"

"I see. But Seamus and—"

"There are exceptions, but not many. A few couples in the Fringe. I'm rare because both my parents were witch-bloods. Everyone warned them against having a kid," she said, not looking up from her work. "Never mind that Mama was one of the best crafters out there. Both of them were smart folks. *Good* folks. But everyone said it'd be a bad idea." She picked up the damp towel and frowned as she cleared his blood away. "They tried anyway. Mama told me they'd hoped I'd swing one way or the other—preferably wizard, I guess. But I was just another witch-blood like them, and they didn't try again."

"You—"

"I'm an abomination. Or so said my dad's mother, the one time she bothered to see me. Mama's mom never came around. My parents both have half siblings, too, but they never wanted to meet me. See, Mama and Daddy were *unfortunate*," she explained as she dabbed. "A bad thing that happened. Train them a little and let them go, maybe they'll be crafters, but in any case, their families won't have to live with the stigma forever. But then they had the audacity to have me—they made a witch-blood on purpose, and as far as most of the community's concerned, that's just wrong." She scowled at a stubborn streak on his heel and rubbed harder. "I mean, I can't blame my grandmas for not being there, but it's horrible to go through life pretending you don't hear when people call you a mongrel."

"What is—"

"A mongrel? It's what you call a mixed-breed dog. They're not worth as much as pedigreed dogs, even if they're sweet and smart and cute. But yeah, that's what they call us. Even some of the Fringers let it slip every now and then. Mongrels really shouldn't make more mongrels," she said as she shook the spray. "I've been hearing that ever since I decided that boys weren't completely gross. And since I don't want to make another kid grow up comparing herself to a dog, I've never looked for a boyfriend. My grades were *great*, though," she said bitterly.

"But...your friend, the one who sends you messages…"

"Aiden?" She chuckled. "He's nice, and Miss Hannah thinks he's flirting with me, but we just talk about computer stuff. Besides, that would never work," she added as she reached for the plasters again. "A witch-blood, plus a witch-blooded high lord? It'd never happen."

While Amy busied herself, I watched Kip's face twitch until he finally blurted, "Your people are idiots, and I think you are marvelous."

Startled, she froze, then raised her eyes again. "Thanks, Kip," she murmured. "I think you're pretty marvelous, too."

"You would have strong sons."

"Excuse me?"

Seeing her bemusement, he paused. "If you would know the son, look to his mother. If you would know the daughter, look to her father. This is known here, yes?"

Amy grinned and opened another plaster, but I could see her pleased flush. "Not exactly. I'll take your word for it."

As she finished doctoring his feet, I stepped back from the wall, and Seamus followed my lead. "I don't suppose they're starving," I whispered when we were out of earshot of the barn.

"Think you're right." He shifted the bowls in his arms and nodded toward the house. "Late-night snack, then? You and me?"

We slipped inside the house and raided the leftovers, then settled in at the table in the dark. Seamus conjured a little fireball and floated it into the air between us, then shrugged. "Mood lighting? With my luck, it'll burn through the table."

I laughed to myself and tucked in. "Remember that vile hole in the wall, what was it, with the gyros—"

"Durham Doner," he said with a grin, "home of the Cat Kebab! God, please tell me it's gone."

"It's a Taco Bell now."

"Oh, that's almost worse." He shook his head and bit into his sandwich. "I took you on some shite dates, didn't I?"

"Eh, came with the job. And it's not like we had any money."

"True." He swallowed, then put the sandwich down and looked me in the eye. "Maybe it's best that we never had those three kids and a house in the country," he said softly.

"Maybe," I admitted, hearing Amy's voice echo in my mind. "But if we had, and they were all witch-bloods...would you have wanted—"

"Of course I'd have wanted them," he said, then hesitated. "Would you?"

"Yeah."

Seamus toyed with his food. "I think you'd have been a great mother, Badger."

"You, too. Father, I mean," I rushed to hide the gaffe.

He smiled sadly and took another bite. "Never had time?"

It was my turn to mull over the many implications before I spoke again. "There was never anyone else."

"Oh," he murmured, studying his plate. "I'm sorry."

"I know."

"Ehm...I don't mean to pry, but is it..."

He left the question unfinished, but I knew what he was thinking. "It's too late for me. Then again," I added, scrambling to prevent the inevitable uncomfortable silence that would follow an answer like that, "can you imagine having children right now in the middle of this mess? They'd be, what, teenagers? Maybe twenty? Or, you know, what if we'd both been in the Fringe database, and I hadn't been away on training, and the hit squad had come for us and our kids? Can you imagine having lost your kids in all of this?"

While I babbled, Seamus took my hand and squeezed until my hypotheticals petered out. "I'm sorry. I'm so very sorry, love," he said. "I fucked that up for both of us, and you...you deserved better than that. Better than me." With a last squeeze, he released me and pushed back from the table. "I think I'll turn in. Not as peckish as I thought I was."

He was almost to the hallway when I said, "Seamie?"

As he turned, I pulled my necklace from beneath my shirt, unlatched the clasp, and held it out to show him. He frowned and drew nearer to see what I was presenting, and his eyes went wide when he saw my old engagement ring. "You *kept* it?" he whispered in disbelief.

"I never took it off. Well, showers and such, but—"

"After everything I did…"

Try as I might, I couldn't stop my eyes from stinging. "I just wanted you back, Seamie. I kept hoping you'd come home…"

On reflection, I think I broke down once I was in his arms, but it all happened so quickly that I may very well have started sobbing before he embraced me. But I do know that when the worst passed, I heard him mumbling over and over into my hair: "Take me back. Please take me back. I'm sorry, I'll do anything, just take me back."

I looked up, saw that his eyes were also wet, tried to smile, and instead broke into hiccups. "I never let you go," I managed between spasms. "But my finger's got too fat for that ring."

Seamus laughed, and I laughed, which only made the hiccups worse, and he pulled me back against him. "We're two freaks of nature," he said. "You'd think we could find a way to resize that thing—or make a better one. A bigger one. Like, a solid diamond boxing glove."

"Practical *and* posh," I said, then pointed to the abandoned table. "By the way, you forgot to put the fire out."

"What fi—oh, fuck," he muttered, and waved our mood lighting into oblivion.

"Faeries," I said with my best pained sigh. "Honestly, I can't take you anywhere."

"No?" Before I knew it, he'd scooped me up like a distressed damsel and grinned as I hiccupped my protestations. "Well, now, I can think of a few places I'd like to take *you*, starting with—"

The back door squealed as it opened, and Seamus turned to find Amy in the doorway, looking flummoxed at the scene onto which she'd just walked in. "Uh…hey," she said, and pointed to the fridge. "I'm just, uh…I'm gonna see if there are any leftovers from dinner. Okay?"

"Sure," I said, wrapping my arm around Seamus's neck as if all of this were perfectly normal. "How's it going?"

"Oh, fine. Kip's going to need some moleskin." She grabbed a few dishes out of the fridge and a pair of forks from the drawer, then hurried for the door. "Um...y'all have fun?"

I flashed my thumb, and she ran off, wearing the haunted look of a young person confronted with the realization that she is not, in fact, the result of a virgin birth.

"So..." said Seamus as Amy's rapid footsteps faded, "I think we may have scarred the little lamb."

"Eh, she's a big girl, she'll get over it." I turned his face toward mine, hiccupped again, and smiled. "You were saying?"

There was no swelling romantic backing track to the kiss that followed, but there was fire in his touch, and that was good enough for me.

I wanted Seamus, and I know he wanted me, but I also wanted to have a place to stay in the morning. There are simply some things one does not do in a strange house, and as we'd been the Joneses' guests for nearly a week already, I didn't wish to give them cause to throw us to the curb. And so, though mutually frustrated, Seamus and I settled for cuddling in the dark and listening to the fan blades whip overhead.

"You know," he said after a time, "there *is* a second barn."

"Seamie."

"And the basement, yes? If we're quiet, Cousin Arnie won't hear a thing." I rolled over and faced his teasing grin. "Heavens," he said with false sanctimony, "what would he think if he knew?"

"Nothing positive, I'm sure."

"You've gone and besmirched the good Parsons name forever, Badger. *Tsk.*"

"Yeah?" I poked back. "What about you, eh? Lord Seamus, slumming with a wizard."

"*Lord?*" He chuckled. "My, aren't we generous tonight."

"Your granny was a queen, wasn't she?"

"And exiled, if I've been hearing correctly. But you can call me whatever you like if it'll get me back into your good graces."

"And my pants, I suppose."

"I can only hope."

I smacked him with a throw pillow, then snuggled closer to him as he laughed to himself. "Probably for the best that we don't fool around tonight. Carey's going to torture me again tomorrow morning, just watch. She's had her little holiday, so it's time for me to prove once again what a great wizard I'm not."

"You can do it, love. I know you can."

"But what if I can't? I've been trying for days, and I can't make it work!"

"You will." His arm slid over me, pulling me against him as his body conformed to mine. "I believe in you, Badger. Even if you don't believe in yourself right now, I believe in you. I will *always* believe in you."

My fingers brushed his dangling arm and found his hand. "Don't leave me," I whispered as our hands locked together. "I don't know what I'll do if you run away again."

"I'm not going anywhere." His breath was warm in my hair, his voice muting toward a mumble. "Never again, love. Never again."

Absolutely not."

"Hear me out," I said as Carey shook her head and crossed her arms. "Whatever talent I have is little better than raw right now. Arnold has the background, he's familiar with large-scale magic—"

"And he's a friggin' magus. Forget it." Grunting her displeasure, she turned back to her bran flakes. "I told you, the mental focus you need to sleepwalk runs counter to the vast majority of Arcanum training. Even if I weren't fundamentally opposed to giving a magus access to the dream space—"

"He's on our side."

"You think. And if he is, there's no guarantee he wouldn't change his mind if his buddies caught him and brought out the thumbscrews. We're not making the mistake you people made," she continued around a spoonful of cereal. "You gave them the keys to your own undoing."

"Grand Magus Harrison worked with us—"

"Until he destroyed you." She scooped up another bite and gave me a look. "The Fringe is learning the lesson now that my people learned from Simon Magus. There's no way in hell that I'd teach any Arcanum wizard, let alone a *magus*, how to sleepwalk—and if they ever mastered it, God forbid that any of them should learn to cast in the dream space," she added with a shudder.

I poked at my oatmeal. "Maybe I'm an idiot, then, but I refuse to believe that every member of that organization is a heartless killer. There must be good people in the Arcanum. Somewhere…"

"I didn't say there weren't. The bulk of them may be delightful," said Carey. "But I'll be damned if I hand any of them a loaded gun and pin a target on my chest." She pushed her bowl aside and leaned across the table to clasp my shoulder. "You're going to get this, Hannah," she murmured. "Someday, it'll click for you. Maybe not today…maybe not for a year…but someday, you'll get it."

"And while I'm trying to figure it out, my people are out there, scattered, hiding, maybe dying…"

She sighed as she retreated. "I hear you, I do, but I

can't take that risk."

"The Arcanum isn't going to know—"

"What if they do? What if they trace it back to me? Let's say they kidnap me—what's to stop them from going after Zeb? Jimmy? They don't know that we exist," she stressed, staring me in the eye. "How long do you think it would take them to decide to eradicate the Minor Arcanum? We don't have the numbers for that sort of fight, even if every one of us was qualified for combat— and believe me, that isn't the case. We've got witches in our ranks. Kids. People like me who're shit with offensive spells. And I can't drag a bunch of unaware, untrained people into this war."

"They're trying to kill us," I snapped.

"Yeah. And if they find out about us, then they'll try to kill us, too. I don't have the right…"

Carey's voice trailed off as the back door opened, and we goggled as Amy and Kip slowly walked inside. Though they moved at a geriatric pace and Kip kept his hand on Amy's shoulder, he was upright and ambulatory—and barefoot, I noticed, seeing the mass of plasters and homemade bandages covering his feet.

"Morning," said Amy with a weary grin. "Any coffee left?"

But Carey was already out of her chair. "*Sit*," she insisted, guiding Kip to her vacated seat, then squatted and picked up one of his feet. "How are you even walking? You're a bloody mess!"

"Much of that is old—" he began.

"Not that old. Wow, guys, did you leave me any band-aids?"

"Maybe four," Amy admitted as she hurried toward the coffeemaker. "Sorry, Dr. Carey, I found the first-aid kit in the barn, and I—"

"Don't worry about it. Just…my wand is on my dresser, please grab it for me." She rubbed her head as Amy hurried down the hall, then looked up at Kip, who watched worriedly. "Scale of one to ten, with ten being the worst pain imaginable, how badly are you hurting?"

He mulled that over. "About six. But I can walk now, so—"

"Honey, you're going to be limping as soon as you rest. Ah, thanks," she said as Amy returned with the wand. Working quickly, she put a numbing spell in place, then pulled Kip to his new feet and wrapped a steadying arm around his waist. "Back in a bit, Hannah, I'm going to get the bandages off and put these two to bed—nope, drop the coffee," she added, catching Amy in proximity to the pot. "You, get some sleep. Kip…well, there's bound to be a couch with your name on it once I make sure you're not headed for gangrene. Come on, walk with me."

When I'd been left to my own devices, I took my time at the breakfast table, making a second cup of tea and checking the BBC's headlines on my mobile. From down the hall, I could hear occasional splashes and the hiss of a spray can as Carey worked, plus a few yelps as she pulled off the worst of the soaked-through plasters. Once I'd reassured myself that the world had yet to come to a fiery end, I tidied up, then thought about heading out into the warm morning to find the boys. Zeb had gone to see about the mares, and Arnold, who had nearly healed from his encounter with the gate, had tagged along out of boredom. But Seamus had gone to the barn, I thought, maybe to check on the kids…

Before I had a chance to fret, he came bounding in the back door with my laptop in his hands. "There you are," I said, raising my mug. "Tea?"

"No time for that." He dropped the computer on my cleared placemat and raised the screen. "You've got mail."

CHAPTER 20

Seamus had, in fact, gone out to the barn to find Kip and Amy, but he'd met them halfway up the short trail as they made their slow, stubborn progress toward the house. Sensing that neither wanted his help, he'd continued on to the barn to make sure they hadn't left a trail of bloody footprints behind them. But the floor was unstained, and Seamus, seeing my abandoned laptop and remembering the mostly neglected task I'd set for him five days before, had taken a few minutes to log into the Fringe network and check for activity. What he'd discovered had sent him running to the house to find me.

I marveled at the time stamp on the message board's latest posting, the first new one in weeks. "I don't believe it. This went up last night."

He stooped to read over my shoulder. "Who posted it?"

"Don't know, it's anonymous," I said as I turned to look up at him. "The only way to post an anonymous message is to do so from ghost mode. You know what that means? This came from a *coordinator*, Seamie."

His eyes narrowed. "Or an Arcanum plant. Let's not forget your old pal Gerri."

He was right, though I hated to admit it. "Let's assume for the moment that it's a genuine message."

"From whom, a robot?" He tapped the screen, and the message opened to reveal an unbroken block of zeroes and ones. "Either that's binary or someone's cat slept on a keyboard."

I stared at the numbers for only a moment before the realization dawned. "A cipher. This is the first activity on the network since the unravelling—whoever wrote this is concerned for security."

"Rightly so," he muttered. "What's the key, then?"

"Don't know yet. Carey!" I bellowed down the corridor. "Have you got a printer handy?"

Ten minutes later, I'd coaxed the laptop to talk to the Joneses' old machine, and all seven of us gathered around the kitchen table to examine the printouts. "Binary," Amy mumbled, clutching her fluffy bathrobe closed. "Well, this should be fun."

"Can you read it?" Arnold asked her.

She shot him a look of disbelief. "Uh, no. You have to know where the numbers *end* to know what they are in base two. Put a few spaces in, now, and I'll convert it for you."

He made a face and stared glumly at the copy in his hands. "I was always rubbish at maths…"

"Please," Amy scoffed, "converting from binary barely takes multiplication." Seeing Kip's bewilderment, she explained, "This is just a different way to write numbers. Let me…ah." She snatched a pen from the sideboard, flipped over one of the copies, and began scribbling. "We normally write numbers in base ten—each digit can be anything from zero to nine," she said as she scrawled the numbers in a line, "and each time you add a digit, it's ten times bigger than the one before. So, like, here…" She wrote *123* and pointed to the digits in turn. "One hundred twenty-three. You have three ones, two tens, and one hundred. Get it?"

His brow furrowed, but he nodded. "Yes, I think so."

"Okay, that's base ten. Base two only has two numbers, zero and one, and every digit is two times as big as the one before." She wrote *10101*, then worked from right to left. "We've got one in the ones' place, no twos, one four, no eights, and one sixteen. So in base ten, this would be twenty-one," she added, writing the numeral on the next line. "Yeah? Base two's easy. Base *sixteen*, now—that's fun."

Arnold's nose wrinkled as he watched her work. "You actually *like* this stuff?"

"What's not to like? It's easy." She turned to look at the rest of us, saw similar expressions of mild disbelief, and shrugged. "We can't all be cool, y'all."

I examined my copy again, seeing no pattern among the unpunctuated block. "Since my tea is still kicking in, what would this be?" I asked Amy, pointing to the message title: *1101110010110011101*.

She pursed her lips, carefully copied the title on one line, then added a second line of digit values below it. "Starts with 1, 4, 8, 16…128, 256…who has a calculator?"

After a minute of work, Zeb held out his mobile. "I get 451,997. Does that mean anything to anyone?"

"No," I mumbled, staring at the line of digits, then froze as an idea struck. "Amy, let me borrow your pen."

The others watched as I scribbled at the bottom of the page. "Maybe it's not all one number," I said, and tapped out my sums. "Look, break it up. The first 1 is 1. Next is 10, or 2."

"Then 11—3," said Seamus, picking up the thread.

Amy squealed and checked my work. "It's 1–2–3–4–5–4–3–2–1," she declared. "1, 10, 11, 100, 101, 100, 11, 10, 1. *Duh*."

"Yeah…duh," Arnold muttered. "What about the actual message, then?"

As one, we bent to look at the block of numbers. "Well," said Amy after a long moment of silence, "This starts with 100…"

"So it is 4," Kip concluded.

"Maybe. Unless it's 1001, which would be 9. Or 10011, 19. Or 100111, which is…40. Like I said, without any breaks in the text, I can't tell where each number ends."

"Unless we only have a finite group of numbers," I

replied. "Assuming this is a cipher and not just a glitch, every number has to mean something." I looked at Seamus and saw recognition in his eyes. "Mrs. Randolph."

"A1Z26, of course. Easiest code in the book. And whatever happened to the old bat?"

"Retired to the Costa del Sol, last I heard, and good riddance. Ehm…" Catching the blank looks around the table, I dragged myself back from a tangent of reminiscence. "Sorry, we had a nasty teacher when we were in primary school. *Mean* old woman, boring as anything, but nearly blind by the time we got her. Seamie and I used to pass notes in class, and we played with different ciphers to entertain ourselves."

"The starter cipher is A1Z26," he explained. "All you do is substitute numbers for letters. A is 1, B is 2—"

"Zed?" asked Amy, face scrunched.

"*Zee* is 26, got it," said Carey. "Okay. Uh…can we get a key going, here?"

It took only a few minutes to write out a chart converting base two to base ten and the corresponding letters, but that left us no closer to decoding the message. The first letter could have been A, B, D, I, or S, and each of those choices left a different digit pattern for the second letter.

After an unfruitful half hour, Seamus and I worked alone. Carey forced Amy and Kip to bed before they dropped, and she and Zeb had their own chores to do before the day grew too hot. Despite his apparent horror of numbers, Arnold tried to assist for a time, but we took pity and sent him out to Zeb, deciding that the fresh air would stave off any traumatic maths-based flashbacks.

With notepads, pencils, and tea at hand, we plugged through the possibilities, making charts and getting unreasonably excited every time a letter combination seemed to make sense. But our hopes were almost always dashed by the third letter in the sequence, and the morning wore on without any real breakthrough—well, aside from Seamus's discovery of his ability to enchant himself a refill, which we considered useful, if not entirely pertinent to the matter at hand.

As the clock ticked toward eleven, Seamus put down his pen and massaged his shoulders. "There are only so many letter combinations in English. This shouldn't be this difficult."

"Assuming this is written in English, you mean." His face fell, and I shrugged. "When you post in ghost mode, none of the usual identifiers pop up—no name, no location. We've all done it by accident. You log in incognito to read or research without getting half a dozen messages, then you see something that really needs addressing and unintentionally make an anonymous comment. All that's to say this message could have come from anywhere. Whoever sent it knew what he was doing."

He squeezed his eyes shut and sighed. "Well, what can we do to limit the linguistic possibilities? How many coordinators are unaccounted for?"

"None, I thought," I muttered, and opened the Fringe dataset that Aiden had copied for me. Scrolling through, I found only two coordinators who hadn't been ticked off the list as dead—Slim and me. "Maybe it's from Slim," I mused. "He's American, so I assume he'd write in English…"

"Isn't he a hostage, though?" said Seamus. "How would he get a message out?"

"Damned if I know." I pushed the laptop away and groaned. "We're running in circles, and we're missing something. Let's think about the writer. What do we know about him?"

"Well," he replied as he topped up our mugs again, "if we trust the dataset, then he's probably *not* a coordinator. The Arcanum may be murderous, but they're probably not so stupid as to give your colleague a computer, yeah?"

"Presumably."

"Which means we're down to two possibilities, then: either someone in the Arcanum has borrowed a coordinator's credentials and left this as a trap, or someone else in the Fringe has done it. What sounds more likely to you?"

I mulled that over as I sipped my freshened tea. "The latter. Harrison wasn't given coordinator credentials—he can't use ghost mode."

"Slim could have been forced to surrender his, couldn't he?"

"Slim's a tough nut, but more importantly, he could have surrendered his *other* credentials." Seamus looked at me quizzically, and I explained, "That sequence of passwords I gave you logs me into the system in ghost mode. If I use a different final password, I'm visible. The Arcanum would have no reason to know about ghost mode, and if they did pry Slim's codes from him, he could have given them the standard set...which makes me think this is from one of us. Someone who knows ghosting exists and has access to a set of coordinator credentials."

"But not a coordinator." Seamus tapped his pen against his messy notepad. "So—assume it's a Fringer, then. Someone in hiding, someone who hasn't had much information since Easter, someone with a healthy fear of the Arcanum. He doesn't know if the network's safe, but he makes an attempt. Why now?"

"Because he's desperate," I surmised. "Maybe he's hurt. Maybe he knows the Arcanum's on to him. He'd have to be desperate to be the first person back on the network after the unravelling. Whenever we've had problems in the past, everyone knew to stay off until a coordinator gave the all-clear. That obviously didn't go out this time, so our writer's in a bad situation."

He started to gnaw on his pen cap, a habit he'd picked up in school and apparently never cured, then paused and stared into space. "Did any of the coordinators have children?"

"Sure. I can't give you a complete list, but I know of several offhand who had families…" I nearly dropped my mug as the proverbial lightbulb popped on. "A child. This came from a *child*."

"A coordinator's child," said Seamus, picking up speed. "He doesn't have his own credentials yet, but he knows his parents' passwords—"

"Or he knows where they're written down, most like. Either he used ghost mode by accident—"

"Or he's old enough to be clever about it," Seamus finished. "Old enough to log in, to have taken care of himself—"

"Three months," I muttered. "And he's old enough to have seen binary in maths. So he wants to send out a coded message," I continued, thinking aloud, "but not *too* coded. Nothing that the average Fringer couldn't figure out. He uses the old alphanumeric substitution—"

"But that's not secure enough, so he puts it in binary."

"And then he runs everything together. Now it's nice and secure, but maybe he didn't realize what a pain in the arse it turned out to be."

Seamus sucked on the pen cap and scowled at the message. "Clever kid. I'd probably have gone with a Caesar and called it a day, and then I'd be up to my eyeballs in wizards."

"A Caesar," I mumbled.

"Yeah, remember, it was in that code book Dad got us? You just shift all the letters down. Like, maybe A is D, B is E…right?"

"I know what a Caesar is," I said impatiently. "Seamie, what if we're overlooking a fourth level of encryption? A1Z26 turns letters to numbers, putting those numbers in base two makes them harder to read, and running them together means you can't use the old 'figure out which of these words is *the*' approach to code-breaking. What if there's a Caesar shift here, too?"

"Bloody hell," he groaned, and rested his head on his

folded arms. "If there's a Caesar involved, we're going to be here all night. Nothing in the key told us how big the shift was."

I stared again at the message title, then finally realized what I was seeing. "The key *did* tell us. It's not a Caesar."

He looked up from the table, perplexed. "Then what?"

"Something less secure—something a child would do. Read the key. The numbers rise, then flip. I think it's in A26Z1."

Seamus blinked, then picked up his pen again, turned to a clean piece of paper, and grabbed at the air. "Chart. Need to add another column."

I handed him our notes and checked his work. With the flipped letters written out, we turned again to the first digits of the message and hoped for a hint. "Okay," I said, scanning our table of values. "If it's 1, it's Z. 10 is Y, 100 is W, 1001 is R, and 10011 is H."

"Probably W or R, but…hang on. Look for common letters—E, A, R, S, T…"

Working with as-yet unsullied copies and a selection of colored pens I conjured up for the occasion, we began scouring the block, marking potential occurrences throughout the text. With the overlap in patterns, however, we didn't make much immediate headway until Seamus said, "I've found an E early in this, digits six through ten. If that's really an E, then the first five digits are probably a consonant or two—"

"Which would be…hang on…H, or R–Z, or W–Z–Z. Has to be H."

"So H–E…what are the choices for our next letter?"

I held my page close to our decoding chart. "Next sequence is 11111, so Z, X, T, L…that's it."

"Probably H–E–L, unless you think this kid's trying to hex us."

"Spells don't work that way, Seamie," I muttered, already looking down the line. "Okay, assume L. Then the next contenders come from 10111. That's Z again, Y, V, P, and D."

"*Held* or *help*."

It took us a few minutes and a bit of trial and error to work through the next two letters, but once we picked *HELP US* from the line, I knew we'd cracked it. When Zeb and Arnold came inside at half-twelve to clean up and start lunch, they found Seamus and me hunched over the table, yelling numbers and letters at each other as we picked our way through the end of the message. "Any progress?" Zeb asked when we fell silent.

I ripped our working paper off the pad and held it in front of his face. "*Help us. Three kids at Mountain View. No food left. Sick. Please help*. It's an SOS, Zeb. We've got to find them."

For ease of reading—and because Kip was still dead to the world on the couch in the den—Zeb carried my computer into the basement, then ensorcelled the screen to project onto the wall between a pair of antique weavings. "Okay," he said as Carey dropped a pair of pins onto the online map, "it looks there are two notable towns called Mountain View, in Arkansas and California."

"The one in California's a lot bigger," Carey offered. "And there was *nothing* else in that note to show us where they are?"

"Nothing," Seamus confirmed. "What if we drove to those two towns and had a look about? How far are they?"

Carey grimaced and mapped the routes. "Going to California, you're looking at an eighteen-hour drive, at least. Going to Arkansas...at least thirteen hours."

"This bloody country is huge," Arnold muttered from his perch on the back of the couch.

"Tell us about it," said Zeb. "You haven't lived until you've schlepped a horse home from North Dakota."

"A motion-sick horse," Carey added with a shudder. "But back to the Mountain Views—you're in for a haul, whichever you want to hit." She paused, then cocked her head. "You're awfully quiet, Hannah. Got a preference?"

"Maybe," I replied. "May I see the computer?" Carey passed it my way, and I opened the Fringe dataset again and began to scroll down. "The writer of that message has access to a coordinator's codes. Assuming these kids are in the States, they probably got the codes from one of the American coordinators. Slim handled the East Coast, but he was taken. For the rest of the States, that was...okay, Blue Boy had the middle bits, and Ranger took the west. They're both supposedly dead."

"Arkansas would be in the middle, wouldn't it?" said Zeb. "And California's definitely the west. Either Mountain View would fit."

"But they didn't say they were in Mountain View." I held up the deciphered note and read it again. "They're *at* Mountain View. And if I'm remembering correctly..."

The wall projection changed to a picture of a sprawling valley, surrounded by jagged, snow-topped peaks that faded to hazy blue and brown at the horizon. "Ranger was always active on the network because he was basically a playboy. Inherited old oil money or some such, speculated well, never hurt for cash. He was an amateur nature photographer on the side—used to go on photo safaris all over the place, lovely work—and every so often, he'd put up a shot or two from his back garden. And if I tab over to the last address..."

The picture switched to the dataset, and I found Ranger—Walker Gerhardt—in the list.

"Well, I'll be damned," said Zeb. "He named his *house*."

"Mountain View," I read. "Pike Ridge, Colorado. How far?"

Carey took the computer back and plotted the route. "Five or six hours. You could make it by nightfall if you don't dawdle."

"Right," I said, and rose. "I'm going. Seamie?"

"I'm in," he replied.

"As am I," said Arnold, raising one finger, then sped up before I could protest. "In case you're mistaken and this is all a trap, you'll want backup."

Seamus looked at me and raised one eyebrow, but I nodded. "All right, then. Carey, Zeb...we'll phone you when we arrive."

"Hang on, now," said Zeb, "Arnie's right—if this is a setup, you're going want some firepower behind you."

"If this is a setup, I don't want you two anywhere near it," I countered. "You've done more than your fair bit, and I'm not dragging the Minor Arcanum into this mess." Though they looked somewhat disquieted, the Joneses nodded, and I gathered up my computer. "Now all we need to do is get out of the house without waking the kids. Meet me in the foyer in ten minutes."

But when we emerged from the basement, we found Amy and Kip waiting in the den, halfway through a box of cold Pop-Tarts. "Did you figure out the note?" Amy asked through a yawn. "I heard the yelling."

"Ehm...yeah, we did," said Seamus. "Going to make a quick drive. We'll be back tomorrow—"

"Oh, *heck* no," she interrupted. "I sat out on the gate trip. Y'all aren't leaving me behind again."

"Amy, love—"

"I'm going." She crossed her arms and glared up at us. "Look, I'm here to either burn the Arcanum to the ground or rescue Fringers. Let me do one or the other."

"You're barely awake," I tried, but she wasn't to be dissuaded.

"I'm a fantastic car sleeper. Missed all of Tennessee once, going the long way. Come on, let me help."

As I waffled, Arnold cleared his throat and stepped forward. "Young lady, can you actually handle a firearm, or were those guns you two pointed at me just for show?"

"Pistol, rifle, shotgun, and crossbow. Take your pick."

He looked at Seamus and me and shrugged. "Can't hurt. Ah"—he held up his hand before Kip could interject—"I know, lad, you're coming with her. We can all squeeze into one vehicle, yeah?"

I gave him a long, hard look. "You're forgetting the kids we're supposed to be finding. I don't have a car that seats eight."

At that, Amy turned pathetic puppy eyes on Zeb, who sighed and muttered, "We've got an extra SUV you can borrow. It's not new, but it'll get you there."

"Yay!" said Amy, and shoved the last of her Pop-Tart in her mouth. "Back in a minute," she added, and ran off in a spray of crumbs.

The rest of us looked at Kip, who remained on the couch with an afghan in his lap. After a pause, Carey pulled out her wand and muttered, "You're going to need new shoes, buddy. These aren't going to be pretty, but sheepskin should feel good on those sores."

After a brief chat, Seamus and I decided the driving arrangements. I sent the kids with him and took Arnold with me, hoping that if I'd been wrong about my cousin, at least the others would have a chance to get away.

But Arnold gave me no cause for concern while we followed I-25 north to Colorado, making good time in the Sunday afternoon traffic. Recognizing his duties as copilot, he kept the radio on an inoffensive station and the conversation light, asking me about the Constabulary and the north, with which he had little personal experience. The talk then turned to the slightly riskier subject of football—to my surprise, we both followed Man U—and then, ever so gradually, to our respective families. "I love my mum and dad," he told me as we crossed the state line that afternoon. "I'd never want to hurt them. But I have no idea where they think I've gone, or even if they think I'm still alive. At the rate Mulligan's going, it's possible they've been told I'm dead." He leaned back in his seat and stared out the window. "Might be the kinder option. If they knew what I've been doing…well, they'd probably think me a traitor to the cause. And Grandfather would never forgive me for embarrassing the family so publicly."

"Even if he knew what you know?" I pressed.

Arnold shrugged at that. "If I sat him down today and told him Carver's still alive somewhere, Mulligan's got a bunch of witches locked away, and the Arcanum's been killing off Fringers since March…no, he'd probably still be peeved. Image means everything, you know how it is."

"No, but I can guess."

"Right," he muttered, hearing the edge in my tone. "Hannah, listen…it's unfortunate that things, you know, are the way they are with the family, but you shouldn't take it personally. All of the old-blooded families pretend their witches and duds don't exist. It's nothing you've done wrong."

I gripped the steering wheel to hold my temper in check. "I shouldn't take it personally that my existence is such an affront to the family that they'd rather pretend I'd never been born? Is that what you're telling me?"

"I mean—"

"You don't get to tell me what should and shouldn't offend me, *Arnie*! You've got no fucking clue what it's like on this side, so don't sit there and preach at me about how I should feel!"

He made no reply as the radio went to commercial, and we sat through five long minutes of adverts for car dealerships and herbal supplements before he found his voice again. "That was, perhaps, insensitive of me."

"Perhaps?"

"I'm sorry."

"All right." I cut my eyes to him across the armrests. "As long as we're both embarrassing the family, I suppose we can try to be civil to each other."

I drove on, cringing inside to hear songs from my youth on the adult contemporary station, when Arnold broke the silence again. "May I ask one personal question without getting thrown from a moving vehicle?"

Anticipating the enquiry ahead, I couldn't suppress a sigh. "I suppose…"

"Should we live to see Mulligan out of a job, how open would you and Seamus be to coming home with me and letting me introduce you as my Fringer cousin and her fae partner?"

That was hardly the question I'd expected, and I looked at him again to see Arnold grinning back at me. "I'd consider it. How open would you be to standing back and watching me tell our grandparents exactly what I think of them?"

"Sounds fair." He hesitated, then asked, "You and Seamus, are you really…you know?"

"Most definitely. Have you got a problem with that?"

"To be honest, at this juncture, I don't think I'd tell you if I had. What's the deal with his court affiliation, anyway? Does he really not have one?"

"Well, seeing as he's Mab's grandson…"

"Very funny," he scoffed, then looked at me again and sobered. "Oh. Oh, that…*wasn't* a joke?"

"It was a surprise to us both."

"Bloody *hell*," he muttered, then caught himself and coughed. "I'm, ehm…I'm sure you two make each other very happy. Lovely couple. And I'll just go stick my foot in my mouth now, yes?"

Around seven that evening, we pulled into Pike Ridge, a wide gap in the mountains specializing in skiing gear and alcohol. As we disembarked at a petrol station to pick up rations, I joined Seamus at his pump and leaned my head against his shoulder. "Long drive?" he asked.

"Tedious. How were the kids?"

"Not bad. They slept most of the way, and then Amy woke and found a pop station, and she tried to start a singalong. I wasn't much help, and Kip was useless, but at least she entertained herself."

"How's her singing?"

The look on his face was pained. "*Lusty*, I believe, would be the kindest word for it." He glanced toward the side of the shop, where Arnold had disappeared with limping Kip in search of the toilets. "We should get a proper meal, if we can. Think I saw a McDonald's back up the road."

"*That* is your definition of a proper meal, Malone?"

"Let me rephrase: a meal that isn't just a packet of crisps." The pump shut off, and he closed the tank hatch. "And a motel."

"What for?" I asked, taken aback. "We find the house, we get the kids, we hit the road again. There's no need to overnight unless you're not up to making the drive back."

He hesitated before answering me. "Badger…you know this could still be a trap, right? A little puzzle to pique your interest, a story about sick and hungry children to push your buttons…"

"It doesn't feel like a trap."

"Neither did Gerri, as I recall. Look," he sighed, brushing off his driving gloves, "we're losing the light, *fast*. Tonight's not the time to do anything. We'll check in with Carey and Zeb, get a few rooms, and start in the morning. Surveil for a few days, if need be. Make sure we know what we're running into."

"Seamie, they may not *have* a few days," I protested. "If we ignore three sick kids—"

"Who may not even exist. That's all I'm saying." He pulled out his wallet and headed toward the shop. "We'll think better after a night's rest, anyway. Want something to drink?"

I grabbed him before he reached the doors and pinned him against the painted cinderblock wall. "We're not waiting until morning," I muttered. "I didn't drive up here to jump at shadows."

He gripped my shoulders and shook his head. "We're

not jumping at shadows, we're being clever about this. Let's make camp, and we'll work out the plan in the morning."

Seamus released me, and I stepped back, smarting. "Whatever happened to 'this is your show, Badger'? This isn't your call."

"Fine. Put it to majority vote, if it'll make you feel better. Or you can trust your partner to have your best interest in mind when I suggest that maybe running around a strange town in the dark, possibly sprinting headlong into a trap, isn't the greatest idea you've ever had." As I struggled for a comeback, he took my hands and closed the gap between us again. "If they're out there, we'll find them. I promise we will. But I love you too much to let you do something that stupid."

"This is what I *do*. This is all part and parcel of the coordinator gig. If someone has to run into the burning building or jump out of the plane, that someone is me. And come on, like you've never had a risky plan on the job."

"A risky plan might involve a few unexpected knives or a gun," he countered. "You've pissed off the murder wizards. If this is really a trap, how many do you suppose will be waiting? Armed? Badger," he said, lowering his voice, "I know you're talented, but how many wizards do you think you could take on by yourself tonight?" When I said nothing, he squeezed my hands. "I'm in the same boat. In a firefight, our best weapons right now are Arnie and Amy, and in all honesty, my money's on her. Let's wait for daylight, hmm? I've got your back, love, and I'll follow you off a bloody cliff, but at least let me pack the parachutes first."

To my dismay, the rest of our party—and the Joneses, when we checked in—thought reconnaissance was the better strategy. "We can check it out tomorrow," said Amy while I glowered at the traitors. "Maybe I could go scout first thing in the morning. I mean, no one's going to think twice about me."

Kip perked up at that. "I will come—"

"Only if your feet are healing up, and you really aren't going to be able to talk without people asking questions—"

"You know, we can work this out tomorrow," Seamus cut in, then coaxed me back into my vehicle and led us to a largely empty motel. Three rooms with pairs of double beds seemed more than sufficient—Amy and Kip weren't going to be separated, and Arnie took the second room, leaving Seamus alone with me as I paced the floor and muttered to myself.

"Badger," he sighed, patting the undisturbed pillow beside him, "come to bed. You're not going to solve anything by walking in circles all night."

"Sorry, am I bothering you?" I snapped. "I wouldn't be if you'd let me do my damn job!"

He cringed as my voice echoed around the room. "If you'd be reasonable about this—"

"*Reasonable*? There is *nothing* reasonable about any of this! We've got an SOS, we're so close, and we're doing nothing! And it's all your fault, Seamie! You're supposed to be helping me, damn it!"

He sat in bed and watched me seethe. "We're taking basic precautions," he murmured once I'd resumed my circuit. "That's all. If I lost you because of a stupid mistake—"

"This isn't about *you*. None of this is about you!"

"No, it's not. It's about you." He climbed out of bed and caught me in my next loop. "Whoever's in that house, their lives aren't worth more than yours. Or Amy's, or Kip's, or Arnie's, or mine."

"It's my—"

"It is *not* your job to be a martyr, Badge. You and Amy are taking a greater risk right now than anyone else in the whole damn organization. If you insist on dying for the cause, at least make your death mean something. Don't die for carelessness." He searched my eyes, looking for acceptance. "I know how much this means to you, but they can last one more night."

Part of me—the rational part, at least—knew he was making sense, even as the angry part of me itched to throw him through the window. "What if it was your mam and dad up there in that house needing rescuing, huh? Would you wait for morning? Maybe scout around to see if it's safe first?"

"Badger—"

"What if it was me? What if I'd written that message?"

Seamus struggled for an answer, and I watched with grim satisfaction as a storm of emotions flickered across his face. Finally, holding on to my arms so tightly that it hurt, he said, "If you'd been taken and I thought there was even a remote chance that you were somewhere in this town, I'd burn it to the ground if that's what it took to find you. But that's not a rational response, and much as I would fight it, I'd hope someone would have the sense to make me step back and be reasonable. That's all I'm trying to do, love." When I gave no quarter, he softly said, "That's not your parents up there. Throwing yourself into danger isn't going to bring them back. I'm so sorry, but you have to see that. No matter how many Fringers you find, you can't save someone who's already gone."

My vision blurred, and I beat my fist against Seamus's chest as I cried, angry at him for driving me to tears and furious at myself for crumbling. But he held on through the abuse, and when my tears slowed, I heard him say, "If I ever knew Brian and Kathy, they wouldn't want you to blame yourself."

"I could have—"

"There is *nothing* you could have done. You and your old wand against a wizard trained to kill? Come on, now."

I sniffed against his T-shirt. "I did tase that bastard

back in Edinburgh."

"Yes, and beautifully, but before all of this, how often did you carry a Taser?" He raised my chin to look me in the eye. "If you'd been there, all three of you would be dead now. You think that's what your mam and dad wanted? Because I'm fairly confident that they'd rather you still be breathing. Let's go to bed," he coaxed, nudging me toward the pillows. "We'll make a plan at first light, I swear, but you need your sleep."

The fire in my blood had died down, and I let Seamus lead me to bed. He flipped the lights out and curled against me in the darkness, but I stared at the lines of light that slipped past the floral curtain until my eyes grew heavy and the world faded.

I slept.

CHAPTER 21

I *dreamed.*

Vaguely, as I became cognizant that the world around me had shifted, I realized that I was back in the dream space. But this time, there was no black plain, no emptiness above and around me. I was still in my bed in the motel, though the walls had darkened to shadows, and my hand was most definitely aglow.

"I'm sleepwalking," I whispered to myself.

Moving slowly for fear that I'd jar myself awake, I coaxed my dream body out of bed. I seemed to still be wearing the clothes in which I'd fallen asleep. The carpet was still rough and thin beneath my bare feet, the sheets scratchy, and I turned to see what had become of my partner.

Seamus lay still with his arm draped over me—well, a shadowy husk with my face and form—unaware that I'd ever moved. He, too, was now glowing, but while my light shone golden-yellow, his was brighter and whiter, and the face he wore was his true one, young and unglamoured. Even frowning in his sleep, he was beautiful.

Briefly, I contemplated trying to reach him as Carey had reached me, but seeing that I'd been given an opportunity to do my own espionage, I decided not to waste time. That left me with a problem, however: how was I supposed to move about in this dream? Get into the dream version of the Suburban and hope she cranked?

Before I had time to ponder this, I was rising, now hovering just off the floor, now above my bed. "Wait," I said, heading for the ceiling, but before I made impact, I passed through it and found myself hanging in midair above the motel roof.

I caught my breath—metaphorically speaking—and gazed down at the line of rooms. There, visible even through the roof, was Seamus, still holding me in his sleep. And there, next door, was Arnold's golden glow—if I wasn't mistaken, slightly dimmer than mine. I looked into the room where Kip and Amy were sleeping and saw only a faint radiance coming from her, and Kip, who sprawled across the other bed, was as dark as my abandoned body had been. As with Seamus, the dream showed his true form.

Leaving them to sleep, I pressed myself higher to take in the block, then the town. Below me stretched a warren of shadowed streets and alleys, shops and houses, pines and shrubs and expensive tarp-covered toys nestled in the shallow valley. All I could see was dark but for the motel...and then I turned my eyes to the mountain behind me.

Perched two-thirds of the way up its side, at the end of a black ribbon of road, was a massive house overlooking the wilderness around us. The place was huge and gated, the love child of a country estate and a log cabin, but the fence couldn't stop my flight toward the lights within the walls.

Speeding through the trees, I passed through the roof and attic, then found myself in what appeared to be the master bedroom, a room that wouldn't have been out of place in Eleanor's mansion. And there, sleeping together in a pile in the middle of the king-sized bed, were three glowing children.

Their light, like mine, was gold, but it was far fainter than my luminance—they were indeed witches, I assumed, two boys and a girl. The boys were of primary school age, if that; the smaller of the two had his thumb firmly lodged in his mouth, while the larger couldn't have been more than six or seven. The girl sleeping beside them was a few years older, perhaps ten or eleven. All three were thin, and the boys' hair had grown shaggy and unkempt.

Though I wasn't sure what I was doing, I managed to land, then touched the girl's shoulder. Her bare skin was warm under my hand, and with a little start, she opened her eyes and gasped. "It's all right, love, you're dreaming," I told her before she panicked. "My name's Badger. What's yours?"

She sat up and looked around, and I remembered that she was seeing none of the detail of the dream space. As far as she knew, she and I were alone in an empty void. "Jo-Josie," she stammered, blinking rapidly. "Uh…why are you all shiny?"

"Dream thing. You are, too."

Her mouth moved in a silent *Oh* as she examined her glowing arms and tank top. "Who…how…"

"Did you write that message on the Fringe board, dear?"

Josie's eyes widened in excitement. "You found my note?"

"Gave us a fit, but yes, we did." I sat on the bed beside her and took her hand. "I'm a coordinator. We've come to get you out of here."

I was only a little surprised when she threw her arms around me and squeezed for dear life. "Everything's going to be fine," I assured her, stroking her thick hair as she hugged me. "My friends and I are down the mountain. Ehm…" I waited until she looked up, then asked, "Are you Ranger's daughter?"

Josie nodded. "Dad said there were bad wizards coming, and Mom made me hide in the attic. I…I heard a fight downstairs, and when it was quiet again, I came out, and…"

"They got my parents, too," I said when her voice faded. "So we'll just have to take care of each other, won't we? And are those your brothers?"

She looked around in confusion. "Huh?"

"Sorry, I can see more than you can right now. The two boys sleeping beside you, are they your brothers?"

"Oh, no…those are Micah and Manny Schwarzschild, they live in town. When Mom and Dad were…you know…I walked down to see if Mr. and Mrs. Schwarzschild would help me. But they were dead, too, and I found the boys hiding in the toolshed, and I brought them home with me. Manny's just four," she explained, "and I think they're both sick, they feel kind of hot, and their eyes don't look good—"

"What have you been eating?"

"Anything. *Everything.* Mom and Dad kept emergency supplies—we get snowed in up here, see—but we ate it all, and we're down to the last couple boxes of saltines." She gnawed her lip as her eyes turned hopeful. "Do you have any food?"

"Whatever you want," I told her, and hugged her again. "Listen, Josie, I need you to do something for me."

"Sure, okay. What do you need?"

"As soon as you wake, I need you to call a number. Ask for Seamus. Can you do that? Have you got a phone?"

She nodded. "And I'm pretty good at remembering phone numbers. I memorized *all* my friends' numbers in case my phone died."

"Good girl. Let me give you one more to learn…"

As I sank back through the ceiling into my motel room, I landed beside the bed and stared down at my darkened self. How, I wondered, did one wake from sleepwalking? Carey had never mentioned it…unless there was something about this in the mentally transmitted notes that I'd yet to consciously recall. Did I just lie down on myself? Would we squish back together if I got close enough?

Fortunately, before I could get creative, I heard Seamus's mobile ring on his nightstand—a ringing loud enough to wake an exhausted cop. In an instant, I was back in my body and blinking at the room, and Seamus, mumbling apologies, was rolling over to see what the commotion was about. "Please don't be the chief," I heard him say, and then he grunted at the phone and took the call. "Hello?...Speaking."

I sat up, feeling leaden after my effortless flight, and watched Seamus rise from the bed, phone still in hand. "You...I'm sorry, you...yes. Yes, she's, ehm...right here." He stared down at me with saucer eyes, and I smiled.

"Who's that, then?" I asked.

"Wait a second," he told the person on the phone, then covered the mouthpiece. "Someone called Josie? She said she just spoke with you, and you gave her my number."

"Might have done."

Seamus slid onto the bed beside me and broke into a wide grin. "Did you *sleepwalk*?" he whispered. I nodded, and he threw one arm around me while he raised the phone again. "All right, Josie, whatever she told you, we're on our way. Do us a favor and text the address, yeah?"

"Ask her to open the gate," I added.

"And the gate, Badger says...right. Very good. We'll be along shortly."

He tapped to end the call, tossed his mobile onto the duvet, then looked at me and shook his head. "You actually did it," he said with a note of awe in his sleep-graveled voice. "How the hell did you *do* that?"

"I'm not entirely sure," I admitted, "but I can promise you that it's not a trap. So, what was that about waiting for morning?"

He kissed me before he let me go. "You are *such* a gracious winner. Have you seen my trousers?"

It took us ten minutes to rouse the others and load into the vehicles, and then we sped through the midnight stillness up the hill to the Gerhardt mansion. We barely slowed at the open gate, and I'd only just pulled into the circular drive and cut the ignition before Amy was climbing out of Seamus's car, disheveled and far too perky for the hour. Kip was right behind her and quickly caught up, even as he shambled on his sore and still unsteady feet, and the rest of us hurried to join the pack.

Before we could cross the wide front porch, the door opened, and Josie appeared on the threshold, holding the yawning boys' hands. "You came!" She beamed, sounding by turns thrilled and shocked. "I thought maybe I'd imagined it all, but..."

Amy ran up and gave the three of them the biggest hug she could manage. "Let's get you out of here, okay?" she said, stooping slightly to look the boys in the eye. "We've got some friends in New Mexico, and they're really nice, and the food is *really* good."

The boys brightened at that, and Amy and Kip helped them into my vehicle while I had a quick word with Josie. "Is there anything here you can't live without?" I murmured. "The plan is to get you three into Faerie. You'll be safe there until the Arcanum comes to its senses."

She shook her head and pivoted slightly, showing off her loaded backpack. "I got my toothbrush and some pictures and things. Micah didn't bring much, and as long as Manny has Mr. Ears"—she pointed to the little boy and his stuffed elephant—"he'll be fine. Um..." She paused, suddenly worried, and looked up at the ring of adults around her. "I didn't know what to do with Mom and Dad," she whispered. "I think the police found the Schwarzschilds, but I...I had to do something with the bodies here, and..."

Seamus took a knee and clasped her hands. "Whatever you did, it's all right," he said, employing the tone we all cultivated for child witnesses. "Where are they, Josie?"

"Basement," she said softly. "They're in a big chest freezer down there."

I started to imagine the horror of that little girl dragging her parents' corpses downstairs and somehow wrangling them into the freezer, but I quickly drove that unpleasant image from my mind. "We'll take care of them," I told her, and nudged her toward the car. "Go on, grab a seat with the boys. We'll be back in a mo."

Relieved, she hurried to join her charges, and Seamus, Arnold, and I headed into the house to handle the cleanup. As Josie had promised, we found the elder Gerhardts frozen in their temporary tomb, and I pulled out my wand. "The floor's concrete. If we incinerate them here, the house probably won't catch fire—"

But Arnold had beaten me to it, and the bodies were already floating toward the floor. "Seeing as it's half-one and I am, technically, a magus, how about I take care of this?"

"Be my guest," Seamus muttered.

Arnold's wand flicked once, and the bodies disappeared in a flash of orange light. "Matter conversion," he explained, closing the freezer lid. "It's a helpful technique if you can master it. Take whatever solid or liquid you like and render it a harmless gas. But seeing as this is a closed room and we're now basically, ehm, breathing the deceased…"

"Yeah," I said, "time to go. And that's disgusting, Arnie."

"Less breathing, more walking," he replied, and hurried for the surface.

At least McDonald's was open all night. I bought a sack full of burgers and fries, plus half a dozen Happy Meals for the boys, and passed the lot to the kids once we were out of town. As I concentrated on the winding road through the mountains, Arnold slid into the back seat and chatted with the other passengers, making remarkable conversation, considering the hour and the circumstances. By the time we reached New Mexico, the little ones were asleep with full bellies, and even Arnold had begun to snore. I turned the radio on, grateful for a distraction in the wee hours, and nearly jumped when I got a text from Seamus: *Reached Carey. They're expecting us. Don't leave me out here, F-1.*

I chuckled and set my cruise control slightly over the speed limit.

The sun was well up by the time we drove onto the ranch. As we disembarked on stiff legs, the Joneses hurried out to meet us. Throwing open one of my back doors, Carey found Manny squinting at the sunlight in confusion and caught her breath. "Oh, *sweetie*," she said, lifting him out of the seat and into her arms, "you could use a good breakfast, couldn't you? And you two," she said, spotting Micah and Josie as they shuffled around the back of the old Suburban. "My goodness, what a night. Who here likes pancakes?"

That woke them enough to get a proper response, and Carey ushered them inside for breakfast, leaving Zeb to get the update. "Scrawny little things, aren't they?" he said once the door closed behind Carey.

"Josie thinks the boys are ill," I replied, stretching my calves. "I don't think she looks too healthy, either. She said they've been living on powdered potatoes and tinned slop for weeks."

"Be that as it may, they're in good hands now." Zeb took his keys back from Seamus and patted my shoulder. "Get some shut-eye, folks. I think you've earned it."

That was all the convincing I needed. I wasn't getting any younger, and aside from my brief sleepwalking episode, I'd been up for a solid day at that point. With Seamus right behind me, I kicked off my shoes and crashed, waking again only once the sun was down. Groggy and disoriented, I left my partner where he was, wrapped myself in a robe, and checked on Amy in the room next door—only to find Kip camping on the carpet beside her bed, having borrowed a pillow and a couple of afghans. My cousin, though, had made it to the kitchen for a plate of beef stew, and the little witches crowded around him at the table, working their way through generous bowls of the stuff and, in the boys' case, playing with their Happy Meal toys. I could see Carey's healing spells at work around each of the children, and she had parked herself at the table, encouraging the boys to play less and eat more while Josie rolled her eyes at their antics. Zeb, who was on kitchen duty, handed me a bowl, and I took my place in the warm chaos.

"The little guys have colds," Carey told me once Zeb had taken the boys off for a bath. "And there's definitely some malnutrition there—"

"Sorry," Josie mumbled.

She reached across the table and squeezed her hand. "You did the best you could, dear, and we're all very proud of you. Go on, have thirds. There's plenty."

As Josie headed toward the stove, Carey turned to me and smiled. "And as for you…nice work, Hannah. I knew you had it in you."

"Yeah," Arnold piped up around a mouthful of bread, "that's impressive. I don't know how to do…whatever it was you did."

"*Good*," said Carey.

"How soon will you clear them to go to Faerie?" I asked.

She mulled that over while Josie reclaimed her seat and spoon. "They should be feeling much better by morning. You're all a little too skinny for my taste," she told the girl, "but they can fatten you up over there just as easily as we can here. And speaking of Faerie," she said, turning back to me, "how are we getting them there?"

"I don't know. I have no idea where the closest gate is, but Seamus or I will call first thing tomorrow. They're a few hours ahead of us, and there's no reason to wake anyone right now."

Arnold looked slightly uncomfortable. "You *really* think

dropping them in Faerie is wise? Isn't there somewhere around here that we could—"

"There's an entire Fringe settlement over there," I interrupted, "with a coordinator in charge and her dozen *very* fae brothers providing security. It's a hell of a lot safer than hiding them here." I paused and smirked at him. "If you're worried about your own safety, I could put in a good word for you. Maybe the settlement needs a resident wizard."

"Thank you," he snapped, "but I'm not going down as the magus who ran away to Faerie when this realm needed him."

"You think it does?"

"I think someone should keep an eye on the Gray Lands situation, yes. Don't know where the next gate will open, but—"

"But until then, you're welcome to stay here," said Carey, catching him off guard. "We've got room."

"Ehm…thank you," he said, and smiled at her. "That's most kind of—"

"Do anything to sabotage the Minor Arcanum or the Fringe recovery effort, and I'll disembowel you. Sorry, Josie, pretend you didn't hear that."

I wasn't sure whose eyes were wider, the girl's or Arnold's, but he managed to nod before he concentrated heavily on his dinner.

"Okay," said Aiden, "here's the deal."

Sitting around the breakfast dishes, we leaned closer to the phone to hear him, and I held a notepad at the ready.

"The nearest natural gate is in Sedona, Arizona."

"That's not too far," said Zeb. "Relatively speaking."

"About five hundred miles," said Carey, who was already mapping a route on her mobile.

"Yeah…but there's a catch." Aiden cleared his throat. "Are you guys familiar with Boynton Canyon?"

"Not particularly," said Carey. "Why?"

"Give me that," said a female voice behind him—American, I guessed—and we heard the shuffle of a phone changing hands. "Hi," she said, "I'm Poppy. Former Dark Company. You're going to have to jump off a cliff."

Seamus groaned beside me. "Not *again*. Can't you send the dragon?"

"Not to Sedona. There's too much foot traffic to risk that, even at night. But if you'll quit whining, I'll tell you how to find it. Besides, aren't you fae? Ever heard of levitation?"

"I'm not using the kids as test subjects while I figure it out," he protested.

"We can do it," said Zeb, and Carey and Arnold nodded their agreement. "Give us the details."

Five minutes later, I'd drawn a rough map dotted with landmarks, and Poppy signed off. "We'll have people waiting on this side," Aiden assured us. "How long until you get there?"

Carey made a face and consulted the mapped route. "Well, obviously, we can't do anything until dark, and we'll have to hike in…let's aim for midnight on this side. About fourteen hours."

"Can do. See you then," he replied, and hung up.

"Well," said Zeb, looking around the table, "time's wasting, folks. Who's ready for another fun-filled day behind the wheel?"

The answer to that was *no one*, but we quickly cleaned up the kitchen and loaded into the vehicles—Zeb, Carey, Arnold, and the little ones in the Joneses' nicer SUV, and Seamus, Amy, Kip, and me in our Suburban. Driving in shifts, we made good time through the desert, stopped for a leisurely lunch and dinner, then cruised around Sedona as the sun set and the stars came out in the moonless sky.

Around ten that night, kitted out with hiking boots and head torches, we followed Poppy's directions to the trailhead and began the long hike out into the wilderness in search of the canyon. Twenty minutes in, Zeb and Seamus were each carrying a Schwarzschild boy, and Arnold had taken Josie's little pack of mementos to help her along. I'd worried about bringing Kip onto the uneven trail, but he'd proven a quick study under Amy, and he navigated almost as well as we did in the near-dark. Still, she hung back to spot him through the roughest patches, and they quietly joked as we hiked on.

And then, around a bend, I saw the outcropping to which Poppy had directed us and wondered how the hell the Company, an organization of magic-blind shifters, had ever located the gate. The ledge she'd described was accessible only by climbing a narrow passage up the rock wall, the sort of ascent that might give a mountain goat pause. At the top of the passage was a shelf perhaps only half a meter wide with a sheer cliff behind it. Standing below, I could make out the gate in the dark by the colorful tendrils of magic that pulsed from the opening above us. Unlike the conveniently vertical Gray Lands gate or the flat gate off Skye, this one was slightly skewed from horizontal, a meter-wide hole a bit lower than the ledge but tilted perhaps fifteen degrees *away* from the cliff. In other words, there was no room for error in one's trajectory.

"I'll go first," I told the others, then made the slow climb and looked over the distance into the gate, which stood out even further because of the faint predawn light on the other side. I seemed to be staring down at the top of a primeval forest—nothing into which I wanted to jump, especially as the hole was several meters away, and missing the gate would mean a long drop to the canyon floor. I couldn't even get a running start from my perch.

"It's here," I called down to the rest of our party. "Tight squeeze on the ledge, though. And I don't know how easy—"

I stopped as I saw motion from the corner of my eye, and then a dark-haired woman in a warm-up jacket was rising from the gate. "Hey," she said, waving to me. "Badger, right? I'm Poppy."

"How—"

"My boyfriend's holding me up. Where are the—*ah*," she said, looking over the side of the gate to find the children. "Send them up one at a time, and I'll take it from there."

The rest of our party hesitated, thinking this through, but Josie put on a brave face. "I'll go first," she told the boys. "This isn't going to be scary." Taking his cue, Arnold grabbed his wand and muttered, and Josie slowly sailed over the canyon with her backpack, rising to meet Poppy at the gate. The woman caught her and flashed a thumbs-up at Arnold, then hoisted Josie over the side and called to someone below her, "Rufe, first one's ready! Tell me when!"

"When!" came a faint male voice, and Poppy released Josie to the waiting enchantment that carried her to the ground.

I didn't truly breathe again until both of the boys had joined her, and Poppy grinned at my visible relief. "They're going straight to the settlement. Vivi's waiting to get them situated, and we've got a few potential fosters lined up. They're going to be fine."

"Thank you," I said, returning her smile.

"Our pleasure. Also, I was told to tell you that your merry band of miscreants is welcome to come over at any time. I've got four Stowes down here to play catch, if you're interested."

Seamus and Amy shook their heads, and I glanced back at Poppy. "Not now. That's only three accounted for—we have work to do yet."

"Got it." With a little salute, she disappeared through the gate again, and I took a last look at the quiet serenity of the canyon before climbing down to hike back to the vehicles.

With any luck, I mused, I'd be returning soon.

"**H**ere's the thing," said Carey. "Sedona's a heck of a trip if you're making it on a regular basis."

Seamus held my mobile in his outstretched palm, the better for me to talk and drive. "There isn't a closer gate," I told her. "Not unless something spontaneously opens."

"I'm aware of that. What I'm suggesting is that we make fewer trips. Consolidate them, as it were."

I paused. "Wait, *we?*"

"We want to help," said Zeb. "Seeing those kids this morning…that isn't right. It's just not *right.*"

I could hear his agitation. "You're already doing us a great favor by letting us squat and steal your food."

"And traumatize your horses," Seamus added.

"But we could be doing more," said Carey. "Zeb and I were talking about this a few minutes ago, and we have an idea. What if we built a guesthouse at the ranch? Nothing fancy, bunks and bathrooms and such, but anyone you find could stay with us for a while, get a hot meal and a shower, let me patch them up, et cetera. When you had a few people together, we could make another trip out to the canyon. It'd save time and gas, at least."

"That's very generous," Seamus replied, "but are you sure—"

"I'm sure that I had sick, malnourished orphans in my house this morning," she interrupted, "and Arnold tells me that little girl was keeping her parents in an ice chest. Yeah, we're sure."

"If we worked together," Arnold added, "we could erect a bunkhouse in an afternoon. I can do a fair bit of heavy lifting, Zeb says he's done spellcraft construction before, Carey's no slouch, and Hannah…we could show you a few tricks, eh? What do you say?"

"And then all of us could move out of your guestrooms and into the building next door," I said. "I mean, I can't imagine why you'd want your privacy back…"

Carey chuckled at that. "All right, you twisted my arm.

We'll have ourselves a bunkhouse raising tomorrow. And then…"

She hesitated, and I heard Zeb murmur, "Go on."

"I was thinking," said Carey, "that Zeb and I might contact a few friends of ours in the Minor Arcanum. People we trust. We're spread pretty widely—might be that we could run a pickup relay."

Seamus and I looked at each other, and I said, "I thought the goal was to keep the Minor Arcanum out of this mess."

"We wouldn't tell everyone. Just a few of the right people."

"Then I'll trust your judgment," I replied, and caught Amy nodding in the mirror. "You two realize that you're at least honorary Fringe by now, don't you? But you're getting all of the work and none of the perks. You *might* have chosen a better time to enlist."

Carey laughed in earnest. "Do I at least get a membership card, or what?"

The real benefit of constructing a building using magic isn't the speed of construction or the stability of the resulting structure—it's the ability to move in that day and not breathe paint and carpet fumes for weeks to come.

We still had work to do to make the bunkhouse home. True, there were plenty of beds and chairs, and we'd built private bedrooms for longer-term guests like us, but the place needed a decorator's touch. Though I questioned my sanity in doing so, I put Amy in charge of the interior design, with Arnold on hand to implement her changes. When I left them that evening, she and Kip were debating paint colors, and my poor cousin was stuck changing the walls at their direction as each tried to make a point.

Closing the door to our bedroom, I found that Seamus had already drawn the heavy curtains against the night and turned down the bed. "Need your space," he asked, "or might I join the festivities?"

I stroked my chin. "Distracting, but cute. I guess you can stay."

Grinning, he slid beneath the blanket, and I burrowed down next to him, fully dressed and hopeful that I could replicate my accidental sleepwalk. As if sensing my nerves, Seamus pulled me close and murmured, "You're going to be marvelous, Badger. I'll be here when you wake."

"Promise?" I mumbled, closing my eyes. "This could be dull."

His fingers rose toward my throat, then brushed against the ring beneath my shirt. "Promise," he said, and reached for my hand.

I held on to him as I fell asleep, letting the steady rhythm of his breathing lull me into a stupor. And then, suddenly, my eyes shot open to find the world changed once more to shadows.

There was no hesitation that time as I extricated myself from my body. Seamus slept on beside me, and I blew him a kiss as I rose through the ceiling to survey the land around me.

Through the roof, I could see Arnold in the middle of the room, standing beside faintly glowing Amy and shadowed Kip. In the house, I spotted Zeb and Carey, who'd settled in the basement in front of the television for a night of peace. I rose higher and turned to the southwest, squinting until I picked out a glow that had to be Jim. Satisfied that I knew where my people were, I rose higher against the night until a light at the horizon caught my eye.

As I neared it, the shadows resolved themselves into the walls of a dingy motel, the sort of place where one can rent accommodations by the hour. And there, in a lonely room near the back of the complex, a young woman lay curled up on her bed, still wearing her trainers and a jacket. On the duvet in front of her was a wand—judging by the girl's dim glow, at least a unicorn-horn model. A backpack sat on the floor within easy reach.

I let myself in and landed beside her, recognizing too well what I was seeing. Ready for a quick run or a desperate last stand, barely sleeping for fear of being caught off guard…hell, I supposed she'd been washing her pants in the sink for at least a few months.

Slowly, I shook her shoulder until she opened her eyes in the dream space and saw me standing over her. "What the—" she managed, and grabbed for her wand.

"It's okay, I'm here to help," I said, catching her wrist. "You're all right, you're just dreaming. I'm a coordinator. Let me bring you someplace where you'll be safe from the Arcanum."

She stared up at me, shocked and fearful, and then her eyes began to fill. "Safe?" she choked out. "You…you know somewhere safe?"

"Absolutely." I sat beside her and smiled. "I'm Badger, and I promise, I'm coming for you."

ACKNOWLEDGEMENTS

Here we are once again, you and me, at the back of the book, the odd blip at the end of the story where I get a chance to say hello and goodbye. Thank you so much for coming along on this strange trip, and I hope to see you next time.

As always, my gratitude goes to the Novel Chicks for their advice and friendship. Once again, I owe thanks to Adam Domby, beta reader extraordinaire.

And yes, here's to you, Mom and Dad.

ABOUT THE AUTHOR

When not writing fiction, Ash Fitzsimmons is an appellate attorney and an unrepentant car singer.

Find her online:
www.ashfitzsimmons.com